AMBULANCE

Other books by this author available from New English Library:

KINGPIN

Ambulance

HUGH MILLER

NEW ENGLISH LIBRARY
TIMES MIRROR

All characters in this book are fictitious. Any resemblance to real persons, whether living or dead, is purely coincidental

First published in Great Britain by New English Library 1975

*

FIRST NEL PAPERBACK EDITION FEBRUARY 1976

*

NEL Books are published by The New English Library Limited from Barnard's Inn, Holborn, London E.C.1. Made and printed in Great Britain by C. Nicholls & Company Ltd

45002655 8

ACKNOWLEDGEMENTS

The author wishes to thank the following for their generous advice and assistance in the preparation of this book; a few names have been omitted by request but none, I trust, by accident.

Isabel and Ann, Jean Wright, Marilyn Pipkin, Professor Ira Moss, Alan Bertin, Maggie Miller, Messrs Herbert Lomas Ltd, and Jack Cowley, who kept the juices flowing.

I am also grateful to Stephanie Dowrick, who proposed the novel in the first place, and whose deft editorial stroke keeps my literary shortcomings to a minimum.

For my people,
North and South

For we wrestle not against flesh and blood, but against principalities, against powers, against the rulers of the darkness of this world, against spiritual wickedness in high places.

Ephesians, 6:12

1

At that hour, with only the sounds of early birds and the closer, comforting purr of Amy's breath close to his ear, Henry Madison was always at peace. It was a state of grace, a time lasting no more than minutes when his mind was awake and reacting to the world, before the infirmities of the body and the barbs within the memory could rear up and apply their inevitable distortions. He turned his head and looked at Amy's sleeping face, the lines softened by the diffuse yellow light from the curtains. In the seasons of their life together, he had never been aware of change in her. Her nature, voice, movement and even her face had shifted subtly to remain in tune with the advancing maturity of his own outlook. She was still pretty, and when she was sleeping there were clear signs of youth in her smooth forehead and full generous mouth. The hair, always fair, had turned white by the most subtle of degrees, and it still maintained the lustre of those early days when she was among the first of the prizes Henry pursued with his unique vigour. She was fifty-eight now, five years his junior. Childless, she had nevertheless been a source of great strength. She was the healthiest person Henry had ever known, and he knew perfectly well that he would be spared the misery of losing her. He would go first; beyond that certainty, he did not care to speculate.

He examined the clock on the bedside table. Seven-fifteen. When he was younger, perhaps thirty years younger, he thought nothing of rising at five, so that he could have that much more day to use. In those days he always slept well and derived the same benefit from four hours in bed as he would from eight. Now he was exhausted by nine in the evening, and even though he would always turn in by ten it took an hour for him to fall asleep and no more than a creaking floorboard to wake him. Age was a ruinous valley, he thought. A man was always reduced by time, no matter how many safeguards he had built. The best that could be accomplished was delay, and that eventually required more energy than a sixty-three-year-old system could muster. Among the less respectable of his regrets was a nagging sorrow that he had never taken more kindly to alcohol. Facing old age constantly sober was like having an operation without anaesthetic.

Henry shifted his legs and felt the familiar stiffness in his right knee. He had found that it was aggravated if he slept on his back. That was unfortunate, because he had never been able to sleep on his left side and his right shoulder was mildly arthritic. The stiff knee was a lesser evil than a locked shoulder. He stretched out his legs and made his customary attempt to lift them in the air, against the pressure of the bedclothes. It was a good exercise, one of the few he had continued to perform past the age of fifty, and it had ensured that his abdominal muscles remained firm, a good deal firmer than those which flabbily contained the innards of the majority of his contemporaries. At the same time he worked his jaw up and down, back and forth, in an alternating rhythm aimed at keeping his features elastic and, if not youthful, at least tight. There was nothing worse than a man trying to exert his authority with a face that kept failing him, expressions trailing behind the immediacy of his approach. Mid-way through his exercises, he remembered what day it was and he stopped moving, his mind springing to attention. Tuesday, February 19. The resentment that had taken so long to depart the night before came back, its colours, shades and echoes intact.

He drew back the bedclothes and swung his legs over the side. Rising carefully, he took his robe from the chair and slipped it around his shoulders, taking a sliver of comfort from the warmth. He strode past the dressing table, trying to ignore the pieces of paper lying there in a neat pile. But he was compelled to look at them again, like a person unable to resist probing a wound just one more time, to test the pain. Henry snatched them up and took the sheaf with him into the bathroom.

While the taps trickled he stood under the heat-and-light unit, wrinkling his eyes against the glare given off by the crisp official notepaper. The first sheet was a memo, curt and precise.

To Mr Henry Madison, MRCP, FRCS: From the Office of the Medical Superintendent, Westfield General Hospital. 10th September, 1972.

At a meeting of the Regional Hospital Board held today, the plans drawn up by Dr Paul Avery, with a view to establishing a mobile life-support unit based at this hospital, were discussed and provisionally approved. Your objections to the scheme were noted, but the Board members are still unanimously of the opinion that Dr Avery's recommendations are far-sighted and in line with the current drive to improve efficiency in Casualty units throughout the country. Should you wish to press your points more firmly, may I suggest that you make direct contact with the Chairman of the Board, Sir Albert Macauley, as soon as possible. Costing of the proposed vehicle is already underway, and I would point out that the Board is applying unusual haste to the pre-implementation stages of this matter.

James Towers
Medical Superintendent

Henry glanced briefly at the second letter, a copy of the one he had spent an hour composing, a plea for sanity in a world unbalanced by the cult of gimmickry. In essence, he had pointed out that the time was wrong for the introduction of a complex, costly and personnel-absorbing scheme which, after all, amounted to no more than a rather flashy ambulance with some clever machinery built into it and badly needed medical staff manning it. He went on to indicate that efficiency within the hospital itself needed a thorough overhaul; no amount of four-wheeled wizardry would alter that fact, and it could well worsen the situation. The proposals called for a driver, an ambulance attendant, a senior nurse and a doctor to be on hand at all times to operate the rescue machinery. Doctors and nurses were hard enough to find as it was, without squandering them on a job best left to the existing ambulance service. Already, grave doubts were being expressed in several quarters, as to the usefulness of such a scheme. In the particular instance of coronary care, prompt aid should theoretically help in reducing the immediate mortality rate of between 18 and 22 per cent; with appropriate emergency attention and follow-up care, the figure should drop to less than 14 per cent. Despite the attractive and convincing theory, Henry had pointed out, in practice it had been difficult to demonstrate any benefit at all from the use of Mobile Coronary Care Units. There were figures abounding to show that doctors in general practice simply did not make use of a mobile service, and in the face of their reluctance, plus the doubtful virtues of the units, he suggested that it was less than sensible to squander money and personnel that could be deployed in so many other already proven directions. As to motorway accident work, for which Dr Avery was pleased to imagine the super-ambulance would prove admirable, Henry stressed that his long experience of accident surgery had led him to believe that little of any value could be done for a patient until he was safely within the stable confines of an operating theatre.

He turned off the taps and lingered for a few minutes longer, warming himself under the lamp, casting a scathing eye over the rest of the letters. From his laconic reply to Henry's exhortations, Sir Albert Macauley appeared to be as little gifted with patience and insight as he was with simple intelligence. His letter was handwritten, on pale blue notepaper bearing his family crest. The vulgarity of the man, Henry thought. Laden with badges and escutcheons and a titular heritage that stretched into the mists of English history, he still possessed no more idea of the meaning of tradition and authority than a street-corner thug.

Dear Mr Madison,

Thank you for your long, interesting letter. Although your points are well made, I must tell you that the Board did consider your objections very carefully at our last meeting. I would remind you that Dr Avery's idea is to produce a mobile unit that provides medical attention—expert attention—right at the scene of an accident, and to continue that attention up to the moment of arrival at the hospital. Surely, whatever facts and figures may be put forward to express a contrary view, it must be admitted that the scheme fills an area of practice until now quite neglected. Direct medical assistance cannot be a bad

or an inefficient aim. Coronary care raises some special problems I will admit, but Dr Avery's ambulance is not principally aimed in that direction.
As to your remarks concerning inefficiency within the hospital itself, and the sad shortage of personnel, may I just say that progress cannot be hindered while the administration gathers up its skirts and limps into action. The new unit would, I feel sure, act as a prompt to a more efficient hospital procedure.
Thank you again for making your points so clearly and forcibly. Opposition is healthy, and it is comforting to see that it can be so vigorous in this day and age of laissez faire.

From that point, the correspondence was a sharp indication of Henry's failure. They stopped listening to him. As a senior consultant he was kept informed of progress, and Dr Avery, with his best vote-winning style, had even had the cheek to send him a detailed specification of the damnable vehicle, but there was no doubt about it, Henry Madison was being steadfastly ignored as the upstart American pushed ahead to the loud applause of the entire hospital Board.

The other scraps of paper were too depressing. He laid them aside and slipped off his robe, taking a brief look at his face in the mirror before getting into the tub. It was the sort of face he had admired as a child. Wiry grey hair, firmly lined cheeks, a wide mouth and deep-set grey eyes. A dominant face. The emphases of character had been put there by years of dedication, years of fighting to attain the status he had always known his skill deserved. Now, with a lifetime of hard work and sterling service behind him, with a professional standing second to none, he was being not-too-gently edged out of the picture; and that was more than irritating, more than humiliating, for the picture would not have been there at all but for himself and others like him.

In the tub he lay back and tried to forget the annoyances. A few minutes of thoughtless calm, up to the neck in warm water, was one way to ensure a long life and a sound digestion. His mother had told him that, and her instinct, although it had run clean across most established theories, had always supported Henry. He closed his eyes and tried to forget the date, just for a short time. Tuesday, February 19. The day they were inaugurating their mobile box of tricks.

In his rented bungalow, two miles from Westfield General, on an estate mainly populated by young professional men and their chirpy wives, Paul Avery had already bathed, shaved and dressed. Breakfast—one cup of coffee and a Rothman's King Size cigarette—was accompanied by a hasty reading of the journals. Tuesdays and Fridays he read the professional papers; Wednesdays and Thursdays were reserved for personal letter writing. Mondays, Saturdays and Sundays he worked on projects that he hoped, one day, would carry him back to America on an accelerated wave of senior appointment potential.

He was thirty-four, an age traditionally linked with promise and abundant horizons, a time for a man, especially a medical man, to start hammering home the spikes. By rights he should have been back home, consolidating himself, changing to top gear among people who would have grown accustomed to his style. But he had decided to stay on in England for another three years, to try for just one more distinction, one additional gold star in his record book. That was the way to do things; his personal vision of how a life should be organised contained a number of obvious, shining pointers. *Never* take the standard route, that was a very important rule. It could be argued that his success, already far from standard in pattern, was an indication that he was well away from any danger of being ordinary. But that was the kind of argument Paul rejected. Even the high road to success was threaded with convention. A different approach would bring a different kind of triumph. So in everything he did, he strove for a method and a style that would keep him off trodden land.

He had learned the lesson first from his father, by negative example. For thirty-nine years John Avery had worked at the same bench in a Boston instrument manufacturer's workshop. In all that time he saw promotion twice, tolerating the meagreness of his advance in the interests of security. 'They couldn't get by without me, now,' he would say, when the world seemed to be moving so fast and he appeared not to move at all. 'I've made myself indispensable, son.' An indispensable drudge, a man with enough inside knowledge of his business to go and work wherever he wanted, but content instead to stay where he was, because he felt safe and roots had grown. Paul's fury, starting at eighteen and burning down to exasperation by the time he was twenty-five, had put him at a distance from everything his father loved and respected. Within the lattices of old John's viewpoint, Paul knew there was a formula for mediocrity. In time, he came to define the downgrade tendency as being a result of standardised thinking. With that view established, the youth had deliberately gone against every predictable trend. Instead of studying business administration (his father's idea, for old John had a strong admiration for the managers of this world) Paul went to medical school. Instead of slipping into one of the comfortable lucrative streams of the profession, he chose to spend his energies on the unrewarding business of accident surgery. The crowning cataclysm was his decision to spend two years in England, where he thought they had sufficient disregard for cash to have the patients' interests still reasonably well to the fore. His father, retired now and despairing of ever having the chance to be conventionally proud of his son, had told Paul he was crazy. In medicine a man had to stay around, he couldn't just disappear for a couple of years then pop back, expecting to take up where he left off. You had to do your growing in the same place, old John insisted. Grasshoppers never did do no good.

Now he was extending the stay to five years. The reasons were simple and complex at the same time. He liked England, he found that there were fewer barriers to advancement, and he knew that his American accent put a certain zip into his bearing among the white-coated knights of the scalpel. At a deeper level, tied closely to the reputation he was earning himself, Paul was learning something about his ambition that only an exile could know. At a distance from the country where he intended to spend the mature years of his career, he could see his own image very clearly. His tall lean body, the curly brown hair, the face that would always be youthful and the soft, husky voice would put Paul Avery into a slot that was already full of clear-eyed winners. Only from England could he see where his type fitted in the total picture of American medical practice. His determination to fill no ready-made pocket made him cling more tightly to England and to the changes it could make in him. He would still be the same physical and emotional type when he went back, but he would return equipped with a record and a behaviour curve that would blow the sides out of any pigeonhole. On his own terms, he would make it to the top; and even the top, he had decided, would be different from the standard pinnacles.

The morning's reading was more difficult than usual. At the back of his calm perusal there was the excitement of launch day. It had happened; he had swung the kind of deal that might have taken the average doctor, with the average respect for tradition, half a lifetime to even suggest. By involving other people in his enthusiasm he had triggered responses at committee level that had virtually raced the scheme through. There was another point he always remembered; enthusiasm is infectious, as long as it's genuine. The Life-Support Unit was something he believed in, all the way through to his instinct, and his energetic campaigning had even overcome the grumbling objections of Henry Madison. There was reason enough to feel excited, but he was careful to go easy on the pride. Pride, like rest, was for people who had finished. Paul would settle for a passing satisfaction.

An item in a weekly paper caught his eye. In a case of psychomotor epilepsy occurring in a boy of twelve, the drug L-dopa was administered to control his difficult behaviour. The child, it appeared, had become very aggressive in a sexual way, and the dosage was reduced. A few months later, however, it was noted that the lad's penis had grown alarmingly, and was in fact three times longer than his twin brother's. The technical name for the condition was hypergenitalism, and Paul knew, by a sort of instinct arising from his own casual study of L-dopa, that the drug had simply raised the production of the boy's growth hormones. It could not happen in adults. Paul grinned. He could think of one or two housemen who would think of giving it a try, just the same.

Paul looked at his watch. He was not due to appear at the hospital for an hour yet. He decided to abandon the journals and spend twenty minutes cleaning up the place.

The sitting room was a mess. There was a pattern of linked sticky rings on the coffee table and some cigarette ash had been blown across the design making it look, in places, as if it were bearing fur. Two ashtrays were piled with squashed filter tips, tissues and cigarette packets. There was a girl's scarf draped across the top of the water jug and a glove in the fireplace. Records lay out of their sleeves, a half-empty gin bottle propped up the smeared plastic lid of the turntable and some stained glasses were huddled beneath the legs of a chair. The room smelt as if it had been closed for years and occupied non-stop by a gang of chain-smoking alcoholics. Paul opened a window and began to put things back where they belonged. Tucked down the side of a cushion, on a chair he tended to think of as his own, he found a wad of blue woven nylon. Incredulous, he unwound it and found himself holding a pair of very tiny panties. He turned them around and felt their texture, his mind racing over what he could recall of the previous night. He had been with Ernie Hale, Ernie's girl and Edith Roberts. They had a lot to drink, that he could remember. They always had a lot. Then they had started playing kids' games. Musical chairs, hot potato, all kinds of retarded nonsense that has been very funny at the time.

Paul looked at the panties again. Surely he hadn't . . . ? Then he remembered that when it was very late Ernie had suggested they play strip dominoes. The very sound of the game had sent Paul, shuddering with laughter, out to the kitchen to try, for the third time, to make some sandwiches. When he got back to the sitting room, Edith was making eye-signals, very elaborate and no doubt significant, in the direction of Ernie and his little blonde. All that Paul could remember now was Ernie kneeling on the carpet, tipping out the dominoes and giggling while his girl reclined, less than fully conscious, on the divan. From that point on, nothing was very clear, but he was prepared to bet that those pants did not belong to Edith. He was equally prepared to lay odds that they had come off the firm buttocks of the randy psychiatrist's friend.

'Oh, boy.' He shook his head and folded the garment carefully, placing it snugly between two thick volumes of *Surgical Practice* on the book shelf. That Ernie. There were times when he behaved like one of his own patients. Edith would have to be contacted discreetly and asked just what went on. An orgy was unlikely; Paul had awakened on his own bed, half-undressed and definitely lacking any post-coital ease in his lower parts. There were no traces of Edith, no tell-tale indentations on the next pillow or damp bars of soap in the bathroom. She must have gone home without any afters. But she would not have gone while Ernie and his sexy sidekick had still been there. She looked after Paul like that, whenever he had too much to drink she stayed around until the guests had gone, just in case anything went wrong. He sighed and looked around him. It was a pity, he thought, that she did not extend her loving care to little things like cleaning up. He would have to start employing a daily cleaner, after all.

The telephone rang while he was still trying to straighten the place. It was Edith. She sounded cool.

'How's your head this morning?' She was definitely cool. He could always tell by the way she clipped her words, like someone learning to speak Afrikaans.

'Not bad. I never really suffer—'

'Well you should start.' He heard her sniff. 'That was a terrible exhibition last night.'

'Tell me about it. I was going to ask you, anyway.'

'You mean you don't remember? You don't remember that little trollop running around the place half naked and that idiot Ernie chasing after her like a defective ten year old?'

He tried to construct the image from her description, but nothing came up that was in any way familiar. 'Sorry. I must get mental blocks in place of hangovers.' He looked down and saw a fresh cigarette burn on the arm of the couch. 'I think we better stop these get-togethers, Edith. For a while, at least.'

'For good.' She was being very firm. He wondered what it was like to be one of her patients. A lot, he supposed, would depend on her mood. This morning, he would not have liked to be on the receiving end of her professional attention. 'You lay on your house and your food and your drink just so that Ernie Hale can bring along his latest tart and show her a good time. And *I* have to sit around like a lemon while you all get drunk and incapable.'

'You don't *have* to, Edith . . .' Time for the brake, he decided. She may be quite right to boil over, but Paul Avery was nobody's release valve. Not even Edith's. 'If you want to play big sister, I suggest you try it on your brother. God knows he could use some attention.'

'Oh—' She stopped before the flood started and controlled her breathing before going on. 'There's no need to get mad with me. I was simply annoyed to see you being treated so badly. You don't make people show you enough respect, Paul. I mean that.

They're nice at first, then they start to abuse you because you don't complain. You should put up barriers, like everyone else.'

He thought, without giving it sound, that if everybody else did it, it was not for him. Then he wondered for an instant if he was not, maybe, getting a trifle smug about his own-bag attitude. 'Okay, let's just forget last night. I'll have a word with Ernie, and we'll probably never see the girl again anyway.'

'We can hardly avoid that, I'm afraid. She's a second year nurse in Essex Ward. I tried to tell you that last night, but you were too far gone to—'

'Edith . . .' His voice was a warning, soft but redolent of the temper she had already seen twice.

'Right, sorry, sorry. I really called up to say that I've just seen it.'

'It? What it?'

'Your transistorised blood-wagon. It went past the residency ten minutes ago.'

'Oh shit. I didn't want you to see it until the little ceremony. We've had the damned thing under wraps for weeks, and now they blow everything by driving it round the hospital.'

'They have to get it to the quadrangle *some* way, don't they?'

He nodded to the mouthpiece. 'Yeah, I guess so. I'm looking forward to the unveiling. Hey, that's it. That's why I had the feeling no one would be able to see it until the big moment. I had this dopey mental picture of it all covered in a white sheet.'

'You're very childish in some ways, Paul.' He side-stepped the embarrassment her endearment brought on. Every time a woman was nice to him, he started to feel vulnerable, as if he was about to be knifed. 'That's a word that's going to lose a lot of its meaning soon, Edith. Childish. If they go on using L-dopa for boys under the age of puberty, childish will mean—'

'I read the article.'

'Oh. Well, thanks for ringing. Nice to know we're still speaking to each other. I'll see you later. Okay?'

'Fine. And Paul—don't be mad if I get protective sometimes, mm?'

'I'll try, dearest heart,' he gagged. 'It's all the iron in my diet, it makes me kind of edgy.'

Thirty-five minutes later he was ready to go. Pin-striped, white shirted, tie knotted a fraction smaller than was fashionable; the perfect image of an English doctor. The fact that he would have preferred to wear jeans, sandals and a sweat shirt was beside the point. Paul observed tradition when it served his ends to do so. He picked up his briefcase and left, rattling the car keys as he walked along the side of the house to the garage, trying to dissipate his feeling of excitement through the jangling metre of the keys. Another day, another small triumph, he kept telling himself. This was no summit, merely a firm foothold on the way. All the real work was up ahead.

Amy Madison waited until Henry had gone before she tapped Katie's door and told her it was almost nine o'clock. Inside, Katie was lying in a face-down tangle across the bed, her nightdress wound like a rope across her back. She lifted her head at the sound of her aunt's voice and grunted a response, then dropped down again and tried to recapture her dream. But it had gone, the door had slammed on whatever had been making her feel good. She rolled onto her back and blinked. Day, first of all. Tuesday. Yellow. Tuesday was yellow now, it had been green when she was younger. Wednesday was a shiny black, Thursday was brown and Friday red. Saturday had always been silver, Sunday was grey and Monday, that was white. She shook her head from side to side, leaving auburn strands across the pillow. There was a taste in her mouth like aniseed, and her tongue found a substantial fur across the front of her teeth. She would be sixteen in four months, and she could depress herself terribly by imagining how long it would be until she landed on twenty. If the papers and magazines were to be believed, everything seemed to happen to girls who were twenty. They always looked better, too. Katie was pretty sure they did not wake up with furry teeth and an odd taste in their mouths. All that mess went away when a girl was properly grown up. The way she saw it, growing to some kind of maturity meant a steady reduction of mess. First it was nappies, then the stickiness of the sweets and buns period, then the tremendous sweating of schooldays on hockey pitches and in gyms and classrooms with big windows and no ventilation. Then it became cooler, and cleaner, and suddenly a girl would be twenty and she would move in a cloud of freshness and perfection, unable to put a foot wrong and incapable of anything but beautiful movement and elegance that went right through to the centre. Of course, that was only in her head, she knew that nobody alive was like that. But that was what became possible, that was the sort of freedom twenty represented.

Her intellectual make-up was a special blend of romance and candour. She had been brought up by a widowed mother until she was ten, then her mother had died from a cervical carcinoma and she had come to stay with her late father's brother, Uncle Henry, and his wife Amy. The contrast of life-styles was sharp but not at all unbearable. Her mother had taught her to read Scott and Defoe and R. M. Ballantine, and she had supplemented the romantic diet with stories her own mother had told, tales of good and evil where the good was always physically beautiful and the bad was black and ugly and foul. Set against the reality of her early schooldays, the floral fictions settled with Katie as a comforting shield from the harsher aspects of enforced education. At Uncle Henry's she found herself in a much more practical environment, a household run to a timetable, with an emphasis on the importance of sound qualifications taking precedence over any wishy-washy dabbling in the arts. Being a flexible girl she fitted into the layout very well; in the process, her romantic background became simply a convenient stained glass window, which cast a pleasing light on her thoughts.

She climbed out of bed and hoisted the knotted garment over her head in a flying arc, aiming it accurately into the mouth of the wicker laundry basket by the window. The room was warm, warmer than her uncle thought healthy, but he doted on her like a daughter and she had no difficulty in being allowed to keep her heater on all night. Getting up in a cold room was horrible, even to think about it was enough to make her shiver. But here she was, bang in the middle of February, able to walk about the room stark naked without the slightest discomfort.

There was no school again for a week, and filling the time on her own initiative had been difficult at first. The evenings were not so bad, she was allowed to go round to a friend's house—or that was where Uncle Henry and Aunt Amy thought she went—and there was the freedom to really do her own thing for four or five hours on a stretch. During the day, her instincts had to be limited by the fact that she was with her aunt most of the time, and that meant finding things to do which did not touch too closely on what she really liked.

She crossed the carpet and fumbled in her handbag for a cigarette which she lit from the lighter she kept tucked in the centre of her box of tissues. Smoking, that would give Uncle Henry a heart attack if he know. She always had one when she got up, another in the loo at lunch time, and in the evening she smoked all the time; three evenings a week she had to stay at home, and the need for a cigarette sometimes drove her to bed early, just so she could sit by the open window and puff. She sat down on the edge of the dressing-table stool, her feet spread out and an elbow propped on her knee. Her legs were quite pale now, she noticed, and a couple of little razor nicks stood out as if they had been added by a make-up technician. Last summer she had been brown, deep brown, but the winter and the cold had bleached it all away. Idly, she put a hand under one breast and lifted it, pleased by the weight and the firmness. Andy said her breasts were perfect. Put like that, it was charming, but that was not really the way Andy said anything. He was coarse, she supposed, and he was certainly very working class. But he was very beautiful too; he would have looked perfect in the old days with a doublet and a ruff and one of those little flat hats on his long hair. The uniform he wore wasn't bad, as it happened. The disco had them specially made and all three attendants wore them, but Andy looked best of all.

She drew deeply on the cigarette and pressed her thumb hard against her nipple, feeling a little tingle of response. She released the pressure and watched the little cone begin to harden. With finger and thumb, she teased it until it was rigid. It was very soothing, like the effects of gin, which she had tried a couple of times recently. She shifted her hand to the other breast and brought that nipple up to match the other. Viewed from above, they did look perfect. She ran her palm across them, aware of the intensified sensation. Tits, that was what Andy said sometimes. Breast was a word that embarrassed him, he told her. It excited him to say tits, if she was there and listening. Katie did not mind. His admiration was what mattered, not the way he expressed it. She took the cigarette end to the potted plant on the window sill and buried it in the earth, then returned to her seat, dwelling over the delicate sensations she had drawn from her engorged breasts.

Aunt Amy knocked at the door again.

'I'm up, Auntie.'

'All right, dear. Don't be too long, breakfast's on the table.'

Struggling to hold the mood, Katie closed a hand round each breast and squeezed, the way *he* did, and tried to imagine him standing behind her, his hard stomach pressed against her back, his thing all pushy and frantic at the cleft of her buttocks. He didn't like her to say thing. She had to say it properly, she had to put her mouth to his ear and say the words he liked, the ones that turned him on: cock, prick, fuck, cunt, and he would nearly explode because it excited him so much and it sounded so much better, he said, because her voice was so cultured and her accent was so refined. Katie took away her hands and stood up, drawing in a trembling breath and forcing herself to move, bullying her mind back up to the surface. She pulled open a drawer and fumbled around among the clothes inside. There was no point in getting herself all worked up. Tonight was Tuesday night, yellow night. A stay-in night.

At breakfast she chomped hungrily on her toast while Aunt Amy sat by the window, reading the newspaper. It had become a little ritual; Katie ate for ten minutes and her aunt stayed nearby, reading. She had been a blessing to them both and she was aware of that, but they were important to her too. Sometimes Katie felt a shaft of guilt at the way she cheated on them, but she could suppress it by recalling that every girl she knew practised *some* kind of deception on her family.

The house must have been a terribly quiet place before her arrival. Even now there was a feeling of a silence you could touch. It seemed to creep forward every time the sounds of eating and clinking crockery stopped. The place was very big, and Katie's stock of tales concerning such houses had provided her with the fantasy that when it was built the designer had used it as a place to store all the silence he had left over from other buildings.

'Would you like to go round to Anna's tonight, dear?'

Katie could hardly believe her ears. 'Well, yes. But I thought—'

Aunt Amy nodded, the fine eyes squarely meeting the girl's. 'I know, Tuesday you stay at home. But I think Uncle Henry wants to bring home some people this evening, and he would appreciate it if you and I weren't here.' She smiled to quell any oddity the statement may have seemed to contain. 'This is the way it has been for a long time, Katie. Over the years, whenever there has been any sort of crisis, your uncle has called a meeting. I understand he is opposed to something that's taking place at the hospital just now, and he wants to have a discussion with some friends. When that happens, I always go out. I go to a guild meeting, or I visit a friend—anything, but I go out. It's somehow very important that he has the place to himself. I think he feels that work should always be free of any domestic trappings. Without you or me here, he'll be able to feel that he's still at work.'

Katie entertained a makeshift fantasy of her uncle and half a dozen other surgeons, all gathered in the study, clad in animal skins and brandishing long medical knives over the prostrate form of a virgin tied down to the floor. 'I don't think Anna's got anything important to do this evening,' she said brightly. 'We can get on with our revision and listen to some records. I'll give her a ring later.' The phone number of Andy's digs was printed on her brain, but she would wait until Aunt Amy was having her nap before she risked calling him with the joyous news.

Keeping matters casual, she asked, 'What do you think it is that's bothering Uncle Henry?'

Aunt Amy put down the paper and shook her head. 'I'm not sure, but I gather he's opposed to some new ambulance the Hospital Board have bought. I always try to keep my nose out of these things.'

Katie swallowed a mouthful of toast and wiped her fingers on a napkin. 'That's funny. I mean, imagine a surgeon being against an ambulance.'

'Yes, on the surface it doesn't make a lot of sense.' Aunt Amy rose and began to clear the table. 'But the surface never tells us much, does it? To us the ambulance is something to carry sick people to hospital. Goodness knows what it represents to a man like your uncle.'

2

The abuse of alcohol is not necessarily an indication of alcoholism. Ernie Hale had been keeping that fact foremost in his mind ever since the first out-patient had swept into the room. His head was heavy. It felt as if someone had decided to do a cavity-wall filling job on it. There was thick foam permeating every crevice, and his reactions, although intact and as incisive as ever, drew so much energy for their function that he was sure he would not be able to complete the day's work. He had no idea how much he had consumed at Paul Avery's place, but it must have been a lot. Long practice had toughened his liver to the point where less than a bottle of scotch would ensure no more than a good night's sleep and a sensation of well-being the following morning.

And there was Cynthia. Little Cynthia, all breasts and legs and a dangerous accumulation of late-awakening urges, who had been prepared to go along with everything he wanted to do, instead of slapping him down like any sensible girl would. He remembered everything, but in an enlarged way. No angry voices had been raised, he remembered that with a feeling of gratitude, but Edith must have been annoyed. She always was, when Ernie did something that nice people were not supposed to do. He could remember that she was calm, she had been drinking very little and acting as stabiliser. That meant she would have a balanced breach-list to convey to Paul, a detailed summary of every lapse. She would use it like a hammer to beat Paul about the head. Ernie did not like Edith. It was not her primness, or her intellectual superiority (which was largely a fake anyway), it had nothing to do with the fact that she obviously thought Ernie was a very inferior sort of man. The root of his dislike was tangled around the calculation he found in her, the cold-blooded manner of her drive to dominate Ernie's best friend. A psychiatrist could be good at that kind of thing. Ordinary perceptive people could detect that viciousness, that pushy impulse some women had in regard to the men thay wanted to own; Ernie could understand the basis of it, and his analytical faculty could make him more apprehensive than was usual—or healthy—for a man of his age. Some day soon, he would have to get around to easing Paul away from that aseptic bitch. In the meantime, he had the oppressive memories to deal with.

He had made it with Cynthia right across the couch. He recalled how she helped him to ease off her paint-tight panties and how he had nearly suffocated before she decided she had taken enough oral-genital foreplay. What he could not clearly recall was whether or not Edith had gone by that time. Paul had vanished, probably to his bed, but just where Edith had been was dubious. She usually hung around until the end, like some kind of door keeper, so perhaps she had been in the house when he was screwing his eyes out with Cynthia. The thought of her being in the house—*perhaps she was even in the room*?—made his head feel worse. Maybe Edith was a peeper? Maybe the early stuff, Cynthia running about without her blouse and with her skirt hanging off had blown some safety bolt in Edith's head and she had squatted behind a chair and watched the little drama of heaving bodies and interlocked intentions on the frail-legged couch? But that smacked too much of neurosis, the 'what-if' land of rampant anxiety states. Ernie folded his hands across his lean knees and tried hard to listen to the man on the couch. He knew that case well, and he also knew that he was doing no more for the patient than providing a vacant ear. Cuthbert Alderton was a raving nut case, and in his way was much more entertaining than any amount of worrying about Edith Roberts.

Scratching the tight nap of ginger hair that sat on his head like a curly helmet, he cleared his throat to interrupt the flow of talk from the corner. 'I'd like you to tell me that again, Mr Alderton. Slowly.' He had not picked up a word of it, but something in the deranged stream had struck a responsive nerve.

The patient sighed and tightened his grip on the cloth cap that rested on his chest. He was in his forties, a cheerless man with candle wax skin and eyes like glazed grapes. 'My medicine,' he said, making an elaborate display of patience. 'It's becoming so complicated, you see. I store it all in my head, because I want to have proper protection before I write it down. I want to patent it. The trouble is, it's very intricate now, I've devised so much, and I discover something new every day. I can't sleep. I'm afraid I'll forget something.'

'What about the shaking fits? Have they gone away?'

'Only because I cured them. You were no help at all. It's my medicine that's giving me the trouble now.'

'Tell me about it.'

'It's like a fountain. A gushing jet of knowledge. I think I may have tapped something outside of human experience, you know. There could be a great sea of wisdom beyond the limits of our awareness, and I believe I may well have tuned into it. I can even feel the information accumulating, forming big pools, which I have to drink from to absorb their content.'

'Why don't you just leave them there?' Ernie spoke as reasonably as he would to a grocer explaining the high cost of rice. 'Can't the pools just be allowed to stand?'

'Of course not! They would overflow and drown me! I have to keep taking in their richness, to preserve my own life. But holding it all is such a strain.' He shifted on the couch, warming to the topic. 'Take the digestive system. One small example. Ulcers are caused by the stomach beginning to digest itself. If the food it receives is not welcome, if it is wrong for the humour of the stomach, then the organ will begin to eat itself, in an attempt to have that kind of sustenance which will be truly agreeable. Now I have to hold that knowledge, and link it to the information I possess concerning the way in which the other organs have to adjust to accommodate this behaviour on the part of the stomach. The spleen, it has to fill up with mercy fluid—'

'Mercy fluid?'

Alderton nodded impatiently. 'One of the three vital juices. There's the mercy fluid, the balance oil and the pulse water. Mercy fluid is contained in the blood, and it can be drawn-off by any organ that needs it. In concentration, it will heal almost any complaint within the body.'

Ernie was glad Alderton was the first patient. A touch of

galloping lunacy was just the thing to deal with the all too solid blues of this kind of morning. The man had been referred by a magistrate's court after he had been found eating flowers in a local park. He had explained to the astonished bench that he required the blooms in order to cope with his shaking sickness. Dahlias, he assured the court, had the power to alleviate the pressure on his brain. The perfume in particular could bring happiness to cells that were under stress. He was fined two pounds for consuming council property and ordered to seek psychiatric help. Since his first session five months before, he had explained the ramifications of his inner universe in ever-wilder detail. He had one constant reference point which kept him in a state of near-sanity. In all things, under all manner of assault from his bizarre imagination, he saw himself as the instrument of great forces, a channel through which the airborne mythologies could become concrete. He was victimised, he knew it and complained of it often, but he could still do little more than accept his purpose. The shaking attacks had gradually withdrawn, but they were now replaced with this exhausting need to catalogue the cosmic medicine. In a way, Ernie looked forward to each new phase. Cuthbert Alderton was a talking book of brand new fairy tales.

'And can this mercy fluid really heal an ulcer?'

'Of course. It rarely does, though.' Cuthbert shook his head sadly. 'People interfere, you see. They tamper. And that renders the mercy fluid helpless. It's tragic, really.'

Ernie was aware that they were veering off the main track, but it did not matter. Whether Cuthbert detailed the general principle of his medicine or concentrated on one tiny aspect would make little difference to the outcome. For as long as he lived he would be a victim of obsession, that die was cast and only the crudest of shock therapy would alter it. With a psychiatrist to talk to and occasionally argue with, he would remain safe enough; in Ernie's estimation, the Cuthbert Aldertons had as much right to their freedom as the murderous psychopaths who constituted the ruling forces in the world.

'In what way do they interfere, Mr Alderton?'

'By using their own stupid medicines. They are poison to the system. Mercy fluid can heal, it is a balm that carries the gift of wholeness. Given a chance, the body's natural mechanisms can correct any and all defects.'

Don't argue, Ernie thought. More than one health fad was based on that very premise. The byways of folk-medicine were too tortuous to be explored by a shrinker with a hangover. 'That's very interesting. Tell me, have you any plan for coping with the work load? I mean, you can't go on taking in all that knowledge indefinitely. Isn't there a clue within the medicine itself, maybe an exercise that would help you to absorb faster or with less effort?'

'I'm glad you mentioned that.' Alderton's voice had dropped to a rumble, which usually meant he was about to leak some very profound discovery. 'There *is* one way. It's called brain division.'

'Sounds interesting.'

'It means I have to split my brain. I have to divide it in two, but instead of making two halves, I make two complete minds. I double my capacity.'

'How do you do it?'

'I have to do two things. First of all, I must spend a week duplicating every thought. Everything that goes through my mind must be re-run. That is a fierce discipline, as you'll appreciate. I would have to spend days preparing myself for the effort. Only the most rigorous adherence to the technique will make it work.'

Ernie tried to picture it, this man going about with his head constantly full of inverted reality, duplicating every batty notion that occurred to him. Obsession probably had a limit, but where? 'What's the other thing you have to do?'

'Eat meat.'

That was a surprise. Alderton was a dedicated vegetarian. He took it further than most people. He only ate those plants and herbs which were, as he put it, designed to match the body's chemistry. Things like lettuce, cucumber, turnip, cabbage and carrot were out. They were not meant for man. Cuthbert's diet consisted mainly of weeds, flowers and mushrooms, grudgingly supplemented with bread. He drank large quantities of milk, which Ernie supposed kept him alive. But meat, that was such a taboo that Cuthbert would turn blue just discussing it. 'Why would you have to do that?'

'To effect duplication of my brain cells. I would have to build another brain, a truly physical organic reality.'

'Where would it be housed?'

'Well, there's no room to put it side by side with the brain I have. It would exist within the present structure. In other words, my brain would thicken, it would double its density, one organ would live right within the confines of the other.'

He certainly had it all worked out, Ernie reflected. A brain within a brain. Not a particularly crazy idea, when it was set alongside the rest of Alderton's fancies. 'Do you plan to do this?'

'I think I must.' He raised a long white hand and drew it across his forehead. 'As soon as I can locate the right kind of meat, I'll probably go through with it.'

'What kind of meat?' Cannibalism had not, so far, figured in their talks.

'It would have to be a cat.'

'Why?'

'Because the flesh of cats has the faculty of rebirth. The old story about cats having nine lives is based on a very real discovery, made by the Egyptians. Other meat, when consumed by men, merely turns to mush and interferes with the normal functioning of the body. The muscles of the cat, on the other hand, are first of all reduced, then the liberated cells re-form and acquire a continuing potency.'

It would be a bad mistake, Ernie knew, to push this man into a corner where he could not explain his way out. He was not improvising, he was obviously repeating some revelation that had been with him for a while. But a little too much prodding could put him on the margins of his doctrine where he would have to struggle to locate his facts. Just one more probe, Ernie thought, giving way to an impulse that was less professional than it should have been. 'How do you reconcile cat-eating with your principles about meat?'

Alderton did not hesitate. 'Special exemption, doctor. My case is unique, after all. Every and any course should be adopted to maintain my efficiency. If I am to be an instrument of extra-terrestrial influence, if I am to go on, day after day, collecting the liberating wisdom from beyond, I have to be kept in good working order. The knowledge about cats would not have been vouchsafed me unless it was intended to be used. But I must admit I'm a shade reluctant, nevertheless.'

'About the necessity to kill a cat?'

'No, not that. That won't be much of a problem. There's an old lady who lives near me, she sometimes comes in and cleans my place. She told me that if I go to the shop on Brent Road that sells Chinese food to take away, I only have to ask for a portion of fried chicken. The old lady assures me it is really cat.'

Even the nastier of the popular myths could serve a purpose, Ernie thought. 'What's the worry, then?'

'The superiority, doctor. I will become even more intellectually superior. It is a lonely state. I must admit that even now, I find you rather a weak foil for my ability. Everyone I meet is so ignorant. They are crippled by the narrowness of their abilities. I think the loneliness will be excruciating.'

In passing, he had touched the core of his problem. The surrounding woodland, sadly, was too strong ever to be cleared now. Loneliness wore as many faces as an uncauterised hydra, and it was the one disease which, if ever banished, would take forty per cent of the rest with it.

'I'm sure your increased mental ability will find an answer to that,' Ernie said. 'Perhaps, in my limited way, I can help you through any problems that crop up.'

'Thank you. I really appreciate that.' Alderton turned his head. 'Now, can I tell you about the new area of knowledge I am being used to communicate? It won't take very long.' The time was officially up, but the glint of pleading in his eye always assured him an extra ten minutes when he wanted it.

'Very well. What's it all about?'

'The nature of Christ,' Alderton said. 'He was really a woman.'

For the remainder of the session Ernie sat back in his chair and let it all roll over his head. Alderton's notes were already filled in, and a fat bundle still waited for attention. Sick minds, troubled minds, minds cut loose from the realities, minds that were trying to kill their owners; his unending daily bread, yet whatever he did, at whatever expense of his energy, was never a tenth of what was necessary. In the morning he always had to face that. By afternoon it was different, of course, he was sailing towards evening and what lay ahead was some kind of escape, not a long string of ailing humanity.

When Alderton had put on his cap and gone, Ernie checked the time. In five minutes the small ceremony to inaugurate the ambulance would begin. He wanted to go down, but he wanted to get on with his work as well. He had three patients to see before lunch, then a protracted ward round in the afternoon. Paul Avery did not know how lucky he was. He could see what he was working with, he could dip his fingers into the wounds and say 'Look, this is a hole in somebody and I'm going to sew it up.' Ernie's professional style consisted in the main of trying to catch wet fish in the dark. What innovations could *he* push through, he wondered? A shock-box that passed music across a patient's brain matter in tandem with the jolting electricity? Perhaps a whole programme of treatment that involved the copious use of erotic ink blots and therapeutic gang bangs? He could always campaign for the introduction of painless suicide kits, consisting of a bottle of gin, some LSD and a few heroin lozenges, to be issued to all depressives in little transparent cases bearing the legend, 'In Case Of Emergency, Break Glass'. How many psychiatrists graced the hoardings outside places of entertainment? Wasn't it always the surgeon, the adonis with the knife and the tense forehead, who captured the public imagination? Psychiatric work only fascinated the kind of people who were in need of having their bumps felt. Cinderellas, from Freud all the way down, the men and women of the Bewilderment Brigade could only ever hope to acquire some commercial sheen by using their qualifications to foist some hoax on the public.

Ernie paused for a moment to consider his own forthcoming hoax. Born of a desire to resist stagnation, and growing rapidly to completion now, his book would break a few windows and perhaps finish his career in Westfield General. It was only a hoax when it was viewed from his own position as author. No one else would argue very forcibly that it was less than sincere. Under the title *The Marshes of Disquiet*, he was in course of presenting a string of lurid case histories aimed at proving what everyone knew anyway, that suppression of natural tendencies could be harmful. Under carefully-stitched cloaks of anonymity, a score of patients—some his own, some borrowed—paraded their peculiarities in titilating detail, rescuing the consciences of the readers and the credentials of the author by having a long boring analysis at the end of each action-packed episode. Ernie had played with the idea of the book for two years before starting it, and he had only been able to confess to its slightly fraudulent purpose when he was halfway through. By a not-too-difficult editorial slanting, he had rendered the material quite sensational; by putting the meatier parts in first-person prose, he had detached himself from the indignity of sordid description. The whole thing was a promotion job, he knew that and he suffered little in consequence of the knowledge. Ernest Hale was creating a place for himself among the lists of popular medicos; the edge he would gain, he felt confident, was that his sexual episodes, unlike those in the welter of sex-manuals, were not limited by the bounds of reality. He had included a rapist, a teenage voyeur, a girl with fixations about older women, two masochists and a number of others whose specialities read like an index page from Krafft Ebbing. The nub of the fraud was that the conclusions drawn were practically random. By a process that was instinctive Ernie could either prove, in a superficial way, that a baby-molester was rebelling against the way he was treated as a child, or that his behaviour was symptomatic of a desire to be reunited to the conditions and sensations of infancy. At a deeper, more carefully analytical level, iron-clad proofs probably could be determined; but that kind of writing was laborious and it left little room for the nitty-gritty the readers would want.

He could hear sounds in the quadrangle twenty yards from his office window. They were gathering to heap bouquets on Paul. Ernie did not begrudge him the applause. Paul was a straight man, he deserved to get on. He was also a good friend. His method was enviable, too, he did the sort of things that no one could complain about, he advanced his life's mission of healing by introducing plans and schemes to alleviate suffering. By comparison, Ernie sometimes felt like a clown. But a man had to do what he was good at doing, and if he happened to be doing something that did not easily attract a glimmer of fame—and if he dearly *wanted* some kudos—then he had to go where-ever the glory flower grew, even if it was dangerously near the quicksands.

Work on, he decided, taking the top file from the bundle and swallowing a groan as he sighted the name. Valerie Brown. A walking snake-pit. He pressed the button that told the nurse he was ready. At least, he thought, he had shown some integrity in the writing of his book. He had put no Valerie Browns in it at all. There were some things the public should not know about just yet.

3

The ambulance was parked in the middle of the quadrangle, directly opposite the central doors of the main administration block. The black tarmac and surrounding green verges set off the stark whiteness and gave the vehicle some measure of the symbolism Paul Avery had evoked in his spirited arguments for its introduction. Basically, it was built from a Ford Transit chassis weighing twenty-five hundredweights, with a one-hundred-and-eighteen inch wheelbase, and a fibreglass body custom-styled and fitted by Herbert Lomas of Wilmslow. The driver's cabin had angled safety seats, designed by a Canadian physiotherapist, a collapsible steering wheel, an instrument dash that incorporated switching for supplementary electrical power, a radio tuned to link with a transmission-reception unit in Westfield Casualty Department, a rescue kit accessible from inside or outside of the cab, spare working lights and a swivel spotlight control. The engine had been carefully tuned by a specialist in Coventry, with a view to improve acceleration, and steering was power-assisted. The working area at the rear was the outcome of collaboration between Paul Avery, a functional designer from London and two consultants in emergency vehicle design. Factors of cost, available space, load distribution, and smooth deployment of instruments and machinery had to be considered carefully. Within the nine-foot-six by six-foot by five-foot-eight space, a fine compromise had been achieved. The panelling was plastic, pale-green and carefully padded. The floor was covered in dark green, non-static plastic tread material. On one side wall directly behind the driver's position, large slap-lock clamps held a wheeled stretcher in position; the stretcher itself was a showpiece of up-to-date functional design principles. It was made from a light, strong alloy, covered in firmly padded leather. The height could be adjusted, by means of a geared winding handle, and the bed was articulated, enabling an operator to place a patient in an infinitely variable number of positions. Fitted directly beneath the stretcher was another, lighter model, designed to split apart and re-assemble around an accident victim; a clamped, foldaway skeleton trolley on the opposite side wall was ready, at a moment's notice, to be sprung into position and accept the second stretcher. Transfusion bottle holders were attached to each side wall, and three stainless steel clips above the main stretcher held fibreglass-shrouded thermos bottles.

The overriding principle in the design of the ambulance was that it should provide broad-spectrum emergency care right at the scene of an accident. Paul Avery had spent sufficient time in casualty work to know the heartbreak of receiving an injured man, woman or child minutes too late on the treatment trolley. The time to provide the most effective assistance to any victim of a road accident was immediately after that accident had occurred. The closest approach to the ideal, clearly, was a mobile life-support unit, a hand stretching out from the hospital to give immediate help that would be continued all the way back to the hospital and right through to the moment when, should it be necessary, the patient was wheeled into an operating theatre. The existing ambulance service was quite inadequate in the circumstances. Patients could be carried quickly from the place where they had been injured, and a measure of comfort could be provided; in cases that were not too serious, rudimentary treatment could be administered. But the truth was obvious and the shortcomings demonstrable; ambulances, in the main, were no more than vehicles for the transportation of patients to a hospital.

Treatment, in any real sense, did not begin until the injured citizen was wheeled through the doors of the casualty department. In proposing the creation of the ambulance that now stood revealed on the quadrangle, Paul Avery had stressed that he saw it as a beginning, the start of a potent line of approach in accident work that was aimed at reducing pain, disfigurement and the lamentable death rate that haunted the motorways. The new ambulance was, in its way, like a fine camera or any other expensive, efficient tool; it enabled the skill of the operators to be exercised with mimimum impediment. It had not to be valued for the excellence of what it was, but for the way it removed obstacles from the merciful function of its team. In keeping with this firm specification, the equipment within the lockers, drawers, cabinets and boxes had been chosen with meticulous care.

Wherever possible, kits had been duplicated. On the floor, to the left of the door connecting with the driver's cab, a fibreglass box contained the basic emergency medical equipment: one compartment held a dozen pre-sterilised syringes and two dozen sterilised needles of various sizes; next to it, sterile dressing packs were stacked according to size and function; another well contained a stethoscope and a sphygmo manometer, surrounded by swab packs and plastic-cased forceps; a removable drawered case held drugs—Morphine, Fortal, Atropine, Lignocaine, Xylocaine, Isoprenaline, a variety of pain-killers, anaesthetics and stimulants designed to meet almost every emergency requirement; ampoules of Paraldehyde, an efficient sedative, were stored separately, together with glass syringes for administration of the drug—this was necessary because the colourless, odourless substance had the unfortunate capacity to dissolve the standard disposable syringes; the final compartment of the box contained an innovation suggested to Avery in his student days in the States and now possible via the technology of the Japanese electronics industry. It was a small, clip-on tape-recorder, fitted with a condenser microphone. Observations could be made while an operator worked, signs that might later disappear and be forgotten would be recorded for subsequent consultation; above all else, the clinical habit of note-taking could be sustained even while the hands were fully occupied.

On the opposite side of the through-door, shatter-proof housing surrounded a rechargeable power unit, with five outlets set into the wall immediately above it. Into these could be plugged the portable defibrillator, via its transformer unit (another Japanese touch which modified the power flow and changed it from direct to alternating current); this instrument was mildly spectacular, and consisted principally of two large circular pads with handles, connected by cables to the power source. When the pads were applied to the chest of a patient whose heart had either stopped or was showing distressing signs of imminent collapse, the resulting electric shock could, in many cases, put matters right. Other apparatus requiring electrical power included a small suction pump, a drill, a humidifying unit used in connection with ventilation equipment, lamps and the movable fan heater.

Most of the electrical equipment was stored in lockers forward of the rear wheel housings. Alongside these, just above floor level, ingeniously compact drawer units held various outfits—cutting-down sets for locating veins, tracheostomy kits, giving-sets for attachment to blood and plasma bottles, Dextrostix packs for determining blood-sugar levels, packets containing Brooke's airways to aid in mouth-to-mouth respiration, plus various sizes of disposable rubber gloves and finger stalls. Beneath the main and auxiliary stretcher bays, ample accommodation was provided for splints both wooden and inflatable, and two large plasma crates were bolted to wall and floor at the angles of the wall separating the driver from the working area. Within securing hooks beneath the long narrow side windows, two Portagen oxygen units were sited, while a lipped shelf above the connecting door held two perspex-fronted boxes containing Penlon infant resuscitators.

To add ballast to the vehicle, as an incidental to providing it with a valuable clinical aid, four oxygen cylinders were secured in a heavily insulated compartment beneath the floor. The outlet was set in the side wall at the head-end of the main stretcher, and was fitted to accept two face-mask attachments, via a pressure reduction valve. A safety device incorporated in the design ensured that oxygen could not be leaked from the outlet until a face mask was attached. One final piece of equipment, carried in a box to which Paul Avery kept the key, was a Polaroid camera; every scheme with which he concerned himself usually harboured the germ of a future venture.

Outside, the ambulance was white and shiny, with the name of the hospital on the sides in gold, and the words, 'ACCIDENT UNIT' painted beneath in fluorescent red. Lights on the roof, fore and aft, could be switched on to provide flood illumination where needed. A square box, situated in the very centre of the roof, flared the word 'EMERGENCY' on all four sides when the appropriate switch was touched by the driver, and a special siren, with an urgent piercing note like a whooping banshee was fitted to distinguish this unit from its lesser brethren. The cost had been difficult to estimate beforehand, and now that the unit was complete, no one had a clue. Some costs had overlapped with those occurring within the casualty department, others had been deliberately spread over total hospital expenditure by an administration that was determined to see the scheme succeed; in Paul Avery's private opinion, the original tentative figure of twenty thousand pounds had probably been overshot. But it had happened, the machine had become a gleaming, spotless reality. As it sat quietly at the centre of an admiring group of invited well-wishers, the subtle urgency of its lines put a spark of excitement in the hearts of Avery and the team chosen to support him.

At a distinguishing distance from the sixty-odd others, Avery stood by the eroded statue of the hospital's founder, flanked by his staff. He knew them all, he had spent months devising the short-list that had brought them together. The real difficulty had been to match the pairs; the service was to be on twenty-four hour call, and Avery was determined that day or night, the team in charge would operate with the same efficiency and the same level of co-ordination as the one following. Two different sets of ideas would not work within a scheme that was intended to be single-minded.

The drivers were both in their forties, men with long experience of the ambulance service, both with commendations for safe driving. Dan McGoldrick, a Dubliner who had not seen his land of birth for fifteen years, nevertheless spoke with an accent thick enough to confuse most English ears. Avery had no difficulty understanding him, as was often the case with men who had spent time with members of the New York police force. Dan was a strong man and at accidents he showed a measure of coolheadedness that was never less than reassuring. Because he had a flattened nose and because he was Irish most people were inclined to assume that he was a man for a spot of roistering; in fact, he hardly drank at all and his disfigurement had been caused in the line of duty, when the rear door of an elderly ambulance had slammed on his face.

Dan's colleague was Ferdie Nesbit, another man from a foreign land. He was among the blackest of all the Nigerians that anyone in Westfield General had ever seen, and he spoke with a melodious inflection that was backed by a gentle eternal sense of humour. He had lived in England since he was a very young boy, and the irony of his status, the long-boned, swing-hipped, curly-headed native of the dark continent, growing to maturity among the paler, rhythmless denizens of a cold island that could be sunk in one of his African lakes, had not been lost on him. He did not feel like an alien, but he had told Paul Avery, when he had first known him, that it was advisable occasionally to behave as if he were inferior; 'Saves a lot of people the trouble of treatin' me that way,' he explained.

The two attendants, Bill Davis and Lester Hill, were local men, both in the mid-thirities. They had all the appropriate qualifications and an endearing disregard for authority. They had joined the service together and now, appointed to identical posts with the Life-Support Unit, their sense of partnership was being consolidated. Off-duty, they spent as much time together as possible. They shared an enthusiasm for beer and card playing, and suffered jointly under the lashes of their wives' disapproval. United from the start by the kind of similarities and differences that always ensure real friendship, they had become virtual blood brothers in their domestic alienation. Lester, short and stocky with the face of a rumpled Brando, was the more vocal of the pair. Bill had a brooding offhand expression that suited his long nose and small sunken eyes. He was content a great deal of the time to nod heavily as underscore to Lester's pithy summaries of life in general and theirs in particular; the married state was one topic that could keep the one firing barbs and the other jerking his head up and down for long stretches of time. 'We get married when we're carefree,' Lester would quip; 'because human beings can't survive without a lot of misery.'

The ladies of the team were both State Registered, both senior staff nurses. Ellen Haxton was twenty-seven, a product of London training and so good at her job that she made some ward sisters nervous. She had a round face with the aggressive look of a female soldier. Dark eyes, a very straight nose and a tight mouth, with hair cut shorter than male fashion dictated. Despite the forbidding look, Avery knew her to be a sensitive person whose training had done nothing to reduce her natural concern for humanity. She was a Catholic who believed in sticking by the letter of her faith; that could sometimes create problems, but her abundant skill compensated heavily for the occasional awkwardness.

Mary Scott's abilities as a nurse were a match for Ellen Haxton's, but her personality was a direct opposite. She was a small long-haired redhead, a twenty-five-year-old fireball with a pleasing shape and a reputation for carnal generosity. Paul Avery had set the legend in abeyance, having met no one who had actually laid Nurse Scott. She gave every indication that the dark hints of deprived housemen might well be correct, but so did most teasers. In ward and theatre she conducted herself with professional decorum and a confident skill, and she had the ability to get along with everyone. Paul had convinced himself that his reasons for selecting her to serve on his unit were all perfectly proper and based on the most objective reasoning.

Everyone was waiting for the Superintendent, Dr Towers, who had a nervous habit of checking the mail every day before he would do anything else. Sir Albert Macauley, chairman of the Board, was already present, as were three other Board members and some senior members of the hospital staff. Matron had clustered about her the two assistant matrons, known throughout the hospital as Tweedledum and Tweedledee, and a curious clutch of sisters flirted stiffly with consultants and senior registrars. The porters were out in force, Avery noticed. They were the experts, of course, the men with lengthy opinions of everything. He could see them passing various judgments, their brown coats flapping in the wind like magistrates' gowns, their heads jerking in the direction of the vehicle, jaws wagging. They probably *did* have a few valid points to make, and anything they said would be uncoloured by political motive or bias—which, Avery realised, was a good deal more than could be said for the expensively-suited consultants who managed, by years of practice, to keep their real feelings and opinions covered by layers of protocol and guile. So far as Paul knew, only Mr Madison had voiced any strong objection to the scheme. The others, by saying little, had thereby demonstrated their general approval. That was the way consultants did things. Say nothing, the rule went, and you will have agreed. If agreement proves, in time, to have been unwise, then it can always be pointed out later that no opinion was ever expressed, although there *had* been nagging doubts. Avery did not object to the convention. It was a protective device, and as such it worked very well. Every man had his own kind of armour, after all.

Mr Madison was not present. Ernie Hale had suggested to Paul that the old man's opposition to the new ambulance might possibly run deeper than most people expected. The opinion was founded on Ernie's capacity for reading human motive very accurately and it was reinforced by his past experience of Madison. A very dodgy man, Ernie claimed. A person without the usual capacity for climbing down. Once, in a case of psycho-somatic disturbance where the patient was presenting all the symptoms of bowel obstruction, Ernie had argued heatedly with Madison that it was a no more than a transient phase in the patient's mental condition. Severe constipation, as all psychiatrists know, can be caused by a fierce possessiveness on the part of a man or woman unwilling to part with anything of themselves, even their excrement. Madison, who had used the term mumbo-jumbo more than once to describe psychiatry, had swept Ernie's diagnosis aside. An exploratory operation revealed a wad of impacted faeces the size of a football, but no obstruction. Madison blithely announced that, far from confirming Ernie's original assertion, the findings of the operation suggested that there was some temporary paralysis of the nerve plexuses in the colon and the rectum. Ernie's insistence met with a granite-faced adherence to the clinical explanation. Madison escalated his claim by making reference to aberrant or even absent nerve-chain cells, and he threw around names like Auerbach and Meissner, laying a thick coat of informed scientific opinion over what he called, with due disdain, Ernie's 'guess'. And that was not the only instance Ernie could cite. It appeared that Mr Madison did not care, ever, to argue. He would glide along his chosen path and in time, by dint of authority, experience and a talent for appearing very wise, he would prevail. Ernie had told Paul that Madison took nothing lightly, for he disliked loose ends and he would see them tied, wrongly or not. In the present circumstances where his objections to the ambulance had been rejected, he would be seeking some means to restore the balance, to cancel the slight to his name and dignity. Paul was not so sure. In his dealings with Madison he had always found him stuffy, an adherent to the tiniest details of procedure, but nevertheless a man of broad learning and clear reason. His arguments against the new unit were reasoned, he probably felt that he was right. Somebody had to win the little struggle, and this time it had been Paul; he could not see that Madison would take it very badly, for he must have lost hundreds of policy decisions in his time. He could not be expected to turn out to cheer the machine he had opposed, but it would probably end there. The trouble with Ernie Hale, Paul reckoned, was that he analysed everything out of proportion.

'My backside's freezing.'

Paul and the rest of the team turned with wide eyes to regard the source of the remark, Nurse Scott, who was hugging herself with crossed arms and hopping from foot to foot. Nurse Haxton had mustered a blush, while the drivers and the attendants were simply grinning. Nurse Scott heaved a despairing sigh and jerked her pointed hat towards the main office. 'Has old Towers got a letter bomb, do you think?'

'Probably rehearsing his speech,' Paul muttered. It *was* cold, and any further delay was going to put a strong damper on the occasion. 'You should wear thicker tights,' he told Nurse Scott. Nurse Haxton smiled thinly, anxious not to seem out of things, but clearly uncomfortable in this area of banter.

'I don't wear them at all.'

Speculation danced behind five sets of male eyes. Paul could not recall when he had last seen a pair of stockings and a garter belt.

'I'm taking that report seriously,' Scott continued. 'Aren't you. Haxton?' She referred to an article that had been the subject of some discussion at Westfield privately and at open nursing forums. A team of doctors had determined, to their own satisfaction, that the wearing of tights, in addition, sometimes, to two pair of pants, was responsible for many cases of cystitis among young women. At an instinctive level, Paul Avery found the theory credible. Nurse Haxton was wearing her blush again. 'I hadn't really given it much thought,' she said, looking impatiently at her watch.

Dr Towers arrived, answering Haxton's prayer, marching with customary dignity towards the spot where the board officials were gathered. He gave Paul a small wave in passing, his severe clipped hair and toothbrush moustache giving him the air of some colonel on his way to take a salute. He was greeted warmly by the plump, rosy-faced Sir Albert, and after some polite exchanges with the others, he turned to face the semi-circular crowd with a raised hand that appealed for silence.

'Ladies and gentlemen, today we have come together to mark an occasion that may well have far-reaching effects on the future of casualty work in this country. The magnificent ambulance you see is the fore-runner, we hope, of many such vehicles, a sophisticated mobile emergency room that can provide advanced medical aid within minutes of an accident occurring. I don't need to tell any of you that, in theory, such an ambulance is a straightforward proposition. Given the opportunity, any number of laymen and doctors alike would design one within minutes. It would be filled with miraculous electronic gadgetry, it would travel with perfect stability at over a hundred miles an hour, and it would be staffed by a team of clean-cut young people who would perform open-heart surgery in an air-conditioned compartment while the ambulance sped back to the hospital.' Towers paused for the ripple of laughter, adding his own wry smile. 'But pipe dreams require dream surroundings. Our hospital lies three miles from a major motorway. Every week, we see the results of careless driving, drunken driving, safe driving caught up in one or both of the other kinds. We see some terrible tragedies. Among the tragedies, a fair proportion are avoidable. People have died because of the time it took for them to be brought here, time during which only the barest minimum of emergency treatment has been possible. Reduction of motorway fatalities requires on-the-spot aid, and to provide that, we must provide a practical, down-to-earth life-support service, based on the knowledge gained from the errors and shortcomings of past procedure. Above all, we must base our system on realistic principles.'

'He's not going to list all the gear, is he?' It was Nurse Scott again, leaning forward and whispering in Paul's ear. 'He sounds as if he's just getting warmed up.'

'He promised a short speech,' Paul whispered back, 'but you know what his promises are like.' Dr Towers, in the manner of his kind, was notorious for the way in which he would agree to implement a scheme, or look into a grievance, or put right any wrong, just so long as the promise would placate a complainant and get him or her out of the office.

'Well, he might end up with my frostbitten behind on his conscience.' Scott warned.

Paul found it pleasant to contemplate that behind. But more and more, she sounded like the kind of teaser he had suspected. The talk was as clear a sign as any label.

Dr Towers was pressing on. 'It would be foolish, within the confines of our overtaxed, understaffed and harrassed profession, to postulate the formation of some advanced hospital on wheels. Such an idea would create more problems than it would ever solve. With laudable regard for essential requirements, Dr Paul Avery set about designing a unit—indeed a service—to offset the sometimes catastrophic effect of delay. What this ambulance and its staff offer to the accident victim is time. In one sense, it is ironical. With our unit we hope to combat delay with delay. By delaying the onrush of complications, we can reduce the damage caused by delayed medical treatment.' He paused to let this small morsel of erudition soak in. Sir Albert Macauley was beaming to left and right. His girth, plus his expensive dark blue overcoat, appeared to insulate him against the sharpness of the air. Watching him, Paul recalled with some gratitude the way Sir Albert had given the ambulance his undiluted support. He was said to be a terrible driver, so perhaps his enthusiasm was laced with self-interest.

'I don't wish to be a source of delay myself,' Towers went on; 'so I will first of all express my own pleasure at seeing the new ambulance complete and ready for action, and my confidence that it will fulfil its proposed task. Next, I wish to record my admiration for the way in which Dr Avery and his assistants on this scheme have demonstrated skill, energy and dedication throughout the long months of planning and revision. Finally, I would like to ask Sir Albert Macauley, chairman of our Board of Governors, to officially inaugurate the new ambulance.'

The applause was spirited, providing as it did an opportunity for people to enliven their circulations. Sir Albert stepped forward, empty-handed, which meant he was going to say very little. It was his usual practice, even when delivering the most cursory address, to work from notes.

'My friends, in a few minutes, you will be able to inspect this marvellous vehicle for yourselves, and Dr Avery, I understand, will answer any questions you may wish to ask.' His voice was rich with the port-wine imagery of his class, and he swung his eyes around the congregation with the confident glassy stare of one who had never been inconvenienced by poverty or struggle. In Avery's book, that was a good point. A man like Macauley had none of the social cleat marks on him, he was immersed in privilege, so no bitterness was likely ever to cloud his reason. He could afford to be totally fair. 'When you examine the ambulance, try to bear in mind that it is an adjunct to the skill of those who will operate it.' Avery liked that; the point he had made back at the start had not been forgotten. 'And remember, also, that it is no static exhibition piece. It is poised, ready to take off on whatever mission of mercy may come crying over the air waves. You will be inspecting a finely tooled weapon in man's struggle against forces which, thankfully, he still refused to regard as inevitable.' He cleared his throat and straightened his back, creating the illusion of having gained a foot in height. 'Ladies and gentlemen, I declare the Avery Life-Support Unit officially in service.'

While the hands clapped and a few voices cheered, Paul found himself growing warm, his face and neck suffused with the blood that had rushed to accommodate his sudden unbelieving pleasure. The Avery Life-Support Unit. It was hard to believe. They had put his name on it. Of all people, an American registrar in an English hospital had the least expectation of that acclaim. Sensations raced across his mind; pride, gratitude, astonishment and finally the safe one again, a satisfaction with no overtones of contentment. He thought of his father and wondered what he would say about his lunatic son now; he thought of the future, years into the future when he would be back in the States and something called the Avery Life-Support Unit would be racing up and down the highways, right here in England. It was like being given a slice of eternity.

'Are you pleased?' It was Sir Albert, *noblesse oblige* written large across his smiling countenance. 'It was my idea to give it your name, but I assure you no one objected.'

'I'm very grateful, sir. I was always under the impression that things like this only happened in England when you got to be around a hundred years old.'

'Oh, you malign us, doctor. In this country, the honours are only handed out where and when they are deserved. I think the least we could do in this case was put your name to something you'd spent so much time and energy on.' He tapped Paul's shoulder with a finger tip. 'Just you see to it that this unit lives up to expectation.'

'I will, sir. Thank you again.'

As Sir Albert wandered off, Paul turned and faced the team, who looked as gratified as he felt. 'That's it, people. We're launched.'

'When's the party?' Nurse Scott again, still looking frozen.

'My place, Saturday.' He made the decision on the spur. Why not? If Edith blew a fuse, she could go ahead. They had all gone through a lot to get this wagon on the road. They were entitled to have a little celebration, something more than the cocktails and salmon sandwiches Dr Towers was laying on later.

'I'll come if you don't let my wife know,' Lester Hill said, and Bill Davis nodded behind him.

'We'll make it look like an emergency,' Paul assured him. 'Dan, Ferdie? Will you come along?'

Dan shrugged. 'I'm not a boozin' man, but I like watchin' other folk make fools of themselves. Yes, I'll pop along.'

'Ferdie?'

The big black face split in a wide smile. 'I'll bring my limbo poles.'

Nurse Haxton had moved off to the edge of the group, anxious again to be excluded from the topic. Paul touched her arm. 'You'll come, won't you?'

She fought with two expressions and settled on the one that showed forced enthusiasm. 'That would be very nice, yes . . .'

For the next hour Paul answered questions and cleared up doubtful points. He was to be the only doctor on the unit. For many reasons, a second doctor would not be a practical proposition. Since he was calling the shots, Paul pointed out that he could put as much strain on himself as he wanted. On the question of priorities, he explained that the unit would attend any emergency motorway calls—or others, on other roads, of similar seriousness—within a ten mile radius. Motorway police could make contact with the unit via their own central transmitter, and if there was a double call, priority would be given to the one which, in the estimation of the police, was the more serious. Rate and distribution of accidents being what they were, Paul felt confident that the team could attend to well over eighty-per cent occurring in the specified area. The members of the team, including himself, would carry on normal hospital duties when the unit was not on call. The nurses were normally engaged on casualty duty anyway, so there would be no long-stretch routine breaks when they left on a call. Drivers and attendants would be on stand-by, and their non-active periods would be adequately filled by maintaining the ambulance itself.

As the crowd started to drift towards the warmth of the superintendent's office and the waiting refreshments, Paul fell in behind them. At the door he paused and looked back at the vehicle, taking pleasure in its whiteness, feeling a closeness to it, a kinship already shared by Dan and Ferdie who were running duster's along its smooth lines. Then, on the road beyond the quadrangle, he saw someone standing quite still, staring at the unit. It was Mr Madison. His expression, even from where Paul stood, was grim. He looked for a few moments longer, then moved slowly away, head down, hands clasped tightly at his back. Paul thought for an instant about what Ernie had said, then he rejected the idea. Madison always looked like that. He would accept the unit, in time, just like everyone else in the hospital.

4

On Wednesday morning Mr Madison was particularly difficult on ward round. Sister Cunningham, who was sensitive to most of his ways, found that he was deliberately by-passing her efforts at path-smoothing, creating difficulties and reasons for complaint where none had existed before.

It started with the third patient. He was elderly, a man who had turned up in his doctor's surgery with a severe pain in his stomach. He explained that it had been coming and going for a considerable time; he had been forced by the increase in pain to consult a physician. It was determined that he had a hiatus hernia—a portion of his stomach had passed through his diaphragm and into the cavity of his chest. In theatre, Mr Madison had restored the anatomy to normal and repaired the damage to the patient's diaphragm, from which his oesophagus had become detached, causing the initial trouble. Now, the old gentleman was making progress, but Mr Madison maintained that he was not being kept to his 'sloppy diet,' essential to post-operative recovery.

'But he has, sir. You gave strict instructions—'

'And they have been disregarded.' Madison sniffed and consulted the man's chart. 'It's possible to detect things like this, sister. This man is not receiving the appropriate diet, or he is supplementing it on the quiet.'

Sister looked at the patient's uncomprehending face. Madison knew who he could dominate. The man looked as if he would agree to any accusation the consultant cared to fling at him. She touched the thin shoulder gently. 'Have you been eating anything you shouldn't, Mr Higgins?'

He shook his head.

'Nonsense.' Madison replaced the chart on the bed and swept on, followed by a blushing sister and a second-year nurse. This morning he had decided to make the round on his own. His registrar, Dr Edith Roberts, had been asked to assist the senior registrar in theatre; to clear the floor completely, Madison had sent the housemen to the library to collect all the data they could on radical mastectomy operations. The errand was a disheartening one, for he had not indicated which aspect of the operation interested him, or which period in the history of the technique he wished to have researched. Alone on the ward, attended only by the two quailing nurses, he was subdividing his anger, transferring much of it into his surroundings. No one could guess what was wrong, for Mr Madison never talked about personal matters. He did believe, though, in letting personal upset interfere with the running of his department.

'What the devil is this?' He was pointing to a bottle standing beside the radiator between two beds.

Sister Cunningham gulped, uncomfortable and annoyed at being kept off guard. 'It looks like lemonade . . .'

'It's mine.' The patient in the bed nearest the offending bottle was a young man with lank hair and a spotty complexion. He was glaring defensively at Madison, prepared to stand by his lemonade whatever happened. As was his usual practice when tackling matters not directly connected with a patient's illness, Madison addressed himself to the sister:

'See that bottles and such like are kept in the lockers, will you? This ward is a disgrace.'

In the ensuing thirty minutes, almost a dozen other causes for complaint were located. A dressing was improperly applied, there were minute dried spill marks beside a bed, a patient fitted with a naso-gastric tube was lying at the wrong angle, some lurid reading matter lying on a locker was condemned, the student nurse was shouted at because she leaned on Madison's arm as she held back the covers to allow him to examine a distended abdomen, the sister was hissingly told that she should pay more attention to one patient's bodily hygiene and, in a rare deviation from custom, Madison told a man directly that he was hindering the progress of his recovery by smoking too much—the evidence for the assertion being a nicotine stain on his index finger.

Finally, at eleven o'clock, Madison stamped out of the ward, leaving sister and her nurse close to tears. He went straight to his private office and installed himself behind the desk, placing a case report directly before him and staring at it without seeing a single word. As a man grows older, things that were formerly important become intensified, mere significance can grow to the proportion of cardinal concern. Henry Madison had long known that he was moving into an area of his life where his principles and his status were no longer trappings, they were being transformed into vital supports. In the old days, the younger flexible days, a slight was a slight and even then Henry had always felt the sting. Now the smallest assault on his authority or judgment was a body blow that left him reeling. Lesser men, he presumed, would learn to accept the inevitable decline, the dwindling brought about by too many attacks on the flimsy supports. That course was not for him. The briefest reading of the surgical texts, a mere glance through bound volumes of the journals, showed that if he was not a sparkling star in the annals of surgery, Henry Madison was at the very least a substantial contributor to the progress of his craft. His steady devotion and his prodigious application had made him a force, a potent dignitary to be respected and honoured. He would never allow that hard-won distinction to be eroded or dismantled. At that very moment he was feeling, as he had been feeling for many hours, the soul-pain of a man whose power had been diminished. He was not sorrowing; he was scanning the breadth of his capacity for retaliation.

The evening before, the humiliation of being disregarded in the matters of the new ambulance had been driven deeper into his heart. He had invited to his home a number of senior colleagues, impressing on them that their attendance was extremely important; he had not said beforehand what it was that made the meeting necessary. In the past, he had called his own kind about him to discuss and plot whenever he had felt that a collective effort was required to deal with political or procedural matters within Westfield General. His authority ensured, usually, a full attendance. The previous night six fellow consultants had sat round the fire in his study, sipping Henry's sherry, listening to his argument. The ambulance, the so-called Life Support Unit, had to be crushed. On his own, he had not been able to make the Board see sense. Collectively, the senior men could produce the requisite weight to ensure that the vehicle was garaged for good. He reminded his fellows that several expensive pieces of equipment lay idle all over Westfield, because it had been deemed better to abandon them than to go through with the costly and impractical business of using them. The decision to purchase did not always means that a point was reached where implementation was inevitable. They had done it before and they could, Henry emphasised, do it again. The power to cancel a decision made at Board level was an important tool; it must be used in this case.

He had gone on to outline the reasons for his disapproval of the scheme. Cost versus questionable value. A disruption, too, he said. The ambulance would alter the established casualty and theatre routine. It would cause unrest. Avery's plan virtually created an êlite, and jealousy would be rife. Henry said that he could foresee union troubles, on the ambulance and nursing sides. He went on for an hour, heaping disadvantage on disadvantage, constantly setting the dark omens against the puny, perhaps imaginary virtues of the new scheme.

Then, incredibly, they had started to argue with him. Instead of putting their heads together to frame their official objection, they had started to speak up in open favour of the brainchild of the gadget-happy, immature, misguided American upstart. Henry could scarcely believe his ears. Men of their standing, men whose loyalties belonged within their own camp, jabbering on about how advanced, how efficient, how *marvellous* the unit was. He answered them with the same arguments he had been using all night, but they were not impressed. They behaved like girls whose heads had been turned. Avery, with his winning graces, his charm that was used as a substitute for concrete ability, had seduced them, all of them.

When they had gone, he sat alone in the house and felt his bewilderment shore up his bitterness. For forty years he had worked to strengthen the establishment, for decades he had helped maintain the ancient dignity and etiquette of his calling. Now, the barbarians were at the door, the age of the jackass was dawning, and men who should have known better were waving the banners of the cult that would wipe out everything they had represented.

He would not give in. If he was to be the only opponent, it simply meant that he would have to adopt more resources to equalise his position. Sitting at his desk, gazing blindly at the report open before him, he found that his mind was arranging the facts, setting out the battlefield. It was an old habit, practically automatic. Hours and hours of anger and fuming would pass away, leaving a calm calculation. A feature of such times was a rather fearful honesty. To be accurate, a plan of campaign should not encounter the risky ground of self-delusion. Glad now that no one could see him as the truth seared across his conscience, Henry faced the central fact of his unrest; his authority was his most precious jewel, he had nothing else of similar value. He would defend it at any cost and by any means, for without it he would be nothing

The first call came in while Paul Avery was removing a splinter of steel from a road worker's thumb. The emergency note screamed out from his adapted communicator and before it had died, a nurse was finishing Paul's task and he was clambering into the cab beside Ferdie Nesbitt and Lester Hill. In the back, Nurse Scott was sitting on a foldaway chair, grasping the connecting door handle for support as the ambulance took the long sweep down from casualty reception and accelerated through the gates, taking the access road towards the motorway.

'Sounds messy,' Lester grunted. 'The copper didn't say much. He sounded sick. A lorry's had a blowout and crossed the reservation. He's hit two cars.'

Within ten minutes they were in sight of the accident. The lorry, like some dead predator, lay across the soft shoulder of the up-stream lane, its nose flattened against the unyielding rock that sloped up sharply towards the fields beyond. A pale green saloon car sat squarely in the middle of the road, its tyres torn open on the nearside, a violent series of criss-crossing arcs, painted in rubber across the light grey tarmac, indicating that it had been spun in a complete circle. The bonnet was twisted and fragments of the ruptured engine peeped past the edge of the crumpled radiator grille. A second car lay on the far side of the lorry, and as the ambulance drew level and Ferdie pulled it across the torn grass and earth of the central reservation, Paul could see that the vehicle was a mini. It gave the appearance of having run part of the way into the rock, but in fact the bonnet and engine housing had been telescoped back into the cabin. There were four people standing on the road beside the lorry, watching in glazed incomprehension as the police tried to effect a diversion.

Ferdie parked the vehicle on the shoulder, ten feet away from the lorry. Paul jumped out and approached the nearest policeman.

'What's the damage?'

The constable was young. From his colour, Paul guesssed this might be his first accident. 'The man in the mini's dead. The engine landed on his legs. There's a girl over there—' he pointed to a blanketed figure beside the squad car, '—I think her legs are broken and she can't breathe very well. Two kids and their mother from the saloon, they're shaken up but no bones broken. The father's unconscious. Blood all over him.'

Mary Scott appeared, carrying an emergency bag, stocked from the equipment in the ambulance. Paul indicated the girl by the police car. 'You take a look over there. Lester, go with her. Ferdie, you come with me.'

The windshield of the saloon had shattered, and Paul gently eased aside the lorry driver who had pushed his head through the opening.

'He looks bad.' the driver said. He was middle-aged, frightened, a man who would never do his job particularly well again. 'Christ, I tried to dodge him, but he was right in front of me, and the mini was at his back. If I'd been able to pull myself round—'

'Just go and sit down. I'll give you something in a minute.' Paul buttoned his white coat about him and leaned across the bulging bonnet of the car. A man was lying back in the driving seat, his hands open at his sides in an attitude of surrender. His chin was gashed and fragments of glass twinkled like rubies on his blood-soaked neck and shirt. Sliding closer, Paul lifted one hand and felt for a pulse. It was there, but it was weak and irregular. There was an acrid odour in the space between the man and the dashboard. Paul assumed that his bowels had voided.

'Ferdie, can you get that door open?'

The handle was distorted, and from the shape of the side frame it looked as if the door might be jammed on to its lock. Ferdie gripped with both hands and heaved, shaking the entire vehicle as he attempted to free the dented metal from the vice grip surrounding it. After a minute he gave up. 'No good, doc. It's solid.'

'Right. We better try the window, then.' There were only two doors, and the one on the passenger side was hopelessly jammed. Glancing quickly towards the injured man's wife and children, he could see scratches on their legs, which they must have sustained when they were lifted through the windscreen cavity. Paul ran his hand along the shattered edge. It was like a razor. He raised himself on hands and knees on the bonnet and examined the upper part of the unconscious man's face. As he suspected, there was a deep cut above the eyes, from which the blood oozed very slowly, seeping into the hair. The man must have smashed the window with his head. Leaning right inside, Paul turned the side window handle. It moved stiffly at first, then it began to lower quite freely until it hit an obstruction two thirds of the way down.

'That'll do.' He jumped back on to the road and heard the woman shout something. Through all the shock following an accident, the concern of one partner always managed to surface. He made a placating sign with both hands and turned to Ferdie. 'I don't want to move him until I've had a look at his head. Get me some dressing packs and bring the number two stretcher.'

Through the lowered side window, Paul carefully palpated the man's skull. He could find no evidence of fracture, but something in the almost stylised posture, the openness of the hands and the spread knees, the apparent tension in the neck alerted him to the possibility of trouble within the skull.

The laceration on the forehead was bad. It was low enough to have possibly involved the structure supporting the eyes. When Ferdie arrived, Paul took a large dressing from him and strapped it across the patient's brow. Another, narrower dressing, designed to hold the edges of a would together, was placed across the lacerated chin, after the particles of glass had first been carefully removed.

'Something's badly wrong with this one, Ferdie. Put the stretcher down by the side of the car. We'll try and rotate him through the hole in the front.' A blinker was flashing dimly in Paul's memory. So far, it was too dim to be recognised.

With considerable difficulty, they managed at last to get the patient out of the car and on to the stretcher. Another ambulance arrived and the driver was directed to take the woman and children back to Westfield casualty department. 'Don't take the lorry driver,' Paul murmured. 'The last thing she wants is him sitting in the back with her. I'll get someone to take him in later.

The man on the stretcher, now that he was in the full daylight, looked quite young. The smell of excrement surrounding him was strong, even in the open air. Paul bent and raised an eyelid. The pupils were distended and even; damage to the eyes had perhaps been avoided. But what was it, what was the flicker of recognition? More and more, as his experience of accident work increased, Paul found himself reacting to general features that could not be pinned down, instincts that were made up of a dozen or more small signals in a specific combination. Back home, they called it gut knowledge, the special sense that attached itself to a man when his professional stature began to fill out. 'Let's get him into the wagon, Ferdie.'

Mary Scott and Lester were already there. Their patient was a girl in her teens, pretty and fresh skinned. She appeared to be unconscious. 'I gave her morphine,' Scott announced, as she busied herself at the patient's legs, checking the inflated splints and making sure there was no tension in her posture. 'Fractures both legs. Impacted right femur, comminuted fractures to right tib and fib. Left femur impacted, and I think there's a Pott's fracture on the left ankle. Her chest took a wallop, but I don't think anything's broken.' She turned for a moment and looked at Paul. 'Did you see her boyfriend?'

'The man in the mini?'

'That's him. The engine block nearly cut him in half.' She sighed. 'They were probably enjoying themselves. Then bang, nothing's the same again.'

Paul eased the shirt from his patient's chest and began to swab away the blood and loose glass. Just as he was clipping the stethoscope over his ears, on the precise verge of telling Ferdie that they could go shortly, the flickering light came closer and he began to move by rapid but cautious instinct. He watched the man's neck for a moment, then tried to re-button the collar. It would not fasten, the patient's neck had swelled appreciably. Paul placed the end of his stethoscope to the chest and listened.

Systolic bruit, an abnormal noise as the heart contracted, could be detected over the top of the breast bone and at the base of the neck. The picture was building up. He checked the pulses of the arms, which were altered now, then the legs. There was relative high pressure in the arms. The patient groaned, then came suddenly awake, panic in his pained eyes.

'What's—' he touched the bandages on his head and chin, and his mouth worked in anxious whorls as he took in his surroundings and felt the pain in his body. 'Oh God . . .' He looked frightened, apprehensive. And that did it. Swelling in the neck, systolic murmur, unequal pulses, and a demonstration of foreboding. The man's trouble lay not in his head, but in his chest. He had all the signals of an aortic tear. That great pump, the vital pathway for the blood, was torn open.

'Ferdie, get on the radio and tell casualty to alert Mr Greer. Tell them we've got an aortic tear on board. When you've done that, get us back to Westfield. But not too fast.'

The condition was gravely serious, and seemed to be an increasing feature of motorway accidents. In Wiltshire it had already been determined that one-third of the people who died in road accidents in the county had suffered torn aortas. Four out of nine fatalities in a recent major road accident had died of the same thing. Paul was well acquainted with the difficulties surrounding an accurate diagnosis. So sadly often, the presence of a tear was not suspected until the aorta gave way completely, and then it was too late.

Lester tightened the bolts on the rear doors and signalled the cab that all was secure in back. Mary Scott looked up and sighted the lorry driver, still sitting by his ruined vehicle. 'Shall we give him a lift?'

Paul peered through the window. The man looked dejected, depressed beyond the capacity to do more than droop. 'Sure. Tell Ferdie to pick him up.' That was the worst position to be in, Paul thought, watching the man's limp frame for a moment, taking in the brutalised lines forming round the eyes, the marks of a citizen turned unwillingly into a killer by the bursting of a simple rubber tyre.

On the way back to the hospital, Paul held the patient over on his right side, in an awkward, incomplete posture, necessary to reduce stress on the damaged vessel. He explained the situation to Lester and Mary as they went. 'Most people suffering from a large aortic tear have only an hour or two to live, unless a competent surgeon can attempt a repair. So far as I know, there hasn't been an aortic tear operation performed at Westfield for years. You know why, of course. They usually arrive dead, or without the tell-tale signs. This man has a chance. He's unconscious again, but that's largely shock and the bang he received to his head. If Mr Greer makes it to Westfield on time, I think our first time out might come through as a shining success.'

At casualty, the patient was wheeled carefully through to the theatre ante-room. The injured girl was passed over to an orthopaedic team while the casualty sister, Bridget Clarke, ordered the mobile x-ray apparatus. Paul spent ten minutes preparing his report and handed it in to the typist. First job accomplished, he thought. Now he could feel that the unit was *really* under way.

In the canteen he bumped into Edith. She was carrying an armful of books, her face screwed up in concentration as she tried to negotiate a narrow space between two tables with a coffee cup balanced in one hand. She looked terribly severe at such times, Paul reflected. Yet her broad, intelligent face could soften into the most gloriously radiant expression when she forgot her dignity and let the girl in her show through. Their arrangement, almost a year old, had taken a direction of semi-domesticity. She wanted to get married, but her hesitancy to push matters too much was well founded. Paul could be stubborn when he chose, and if he backed off too quickly she would be hard pushed to find another man who suited her quite so well. From Edith's point of view, they were perhaps in love; from Paul's, he found that he was drawn to her, but he would not put a label so lofty as love on the relationship. She had a lot of faults that only her emotional chemistry could suppress, and in his objective way Paul hankered quietly either for an improvement in her or even another girl to come along before he applied any real thought to his future in the man-woman stakes.

'Carry your books, lady?'

She frowned harder for an instant until she realised who was talking. Edith was eternally preoccupied and recognition always dawned slowly, even when she was confronting the man she thought she loved. When her smile broke, she displayed even white teeth, so regular that Paul had once thought they were false. 'I heard you had a call,' she said, letting him take the books and steer her into a seat.

He sat down opposite and fished in his pocket for a cigarette. 'Yup. Brought in an aortic tear.'

'Who's operating?'

'Greer, I hope.'

'I hope so too. Nobody here has any experience of that technique.'

'It's terrible,' he murmured, lighting his cigarette and blowing the smoke downward towards his lap. 'I'm hoping the guy pulls through, but I'm hoping it for the sake of the unit. First job, and all that.'

'You did well just getting him here. You've made your point already. And you probably gave a prior alert, right?'

'Yes, we did.'

'Super. On-the-spot diagnosis is as advantageous as emergency treatment, sometimes.' She touched his wrist, a considerable intimacy in view of the surroundings and Edith's strict observance of public proprieties. 'You'll be a big-timer one of these days.'

He studied her face, covering his appraisal with half-shut eyelids as he drew deeply on the cigarette. She was like two people, outside and inside. He could see no trace now of the severity and stiff dignity that sometimes took hold of her. She was a pretty, intelligent-looking girl, and her smiling affection seemed permanent. Paul recalled the different Edith who could tighten up and put a cold compress on any situation, however inflammatory. Then her eyes would be tense, her facial muscles so taut that the end of her nose would move as she spoke. Her manner of speech would change too, the teeth staying close together as if they found some strength in close order drill. Taken at a less fanciful level, her duality was purely the outcome of conflict. She had been born with all the physical and mental properties of a happy-go-lucky woman, but her upbringing, which had been designed to teach her the meaning of personal excellence and the value of breeding, had been superimposed on the natural personality; it did not dissolve into her lines, it was altogether too foreign, but it sat cramped within her, taking command whenever the activating nerve was touched. It was curious how much harm could be done to the nature of a child, simply by educating it without considering the needs of individual tendency. He knew that Edith could accept and approve of things that her background would abhor, but it was a self-conscious acceptance, one that fled when she was angry or insecure.

The business of Ernie Hale and his behaviour at Paul's house on Monday night had been diplomatically set aside. Edith just did not like Ernie, and she would not have liked him even if he was a gentleman. The fact that he was a boozing, lecherous, disrespectful hedonist at least gave Edith a reasonable excuse for her dislike. The real reason, as Paul knew, was that Ernie unsettled her. He could always accurately tell what was on her mind, he had sometimes anticipated her deliberately, and to someone with Edith's intellectual vanity that was extremely uncomfortable. Paul believed her when she said that Ernie was an abuser, and he accepted her assertions that Ernie was also a man who did not exercise the proper control over his instincts. To Paul, that made Ernie all the more enjoyable as a person. It boiled down to simple likes and dislikes; wives who had been beaten senseless time and again by their husbands could enumerate the reasons why their men should be forever known as thoroughgoing bastards—but that had little to do with the elementary truth that those women usually loved the creatures who made their lives hell. Ernie, hairy warts and all, would always be a friend of Paul's, and no amount of reforming would ever make Edith like him.

'What's new?' Paul always asked that, or something similarly diversionary, when he saw the softness in Edith's face move on towards the place where she would begin to chip gently at the thin wall sealing off his plans for the future, *their* future.

She planted her elbows on the table and looked thoughtful. 'Everything's rather bitty just now. Mr Madison's being difficult, but that's common enough. I think he'll put forward my recommendations about ward flowers, though. He told me he had been suspicious on that score himself.'

Paul looked blank. He had no idea what she was talking about. No doubt she had told him all about it before, but he could switch off very easily when Edith started on about her enthusiasms along the byways of surgery.

She was accustomed to his memory lapses, and explained.

'Nurses have always been rather uneasy about flowers in a ward, as you know. Their photosynthetic properties are usually blamed for the distrust. Flowers can synthesise quite complex chemical substances from carbon dioxide and water, using the sun as a source of energy.'

'I *have* read up on my botany, Edith.'

'Sorry. Well, I've been following some American research that makes the presence of flowers among sick people a more solid worry. It looks as if they might be a productive source of infection. Samples of tap water that had flowers standing in them for three days produced a mixed growth of Gram-negative bacteria. A high count can be produced within an hour. The researchers in Miami have said that throwing the water from a vase of flowers down a wash basin is tantamount to splashing a broth culture of assorted bugs round the ward.'

'How about tap water left on its own in a vase?'

'They tried that. They got a very low count, but it shot up when they put the flowers in.'

The game of theory testing was automatic. 'How about distilled water, then?'

'Hardly any difference.'

'So relatives will have to say it with plastic flowers from now on. Boy, science is sure taking the romance out of living.'

Edith folded her arms, maintaining the firm pressure of her elbows on the table. 'I think Mr Madison will just ban flowers completely. We've got a test booked at the path lab, and if it comes up with anything like the American results, that'll be that.'

Paul stubbed out his cigarette in the ashtray. He only ever smoked two-thirds, as a small concession to the cancer campaigners. 'Madison will enjoy taking the brightness out of the wards.'

'Oh, that's unfair. He's not so bad.'

She had coloured a little, and that surprised Paul. Very little could put Edith in the position where her emotions affected her blood vessels. Ernie's brief lecture on blushing came to mind; it had been delivered one evening after they had drunk nothing but wine. That always brought forward the best in Ernie's psychiatric theorising. A blush was a response to an emotion too strong or too inappropriate to be expressed. That was the condensation of ten minutes' talking. Edith had expressed her belief that Paul was being unfair to Mr Madison, so she would have *appeared* to mouth her emotion. But the blush came up a little to the rear of her comment. So according to a loose application of the Doctrine of Human Behaviour, as preached by the prophet Hale, Edith harboured some emotion in relation to her boss that she did not think appropriate to mention. It was an amusing theory, and Paul decided to push it a trifle further. 'He probably resents flowers, Edith. He dislikes anything that's cleverer than he is. Flowers can synthesise like crazy, without being told how to, and they're prettier than Madison, too.'

'You're just being childish.' The blush remained, and her bright face was showing signs of giving way to the uptight training again. 'You're simply annoyed because he opposed the ambulance.'

Defensiveness too, he thought. Well, well. 'He doesn't really annoy me, honey. Who can get steamed up about a tired old man?'

In the space of seconds, matters had taken an ugly turn. The change was complete. Edith had moved back, letting her arms slide off the table, and her face was growing taut. And she was still blushing. Ernie would have rubbed his hands and muttered something about schizophrenia. Even her hair looked as if it had changed. That was probably, Paul guessed, the outcome of research, some private experimentation of Edith's to find a hairdo that would complement her two selves. He realised, with a jolt, that he would need very little effort to really cool off with this girl, if the need arose.

'For a man of supposed intelligence, you can talk just like an oaf, Paul. Mr Madison, whatever his faults, is a fine surgeon and he has enough character, enough culture and enough commonsense to make ten of the type of person you find admirable.'

'I take it we're alluding to Ernie Hale again?'

'Why not?' Her voice was under control, but it was being expelled on petulant little gasps of air. 'You would set up that alcohol-soaked, fornicating witch doctor against someone of Mr Madison's stature any day, wouldn't you? You prefer anarchy, don't you? You said it yourself, you prefer not to go on any approved paths. That gives you something in common with the other hooligans of the world.' The outburst was not untypical, but the sudden onset was odd. What Ernie had termed the *Sturm und Drang* element of Edith's temperament, the component that made her start to throw slander around, was normally exposed in stages, following long-term argument. Paul's habit of smiling-off the blows always made her raw; but it took time, lots of time, before she actually began a direct attack on *him*. There was a good deal, surely, in her esteem for Mr Madison. In a way it was encouraging to find that Edith had a weakness he could touch and activate so easily. Weakness and humanity were parts of the same fabric.

'I suppose that's why you hang around with me, Edith. You like a piece of rough occasionally.'

'Don't be so bloody foul-mouthed!'

'Steady, doctor. Think of your blood pressure.' He was tempted to goad her about her fuming defence of Madison but thought it better, for the moment, to reserve comment. She had never before shown a particular loyalty to the man. Like any other doctor she complained about the chief in a lighthearted way, and occasionally she would even say that he was driving her mad. But that was standard, and Paul had assumed, if he had thought about it at all, that her position in relation to the consultant was of the routine kind. He could not remember, either, that she had ever said much about Madison outside of the occasional passing comment. Something in Paul's ability as a surgeon was tied up with his pleasure in probing unpredictable situations. He would go into this one again.

Meanwhile, Edith had to be restored to a state of calm. That was done, usually, by pushing her so far out that she panicked, thinking she would break her mooring, and drifted back, chastened.

'I'm throwing a party at the house on Saturday evening.' The change of subject was a shock to her; the nature of his information called for a different department of her anger.

'Another one?' She shook her head, the way doctors did in bad movies when they speechlessly indicated that there was nothing they could do. 'You're determinded to go on letting yourself down, aren't you?'

That was the precise point where he always tugged the rope. 'No need for you to attend, Edith. There's no chain on you, remember? I'm having the team round, sort of a celebration for them. If you can't bear it, forget it.'

The tension began to leave her face and her eyes softened with caution. Paul made a show of his unconcern, dusting some ash from his sleeve and looking around him, nodding to acquaintances. It was stagey and it was not intended to fool her. Before he was twenty-three, he had found that certain types of women, particularly those who prided themselves on their perception, tended to respond more to overdone, calculated gestures than to the less accentuated signs of unfaked love, hate, pleasure or anger. They accepted the message for what it was, a blown-up communication requiring urgent attention.

'There I go again.' She said it in a small voice, lowering her chin and watching him with upturned eyes. 'I put your back up, didn't I? I don't really mean it when I talk like that, Paul. I over-react.'

He turned on a smile that was intended to look forced. 'Forget it. Let's just say we were both at fault.' Generosity in circumstances like these always floored her.

'No, I was. I try to re-mould you, and really there's nothing wrong with the way you are. No hooligan gets his name added to an ambulance service.'

Again he was tempted to have a dig in the direction of Madison. What would *he* think about the naming of the unit? It had only just occurred to him to wonder. So far as Paul knew, no foundation, no hospital ward, not even an ointment was named after Henry Madison. The man didn't lack any ability; he simply had not learned to arrest his English reserve at the point where it could interfere with his up-front advertising. But no more goading. Edith was back in check and that was the way he wanted her for the time being. 'Okay, let's forget the little spat. Are you going to come to the party?'

To his surprise, she shook her head. 'I can't. Not on Saturday. If I'd known beforehand, Paul—'

'I should have told you. Sorry.' She was making no explanation, he could see and feel it. That was another untypical move. She always poured out her reasons for not being able to make a date. Always. Now she was doing the look-around-at-friends bit herself, and it was genuine, she was embarrassed. He astonished himself by feeling a minute jab of jealous curiosity. But he would not ask her. On balance, he still preferred a mystery that he could work on in his own way. Quite a day, all round.

His communicator started bleeping while he was making up his mind about going or having a coffee. 'See you.' he said, squeezing her shoulder and heading for the door. He carried her parting expression before him as he pushed his way through the canteen doors. It was affection, open warmth, and obvious relief that he was going.

5

The aorta is a great artery issuing from the heart, carrying blood through its branches to the rest of the body. It rises in a supple curve from the left ventricle and descends along the line of the spinal column, to which it is firmly attached from a point adjacent to the fourth thoracic vertebra.

In motoring accidents the aorta frequently tears as a result of sudden whiplike movement in the mobile upper part, which rips open because of the resistance from the lower tethered portion. When a tear occurs—a deep tear penetrating the fibrous, muscular and endotheliel layers that form the artery—blood for the rest of the body begins to leak into the cavity of the chest. At any time, the aorta may divide completely, without prior warning, and death will be instant.

Sufferers from aortic tears are usually, though not always, drivers who have been involved in head-on collisions. Passengers may suffer, too, especially if they have been wearing safety belts. Whoever the victim is, and however his injury was sustained, he is in mortal danger until a competent thoracic surgeon can intervene and attempt to divert the inevitable.

Paul Avery's patient was on the operating table within minutes of arrival at the hospital. Mr Leonard Greer, a surgeon specialising in cardiac work, had been only a few miles away when the emergency call went out. He promptly handed over the relatively simple operation on which he was engaged at a local nursing home, and drove to Westfield, arriving there before the accident victim.

He had repaired aortas before but experience in the work did not produce any great confidence. There was a set procedure, fraught with fairly predictable side emergencies, but the sheer difficulty of the task kept it in the realm of operations that Greer called untidy. Nevertheless, he was a man who always kept up a strict practical line of approach, and he never allowed any lack of confidence to show. Morale in a theatre was largely in the hands of the surgeon, and Mr Greer was aware of his responsibility.

The patient was placed in much the same position as he had travelled to the hospital. Halfway on his back and halfway on his right side, he was carefully supported and his left arm placed high over his face, well clear of the site of operation. First, a knife was used to make a wide incision between the third and fourth ribs, then the ribs were held back out of the way with a rib spreader. Mr Greer's eyes took in the discouraged expressions of his young assistant and the theatre sister. There was blood everywhere, a pulsating pool that obliterated all landmarks, throbbing with the aortic pulsation.

'I shall have to work in the manner of a Victorian gynaecologist.' The assistant did not understand, but the crinkling at the corners of sister's eyes indicated that she did. In the days of more cloying modesty, a doctor who wished to examine a woman's delicate parts had to do so by pushing his hands through a hole in a sheet, held up by a nurse to preserve the holy vision of the patient's pudenda. Similarly handicapped, Mr Greer had to probe with gloved fingers made slimy and insensitive, almost literally grasping at straws, the object of his search barred from sight by a puddle of warm dark blood.

To locate the curve of the aorta, he had first to begin dissecting along the left subclavian artery, a tributary that connects with the aorta at the point where it turns left and dips down behind the heart. By loosening the subclavian from its surrounding tissues, with extreme care, a tiny portion at a time, Mr Greer eventually found his fingers enclosing the mass of the aortic arch. A length of tape was then placed around the top of the aorta, to provide a measure of control, and a clamp applied right across the artery. The lower aorta was then dissected up from the tissue enclosing it and a clamp applied there, too. The damaged portion of the artery had now been effectively shut off, and it was important next to establish a bypass, so that the blood could still pass from the heart to the lower end of the aorta, beyond the point where it was clamped.

'At the expense of probably more than a few lives, we have learned that the bypass is imperative,' Greer said, as much to keep general tension down as to instruct. 'If the kidney goes without its supply of blood, even for a short time, the damage done is usually irreparable. The spinal cord comes off badly, too, without its blood. Even a reduced flow there can cause thrombosis of the spinal arteries, and God knows we have enough to contend with.'

The bypass consisted of little more than a cleverly designed tube. First, purse-string sutures were applied to the left ventricle of the heart and the descending aorta; small stab wounds were then made in the centre of the sutured areas, and the sharp ends of the bypass inserted. Air was released from the tube and blood was then allowed to flow, completing the circulation once again, leaving the damaged portion of the aorta free to be repaired.

Damage was extensive. 'It's holding by a thread.' Mr Greer shook his head, lost in the wonderment that often settled on him at the sight of a ruined artery or organ that could still, by some magic, go on working to keep the body alive. 'I'm afraid we must go to the expense of a graft, sister.'

Although no more than a short tube of woven Dacron, the aortic graft was astonishingly expensive. Mr Greer had known of several cases where, because the patient died after the graft was inserted, it was actually removed again and kept aside to be used on someone else. 'We are lucky here,' he told his assistant. 'There is about a centimetre and a half of aorta beyond the tear which will form a cuff for stitching. Sometimes we get to this stage and there's nothing to attach the blessed graft to.' As he set to preparing the artery for grafting, he winked at the sister. 'One day, the boffins are going to find a way to introduce plastics into the genetic structure of human beings. Then we can just weld in new parts.'

The graft was inserted without event, the mediastinal pleura oversewn and the bypass removed; as this was done, it was only necessary to draw on the ends of the purse-string sutures, and the small holes closed. The chest was then drained and the patient closed up.

Shortly afterwards, Mr Greer approached Paul Avery in the

casualty department where he was stitching the upper lip of a boy who had been kicked by someone he had thought was a friend. Paul finished the job and walked to the reception area with Greer, anxious to hear how the operation had gone.

'I think we can say he'll live. I wanted to congratulate you.'

Paul looked surprised. 'Me? I should be handing round the praise, I think. That's a tricky operation.'

Greer smiled. 'The diagnosis is trickier. You know perfectly well that people have languished on trolleys for hours with aortas leaking away and no one the wiser. If the repair operation is ever to become commonplace, on-the-spot diagnosis will have to be improved.' He frowned. 'What made you think it was a tear?'

Paul shrugged. 'A combination of small things. I think it came from outside actual awareness, though. I was suspicious before I knew what I suspected, if you follow me.'

'Oh yes, I follow. Only too well. Doctor Avery, your reputation has brushed me from time to time, and I think I must couple a small apology with my congratulations.' His face bore the soft lines of a humourous intelligence, and now he was smiling faintly, about to confess in the way that only the deeply honest person ever feels necessary. 'I had you down in my type-chart as an overnight sensation. I've come across them before. Smart, always ready to pick up a point, loaded with energy. My theory is that such people have lost part of their machinery. They use a lifetime's mental and physical energy in a couple of years. Then they fizzle out, for all time. I had you typed as one of those. I heard about the way you could argue at seminars and meetings of the learned colleges, I read the notes of your lecture on emergency treatment of abdominal injuries, and I've seen the teaching films you made for nurses. All very laudable, and you back your professional ability with a likeable personality. For all that, you could still have been a—'

'A bum?'

Greer laughed. 'Yes, a bum. But there are certain things an exceptional doctor or surgeon can do that a bum could never do. Your diagnosis today, that's typical of what I mean. It shows you have a feeling for your profession that goes beyond the talent for innovation and showmanship. I can understand now why you have done so well.'

Paul was feeling embarrassed. 'On just one diagnosis, you've been able to revise your opinion?'

'On a very special diagnosis.' Greer extended his hand. 'Nice to really know you, doctor. And may I say, your ambulance scheme will be a great success, if today's performance is any sample.'

A few minutes after Greer had left, Ernie Hale rang casualty to ask if Paul was doing anything that evening. Paul told him he was free, then he told him what Mr Greer had said.

'Watch your head. Paul. Those doors down there aren't too wide. You can start feeling complacent about the ambulance when Madison shakes your little paw and tells you you're a good kid.'

'You make too much of that, Ernie.' He was growing sick of the idea of Madison. His name seemed to crop up all the time, and every time it did there was some warning or some mystery attached to it.

'Do I? I'm only telling you to keep an eye trained on that quarter. I'm good at smelling types, too. You know that.'

'Right, right. See you tonight.' He hung up and returned to the treatment room. The ambulance was a success. That was the thought to keep. Who could hold out against anything so downright *good* for any length of time?

Katie Madison realised that, by many people's standards, her Andy was rather weird. That did not deter her, it did not make her think that she should take account of the others and what they thought was normal or desirable. It was just an observation. Andy was different in every other way, too, so his weirdness was probably inevitable. In search of a word to sum up his overall inventory of characteristics, she settled for consistent. He was that, all right.

She had never been in his room before. He had often promised that he would take her up there, but it wasn't always convenient. His landlady was one of the kind who didn't like her boarders having guests. She went out two nights a week, and those nights, being random, had never, until now, coincided with Katie's meetings with Andy. Now, at long last, she was there, sitting on his couch, admiring and wondering at the odd collection of mismatched artefacts that composed her lover's home environment.

That was so important, to see how a man lived, especially if he lived on his own. Just before she met Andy, before that great night at the disco when he had sauntered across to her in his uniform and started talking to her in his guttural confident manner, she had been going round with a boy who had sold himself to her as a real swinger, a man who walked his own road. When she had gone to his bed-sitter with him, he turned out to be a totally artificial product of his own daydreams. He had pin-up pictures of girls on the walls, and pages clipped from pop magazines, and even a glossy blow-up of Chelsea football team. There was nothing of *him* in the room, just the shadows of the pitiful idols he used to fill the gaps in his individuality. Katie's primary requirement in a man was individuality. There were other things, of course, but without the individuality they were useless, they did not connect. Andy's unique personality was surrounded by a spooky aura of barely mentionable interests. The whole room was a stunning replica, Katie decided in her colourful way, of the inside of his head.

While she let the place work on her, Andy was making orange-squash drinks to combat the dry-mouthed stage of the joint they were about to smoke. 'What do you think of the lair, chicken?' He spoke with his back to her, measuring the quantities of cordial and water so critically that he might have been working on a precise chemical formula.

'I'll tell you in a minute or two,' she said. Andy sometimes laughed at her artistic conceits, but when she gave any sign of mystic behaviour where their relationship was concerned, he rarely argued. 'There's so much to take in.' There was a lot, indeed, and the major problem was tying it all together. The place could have been the abode of half a dozen different people, so varied and contrasting were the elements.

The couch on which she sat, for a start, seemed to have some significance that went beyond its humble function. It was lumpy and it creaked, but it was covered with what looked like a crocheted Turkish blanket, a huge woollen rectangle that touched the floor on all sides. At the centre of the pattern, in the middle of the back rest, the word PURIFY was woven, not too neatly, in green knitting wool. The same brief command, or perhaps it was a prayer. was written on a large piece of orange cardboard tacked above the sink. The walls were painted matt black, and the floor was covered with a dozen different carpet designs, stitched together from a trade sample book. Above the bed, which was narrow and draped with a black nylon spread, there was a large American poster depicting a naked black girl, her head thrown back, half squatting with a live chicken clutched between her legs. Along the wall facing Katie, there was a long, unpainted book shelf. It held a few books and perhaps a hundred magazines, plus an assortment of film cans and an eight millimetre projector. Beneath the shelf, a battered Indian brass vase sat on top of a pile of Rock and Roll albums. A stuffed mongoose confronted a simulated voodoo mask, and by the door a prim rolled umbrella leaned against a cheap plaster figure of a boy eating cherries. But it was the collection of pictures that affected Katie most. Unlike the pin-ups she had seen in the other boy's room, these were stuck in a random order all over the walls, and no straightforward theme could be detected.

The largest was a reproduction of the Christ of Saint John of the Cross, by Dali. The others were postcards, newspaper clippings and magazine pages. One showed a child, in a hyper-romantic setting, gathering flowers. Another depicted a Biafran soldier, lying by a roadside with half of his head shot away. Above that, there was a sepia of Mr Universe being crowned, and alongside there were three prints showing a schoolgirl in various stages of undress. Elsewhere there were battle scenes, formal portraits of statesmen, a framed postcard of the Queen, clippings of dead tigers, a Norman Rockwell painting of three happy GI's, a little boy with a bunch of balloons, a skinny girl with a hatpin through her cheek, a profile shot of John Wayne, an advertisement for Outspan oranges, an old lady lighting a candle in a room full of polished brass and copper, a man with blood streaming from his nostrils, a pink rabbit with a green bow around its neck and a photograph of an egg. Katie looked at them all, and some others on the wall behind her. She liked the sense of mystery, the rows of reproductions that definitely implied some unity but which, at the same time, defied analysis. It was strange, too, that apart from the few semi-erotic prints, none of them seemed particularly distinguished, they did not appear to be of sufficient interest for anyone to take the trouble of sticking them on display.

Andy came away from the sink and placed two tumblers on the floor in front of the couch. He was about twenty-five, with greasy skin and red-rimmed eyes. In the dim light from the overhead bulb, he had the look of a tired, dishevelled prisoner. He was wearing jeans and a scarred leather jacket, and his shirt was unbuttoned as far as the waist, revealing a tattoo just above his navel. It was a pale blue eagle with spread wings, and it carried in its claws a little banner, bearing the name Toni. His fingers were rough and the nails were bitten and cracked. Katie found them very attractive, they reminded her of a poem she had once read where a workman's hands were described as 'pitted saviours of the world we know'. Andy did not believe in work, as it happened, but that did not make any difference. His essentially physical presence was as eloquent as that of any true labourer.

'Like the gallery, do you?' He sat beside her and squeezed her knee affectionately.

'It has a strange effect on me,' she admitted. 'I don't think I quite understand it, though.'

He waved his hand airily around him. 'It's all me, chicken. I kind of respond to the things you see here. That's not it all, of course.' He winked, a manoeuvre that he did not manage too well; one eye closed and the other almost did, too. 'I don't think about putting on a show, y'know? I put the pictures up for myself. And the rest—' he jerked a thumb towards a scratched tin trunk with a padlock that stood near the bed, '—they're sort of entertainment.'

Katie was enthralled by his inventiveness. He was so much of an individual that his every whim was surprising. She could only guess vaguely at what might be in the trunk. It would be something breathtaking. He had taught her to expect that much. Andy always stepped across the normal barriers, and Katie had learned that she enjoyed accompanying him. Every feature of him that was on the outside was unusual, so anything he chose to keep under lock and key must be really wild.

He lit the joint and passed it to her. Katie took three short puffs, holding the smoke for as long as she could before expelling it in a plume. This would be her third experience of cannabis, or shit as Andy had taught her to call it. The first time she had taken too much and the reaction—anxiety, loss of limb control and eventual sickness—frightened her. But he had insisted she try again, and it had been great, she had known what it was like to step outside of herself, and she had found that physical sensations became heightened to a point where pleasure could be almost unbearable. Now there was a familiar taste to the smoke, a precursor of the voyage to come. She passed back the stick and Andy placed it to his lips, making some show of his smoking technique. After a few drags, he said, 'Did you have any trouble getting out?'

She shook her head. 'None at all. I got Anna to ring and ask Aunt Amy if I could go round to help her out with some maths. Easy.' She grinned, her own quite exceptional beauty forming a strong contrast to the drab, used look of her companion.

'I see you put it on.' He leered openly at her clothing.

'Just as you asked.' She would not have chosen the ensemble herself. But Andy insisted that it turned him on. It was a help, in a way, her aunt was less likely to suspect that anything was going on if Katie left the house wearing clothes which, in her own opinion, suppressed her femininity. A white shirt, school tie, short grey skirt, white ankle socks and black leather flat-heeled shoes, the kind of threads she spent her days in. For reasons of his own, Andy found her attractive like this. She had so many really nice outfits, she even preferred bleached jeans and a tee shirt to this lot, but school garb it had to be, for that was what her man preferred.

'You look great.' He puffed some more and passed the joint back to her. While she gently inhaled through the damp roach, Andy stood up and crossed to the trunk. He produced a bunch of keys and fitted one in the padlock. 'I'll show you a little bit of switch-on, chicken. Nobody else had laid eyes on this but me, until now.' Opening the lid, he fumbled around and withdrew some envelopes. Coming back to the couch, he threw the bundle in her lap. 'Tell me what you think.'

Andy finished the joint as Katie went through the collection. They were all half-plate size glossy prints, more than fifty of them. They were not at all what she had expected. Andy had shown her some pornography before, and she had even managed to pick up some fairly hard-core stuff of her own. But these pictures did not switch her on, they simply mystified her more than the ones hanging on the walls. There was a continuous theme, that was something, but it was so ordinary. Motor-cycles. Dozens of motor-cycles, and they were all smashed up. There was not a complete bike anywhere in the collection. She looked through them twice, taking in the details of smashed Harley Davidsons and mangled Triumphs and distorted Yamahas, her confusion mounting as the cannabis began to affect her. 'I don't understand,' she said finally.

Andy stubbed out the smouldering end of the joint, shaking his head, looking very disappointed. 'I thought you dug that kind of thing.' He took back the prints and slowly replaced them in their envelopes. 'These are all police pictures, you know. Nicked from files, the lot of them.'

He was growing moody, she could sense that. Frantically, she searched her mind for any recent occasion where they might have discussed damaged bikes. It was a silly enough subject to be recalled at once, but she could trace no recollection. 'Honestly, Andy—if I could remember saying anything—'

'Skip it.' He dropped the envelopes on the floor and put a hand across his eyes. Katie watched him, fearful that he might be going into one of his long silences. She always felt insecure when he did that. It was like being excluded from her own home.

'Please, Andy . . .'

'Please what, for fuck's sake.'

'Maybe I just didn't catch on. Bikes, I mean I don't remember talking about bikes, you've never said anything about them to me. Really.'

He removed his hand and stared at her. He was scowling petulantly, and as the softening effect of the cannabis began to make her awareness stretch, she could see every component of the expression; tiny muscles at the edges of his mouth exercised a downward tug, his eyes were wide but the lower lids were remaining tense, his nostrils flared. So much work went into a look of displeasure, she thought. He must mean it, to take all that trouble.

'Last time,' he grunted, 'when we were in my car . . .'

'Oh!' It had suddenly meshed. 'Crashes. We talked about crashes, and you said how they could turn you on—'

'And *you* said—'

'I know I did,' she said urgently, anxious to make amends.

'But in my mind I was seeing crashes *happen*, Andy. They involved people, and they were full of action. That's what I said turned me on.' She watched his face for any sign of change. The whole thing had been his idea. They had been making it in the car, and he had said it would be fantastic to do it in a car while it was being involved in a crash. His power to influence her thinking was considerable. After a few minutes of verbal fantasising, Katie had been able to respond to the oblique eroticism he conjured up. It was like masochism, which she understood very well. The idea of being hurtled through glass and metal while in the throes of sexual ecstacy was very appealing; she would not like to do it, of course, but to contemplate it, to imagine the blood and the bone breaking and the exaggerated postures of bodies in close proximity to twisted metal, that was a fierce turn-on. Andy had told her that he thought about it a good deal . . . he had even hinted that he once tried to crash his car, just to draw on the complex pleasure he detected in the act. Pictures of crashes, static aftermaths, bore no relation to what Katie felt.

'Sorry, kid.' He relaxed and touched her leg. 'I thought you'd been faking.'

Grateful, she leaned across and kissed him, smelling the musky odour of his sweat, mingled with another darker scent as it rose from his shirt. 'I never fake with you, Andy. You should know that. Do the pictures really work for you?'

For answer, he drew her hand roughly to the bulge at his fly. 'Every time, just like that. But it wasn't the pictures this time.

She moved her mouth to his ear, leaving her hand where it was. 'I'll have to ask my uncle if they've got any pictures at the hospital. That new ambulance would be really something for you to ride on, huh?' She was joking, but at the same time she was aware that he was listening intently. He was definitely a talk-man. He had told her that, and she had proved it for herself. She closed her fingers slightly, feeling the tense hardness increase beneath her palm. 'Just imagine, a great big pile-up, bodies all over the place, and you right in the middle of it, touching, seeing . . .'

He groaned. Oh, he was weird, she thought, finding herself delightfully warm, filling with an overpowering gratitude that had started with his decision to forgive her and was now connected to all the things he had taught her, to all the sensations and tastes he had awakened and nurtured. Her weird Andy, her dark man of the shadows, a figure as romantic as any of her former heroes, with the added attraction of sensuality, tempting brush-strokes of evil.

He slid away from her, half-lying on the couch, his legs splayed, his eyes fixed on her body. Katie knew what he was thinking, what he was contemplating, he had told her often enough. Really sailing on the cannabis now, her tongue sticking to her palate—high and dry Andy called it—she reached down for the orange drink and took a quick swallow, moistening her lips and throat. She placed the glass against Andy's mouth and he gulped half of it, sighing and grinning, waiting.

Katie stood up and placed her hands on her hips, her feet spread, her head turned on the side, the dark red hair dropping in a soft curtain and obscuring one eye. Andy bared his teeth and she changed her posture from one hip to the other. She watched him rub his bulge with the flat of his hand, then she stepped forward and planted a knee on either side of his hips, dropping the firm weight of her buttocks on his thighs. Leaning forward, so that her hair brushed his face, she whispered, 'I love you,' and kissed his forehead. His eyes were down, staring at the taut hem of her skirt. She drew it back with one hand, revealing her spread bare thighs and the tight red crotch of the pants that had formed a part of his detailed specification for switch-on dress. Keeping her head bowed, she ran a hand along the inner surface of one thigh and cupped herself, squeezing with hooked fingers.

Abruptly, Andy's hand came up and jerked down his zip. Another odour rose up, an almost dank smell of unwashed clothing and stale skin. He pulled out his penis and grasped it at the root, shaking it, rubbing the tip against her thigh. Katie lowered herself on him, an expert by now, and arched her buttocks, letting him press his member against the thin fabric of the pants. He began to buck and groan and she reached underneath herself, drawing the nylon crotch aside, feeling him guide his erection against the moist opening of her vagina. When she knew it was right she thrust down on him, taking in the length of his penis, feeling it abrasively dry at first, then gloriously smooth as she made tiny up-and-down movements, panting in his face, shuddering at the sensations radiating from between her thighs.

'Talk,' Andy whispered. 'Talk!'

'I adore feeling it,' she said, timing her words to coincide with his upward thrusts; 'your cock, your big fucking cock, rammed inside my tight cunt. I want you to tear me up with it, I want your fat prick to burst through my pussy and squirt all over my insides—' She began to groan, unable to keep herself in check. He was driving so hard against her that the force was raising both their bodies clear of the couch at each stroke. Andy's heels and his shoulders forming the only points of contact. In her head, Katie could see them, as if she were standing beside the couch, she could see the spread of her own thigh, her skirt rucked high with Andy's hands clinging to her buttocks, her head superimposed on his own, her lips whining at his ear.

He came, and a second later she followed. The writhing subsided and became a soft gyration. Andy, as always, had closed his eyes and looked as if he was in some pain. She lay relaxed on top of him, feeling the semen seep from her and mingle with their pubic hair. Her orgasm was still tingling, an echoing pleasure-pain that the cannabis always lengthened. Everything she had, everything she cherished, was right here, wrapped up in what she was doing, whom she was with and how she was feeling. Everything else was unimportant.

Later, when they had straightened themselves and the high was diminishing to the level of no more than a pleasant lightheadedness, Andy produced a folded slip of paper from his pocket.

'I want you to try and do me a favour,' he said, holding her close, his arm tight around her shoulder.

'Mmm?' She stared dreamily at the paper.

'Your uncle, chicken. Does he keep any stuff at home?'

'Stuff?'

'You know. Tablets, drugs.'

She frowned, concentrating. 'I don't really know. He's a surgeon, I don't know if they carry things like that.'

'Could you find out?'

'Yes, I could try.'

'I've got some names written down. Look for those first, and if you find anything else, get me some samples and I'll find out if they're any good.'

It had been money the last time. Not much, just a few pounds. She had taken it from her own savings account. 'Andy, you're not going to start using hard stuff, are you? I don't mind pinching some if there's any about, but I don't like the idea of you experimenting. Remember what happened to the kid from our school?' The girl had been fourteen, quiet and a poor mixer. She had accidentally killed herself with some pep pills.

He laughed softly, nuzzling his face in her hair. 'Dopey drawers. It's not for me. I owe somebody a big favour. Some of these goodies would get me off the hook. Will you try, Katie? Will you?' The wheedling was saved for times like these. She liked it.

'I'll do what I can. But don't be mad if I can't find anything.'

'Just you do your best.' He put a wet kiss on her cheek. 'I don't expect more than that.'

She tucked the paper in her bag. 'Andy, are you going to explain your picture gallery to me? I'd like to know what it all means to you.'

He was offhand now, almost businesslike. He examined his watch. 'My landlady'll be back soon. You'd better be going. I'll talk about the pictures some other time.' He helped her on with her coat and went down to the main door with her. 'Sorry I can't give you a lift, chicken. The car's on the blink again—'

'That's all right, Andy.' She kissed him hard on the mouth, but he drew back when she moved to put an arm round his neck. 'Old dragonface might be along any minute, kid. See you Saturday.' He kissed the tip of his finger and touched it to her nose. 'Go carefully.'

Back home she had a late-night cup of chocolate with Aunt Amy, then had a bath and went to bed. She took the slip of paper with her and lay proped against the pillows reading it. Quite a list, she thought. Apart from one or two names she had heard mentioned at school, the substances were all foreign to her: Sparine, Stelazine, Tised, Prothiaden, Amytal, Tropium, Gardenal, Amitriptyline, Motival, Dexamed, Mandrax—the names covered two closely written columns. All those substances, Katie thought, folding up the paper and putting it in her bag beside the bed, all designed to do people good, yet all capable perhaps of harming people who had nothing really wrong with them, except that they were perhaps slightly inadequate, not fit to face life without a few chemical crutches.

She pulled the light cord and slipped down under the sheets. It was different with her and Andy. They used cannabis to lift them above the world, just for a little while. Nothing wrong with that. They weren't *dependent*. It occurred to her, a few moments before she sank into sleep, that she did have a dependence. Andy. She could never bring herself to think how she would manage without him. He was her drug. The idea was not altogether pleasant.

6

On Thursday and Friday the Avery Life-Support Unit attended five further calls. The first two went smoothly: a collision between two lightweight cars produced two sets of multiple fractures and a suspected fractured skull. On the return trip, assisted by the silent Nurse Haxton, Paul carried out emergency splinting to the broken bodies, and then set to observing the principles of care prescribed for skull fractures. Oddly, the most common reason for deterioration in a patient's condition when his head is injured is obstruction of the airway. The tongue can roll back into the throat, uncontrolled by the normal sentinel devices in the brain, false teeth can become dislodged and effectively stop the passage of air, the contents of the stomach can rise and be inhaled, cementing-off the entry to the lungs. So the patient, a middle-aged woman, was placed on her side with her head at a lower level than her trunk. The mouth was then cleared by Paul's efficiently hooked forefinger, and an endotracheal tube inserted. A simple airway, in his estimation, was not sufficient. For all he knew, the patient's cough reflex might have gone, and a build-up of mucus beneath the short airway tube would have rendered it useless. The endotracheal tube, on the other hand, brought an air inlet right to the point of the trachea where air would enter the lung. The lady arrived in the hsopital alive, breathing freely, her life supported in direct accordance with the unit's avowed function.

The second call, two hours after the first, took Paul and the team to a farmhouse where a young labourer had fallen from a hayloft and had been impaled on a spike jutting up from a binding machine. The one-inch diameter rod had entered his back to the left of the spine and just under the shoulder blade, and made its exit beneath the lower end of his breast bone. He was fully conscious and in great pain. Other farm workers stood round, gaping, half shocked, half fascinated. Paul's procedure startled the spectators even more. After checking the patient's condition, and determining that, miraculously, the lungs were undamaged, he administered a pain-killer and then ordered the attending firemen to remove the spike from the machine, leaving it stuck through the patient. In that condition, with the three foot long spear still skewering him, the young man was carried back to the casualty department, which had been pre-warned. That was another of those first principles, Paul told Ellen Haxton on the way back. However easy it may seem to pull a spike or a steering column out of a man's chest, the best procedure was always to leave it where it was. The moment such a thing was removed, hell would break loose, with haemorrhage and other emergencies in such profusion that only a fully manned operating theatre could cope.

The third, fourth and fifth calls, all occurring between two o'clock on Friday morning and four the same afternoon, taxed the unit to an extent where Paul Avery was almost sure that somebody somewhere was testing him.

He was asleep when the distinct emergency tone rang out. Jumping into his clothes, he quietly cursed the arrangement—his own idea—whereby no deputy was appointed to the Life-Support Unit unless he, Always-On-The-Job-Avery, was out of the hospital. Downstairs in the ambulance bay, Dan McGoldrick was grinning all over his Irish face, looking fresh as a daisy while the duty attendant, Bill Davis, stumbled around, gathering his wits and hunting for his overcoat. Paul climbed into the cab, shivering, and nodded to Dan.

'Nice to see you looking so well,' he growled at the driver.

'And you, sir. It's a blessin' we've got such alert people lookin' after our welfare.'

There was a bump in the back and Paul turned his head, peering into the working area. Mary Scott, looking very lovely but also dead tired, had just tripped on the single step and was regaining her balance, hanging on to the door support. 'Bloody thing! We'll have more accidents inside this crate than outside of it!'

Paul swallowed his smile and waved to Bill Davis. 'Come on, you won't freeze without your coat.'

The sombre face came right up to the open side door and glowered in. 'With respect, doctor, I wish you'd speak for yourself. I've got lousy circulation.' The night casualty sister came up with his coat bundled under her arm and thrust it at Bill. He took it without a word and climbed into the cab.

The call had come from a police motorway patrol operating on a five mile stretch on the limit of the unit's area. It was a multi-ambulance call, which meant something very bad had happened. As soon as they were on the motorway, Dan put his foot down hard, shifting into the fast lane and setting the siren and the flasher going, taking the speed to ninety and holding it there. The legal position of ambulances was curious; they were entitled to priority on the roads, but they could be prosecuted for breaking the speed limit. Dan was a man whose sense of priority permitted him to ignore speed limits, and so far no complaints had been raised.

When they arrived at the spot, Paul was glad that nowadays no patient could have much emotional effect on him. The scene was hideous. Under three police spotlight units, scattered across the glass-twinkling, blood-darkened road, the bodies of five children and three adults were scattered in a pattern of stillness that generated a startling sensation of the violence which had put them there. The adults were women, nuns, their cloaked dignity gone, replaced by sprawling inelegance and the fearful marks of disruption. One lay on her face, the starburst of blood and brain matter around her hood indicating that she had lost her face along with her life. Near her, on her back with one arm bent at an impossible angle beneath her shoulders, another sister breathed with sharp jerks, each expulsion of air producing a little vapour cloud and a faint pained squeak. The third one had a broken spine and lay on her side, jack-knifed backwards, her eyes open and startled, her tongue lolling from the side of her mouth, arms spread out behind her as if she were simulating flight.

Two of the children were dead. A tiny one, a golden-haired

girl no more then three years old, lay in a huddle within her blue anorak, her knees drawn up, one small buckled shoe missing. Her eyes were closed and her expression was quite serene, as if she were asleep. Only the muddy tyre-tread running over one shoulder of her coat gave any clue that she had been injured; her pallor made it clear that she was beyond rescue. Several feet from her, a boy of eight or nine was no more than a loosely-connected bundle of his constituent parts, a resounding, heart-breaking reminder that, in so many ways, the motor car was an obscenity.

The van in which the victims had been travelling was upside down by the verge, and a fireman was aiming the jet from an extinguisher against the smoking engine. Another vehicle, a bright red sports car, was frozen in a swerving turn at the centre of the road, twenty feet from the upturned van. A young man, expensively dressed in suede with a gay yellow scarf tied at his throat, leaned against the side, his face buried in his hands. How many times he had seen that picture, Paul thought. The reality of tragedy could only be fully understood by those involved in it.

A police sergeant wearing a bright orange jerkin stepped up to the ambulance as Paul and Bill Davis were climbing out. 'Five of them still breathing,' he said. Paul looked at the knot of three children, at a distance from the main area of carnage, probably saved from instant death by the grass reservation across which they half lay. They were all moving, but there was no co-ordination. Nerves were simply reacting, making muscles twitch and flail. 'I didn't want to move any of them . . .' The man's face was haggard, tired. 'Those poor kids.'

Nurse Scott had opened the rear doors and came round the side, carrying two emergency bags. 'What happened?'

'A bloody rabbit,' the sergeant said. 'The car driver over there said a rabbit ran across the road. The nun driving the van slewed across the lanes trying to avoid it. She hit the brake too hard, I suppose. The van spun over and the kids and the other two nuns were flung through the side windows. The sports car ran over three of them. Two children and the sister in the middle there. It's the van from the Christie Orphanage. Talk about bloody ironical.' He sighed and followed the team into the illuminated area, where three other policemen and two firemen were trying to spin the van round, on to the verge. By the side of the fire appliance, Paul spotted the chief, in a white helmet, being sick.

Two other ambulances had turned up and were parked on the far side of the circle of light. Attendants carrying stretchers came forward, looking about them, wondering where to start. Paul took charge. Signalling to the attendant from the larger of the two wagons, he pointed to the two dead children. 'Will you take them—I don't want to declare them dead. Get them to the hospital and have a casualty officer look at them.' His reason, which escaped the attendant, was totally bound up with decorum. As a student he had been told that a dead body deserved as much respect as a living one. He had taken the observation to heart and made it one of his humanising rules. The humanising laws, of which Paul had several, were designed simply to keep him in touch with the refinements of behaviour which doctors sometimes lost. If he did not declare the children dead, they would have to be examined by another doctor, which meant their bodies stood a chance of being retained in a hospital mortuary, which was a good deal more civilised than a wayside public mortuary. It made little difference, logically, where the bodies were laid, but Paul always tried to avoid the idea that a dead person was just so much meat, to be dumped whenever and wherever convenient. 'Take the nun over there, too.' He pointed to the sister who had landed on her face.

Mary Scott was bending over the three children by the reservation, gently probing among their tangled bodies, loosening heavy clothing. When she was working she was so unlike the glib Nurse Scott Paul knew that he was tempted to wonder if she was as double-headed as Edith. 'What's the score, nurse?'

'They all seem to be rib-cage injuries,' she announced, squatting by a little boy whose eyes flickered open and shut at regular intervals, shock causing his body to heave in a spastic, puppet-like series of jerks.

'Get airways into them first,' Paul said, and moved to where Dan and Bill were standing over the two nuns in the centre of the road.

'Get the break-apart stretcher, Bill. I want you to carry her into the ambulance very carefully—face down. Keep her that way.' The sister whose back was broken would present a lot of problems for the staff dealing with her back at Westfield. The most Paul could do was ensure that she got there with a minimum of further damage occurring.

As the stretcher was bolted around the prone figure, Paul stooped and inserted a finger into the nun's mouth. Her upper teeth were false and he pulled them out, wrapped them in a tissue and tucked them into the deep pocket on the black habit. 'Put in an airway and make sure she's breathing easily.' He squinted at the woman's face as she was carefully lifted. One pupil looked quite fixed. Probable skull damage, too. 'This is the hardest penance she'll ever do.'

The other woman was almost conscious. Her arm was broken in three places, and she was having difficulty with her breathing. Kneeling by her side, Paul touched the injured arm and she screamed, a sharp, brief rattle of agony. He crossed and picked up one of the emergency bags. Mary Scott was on her knees now, heedless of the dirt, straightening out the three children and passing airways into their mouths. Something about her, Paul thought in passing, looked just right. It was the look some surgeons had when they were working. Their bodies seemed angled and poised in the precise lines of competence. He returned to the nun and rolled up the sleeve on her good arm. From the case he took a syringe and a needle, discarding their sterile packings and fitting the needle firmly over the nozzle of the syringe. He then located an ampoule of DF118, a pain killer, and drew the contents up into the syringe. In view of the circumstances, where the full extent of injury could not be determined until they got to the hospital, he did not feel it wise to do more than inject one millilitre of the preparation. That chest, and the oddness of the woman's breathing pattern, could be an indication of trouble that would not respond well to the heavier pain-killers. Again, he was responding to an instinct that had made its own evaluation. He pushed the point of the needle through the skin and emptied the syringe in a steady, firm stroke. After a few moments, the woman began to look more relaxed. She complained when he touched her broken arm again, but the note was less urgent now.

Paul straightened the arm slowly, assessing the fractures as he did so. The humerus appeared to be broken across the shaft. Using a pair of blunt-nosed scissors, Paul snipped away the sleeve and touched the swelling on the upper arm. Pressing firmly, he detected a clean break. The elbow was smashed and several particles of bone could be felt moving just under the skin. Radius and ulna had snapped close to the wrist. Deftly Paul slipped on an inflatable emergency splint from the bag. He had been on the verge of setting the arm, but the delay would not merit the procedure. The best he could do was immobilise the arm.

Nurse Scott came running across. 'Dr Avery—I think one of the kids has a pneumothorax.'

He followed her and knelt down beside the child. The shirt was already open and Paul tapped the chest wall with two fingers. It was tight as a drum. 'Hyper-resonant,' he muttered. The indication, from the tense state of the child's chest and the distressed breathing, was that a tear had occurred in the lung, permitting air to escape into the pleural cavity. The condition was serious. 'Get me a big hypodermic needle,' Paul snapped. 'The biggest you can find.'

Nurse Scott returned a minute later with the needle. 'I'll take care of this, nurse. You get Dan and Bill organised. Get the broken arm case into the wagon and give her oxygen. Tell Dan I want to take this patient back with us, too.' Scott moved off and, without hesitating, Paul pushed the needle into the child's chest wall. Air immediately began to hiss out of the end.

The driver from the second outside ambulance approached and pointed to the other two children. 'Will I take these, doctor?'

Paul nodded. 'Handle them carefully, won't you?' They don't get to me emotionally, he thought. Yet he was scared in case they got damaged by an ambulance man, a trained individual. Maybe he was a frustrated father.

They arrived back at Westfield, unloaded the patients, wrote up their individual reports, re-set the ambulance and retired to the canteen. Bill Davis, still looking as tired as he had when they left, slumped down on a seat and folded his arms. 'Benzedrine and tea,' he told Dan. 'I'm bloody knackered.'

Mary Scott and Paul sat opposite him. 'What's up, Bill?' Mary patted his elbow. 'Too much bed and not enough sleep, eh?'

'Ha!' The humourless howl made a sleepy night porter by the counter almost drop his coffee. 'Acts of bravery are out of my line, nurse. Anybody that tampers with my missus wants a medal.'

'Don't you sleep during the day when you're on nights?'

'I'm supposed to, I know. But it's my responsibilities, you see. Brenda has all these little jobs for me. If I don't get them done as she thinks of them, they pile up. All day today I was lying about the lounge floor, putting down flaming carpet tiles. Tomorrow, or the next day, I've got to put a new splashguard on the sink.'

'Henpecked,' Scott said.

'Definitely,' Bill replied.

Dan came back with a tray. 'Teas all round, courtesy of the last of the big spenders.' He set out the cups and eased himself into the seat beside Bill. 'That was quite a mess tonight, wasn't it?' He sipped his tea, fixing his eyes on Nurse Scott.

'I've seen worse,' she said lightly.

'So have we all,' Dan droned. 'But it was a mess, just the same.'

Paul was curious about Mary Scott's attitude. When she was not working with patients she always gave the impression of someone hardly concerned at all with human suffering. Yet when she was doing her job, there was no one more dedicated. There had been a doctor like that in Paul's training hospital. The underlying reason for his behaviour, it turned out, was that he was so badly wrapped up in his work, involved to such an unusual extent, that he had to pretend indifference to combat any outward sign of his near obsession. Paul made a mental note to talk to Mary about that sometime, and realised as he did that he had been looking for an excuse to talk to her for quite a while. So far, he had not admitted to himself just how interested he really was. The possibility of Mary turning out to be a teaser was, he partly admitted to himself, making him very cautious. And of course there was Edith. He should show some loyalty to her. He should, but he could not honestly say that he felt any pressure, from his conscience or elsewhere, to do so.

'You know what I think?' Bill had swallowed his tea in two gulps and was waxing untypically talkative. 'I think they should get some bleeding legislation passed double quick, to govern the top speed of car engines. The number of deaths that could have been avoided, this week alone, if the cars had been limited to a top twenty miles an hour.'

'Nice dream, Bill,' Paul said. 'But you're talking about interfering with something very holy. It's like the crazy business in America with guns. You can't ban firearms there now, because people have taken their guns into their personalities, it would be like traumatic amputation to take them away. Cars are worshipped, remember. Some men and women don't come properly to life until they're behind that steering wheel. They'll go on getting more powerful and more deadly, and all we'll be able to do is what we do now. Run behind and pick up the wounded.'

'Bloody disgraceful.'

'I like cars,' Mary Scott said. She was clearly on a provocative tack, for some perverse reason. 'They're not designed to kill people. They're made to give pleasure. It's only human stupidity that causes the killing.'

Paul grinned. 'I think we all accept that. The point is, you don't give explosives to children. If a baby detonates a grenade, it's the baby's stupidity, if you like, that causes the damage. Driving tests should be very much more stringent. I'm sure that's the way to reduce road deaths.'

'How about that accident we just attended?' Mary's eyebrows were high with petulant enquiry. 'Would a tougher driving test have stopped that from happening?'

'Sure. The nun would have been trained to keep right on, she would have learned that swerving to save an animal's life can cost human life.'

Mary shook her head and gazed down into her cup. 'I think you'd have to start interfering with a nun's religious scruples a hell of a lot before you'd get her tuned to the idea of running over an animal, by instinct.'

They fell silent. Talk regularly shot back and forth on the lunacy that haunted motorways. Everyone in casualty had seen mutilations of the kind previously only seen in time of war, and they had usually come in from the motorway. The ambulance drivers and attendants had swept people up in pieces, they had seen mothers blinded, children crippled, fathers with bizarre injuries that sounded funny in gag books, which betokened nothing but horror in real life. High speed driving suffered the same basic defect as galloping disease; it had too much momentum, it could not be stopped when there was danger. To arrest a speeding car, to make it stop instantly, meant that the driver and his passengers would die, almost certainly. To bring it to a halt at a pace consistent with occupant-survival, usually someone outside got killed—that was certainly the case when any irregularity cropped up. The trouble was, Paul knew, although he never cared to argue about it, that the pleasures of fast driving far outweighed the likelihood and the apprehension of accidents. People who knew all the clinical dangers of smoking still went ahead puffing their poisonous cigarettes, because the pleasure pushed the danger over the horizon. Too much in the way of commercial interest and individual self-indulgence stood in the way of reform. The little ones would still die tomorrow and all the days after, people would be blinded and maimed, on a rising scale, because to ask people to defer certain pleasures and certain profits was outside the ability of any power, short of God's.

Another call came in before they had finished their tea.

'What the hell are people doing on the roads at this time of night?' Dan sounded angry. Paul had seen him turn that way before, and he believed it was because Dan disliked bitterly having to deviate from a set intention. He had probably been looking forward to peace and quiet for the rest of his shift.

Bill simply yawned and stretched, resigned to accept whatever was hurled at him. 'When the fairies turn against you, Daniel, they make a job of it.' He slapped Dan's shoulder as they hurried through the door, with Paul and Mary Scott at their backs. 'You probably stepped on a bleedin' leprechaun when you were a kid, and we're all suffering for it now.'

It was another collision. The police were even less specific than usual, they simply indicated that the accident had occurred on a dirt turn-off six miles from the hospital, naming a road which Dan knew very well. 'I used to go courtin' round there,' he mused. 'Lovely spot in summer.'

The place would never be quite so attractive again. A speeding car filled with youths and their girlfriends had rounded a bend in the narrow, hedge-flanked road and struck the rear end of a car that was parked side-on to them, two-thirds of the way into a field. The youths' car had spun and hit a telephone pole, half of the occupants had been thrown into the hedges and the boot and one wheel of the parked vehicle had been ripped off. People were being helped out of the hedges when the ambulance ground to a halt by the torn car. Dan switched on the spot lamps, manipulating the handles inside the cab to achieve a broad flood of illumination. 'Don't see why they sent for us,' he muttered. 'Looks as if they're all walking.'

A policeman explained the graver part when they all got out. 'There's a couple in the back of the car,' he said. He spoke in a low affronted tone, his eyes trying to convey the delicacy that mingled with the emergency of the situation. 'They, ah—they were having it off when the car was hit.'

Pointed enough for a delicate remark, Paul thought. He touched Nurse Scott's elbow. 'Come on. Bring a torch and the small emergency bag. Dan, Bill, have a look at the others, will you? Hand out some first aid.'

The door of the car had been freed from its lock by the twisting impact on the rear end. Paul waited for his nurse to bring the torch, then he switched it on and pointed the beam along the back seat, sticking his head inside at the same time. This one was for the chamber of horrors, he decided. A man was lying on the floor, jammed between the front and back seats, his trousers at his knees. On the seat a girl lay very still, her dark hair in a fan around the arm-rest adjacent to the far door. Her right arm hung down, brushing her companion's shoulder, and her left hand was resting, very relaxed, on her breast. Her skirt was up around her waist and her pants were in a coiled figure of eight round her knees. In the harsh glow of the torch, flecks of semen glinted on her thighs and belly. Paul reached out and touched her. She was very cool. He climbed right inside, wedging a knee on the seat between her feet, propping his elbow on the back of the driver's seat. He lifted one eyelid and shone the torch on the pupil. He did the same with the other eye. Exhaling and arresting his breathing for a few seconds, he placed an ear to the girl's chest. Over his shoulders he saw Mary Scott peering into the cabin.

'Dead,' he said.

The man was alive, indeed he appeared only to be suffering from concussion. With the nurse's help, Paul got him out and on to the grass at the side of the car. He checked the pulse, which was thin and rapid, the pupils dilated and equal. 'Just keep an eye on him, nurse. I think it's simple concussion, but he may go into cerebral compression. Get Dan and Bill to put him on the number one stretcher.' The man looked appreciably older than the dead girl. He had short, oiled hair and a small, neatly trimmed moustache. On an impulse he looked back inside the car. She was wearing a wedding ring. It was odd how many of these wife stealers, especially the ones who stole young wives, had the look of the wicked Squire about them. Romantic imagery, Paul assumed, played a bigger part in the female's sexual outlook than she cared in general to admit.

'Aren't you going to try resuscitating her?' Nurse Scott was keeping a straight professional face on matters. Had the girl been alive, Paul would have been on the receiving end of some coarse comment, he was sure of that.

'No, there's no point.' He bent along the car seat and moved the girl's head. It swung freely, as if it were on an oiled pivot. 'I heard the movement of the vertebrae when I was listening for her heartbeat. Her neck's broken.' Complete lesions above the fifth cervical vertebra were always fatal. Attempts at respiration were fruitless, as respiratory paralysis always occurred at the moment of injury.

As the concussed patient was being transferred to the ambulance, the policeman returned, looking as sheepish as before. 'We've dropped a bollock with this one,' he confided to Paul.

'Why?'

'A man reported this car stolen earlier tonight. He said it was urgent we find it, for there were some valuable papers inside. So when I called the details of the crash through to the station, I pointed out that the stolen car was involved.'

'So?' Paul was interested, but mystified.

'Well,' the policeman spread his leather gloved hands; 'it's a put-up job. The dead woman's name is Mrs Irene Calder. The owner of the car is Reginald Calder. Her old man. My mate in the car recognised the woman, he lives near their house. He reckons the woman's husband put out the theft call just to catch her out. She drives the car all the time, apparently.'

'Drove,' Paul corrected. 'She's dead. Where have you boobed? I still don't get it.'

'When we called in to the station, Calder was there, waiting for word. The dopey kid on the desk told him we'd found his vehicle, told him where, too.'

'Oh, boy.'

'Exactly. The sergeant's just been on the squeak box to tell us that he reckons Calder is on his way over here.'

'We better move fast, then.'

The girl's body was wrapped in a polythene sheet and placed on the floor of the ambulance. Paul called through to ambulance headquarters to ask for another unit to come and bring the shaken, cut and bruised occupants of the second car to Westfield casualty. 'That's it, then,' he told the policeman. I'll leave you to cope with the husband.' A thought occurred to him, just as he was climbing into the cabin. 'You can maybe divert his anger a little by charging him with using the police to further private investigation. There must be a law against it.'

The policeman smiled wanly. 'Thanks a lot.'

On the way back, the man regained consciousness. He was held firmly across the shoulders by a padded strap, and only his head could move with any freedom. Nurse Scott placed herself in such a position that he could not see the body on the floor.

'What happened?'

'You were in an accident.'

He closed his eyes tightly, trying to think. 'I don't remember anything . . .'

'Just relax, you'll be all right.'

'Irene!' He shouted the name and his head and neck craned upwards from the stretcher. 'Where's Irene? Is she all right? Oh suffering Jesus—'

'Now lie still.' Scott was capable of the sour sharp command when it was needed, and the man let his head drop back on the padded rest. His eyes stared at the dim lights in the ceiling of the ambulance, and a look of near terror crept slowly across his face as the minutes passed.

Nobody was prepared for what happened in the ambulance bay outside casualty. A wheeled trolley had been brought for the dead body, but this was kept aside until the concussed patient was brought out, still shielded from the sight of the wrapped corpse. He was able to walk with assistance, and he trotted along towards the entrance door with an arm round Nurse Scott's shoulder.

They were only two feet from the door when a man appeared from the shadows, holding up a long thin knife. He was crouched, walking like a mutant crab, and his face was as wild as any in the violent wing of the psychiatric block. 'Bastard!' he screeched, making straight for the patient. 'Rotten fucking bastard!'

Mary Scott, taken off guard, stood stock still, watching the waving point of the knife. Paul, coming round from the cab, saw the situation and guessed at once that this was the jealous and ingenious Mr Calder. 'Stand just where you are,' he yelled at Mary Scott. 'Don't let go of that patient!' He ran off to the side, his white coat forming a moving diversion that Calder could not ignore, even in his agitated condition. He spun to the side of Mary and grabbed her shoulder, gritting his teeth, trying to push her away from her patient. Paul swallowed hard and made a flying leap at Calder's ankles, catching only one of them as the man jumped clear.

'Get off me! Get off!' The knife flew around in an arc and Mary ducked. The thin edge struck the side of the patient's head and sliced down along his cheek, severing the flesh completely, exposing his back teeth like some grisly anatomical demonstration.

Paul dug in his fingers and drew the captive leg towards him as he rolled over sideways. Calder toppled and landed in a heap by the door of the ambulance. Before anyone could reach him, he was up again, resting his hands on the ambulance step. From behind Paul saw him stiffen. He was staring at a shoe protruding from the polythene bundle on the ambulance floor.

'Dan! Grab him!'

The big Irishman's hands took hold of Calder's shoulders, but the man dropped down, leaving his overcoat behind, and rose again, whipping the flap of the plastic sheet aside. His wife lay exactly as she had died in the car. Calder's head came back, and for an instant it looked as if he would fall over, then he jerked forward, hawking in his throat, and sent a gobbet of spittle across the dead woman's legs.

Dan and Bill grasped his arms and pulled him away. He relaxed and let them carry him through the doors into casualty. The knife lay on the damp tarmac, its edge thick with arterial blood.

It took an hour to straighten matters out. The police collected Calder, Mrs Calder's body was removed to the mortuary, and the damage to the boyfriend's face was assessed and repaired. In the space of time between receiving the injury and getting inside the department, he had lost three pints of blood. The left major and minor cheek muscles had been cut clean through, as had the retromandibular vein and the superior labial and facial arteries. Painstakingly Paul did his best to rebuild the sundered structures, assisted by a houseman and Nurse Scott. Fine stitching, with attention to the original lines of tension, formed the major part of the task. Even so it was fairly certain that despite the care taken over the repair, the man would carry an unsightly scar for the rest of his life. When it was finished, the man was admitted to a surgical ward for observation.

Back in the canteen, where Paul decided it was his breakfast time and treated himself to two eggs and an immoderate amount of bacon, Dan McGoldrick took three cups of tea and twenty-five minutes to lay down his complaints about the madness and the imminent chaos infecting mankind. The old virtues, he kept insisting, had been abandoned at the expense of the oldest regulator of them all, Christian morality. Nobody disagreed with him; half of the time, with the exception of Paul who was too busy eating his breakfast anyway, nobody could make out a word he was saying. Bill was so tired he kept swaying in his seat, and Nurse Scott had gone broody. The end of a perfect day, Paul thought, wiping his hands on his coat. Death, destruction, adultery, jealousy and attempted murder, topped off with a sermon from a disillusioned Irishman.

Paul attended one more call that day. In the company of Ferdie Nesbitt, Lester Hill and Nurse Haxton, he travelled at high speed to the site of a petrol blaze in a garage forecourt. An attendant had been carrying an open can of fuel to a vehicle under repair at the rear of the main building. By the kind of fluke that accounted for most fire tragedies, a spark from a cigar being carried between the teeth of a customer three feet away ignited the vapour at the narrow mouth of the can, and the can exploded. The attendant, a young man of nineteen, was enveloped in fire, and as he ran and crashed into a petrol pump, screaming his agony and his terror, the fanned flames on his clothing and skin set fire to another container at the base of the pump.

Perhaps it was fatigue, or a weak spot in his objectivity, or a combination of both that suddenly put Paul in the grip of a terrible nausea when he saw the victim. He had been laid on the grey cement and extinguisher foam lay in regular pools around him, like some bizarre trimming. He was deep purple and black in irregular patches. His face had been so badly burned that the lips were charred to the consistency of brittle, overdone meat.

His hair was gone, and Paul suspected that the eyes, too, had been lost. The most awful part, the part that seemed to trigger the queasy sensation in Paul's stomach more than the smell and more than the extent of the destruction was the fact, clear from the agitation of the charred form, that the boy was conscious.

'Don't just stand about!' It was unfair that he should try to drive back his sickness by picking on Nurse Haxton, but she was the nearest to him. 'Get him into the wagon. Set up the plasma. Quickly!'

While the driver and attendant moved the patient, Paul went round to the rear of the building, striding purposefully, and found the lavatory. He splashed cold water on his face for almost a minute, until he could feel the circulation surging in his head again. He dried his skin with half a dozen paper towels and looked briefly in the mirror. He was like an older version of himself. He did not pause to wonder why.

In the ambulance he told Ferdie to get back to the hospital as fast as possible. As the vehicle swung out through a gap in the morbid circle of onlookers, Nurse Haxton was setting up the giving set, while Paul prepared the plasma bottle. 'I want it poured into him, nurse. Poured in.' A factor of severe burning, too often overlooked, was the terrible fluid loss. Current thinking insisted that as many as thirty-five or six pints of plasma should be given to a victim as emergency treatment.

While the plasma was going in, Paul gingerly inspected the damage in detail. The chest, arms and legs were roasted. This life must love this body, he thought, to hang on against such odds. He pulled away the charred front of the trousers. The primal dread affected doctors as much as other men. The petrol, running in searing trickles along the natural flow lines of the body, had formed a particularly effective furnace in the youth's groin. Paul felt himself gag. There was no use fighting it, no use suppressing what he knew now and always managed to forget at other times; burns sickened him, the sight of a blister on his own finger could make his knees tremble and bring out the sweat on his brow. What appalled him, when he saw burns in other people, was the way he could almost feel their pain. No other injury produced that reaction. And the boy was still awake, still up in the world, locked inside his tomb of agony.

Swallowing very hard, several times, he moved to the head and examined the mouth, listening to the rhythm of the breathing. While he was stooped over the contorted gap, his ear only inches away, the breath caught; then, shockingly, the voice spoke, clean and uncharred, a moist movement from deep in the throat. 'Oh God, it hurts.'

Paul spun away and threw up. For the rest of the journey, he remained on his knees, clinging to the side of the vacant stretcher.

He was in the residency, lying on the small bed in the room he used when he was on call, when they rang from men's surgical to tell him that the boy had died. It had been a foregone conclusion, but every continuing minute of life had been like a knife stuck in Paul Avery's side. He sighed and put down the phone.

So who was he to say that it was a blessing, who was he to know that any man or woman or child would be better off dead? Doctors, the best of them, were not gods. They had no special knowledge that permitted them to know of any virtue or advantage in death. The temptation to presume was strong, it was put there by the suffering people who placed their faith in the men with stethoscopes and powerful drugs and healing knives. When he was twenty-one, he knew everything. He had positive views. Now he was sure of nothing, which was probably a sign that he had learned a lot over the years. That one case, that one gap in his wall through which he had been compelled to share a patient's agony, had caused a flood as he lay on the bed. Those children, the pure of the earth who had done no harm, scattered like dross across the motorway, the virtuous nuns, broken and twisted, the poor woman who had probably been driven to seek the squalid romance of a back-seat affair with a conniving, just-as-lonely partner, and her demented husband, driven to an act of hate against the remains of perhaps the only person he could love; all that misery on which Paul Avery, by virtue of his special training, was obliged to dance attendance. The irony, the irony that would make the situation laughable were it not so loaded with pain, was that he was just one of the people himself, just as subject to the ills and accidents of the world, yet he was supposed, by some suspect process called hardening, to remain separate.

At times like this—and this was not the first—he knew that his sympathy for his brothers was intact, as whole as if he had never donned the white linen. Even without his humanising rules, he would be the same. It was cause for rejoicing and for lamenting. A sympathetic doctor was as effective as a butcher who loved his animals. Kindness and fellow-feeling could be the erosion of effective medicine.

But tomorrow it would be over, his feelings would be safely under the deadening blanket of procedure, work-pressure and experience. Knowing that, facing it and believing it, he felt better. His ambitions would not be harmed by the odd bout of compassion. And that was another point, he thought, turning on his side and closing his eyes, that was something to be really glad of—his underlying sympathy was not at all standard, and the unconventional routes were the ones he always sought.

7

Among the morning mail Ernie Hale had brought to work with him, there was a letter from his publisher. When he saw the letterhead he read no further, deciding to leave it until last. Whatever it was about, it would get his full attention. The other stuff was the usual collection of invitations to join this or that breakaway body, bills for subscriptions, medical circulars and extracts he had ordered from journals. He held them on his knees and sorted them into two piles, keep and discard, while the first of his three Saturday morning patients settled herself into the chair before him. Dropping one bundle into the waste basket and the other on his desk, he looked up and smiled.

'Good morning. It's Mrs Young, isn't it?'

She was attractive—a well dressed woman with intelligent eyes. It was her first visit. From the clinical notes he had read before she arrived, Ernie had learned that she was thirty-two, the wife of a school teacher and a former teacher herself. Her doctor had been treating her for mild depression, prescribing Librium and, later, Noveril. The focus of the lady's condition had not been uncovered, although it was suspected that she had severe domestic problems. The general practitioner based this suspicion on the fact that she always made an effort to keep off the subject of her husband and children, even when pressed for details of the home life. Her symptoms, as she had related them, were a vague, persistent unrest and feelings of anxiety. She had been referred to the psychiatric outpatient department at Westfield because lately she had complained of numerous obsessions. Mrs Young had been reticent about the details, although she was obviously keen to have treatment for something. The doctor had concluded, in his covering letter, that she had wanted to see a psychiatrist all along, but had been too shy or apprehensive to ask.

She had not spoken yet. She had nodded and smiled, but that was all. In her face Ernie could see the kind of young girl she had been; studious, pretty but not very communicative, anxious to please and probably weighted down with feelings of inadequacy. That kind of background was never cured by marriage; it was simply set on one side for a time. The main features always came back.

'Your doctor tells me you've been having a bit of depression, and he says you're in the grip of one or two obsessions now. Would you like to tell me first about the obsessions?' He kept a pleasant smile on his face, and moved his hands as he spoke, indicating his positive ability to help (moving hands always did that; it was one of his oldest touches of stage dressing).

Defensively, Mrs Young slipped down an inch or two in the chair and folded her white hands in her lap. 'I don't really know where to start—'

'Start wherever you like. There are no hard and fast rules.'

She ran the tip of her tongue along the edge of her upper teeth, a small gesture, probably habitual, which Ernie found enticing. 'Well, I have this thing about sentences I hear. For instance, when you spoke just now, the last word you said was "rules." I immediately started to tack rhymes on to it. I do that for long periods of time. If I'm reading, I ruin the book for myself by doing it, or if I'm listening to something on the radio, I lose the drift because I become attached to one word and I have to apply all the rhymes I can think of. If I force myself to stop it, I feel guilty, I feel that something bad will happen.'

'Can you give me an example?'

'Ample, trample, sample—'

'I see.' A vast area of her mental energy must, he thought, be given over to the habit. 'How long has it been going on?'

'I don't know. I've always had the ability, but I think it got out of control several months ago. It's reached a point now where I find it hard to bear.'

'I can understand that, Mrs Young. What else is troubling you?'

'Oh, there's my funny convictions. Sometimes, I'm convinced that I'm the only person in the world who isn't in on some big secret. Everybody else knows something, something very profound about life, but they all know they have to keep it from me. It's easy to tell you that, and it's easy right now to realise that it's silly. But at other times, when I'm alone . . .'

Ernie nodded his head slowly, sympathetic, understanding, recognising the emerging pattern already. 'What else?'

'The fear of death.' She looked at her hands, spreading the fingers. 'I have the terrible feeling, every time something nice or exciting appears on the horizon, that I'll die either before it happens, or immediately afterwards if I enjoy it too much. And there are plenty of other things. I touch objects, in a certain order, at certain times of day. I also deliberetely balance every pleasure with something unpleasant. It's as if—' her hands came up and clasped together under her chin, '—as if I was constantly trying to please something or somebody, and the terms get harder and harder.'

'How well do you sleep?'

'Not very well at all. The doctor gave me some tablets, but although they rested me, they didn't really make me sleep. I was half-conscious all the time.'

He could see that she was becoming very tense. Probably, knowing that a psychiatrist was her only hope, she was anxious that something be done. 'Mrs Young, if you'll permit me, I'll make a prediction. I'll bet that you already know how you'll behave when you go home today. . . . You'll feel obliged to step up the pressure on yourself, because you've broken the rules by coming to me and hoping that I'll liberate you from your obsessional duties. You'll have to do penance. Then you'll deliberately make yourself distrust me. Just like everybody else, I know a big secret which I'm not going to tell you, so I'm in league with all the others, I won't do you any good. Am I warm?'

'Yes, you are.'

'Then let me tell you some more. Your obsessions are serving a dual function. First, they're totally occupying your intellect, so that you will not dwell on the painful truth, whatever it is, the truth at the bottom of your unrest. Second, the little habits and rituals are being used by you to extract penance for your moral dishonesty. Do you see it? The nasty circle? You produce the obsessions to cover the facts, then you use the same obsessions to beat yourself across the back for *not* facing the truth. How does that sound for a snap diagnosis?'

She relaxed, for the first time since she had come in. 'It makes sense to me, doctor. It sounds right.' She blinked. 'I'd say it's absolutely right.' She looked as if she had come to the end of a long, hard sprint. Then she narrowed her eyes. 'Isn't a psychiatric patient supposed to work things out for himself, with the doctor simply keeping him on the tracks?'

'In general, yes.' Ernie smiled. 'But I don't really think you're a typical psychiatric patient, Mrs Young. I think you're an ordinary, intelligent human being, with no great disturbance, and you happen to suffer from a very common complaint. Right now, you'll be feeling relief, you'll be sure that the problem has departed. Well, in a sense, it has. You've loosened the roots, by letting me talk to you. But unless you drag up your real problem and examine it, work at solving it, you'll be plagued with the gremlins again.'

'What should I do?'

'Tell me, right now, what's really wrong.'

'But I—'

'And don't go smothering it. It's there, you know what it is. Every time you come near it, though, a wall comes up. It's something you're scared to admit.' Ernie had his hands flat on the top of the desk, fingers whitening at the tips as he pressed them against the wood. 'All you have to do, to set yourself on the road out of this cave full of bats, is face the thing you're frightened of. That's all.'

Her mouth moved, it opened and her tongue touched her teeth again, a hesitant preamble. 'My husband . . . '

'Go on. Get it out.'

'I think my husband is a homosexual.' She looked astonished.

'I suppose that's the first time you've let yourself believe that at a conscious level?'

'Yes.'

'And it would be safe to assume that you can't sleep properly in case your subconscious comes up with the truth. Just relax,

Mrs Young. It's not the end of the world. If our masters can rationalise the hydrogen bomb, I think we can make some sense of your husband's little difference.'

To allow her time to catch her breath, he scribbled a few notes on a blank case sheet. When he glanced up, she looked glum, but definitely in control of herself. 'What makes you think he's that way?' He did not want to use the word homosexual; from the way she had reacted to her own pronunciation of it, Mrs Young clearly found it shocking. The time for shocks was past. Now was the period for unemotional, moderate consideration.

'We've been married for six years. I think I've known for about two years. At first, I covered it up. I told myself I was being too jealous. He gives private tutorials, you see, and the students are always rather pretty boys, usually in their late teens. I could detect a sort of rejection in the air whenever one of them was in the house. They would shut themselves in the study and they'd laugh and I'd be shut outside and I'd wonder . . . but I never did get to the point where I'd really give it any hard thought. As it got more blatant, I just pretended harder, I suppose. Then, a few months ago—'

'Around the time when the obsessions started filling your head?'

'That's right. Goodness, you *are* right about this . . .'

'Please go on.'

'A few months ago, I walked into the study—I *made* myself do it, it was like sleepwalking, sort of automatic but somehow inevitable . . . George was sitting at the table, reading aloud from a book, and the boy, a very soft, girlish person, was sitting at the side, and their hands were clasped on the top. I told them I was sorry and I walked out again, and all I could see was George's hand wrapped round that boy's.'

'How did you bury that?'

'I told myself firmly that it was a fatherly gesture on George's part. I never dwelt on it.'

'You couldn't, could you? You were a full-time employee of your mental habits.' He looked at his watch. 'Mrs Young, I think we should have another talk. A longer one. This morning's little meeting was intended merely to serve as an introduction to treatment. But as I said, you are not ill. You've simply needed someone to talk to. If we thrash this out, I'm sure you'll come to proper terms with reality, and an answer will be found, even if it's only a compromise.'

'Would a compromise work?'

'Why not? Thousands of people are in your position. I think your husband probably lives with several compromises. You love him, don't you?'

'Oh yes, dearly.'

'Well then. Some honesty on both sides will work wonders, I'm sure. Just try to believe that he is not possessed by the devil, or that there is anything particularly malignant in the idea of a man being attracted to other men. Socially it's a problem, but so is dandruff. I'm not going to try to tell you what you'll decide. The decision will be the outcome of a lot of things, a lot of soul-searching. I'll lend you my experience and my ear. All right?'

She stood up, pushing back her chair. 'I'm amazed,' she said quietly. 'A lot has been lifted—'

'And a lot's been deposited, too. But rest assured your mind-games won't bother you much now. You know what they are and why they were there. Mental honesty is the best safeguard against problems of that kind.' He checked his desk diary. 'Next Friday, three o'clock?'

'That'll be fine,' she assured him. 'Goodbye, doctor. And thank you.'

When she had gone, he sat still for a moment, thinking about her. Standing at his professional distance from the dramas that came into the office, he could be terribly reasonable. Faced with a homosexual wife of his own, say, he would probably hit the roof. She was a nice woman, a good person, and the Lord, in his wisdom, always saw fit to drop shit on the people who bore nobody ill will. Scoundrels like himself, they got by very well. He glanced at the letter from his publisher, lying on the desk, and he thought about the book. He had the cheek to tell Mrs Young that mental honesty was a mighty, curative virtue, while in an other quarter he was employing a craftily disguised streak of intellectual dishonesty to push himself into the bright lights. On the other hand, his advice regarding mental honesty still stood and he based it on personal experience. No matter what he led other people to believe about him, Ernie never tried to fool himself.

He picked up the letter and read it.

Dear Dr Hale,

Thank you for the revised chapters and the summary of chapters in preparation. I find the material very interesting, and I am sure a wide audience will endorse my enthusiasm. The small fear you express in regard to overstepping the bounds is, I feel, groundless. In the current moral climate, healthy curiosity can safely be met with an equally healthy candour.

One small point that may interest you: we have had an inquiry, from a Henry Madison, FRCS, who expresses interest in the book. He says that he read of it in our advance news circular. He wants to know quite a lot—contents, outline, etc. Is he some kind of official medical snooper? We shall hold back on a reply to him until we hear from you.

Very best wishes,
Logan Miles,
Editor

'That bloody old woman!' Ernie kicked the waste basket, stood up and had a kick at the leg of the desk. He walked across the office, tapping one balled fist in the palm of his other hand, then returned to the desk and picked up the internal telephone.

'Casualty, please.' He drummed his fingers while he waited, glaring with open hostility at the letter, crumpled where he had left it. 'Hello? Oh, could you get Dr Avery to come to the phone, please? It's Dr Hale.'

Paul came on the line after a few moments and Ernie told him about the letter. 'I told you, didn't I Paul? He's the flaming Witchfinder General for this hospital. He's sticking his nose into my affairs, and I'll bet he says it's in the interests of the system.'

'It probably is.' Paul gave every audible evidence of amusement.'

'Balls! He's got his knife in me, the old sod. He'll make this a disciplinary issue before the book even comes out. I expect fireworks, but I want to be published before they start.'

'Why don't you tackle him about it?'

'That would be bright, wouldn't it? Make him think there's something to hide. Get him into the full flush of his crusading spirit. He'd love me to do that. Why couldn't the old butcher come and ask me, to my face? Why couldn't he say "I've heard you're writing a book. Care to tell me about it?" What's wrong with that approach?'

'Look, Ernie, can I talk to you about this later? I've got an attempted overdose on the table right now, and there's a queue growing in the waiting room.' He paused. 'Listen, I'm having a party tonight. All the gang from the Life-Support Unit. By special dispensation they're all off duty, me included. Want to come round?'

Ernie's face brightened. 'Great. I'd love to. I'll bring a bottle. Two bottles. Hey, can I bring Cynthia?'

'If you promise not to—'

'I promise not to.'

'Okay. See you around eight-thirty.'

Ernie put down the receiver and resumed his seat behind the desk. He picked up the publisher's letter and put it in his pocket. Madison. That name had the same effect on him as pork had on a rabbi: taboo, an area of bad feeling. Whatever the consultant was up to, Ernie was determined to see his book come out in the form intended, whatever it cost him professionally. Madison could go and shove a dilator up his arse.

He punched the bell and a moment later the door opened, revealing little Miss Donovan, who suffered from terrible urges to throw stones at people on the street. Ernie folded his arms and gave her a smile. 'Come along in, Minnie. Who have you tried to kill this week?'

The large study was more than a sanctuary, it was a power house and a place of regeneration, a place where Henry could come and sit with a book, half reading, half dreaming, letting the peace heal up the bruises of the day, permitting the civilised company of fine books, fine furniture and an open fire to work on him with the gentleness of a balm. It was in this room that he composed some of his best speeches; it was at the Georgian desk that he wrote the address that had been acclaimed in the professional press as 'fine words in a very fine order, the sentiments expressed with the precision of Madison's craft and elevated by the power of his vision'. That had been fifteen years ago, but the room still worked on him now as it had then.

When he had seen his wife off at the door and bade a cheerful goodnight to his niece as she trotted off to her girlish pursuits, he came straight to the study. For some men, Saturday evening was a time for joining their friends, for going out in search of pleasure. Henry Madison found his pleasure right here, in his own house, within the stimulating confines of his study. His guest, Dr Edith Roberts, was not due to arrive for another hour. He was content to wait in this room and imbue himself with its peaceful, muted atmosphere.

There were nearly five thousand books. Some had come from his father, many had been purchased at auctions, and several hundred had been bought brand new. English literature was well represented, as was the English language, filling three full shelves of encyclopedias and dictionaries, some of them extremely old. Every branch of medicine, with the exception of psychiatry, was covered in an enormous series of texts that were still regularly supplemented. There were fine, expensive volumes on anatomy, anaesthesiology, bacteriology, dermatology, diagnostics, haematology, ophthalmology, pathology, physiology—in addition to one of the largest private collections of surgical manuals, text books and treatises in England.

By the fireside, on a small shelf which had been built for the purpose, there were books Henry had used when he was a student at University. Each one had a special significance. There was a 1930 edition of *Physical Signs in Clinical Surgery* by Hamilton Bailey. Henry had bought it from another student for five shillings, because the chap needed the money. That young man had gone on to become one of the country's most prominent surgeons, and his signature was still clearly inked on the fly leaf. Next to it, there were three books of hand-written notes, presented to Henry by a friend who decided to pack medicine in and join the church. There was a year book, with pictures of all the students. Henry picked it up now and leafed through the pages. There had been two girls in his year, and underneath the picture of one of them, a waggish friend had pencilled, *Molitur per utramque cavernam* which meant, in a loose translation, 'she lets herself be done in either orifice'. Henry smiled, recalling the joker, long since dead. Even the coarseness in those days had bowed to the established virtues; a man could employ Latin then as easily as most used American slang now—a man of learning, of course, a man of some substance. He riffled further through the book and found himself, young, smooth-skinned, serious and keen. It had all been before him then, they had been magnificient days, full of the will and the capacity to learn. He put down the book and picked up a weekly journal instead. Too long at that small shelf meant a flood of regrets and memories of opportunities missed.

He took a high backed chair by the fire and spread the paper before him. They looked like tabloid rags nowadays. There had been a time when every journal was printed on soft paper, in a typeface that bore dignity to match its subject. Not now. Now it was blaring headlines and articles cut down to the length of mere paragraphs. His eye fell on a prominent item. The British Medical Association was setting up a pensions probe. The indignity of it. The BMA was descending to the market place, squabbling over the suspected fact that pension contributions were being nationally invested at four and a half per cent. The article took up more space on the page than any of the medical items. He turned over and found an entire page devoted to personal investment advice. Opposite, there was half a page of holiday advertising, followed by an illustrated list of cut-price toys.

Henry dropped the paper and stood up. There was still some time before Dr Roberts was due. He walked round the shelves, hoping that something appropriate to the restlessness of his mood would catch his eye. He felt in need of something profound, some stimulant for the mind that would set him at the proper distance from the annoyances of the entire working week. Then the bright blue of the publisher's folder, lying on the desk, impinged on his vision. Henry crossed the room and snatched it up, knowing in his bones that the finest ease he could find would be in asserting his proper authority.

ADVANCE NEWS SPECIAL!
AN AUTUMN LIST SENSATION!

The heading appalled him; brash, vulgar, the bray of the sensation vendor. It was bad enough, it was deplorable enough, that such tactics should be employed in the promotion of any commodity. That this fairground technique, should be used to further the sales of a book was almost too saddening. The full shock of the advertisement lay in the paragraph that followed, a paragraph that Henry Madison had been compelled to read twice when he first saw it.

Pemberton and Morris are privileged to announce the forthcoming publication of *The Marshes of Disquiet* by Ernest Hale, a book written by a practicing psychiatrist that rips the lid off the consulting room. Paraded in startling detail are the wayward lusts, deviant acts and twisted dreams of the psychopaths who live alongside all of us.

Sadists, rapists, lesbians, masochists . . . plus many, many more . . . talk freely and openly about their deeds and their horrifying moral codes. Dr Hale spares us nothing in his searching examination of the wickedness that lies at the heart of so many seemingly 'normal' people. The exhaustive case histories are accompaned by clear, easily-understood commentaries, giving laymen, for the first time, a clear understanding of the workings of the sick mind.

Available October.

The list had been lying in the local bookshop, and Henry had almost missed it. Only because someone approached the assistant before him did he bother to pick it up. What a blessing he had! This was ammunition.

The psychiatric department at Westfield General was no direct concern of Henry, but his overall authority within the hierarchy of hospital administration did give him some voice in what he chose to call the Department of Black Magic. The consultant psychiatrist, Dr Freeman, was old and not at all interested in the finer points of discipline. That, Henry thought, was hardly surprising. Any man whose entire professional framework consisted of childishly stupid theories and dangerously irresponsible treatment, could not be expected to understand the requirements of medical ethics. Freeman allowed his staff to do as they pleased. Hale, his registrar, organised group-therapy sessions, patient lectures and clinic timetables to suit himself. He was a man with no respect for seniority, and he had even seriously questioned one or two of Henry's findings in the past. He was a known drinker, a lecher, a devotee of popular music and an arch debunker. The presence of Hale on the staff at Westfield was, to

Henry, the equivalent of an ink stain on a fine, valuable painting. Or, he thought now, perhaps Hale was a nucleus of infection for not too long after he had taken up his appointment in psychiatry, Avery had been assigned to casualty. Another of the same ilk, an iconoclast, and it was no surprise to discover that Hale and Avery were close friends. Birds of a feather, emissaries of the new chaos; just as Avery had flouted Henry's standing and had succeeded in introducing his crowd-pleasing scheme, Hale was using his qualifications as a springboard to popular success. Between them they mocked the finest system of medicine in the world, and they were laying the path for the hordes that would follow, the clinical guerrillas who would smash the old order.

Henry stared at the book list and chewed thoughtfully on a particle of loose skin on his lower lip. As soon as he had more details of this book Hale had written, he would insist upon an inquiry. If that clown had been abusing his position to obtain material, he would suffer. If he had not been using case matter from the hospital files, he would still suffer. Westfield would not be saddled with the embarrassment of a glory-seeker who peddled pornography under the guise of scientific documentation. Just as Avery would be brought down, so would his soul-mate. Henry Madison had already decided that no means within his grasp would be too extreme if, as a result, he maintained the dignity and tradition of Westfield and his own hard-won eminence.

Edith Roberts arrived on time. Henry took her coat in the hall and showed her into the study. She was wearing a dark silk blouse with a softly turned collar and a brown, pleated skirt. She was a very fine looking young woman, Henry reflected as he walked behind her, and she embodied many of the embryonic virtues that would make her a sound member of her profession. Of all the women who had ever graced his staff, she was the one who showed most promise. He could admit to a degree of interest in her that went beyond the purely professional, but there was little harm in a man of mature years taking pleasure in the grace of an attractive girl. Essentially, he admired the intelligent surgeon in her.

'Do have a glass of sherry, doctor. It has an agreeable effect on the circulation.'

'Thank you.' She took the winged chair he indicated and sat with her hands demurely clasped in her lap. Her hair was a surprise. Henry had only ever seen her in the hospital before this evening, and at work she adopted a style which, while not severe, tended to fit in with the seriousness of her calling. Tonight she had combed it down, and its dark sheen lay in soft waves along the lines of her face and shoulders. In the shaded light of the study, viewed against the mellow panelling and rich leather, she looked quite beautiful. Henry was reminded of the way he used to respond to the sight of his Amy when she was a girl, how the presence of her used to make him clumsy and how he would tremble slightly when he touched her skin.

They drank sherry in silence, then Henry put down his glass and rubbed his hands together. 'To business, then. I must say, right away, that I'm grateful to you for giving up your valuable free time like this.'

'It's a pleasure, Mr Madison, it truly is. The venture fascinates me, and I'm glad of the opportunity to be involved.'

He smiled, aware that he had grown a little warm at the neck, and he moved hastily to the desk, fearful quite suddenly that he might make a fool of himself. Without the usual surroundings to suggest his direct authority over Edith Roberts, he felt their relationship to be slightly altered. He picked up the thick folder and brought it to a table by the fireside. Bending over Edith, he held out a sheaf of paper to her. 'This is the index, as far as it goes. I'm afraid it's no more than a skeleton. That's where your help will be so unvaluable—adding the flesh, as it were.'

He had told Edith about the book a week before, and on Wednesday, to interrupt his gloom, he had asked if she would care to assist him in the preparation of the index. She had seemed flattered. In his own way, Henry had been flattered to be asked to do the book. An original work bearing his own name would have been more satisfying to him, but he had never been able, for some reason, to originate more than a few pages on any of the numerous occasions that he had tried. The book was a standard text, written by Sir Owen Lethbridge, who had died two years previously. Massive revision was needed, and out of the blue an acquaintance with connections in the publishing house had asked Henry if he would like to undertake the task. His name would appear on the cover, he was assured. It would say, *Principles of Surgery for the Student Nurse*, by Sir Owen Lethbridge, revised by Henry Madison. There was always the chance, too, that a perceptive reviewer would note just how much Henry had introduced by way of change, and it was not too much to hope that it might be regarded as a practically new work.

'The old index is useless to us, I'm afraid. What I would like you to do is read each article, noting the specific mention of conditions and technique, and refer to the page number. The page proofs are all in the folder.'

Edith sat forward in her chair, leafing through the long galley sheets. The illustrations were admirable. Her chief had discarded all of the old ones and substituted colour and black-and-white pictures from his own collection, plus several from files held by colleagues elsewhere. There were fifty chapters covering six hundred and fifty pages. He must have spent months on the job. Edith had seen the original edition, and beside this it would look like a joke. Her defensive attitude in regard to Madison was reinforced by the weight of this undertaking. Practically everyone she met from ward sisters to doctors had a list of grievances about Mr Madison. They complained that he was old-fashioned, pedantic, dictatorial, bad-tempered and unreasonable. No one, Edith had noticed, ever took the time to praise his dedication, his great skill, his concern for maintaining standards or his continuing record of grinding hard work at a time of his life when he could so easily have delegated the less pleasant surgical chores. When she was a young student she always pictured a consultant surgeon in the terms which Henry Madison embodied: tall, dignified, strict and gifted. That was her boss, and she admired him a lot more than she could ever tell anyone. He had taught her so very much, and now he was crowning the generosity of his teaching by offering her involvement in the revision of this book. She could think of nothing that would have made her refuse to help – certainly, she would have liked to be with Paul, but she did not like parties very much, and Paul would still be there on Monday. A chance to work side by side with a consultant did not occur everyday.

They worked steadily for two hours. While Henry read the proofs and made corrections. Edith went through the individual sections, noting and numbering. Every few minutes she would query a point and from his seat at the opposite side of the fireplace, he would make everything clear with a few softly spoken words. Between them, they created an atmosphere of peaceful industry, and Edith was quite disappointed when it was time to go.

Henry offered her another sherry before parting, and she accepted it. Standing by the fire, feeling its warmth on her back, she was overwhelmed by an old childhood craving to live in a house like this, to hide herself in its folds and absorb its great strength. The house and the man went well together, she thought. She liked stable things and stable people; constancy was security. In the study she could feel the character which the shape and age of the building created, and she was equally aware of how much atmosphere Henry Madison had superimposed. Edith had looked forward to the evening. Now, at its close, she felt that she had not enjoyed anything so much for a very long time. Yet nothing spectacular had happened. A man and a woman had sat down to work together, that was all.

'When would you like me to call again?' The index, she was pleased to note, would take a long time to complete.

'Next Friday, perhaps?' He had been replacing the papers in the folder, and when he turned, Edith caught the brightness of his eyes, something she had not seen before. 'At the same time, if that suits you.'

'That'll be fine, Mr Madison.' She sipped some more sherry and made a show of sighing. 'This is a wonderful house. Do you and Mrs Madison live here alone?'

'We have a niece, Katie, who has been with us since she was orphaned. I'm glad you like the place. I've had it for a long time, and I've never tired of it.'

'It's my dream house,' she said, smiling. 'Not the one I specifically dreamed of, of course. But houses like this have always fascinated me. Even now, my secure dreams always feature a solid house somewhere in the background. I suppose that means I'm basically insecure.'

Madison sniffed, sipping his own sherry. 'If you take any account of what the psychiatrists say, I suppose that's what your dreams do indicate. I'd be more inclined to think, personally, that one's dreams are as random and purposeless as they appear.'

She had heard his views on psychiatry before. 'I suppose you're right.'

He crossed to the desk and picked up the blue folded sheet he had been reading before she arrived. 'Have you seen this if we are turning to the subject of mind healers? Dr Hale appears to be going in for a career of sensational journalism.'

Edith read the advertisement. 'I think that's dreadful.' She would take it up with Paul. If he knew anything about the book, he had not mentioned it to her.

'His breed are a stain on the profession,' Henry muttered, taking back the paper. 'And they're not restricted to psychiatry, either.' He drained his glass. 'Neither of those men should have been appointed to Westfield.'

Edith did not understand. 'Who is the other one?'

'Why, Avery, of course, the star-spangled showman of casualty. He's equipped with all the flair of a ringmaster and none of the decorum that is essential in a doctor.' He ran his hand through his hair and looked directly at her. 'They're a sad comment on the decline of standards, those men.'

It was incredible, Edith thought, that he did not know of her closeness to Paul Avery. They certainly did not make much display of their relationship when they were in the hospital, but Henry Madison had a keen eye. There was a good deal of subterfuge that he could see clean through at a glance. She did not know how to respond. She knew about her chief's objection to the ambulance of course, but she did not realise, until now, that he held such a low opinion of Paul as a person. She felt the warmth of the house diminish and that was saddening. It was her reaction, that was all. To retain some of the good feeling, she decided to put the conflict from her mind. She loved Paul, and she admired Henry Madison. That was enough, any weighing of one against the other would only produce a diminishing, perhaps some loss.

Fortunately, Madison appeared to have dropped the topic. 'This book we are working on should fill a dire need,' he said. 'A detailed text for the nurse has been lacking for some time.'

'We', he had said. That pleased her, the indication that he regarded the work as she did—as a collaboration. Her sensation of well-being came back to almost its full previous level. 'I'll do all I can to make my small part a complete success.'

'I'm sure you will.' He paused in front of her, showing her more openness in his face than he had ever had before. 'May I say, Dr Roberts, that I find you a most stimulating companion. I have enjoyed this evening very much.' His cheeks were pink, and Edith felt her own begin to turn warmer.

'I've enjoyed myself, too.'

At the step, he watched until she was inside her car, then he closed the heavy oak door and returned to the study. Perhaps, he thought as he tidied up the glassware and straightened the papers on his desk, perhaps he had gone a shade too far. He had given in to a momentary impulse, a very strong impulse of a kind he normally avoided. Her face, her eyes particularly, had been so much in sympathy, it was as if he were standing before someone with whom he had been familiar for many years. He had felt strong affection. In the circumstances, what he had said had been very muted indeed. He was sure he had not caused her embarrassment or offence. He also permitted himself to hope that she really had enjoyed herself.

A key turned in the front door and he straightened, shaking his head sharply. It would be Amy. Just in time to keep him from descending into some undignified reverie. It must, he thought, have something to do with his age.

8

Paul had carefully removed everything breakable from the sitting room before his guests arrived. He had a talent for losing fragile things, and tonight, throwing a party for people whose party habits were unknown to him, he did not want to run the risk of a major catastrophe. The record player and speaker were the only items at risk. Apart from those the room had been streamlined down to minimal seating and a large expanse of open carpet. Table lamps and the clever revolving light Edith had given him were removed too. Even at the risk of taking from the atmosphere, he had decided to make do with the ceiling light. Drinks were set up in the kitchen, as were the sandwiches, buns and cakes supplied by the local bakery's catering service. Just after eight o'clock Paul shaved and changed into black slacks, a college sweater and white moccasins. For an instant, looking in the mirror, he felt he was back home, on the threshold of another over-riotous campus shindig. For thirty-five, he was wearing well.

The two attendants, Bill Davis and Lester Hill, arrived first. They were in their best suits and between them had brought a carrier bag full of canned beer and a smaller bag with a bottle of gin and a half bottle of vodka.

'Our wives think we're going to a branch union meeting,' Lester explained, hanging his coat in the hallway and peering about him. 'They had a bit of trouble believing us, of course. Saturday night and all that. Still, I think the suits and ties did the trick.'

Paul started unloading the cans and piling them on a small trolley. 'Your wives don't like you going to parties?'

'Not without them,' Bill grunted. 'And *with* them, Lester and I don't like parties.'

They moved into the sitting room. 'Make yourselves at home, fellas. I'll fix the drinks. What'll it be?'

'Beer,' Bill said. 'A big one.'

'The same,' Lester added. 'A very big one.'

With their glasses in their hands, the two men flipped through the stack of record albums, looking more and more frustrated as they neared the end.

'Don't I have anything you two like?'

Lester shook his head firmly. 'Not a sausage. All this jazz stuff is just great, I suppose, but when I go to a knees-up I like to hear music that knows where it's going. You know, Glen Miller, the Andrews Sisters, that kind of thing.'

Paul grinned. 'When the hell did you last go to a party? That stuff was all put out during the war.'

'Don't rub it in, doc. We know we're getting past it.' Lester folded his arms and shrugged. 'Just put on something noisy.'

Above the thumping melody of a Ramsey Lewis number, Paul heard the bell. On the doorstep, he found Mary Scott and Ellen Haxton. 'Come in, girls. The two swingers of the team are here already.'

When they had removed their coats, the girls stepped into the sitting room behind Paul, to the accompaniment of spirited whistling from Lester. Bill was nodding his agreement. Ellen Haxton was wearing a black dress, quite short and tight, revealing for the first time that she had a good figure. She had combed her short hair down in two tight sweeps at each side of her face, and also for the first time in the recollection of anyone present she was wearing make-up. But beside even this more glamorous Ellen, Mary Scott was looking spectacular. Her red hair was in a style that Paul had once heard Ernie describe as soft frantic worms. Small curls, fluffy and loose, covered her head and formed a silken fringe across her brow. She had really worked on her eyes, using a deep green shadow that merged to white under the eyebrow, and her mouth was an erotic masterpiece of warm rosy-red, lustrous brushwork. Her dress was very thin, a wispy clinging number, dark blue and pale green, cut distractingly low at the neck to reveal the kind of exposed cleavage that Paul had not seen for years. Her legs were bare and her feet were enclosed in tiny sandals, thonged at the ankle.

Breaking the moment of re-discovery Paul said, 'What will you drink, ladies?'

'I'll have a gin and tonic, if you have any,' Mary answered; 'and if you've got a can of air freshener out there, bring that too and I'll see if I can't get rid of the smell of mothballs in here.'

Mock outrage flashed across Lester's face as he fingered the lapel of his jacket defensively. 'This is only two years old, cheeky.'

'Didn't they have one your size?'

Paul touched Ellen Haxton's elbow. She was still standing beside Mary, looking awkward now and ill at ease. 'What would you like?'

'Well, I don't really drink. Do you have any fruit juice?'

Everybody looked at her. 'Yes, I do,' Paul said brightly. 'It's imported, and there's a lot of other things in it—you know, bitters, that sort of stuff. Will that suit?'

She nodded and he went to the kitchen, where he prepared one gin and tonic and one orange juice with a measure of vodka. The idea of Ellen staying sober and stiff all night was too depressing to be entertained. He returned and handed over the glasses. 'Drink up. No calls tonight, I promise.' For maintenance reasons the ambulance had to be off the road for one whole day every week, and Paul had arranged that it be attended to today. In the case of a major emergency maintenance would have to wait and the unit would go out manned, in the absence of the entire team, by whoever could be found.

Dan and Ferdie arrived a few minutes later. Ferdie had brought some wine and a large can of beer. Dan's contribution to the proceedings was a half bottle of Irish whiskey. Everybody made a sour face, and Dan grinned. 'I was hopin' you'd feel that way. It's too good to be wasted on heathens.'

Paul watched Ellen Haxton from the corner of his eye as he went about the room with glasses and sandwiches. She had taken almost half of the drink, in slow sips, and was looking better already. There were small pink spots on her cheeks, just under her eyes, and she actually laughed, letting her mouth go, when Ferdie told Dan that where he came from, they used Irish whiskey for shrinking heads.

Ernie's arrival was heralded by a loud banging on the door; when Paul drew it open, Ernie's head came round the edge, fake-drunk and bleary-eyed. 'Is dis de place?'

He entered the sitting room with arms spread, a bottle clutched in each fist, leaving Paul standing by the open door. 'The party will be a success after all!' he roared. 'Ernest the Shrink is here!' He made a full circuit of the room and came back into the hall, handed the bottles to Paul, and winked.

'Cynthia's still in the car. She's fixing her face.'

'You've been at it already?'

'Now, you made me promise not to get up to any nonsense at your party. All I've done is take the necessary precautions.' He puffed his cheeks and blew noisily through his pursed lips. 'I can't speak for Cynthia, but I've had plenty.'

Cynthia's precarious shoes clip-clopped in the darkness beyond the door and she appeared, flushed and as dangerous looking as ever. She reminded Paul of the big schoolgirl types who were always getting men into trouble. Blonde, large breasted, wide hipped and eternally suggestive, she offered Paul her cheek and drew her long fingernails slowly along Ernie's face at the same time. 'Thank you for inviting us back again,' she said. The possessive pairing in her words, the 'us' said with the ease and casualness of a permanent member of a permanent arrangement, prompted Paul to think that she may not be around for very much longer. Ernie feared, above all else, the idea of being smothered by a woman. He saw too many of the casualties in his office.

'Come on inside, meet the clan.'

The reception was mixed. Everybody liked Ernie, even the withdrawn Ellen Haxton, but Lester, Dan and Mary Scott clearly did not take to Cynthia. She was probably well-known to them, and when the staff of a hospital were inclined to stand off from one of their number, it was usually for one of three reasons; jealousy, a fear of humiliation or caution prompted by hearsay. All three were probably in operation at that particular time. Mary Scott, although a very provocative little lady in her own right, was an intelligent girl who would possess a set of behavioural barriers. Faced with Cynthia, who could take away most men simply because she had the marks of total immorality, Mary would no doubt be experiencing the helpless annoyance of a woman confronted with another who would break any rules in order to score. Dan, a friendly person but angular in his behaviour, would see all the possibilities of being laughed at, an experience men of his kind could not easily shake off, while Lester's caution would be backed by the inflated gossip of porters and ward maids, who dearly loved to pass around the scandal of a loose woman in a dedicated profession. Paul hoped that Ernie and Cynthia would stick close together, for the sake of general harmony.

To mark the taking-off point for the party Paul proposed a toast, to his team and their devotion to duty. Ernie followed with another, to Paul Avery and his ministering angels. 'A mobile repair kit that deserves to succeed.'

Paul located a Tamla Motown album and urged everyone to take the floor. His object was partly therapeutic. People whose work exposed them to suffering and grief required a mindless, energetic form of recreation. So many divisions of their minds and their emotions were involved when they worked that any activity comprising pure, physical involvement, simple response to simple stimuli, gave the responsible and overtaxed areas of their personalities an opportunity for rest and replenishment. There had been a theory, common among some senior students in Paul's training days, that the more intelligent a nurse was, the easier she would be to lay. It did not always work out that way as he could testify, but the fact still stood—people whose lives were lived at a high dramatic pitch frequently preferred to relax like noisy kids, or sexual gluttons.

The dancing went well. Ferdie gave a solo demonstration of free-style Afro choreography that owed nothing to tradition and everything to his long, agile body. Lester partnered Mary Scott in an awkward but hilarious travesty of the conventional ballroom style, while the others, except Ellen Haxton, jiggled about the floor interpreting the music in their own way.

Paul stepped up to Ellen and took the glass from her hand. It was her second bogus fruit juice and, although still subdued, she was more relaxed than he had ever seen her. 'Come on and dance.' Before she could frame her refusal, he had drawn her on to the floor and, with his hands clasped easily round her waist, enforced a rhythm that she was obliged to follow, with gentle movements of her feet and shoulders.

'You don't get around very much, do you?'

Her mild intoxication made it possible for Ellen to hold his eyes. 'No not very much.'

'Why not?' No better time, Paul was thinking, to crack some of her ice. When she made the effort to look a person in the face, she was pretty.

'I don't get on with people too well.'

'But you would, if you tried.'

'No incentive,' she said.

'You mean you're not convinced that you're missing anything?'

'Yes, something like that.'

'Are you enjoying yourself now?'

'Very much.'

'Right. Learn to need enjoyment then.' He said no more. By degrees, as they moved in a slow circle around the others, Paul tightened the grip of his hands, drawing her close, enjoying the idea that he was probably dancing with a real live virgin. Her symmetrical face, usually so forbidding, had undergone a change that had something to do with a release of tension at the corners of her eyes, and as Paul deliberately brought his chest into close contact with her breasts, he watched her lips part slightly and her eyelids lower a fraction. There was nothing wrong with her chemistry. He toyed with the idea that she might be full of pent-up sexual frenzy and that she would be a demon in bed. But that was probably all wrong. Girls of her general build, temperament and age were usually slow and methodical, treating the sex act as something to be handled carefully, in case of damage. It occurred to Paul, as he began to let his knees brush Ellen's thighs, that his thoughts tonight were taking a particularly randy turn. It could, he supposed, be because Edith was not around, keeping her eye on him.

A break was called after thirty minutes. Drinks were topped-up and Ernie Hale announced that he would provide the cabaret. Cynthia, who had rapidly become drunk, sat on the floor, her arms wrapped around one of Bill Davis's legs. Bill sat stiffly in his chair, as if undergoing investigation by a hungry snake. Mary Scott leaned by the door, quite high and smiling all the time, while the others huddled on the big couch, watching Ernie's compact figure as he took his stance in the middle of the floor.

'First,' he said, 'a feat of magic that has baffled scientists and mystics alike. I require the assistance of a young lady.'

Mary Scott volunteered at once. Ernie stood her in front of him, and explained what would happen. 'I am going to place the forefinger of each hand over your closed eyelids. I want you to keep your eyes open until my fingers are almost touching you, then close them tightly. You will be visited by an alien spirit during the period of this mystical contact.'

Mary put her hands behind her back and Ernie made an elaborate show of discomfort as her bosom presented itself a few inches below his nose. Cynthia did not laugh with the others, she pouted and gripped Bill's leg harder. Could this, Paul wondered, be the thin edge of the wedge? Was Ernie beginning to squeeze Cynthia out, using the party as cover? The possessiveness like any tumour, had to be excised at an early stage if a cure was to be effected. It would be interesting to see what happened.

'Now, stare at the tips of my fingers.' Ernie held up his hands, the fingers curled underneath, index fingers pointing straight at Mary's eyes. He began to move them forward, and when they were less than an inch from her pupils, Mary shut her eyes. Ernie immediately dropped one hand to his side and extended the second finger of the pointing hand, touching her eyelids with two fingers of the same hand. As far as she knew, he had both hands occupied. Keeping his fingertips in contact, Ernie raised the free hand and stroked her shoulder. Mary jumped, and Ernie quickly brought up the free hand and set it beside the other as he removed the pressure from her eyelids. The illusion, from Mary's point of view, was perfect. She saw the two hands moving away from her face, the two hands which she fully believed had been pressing her eyes—yet something had touched her, and there was no one nearby.

The audience was highly amused, except for Cynthia, who was looking bored, elaborately bored, which meant she was feeling very jealous. Ernie bowed and offered to repeat the effect.

'Yes, do that,' Mary said. 'I can't quite believe it.'

Again, at the last moment, one hand dropped down and two fingers of the remaining hand came to rest on her eyelids. This time, Ernie drew his free hand down over her waist and squeezed her hip quite firmly. When she opened her eyes, there he was, withdrawing two hands and two pointing index fingers. Dan McGoldrick was laughing so hard that his drink was spilling over his knuckles. Mary's growing amazement was something to see.

'Look, do it just one more time, will you?'

Ernie obliged but this time, he brushed the side of her breast with his knuckles. The spectators whooped, except Cynthia who set her jaw and began to look openly angry, and Mary Scott jumped back. She still did not catch it, and Ernie announced that, in view of the growing boldness of the invisible toucher—'A *really* familiar spirit!'—it would be unwise, and possibly immoral, to go on with the experiment. He dismissed the bemused Mary and called for silence.

'Friends, you have seen nothing yet. Paul, do you have a pack of cards?'

Paul brought a pack and handed it over. 'I am going to demonstrate that I have the talent called dermavision. In fact, I have blindfold dermavision. I can read with my skin. No kidding. I can even read with my skin when it is covered with clothing. Now this talent is hard to develop, as you can imagine, and so far, I can only read simple things, like the faces of playing cards.'

Paul saw something curious happen. Cynthia lost her glaring look and began to brighten. In addition, he observed that Ernie had smiled significantly at her. After a moment, it began to make sense. Ernie was, after all, a psychiatrist. His methods of working were usually less than obvious. The trick he was about to perform was known to Paul. It required the aid of a confederate; it was natural to assume that Cynthia had been clued-up beforehand. So Ernie was not really shedding her. His little performance with Mary Scott had been aimed, Paul would now bet, at establishing a mandate: she was welcome to remain his girl, but within the frame work of behaviour that he chose. She would accept, she was being told, or she would abdicate. It was very neat, for in addition to being quite clear, the technique left Cynthia off-balance.

'I would like some unbribed member of the audience to come forward and choose a card, freely and without pressure from me. Madam?' He pointed to Ellen Haxton, doing his own little bit towards bringing her in from the cold. She stepped up to him and took a card from the pack.

'Now, I'm going to bend forward,' Ernie explained. 'I want you to lay the card face down on my back, after showing it to everybody but me. Then, I will endeavour to read the suit and value right through my jacket, shirt and liberty bodice. Okay?'

Ellen held up the card and showed it round, while Ernie bent forward at the waist, supporting himself with his hands on his shins. Paul noted that when Ernie dropped his head right down, he could see Cynthia through the space between his legs. The confederate theory was correct, but there was a puzzling aspect. For Cynthia to transmit the name of the card, she was supposed to use a simple code, and to do that, she had to be standing. With her foot, she had to tap out a little count, unobtrusively. Sitting on the floor as she was, with her legs over on one side, she would not be able to do it. Ernie seemed unperturbed. He asked if everyone had seen the card, and he also asked if they were all satisfied that he had not seen it. Receiving affirmative answers to both questions, he told Ellen Haxton to go ahead and place the card on his back.

Paul tried to remember the code. He had been taught the trick by Ernie over a year before and they had performed it at a stag party for one of the housemen who had been getting married. To signal the suit, the foot had to be moved once for Clubs, twice for Hearts, three times for Spades and four times for Diamonds. Then there has to be a pause before the foot started up again, moving once for an Ace, twice for a Deuce, three times for a Three and so on, up to thirteen for a King. How the hell was Cynthia going to do it?

Ernie announced that he would need to concentrate very hard, as it normally took quite a lot of mental energy for his skin to see through his clothing. Paul watched Cynthia, waiting. When she started to signal, he had to bite his lip.

She did it with her knees. The right leg, lying curled on the left, lifted twice, indicating Hearts, which was correct. Paul had to fight back the laughter. The card was a ten, so her little flashes of white nylon crotch would prove very tiring. As the knee began to rise and fall, Ernie made groaning noises, as if the concentration were making him suffer. Paul watched the white strip of material between Cynthia's legs switch on and off, like an erotic morse coder. By this time she had reached eight, her face was flushed.

Ernie announced the name of the card in due course and retired to a wave of enthusiastic applause. It began to look as if he had started a trend. Lester Hill was on his feet, offering to show the company a trick with numbers, and Ferdie, full of beer and grinning from high on either cheek, promised to perform an unspecified feat that no one would be able to duplicate. Paul took advantage of the confusion to slip into the kitchen and mix himself a fresh drink.

He was adding the soda when Mary Scott appeared, carrying some soiled plates and a couple of sticky glasses. 'You should have a maid,' she told him, depositing the load in the sink.

Paul turned and looked at her back, instantly able to imagine himself pressing his shape along those inviting lines. Her firmness, coupled with the filmy texture of her dress, opened avenues of misty recall. The way it was, the times there had been, the recollection of the atmosphere surrounding girls now gone heaven knew where—it was a lovely nostalgia that informed Paul's hand as he reached out and touched her arm.

She turned, her face serious. 'Why did you do that?'

'I was playing at mystical spirits.' He was not smiling, he realised.

'Why, really?'

'I suppose because I wanted to. Why I wanted to—well, we can go on all night about that. I did it without thinking.'

'I thought you did.' She dried her hands on the tea towel, peered through the door to see if there was anyone about, then came up close to him and kissed him on the mouth. She lingered, her lips withdrawing a mere fraction and moving against Paul's with the lightness of silk. He closed his arms about her and felt the sleekness of her back with his spread palms.

'Hey,' she whispered; 'where does Dr Roberts come into this?'

'She doesn't.' At that moment, he meant what he said.

She pecked his lips. 'But she's your lady friend, isn't she?'

'It's a very strained arrangement, Mary. Ask Uncle Ernie.'

She leaned closer, her breasts a firm pillow against his chest. 'He's unethical enough to tell me, too.' This time it was Paul's lips that advanced, closing over hers, his tongue lightly probing the firm teeth beyond. He felt light-headed, but confident. Mary put a hand on his waist, her nails digging through the wool of his sweater. She drew her head away and looked at him, squinting to focus his features. 'Do you want me?'

'Three guesses.'

'No adhesions?'

'Adhesions?'

'No ownership. No style-cramping, and no letting work interfere with pleasure, or vice-versa.'

'That's the way I like things,' he said.

She kissed him again, open-mouthed, and drew his hands down to encase her buttocks. He cupped the fullness, feeling the slender raised line of her panties through the thin dress. She groaned deep down in her throat and thrust forward with her pelvis, grinding against him for several seconds while her tongue raped his mouth.

She stood away abruptly and winked at him, her face bright and business-like. 'We know where we stand,' she said. 'That's always a good thing.'

He was about to say something, anything to extend the thread of what had happened, when Ernie came through with his empty glass.

'Excuse me for busting up your private party, children, but Ernie needs more medicine.'

'That's all right,' Mary said. 'I was just going back, anyway.' She cast Paul a smile that summarised their understanding perfectly. 'See you later.'

As she left, Ernie dug his elbow in Paul's ribs and performed an exaggerated leer. 'Dabbling, eh? You dirty American defiler.' He poured himself a large gin, drank some of it and topped up the glass again. 'Great party, Paul. I'll have a hobnail liver in the morning.' He picked up a damp cigarette from the draining board and managed to light it. 'I'm devising a drinking cure for paranoia, you know. I'm going to call the paper 'From Neurosis To Cirrhosis'. How does that sound?'

'It sounds like you're pissed, Ernest.'

'Not really.' He drew hard on the cigarette and dropped it into the strainer by the sink. 'I wanted to have a word with you before I did get drunk, though. About that shit Madison.'

'You worry too much about him, Ernie. You play into his hands. Do what I do. Ignore him. He's just cranky.'

'So was Hitler. Listen, I've told you before, he's the kind of man to take pleasure in ruining somebody. Somebody like me. And you, too. I want to hear your thinking on what could be done to combat any move he makes to get my book blocked.'

Paul thought for a moment. 'Well, he can't do that. Not directly. But he could perhaps get you in the position where you'd rather withdraw the book for the sake of your job.'

'Look, if I lose the job, I lose it. I'd rather keep it, I think, but on the other hand, a private practice in psychiatry is something I fancy, too. I'd never get round to it unless I was forced, so he might be a help there. If he gets me kicked out, I won't go to another hospital.'

'He could scare your publisher off, though. Has that occurred to you? All he has to do is get his pals behind him. They could sign a petition that would frighten the Pope. Unethical, misleading, contrary to accepted medical procedure—you've heard the terms before. I can just see a publisher beginning to wonder if he needs all that trouble.'

'That did occur to me, Paul. The book is hardly on the lines of a standard medical text. Oh, there's a dozen ways the bastard could harrass publication. What I want, really, is some way to stop him.'

'There's no way,' Paul said. 'He's rocket-proof.'

'There's *always* a way, damn it. See, I don't want any trouble at all until the book is out, actually in the retail stream. Then I'll be in the public eye, and Madison will have to go carefully, for he could come out looking very bad. If he starts using the boot before anybody's heard of me or the book, I'm a dead cause before I start.' He slapped a hand on Paul's shoulder. 'Friend, I want that book to work for me. If there's a way of stopping Old Mother Madison from fouling it up, I'm going to find it.'

'Please yourself. But I think he's safe, and I still think you could be making too much of this. That's the way his kind always go on when they see what they think is a breach of ethics. They're obliged to sound off, but nine times out of ten they leave it at that, having made their gesture.'

'Well, I've noted what you've said.' Ernie straightened his tie and ran straightened fingers through his hair. 'But just in case, I'll keep thinking about getting some dirt on him. And if I were you, I'd bear in mind that he has a big down on your white charger.'

'Check. Now let's get back to the party, huh?'

'Marvellous idea. By the way, I notice Edith hasn't graced us with her presence tonight. Did I deter her?'

Paul laughed. 'No, she had another appointment.'

Ernie raised one eyebrow. 'Oh? Saturday night, eh? I wonder if she's walking out with another young man.'

'Ernie, please. Let's go back to the crowd.'

Dan McGoldrick appeared to be the only sober person in the place. He had been clutching the same glass all night, and most of its contents spilled on the carpet. When Paul and Ernie entered the sitting room, Dan was judging a contest between the other three men, to see who could hold a note the longest. The best out of five attempts was to be the winner and so far the score stood at two for Lester, one for Bill and one for Ferdie. The best Bill and Ferdie could hope for was a draw, but Lester was winding up for the last round, determined to win. When Dan shouted 'Go!' they all emitted a grinding din, three levels of sound that combined to make something worse than discord. After thirteen seconds Lester alone was still squeaking, his face blue and his eyes bulging. Amid raucous applause he was presented with a small wreath, created impromptu from a vase of tired flowers still left in the room.

Ernie heaved a sigh. 'Whatever happened to those parties where everybody stood round holding cocktail glasses and indulging in witty patter?'

'The circuit died of boredom.' Paul ran his eye round the room and saw Mary Scott looking at him. Maybe the tease theory was wrong, after all. Even so there was a lot of open space between a quick grope and grind in the kitchen and a full-fledged carnal workout. He looked at her again and saw that serious look. That was sincere, he would bet his degree on it.

An hour or so later, people started to leave. Lester, helping Bill into his coat, was full of foreboding. 'They'll never believe the union meeting story now.'

'We can tell them it was held in a pub,' Bill said, staggering as he missed his sleeve. 'And if they don't believe that, they can go and jump.'

'That's easy to say when you're under the anaesthetic, mate. Wait till the morning, that's all. Just wait.'

Ellen Haxton, looking tired and content, sought out Paul and thanked him for a wonderful evening. 'I haven't enjoyed myself so much for a long time,' she told him.

'A pleasure to be of service,' he replied, and just to put a top on events, he placed a brief kiss on her forehead. One of the really nice people he thought as he watched her flush. It was so odd the way elders and betters always held up nice people and modest behaviour as the standard, while so few actually attained it. Those who did were probably born that way, unable to be anything else, even if they tried.

Dan and Ferdie offered to give Ellen a lift back to the nurses' home, and while they were bustling around the door, Ernie came forward, holding Cynthia by the hand. 'I don't think I'm fit to drive,' he said, smiling as if he were highly satisfied with his condition. Cynthia was wearing a similarly cheerful face.

'You want me to drive you?' Paul had taken plenty of alcohol himself.

'Good heavens, no. I wouldn't dream of such presumption.' Ernie patted his shoulder. 'I wondered if you'd like to put us up for the night. Tomorrow being Sunday, and all—'

'I'm glad you wouldn't dream of being presumptuous.' Paul scratched his head, trying to summon a recollection of the domestic layout. 'Ah—If you don't mind using the room next door to mine—'

'Why should we mind?'

'I'll be lying in there, listening to every sound you make.'

'Groovy,' Cynthia said.

'And I've no spare pyjamas or nightdresses,' Paul added.

'Great,' Ernie assured him.

Paul shrugged and turned back to the door. Dan's car was pulling away; somebody waved from the back. He returned the wave and stepped briskly to the doorway of the sitting room. They had all gone. He came back to Ernie, who was nibbling Cynthia's ear lobe. 'Anybody see Mary Scott leave?'

'I think she went with the ambulance drivers,' Cynthia volunteered.

'Hard luck, brother.' Ernie put his hand on Cynthia's waist and steered her into the sitting room. 'I think I need to sit down. Conserve my energy, you know.'

Paul spent twenty minutes tidying up in the kitchen, feeling low, tired, faintly disappointed. The party, at least, had been a success. The memory of it would stay with all of them and at times when they were hard pressed and ragged-edged, they could recall that at least they had a comradeship. Parties among colleagues were always effective bonding procedures. He was only sorry he'd missed the chance of tightening the bond between himself and Mary Scott. She had not even said good night. Then, of course, she had a lot to drink, and so had he, so perhaps two sets of good intentions evaporated somewhere halfway towards execution.

When he returned to the sitting room Ernie and Cynthia had gone. Edith's little lectures about Ernie and his tendency to abuse came back to him in fragments as he plumped cushions, wiped up spilled drink and generally straightened the place. There was a level at which self-pity came flooding into his life, and he was touching it right now. They had all supped, caroused, and gone, leaving him to set his house in order. Ernie and his tame limpet were in bed, extending their stay and compounding Paul's feeling of isolation. The hell with it! He would go to bed and forget everything. Morning would put it all back in perspective.

He went to the bathroom, stripped and climbed into a pair of old, warm pyjama trousers. He never wore the tops; they wrapped themselves round him in a knot during the night so that he woke up feeling that he was being strangled. Brushing his teeth, he paused suddenly and sniffed. Perfume. It was Cynthia's. She had been in here. A whiff, detached from its source. That was a poignant thing, he thought. The scent of a warm woman who was not at all available. Paul had a strong feeling that the sexual instinct, as it manifested itself in him, was two parts comfort-seeking to one part lust. He hated to be alone sometimes—especially when he was faced with the prospect of listening to a couple nearby thrashing out the celebration of their togetherness.

In the dark, he crawled into his bed and lay back, drawing the covers up to his neck, waiting for his own sounds to subside and the vibrations from next door to filter through. After a minute, he heard it, Cynthia's throaty groaning and Ernie's deep bass counterpoint. That bed made a lot of noise. Paul and a girl he had once known used to share a noisy bed, and they had decided between them that it had been manufactured by a strict Presbyterian organisation, dedicated to reducing the level of immoderate sexual behaviour in society. With people like Ernie Hale and Cynthia around, the mattress would have to be filled with exploding detonators before any reform could be effected. As Cynthia began a long, climbing orgasmic howl, Paul drew the covers around his ears and tried to think of sleep as the one thing he desired.

A hand tapped his shoulder and he almost leapt out of bed. He pulled the light cord instinctively, and blinked in full, sober wakefulness at the figure of Mary Scott, dressed fetchingly in tiny flowered pants. It was almost too much for him. He gulped, and she laughed, drawing the covers aside and climbing in beside him.

'Put out that damned light,' she murmured against his neck.

In the darkness Paul started to respond to the situation. For a couple of minutes he had been stalled by the shock. Her breasts were as large and full as her bulging clothes usually indicated, and the way she was lying, with one arm and one leg across him, had placed the full warm mass of one globe right on the centre of his chest. He brought up a hand and ran it along her back, his fingertips scanning the deep ridge at her spine, pausing on the top edge of her pants. 'Where were you?'

'Out safeguarding appearances. I put on my coat and slipped away among the others. I told Dan and Ferdie that I was being picked up at the end of the road. Plenty of witnesses saw me go.' She giggled and touched his chin with her tongue. 'I made a detour and came back here while you were in the kitchen. I was going to knock at the door, then I saw those two in the sitting room. So I entered by stealth. Your security isn't very good.'

'I'm glad.'

'I've been huddled in that box room across the landing for ages. Mind you, it was different.'

'Where are your clothes?'

'Right by the bed. I stood there and took them off and you didn't even hear me. You were too busy tuning into the programme next door,' Her small hand swept boldly in a cool line down his chest and undid the button of his pyjamas. Paul slid his fingers under her pants now, kneading the roundness of her firm muscle and soft skin.

'I'll keep up the camouflage,' she assured him. 'I have to be on duty by eleven tomorrow morning, anyway.'

'You're very accommodating,' he said.

'That's right.' Her fingers enclosed him and began to move slowly. 'If I like an arrangement, I always do my best to support it.' Her teeth grazed his ear. 'Now stop talking, eh? We've a party to get on with.'

9

At a few minutes after three on Monday afternoon, the Life-Support Unit was called to an accident on a fog-bound stretch of the motorway. There was only one victim, an old man whose car had run off the road and into the banking. Assisted by Bill Davis, Paul eased the patient out on to a stretcher and made a swift examination. He was unconscious and his face was cyanosed, breathing was laboured and Mary Scott was told to bring the Portogen cylinder. She applied the face mask while Paul checked for injuries.

'Pott's fracture, right ankle.' In response to the announcement, Bill returned to the ambulance and brought a splint pack. Paul had insisted at the time of initial procedural study that if it were possible to apply aid before the patient was even in the ambulance, then it would be done. Speedy return to hospital was always desirable, but the primary requirement was that the victim should not be injured any further following his accident, and splinting at the roadside could go a long way to ensuring that.

'Blast!' Mary's face was grim as she detached the face mask again and rose to her feet.

'What's wrong?'

'The cylinder's empty.' She swept through the coiling mist between the stretcher and the ambulance, and a moment later came back, with the duplicate cylinder. After only a few seconds, she cursed and rolled the unit aside. 'That's empty too.'

'Jesus Christ!' Paul glared at her, then at Bill. 'Get him inside, quick. I think his sternum's damaged too. I want oxygen, and quick.'

In the ambulance Mary quickly fitted a mask to the piped oxygen supply and turned it on. The gauge responded for a second, then the needle dropped right back to zero. There was an ominous hissing, up near the top of the pipe, where it was anchored. 'Now what?' Paul snatched the mask from Mary's hand and re-attached it to the system, using the secondary outlet. There was no response at all.

'It's leaking,' Bill pointed out. 'Do you want the hand unit?'

He was referring to the ambi-bag, a manually operated device to induce regular breathing. It was of use, Paul knew, but it did not fill the need of the impending emergency. In air, oxygen forms about twenty per cent of the mixture. In a person with normal respiration and circulation, this is adequate to saturate the haemoglobin of the blood. But this patient's respiratory and cardiovascular systems had suffered interference. So, reduced oxygen intake was causing the condition known as hypoxia. The contributing factors could be many. The man was old, he was injured, he might well be suffering from a heart disease and the extent of his injuries was not yet known. It was imperative that he receive an increased volume of oxygen to his lungs.

'I can't believe all this.' Paul was shouting, irritated by the breakdown in simple routine systems. 'All I want is some god-damned oxygen.' He banged on the connecting door and Ferdie started up the engine. As they swung round in the direction from which they had come, Mary Scott lost her balance and fell back across the empty stretcher.

'For God's sake, haven't you mastered the simple procedure of staying on your feet in a moving vehicle yet?' He saw the hurt cross her eyes and at once wanted to apologise. But the pressing needs of the unconscious patient cut short the charitable impulse. 'Bill, try to see what's up with that pipe.'

Bill found, after groping around the junction point, that the line had separated from its sealing collar. 'It seems bloody impossible,' he commented.

'Impossible? It's happened, man. We're riding in a hot rod super care unit that can't even supply a puff of oxygen. Turn it off, before we have a disaster.'

They arrived at the casualty department in a few minutes. Steps had been taken to immobilise the patient's fracture and shock-preventive measures had been applied. Dr Grace, the duty casualty houseman, took over, aided by Mary Scott, while Paul took Bill and Ferdie into a side room.

'So what happened, gentlemen? How come we've got no oxygen?'

Ferdie's big eyes rolled about, as if he was looking for an answer written on one of the walls. Bill simply drooped the corners of his mouth and shook his head.

'Who attended to maintenance?'

'The technicians from the main workshop, and two mechanics from the garage,' Ferdie said. The technical people were skilled at the routine maintenance of complex theatre equipment; the fittings in the ambulance presented no particular challenge. The hospital garage employed five good mechanics, used to handling ambulances and familiar with the specialised requirements of the unit's tuned engine. It was hard to believe that full cylinders had not been placed in the Portogen kits, and it was even harder to believe that the carefully designed pipe-line could spring a fault without it being detected. Paul felt the sort of frustration he had experienced in the past, working in casualty departments lacking the equipment needed to perform the tasks he could undertake so easily. This ripple in the flow hit at the heart of his guiding principle—skilled assistance must not be impeded by mechanical inadequacy.

'How long was the unit out of our grasp?'

'Two whole days,' Ferdie said. 'Saturday and Sunday. I think the mechanics had it in the morning, then the technicians moved in after lunch.' The routine was carefully laid down. When mechanics were working on the ambulance, all drugs and sterile packs were removed to the pharmacy, where they were replenished. When the technicians took over, they put back the medication and checked every piece of equipment. They were also responsible for replacing the cylinders of oxygen. If the lapse had occurred following a period of accident duty, blame could have been set at the door of the team. As it was, the members had all been away from the ambulance since Friday night; the faults had occurred in the period between then and Monday afternoon.

There followed a painful, strained hour of follow-up during which skilled men were cautiously accused of making glaring mistakes. Their denials were heated and convincing. Paul could not raise any enthusiasm for the idea that technicians who daily serviced the most intricate surgical and anaesthetic equipment could make such stupid mistakes, and eventually he apologised.

In the company of a senior theatre technician, a man with vast experience of the refined electrical and mechanical anatomy of modern surgery, Paul went over the ambulance, checking every particular of equipment, installation and function. The oxygen line from the under-floor area was in perfect shape, except for the small leak at the junction collar. 'It's daft,' the man said. 'If you look at it, you can see it's been knocked.'

'Knocked?' Paul stood on a box and peered at the copper pipe. There was a small dent on one end, where it came from the collar, and a scratch on the rim of the collar itself. 'How could that happen?'

'If you smacked it with something. I'm not up on forensic work, but I'd say it had to be a wallop from a hard object. It couldn't do that by itself.'

'Could it have happened while your men were working on it?'

The man shook his head. 'No chance at all. The last thing they do is check the oxygen. The very last thing.' He held up the check list referring to Saturday's service. 'It's marked off here, and I'll stake my job on what that sheet says. The ambulance was in perfect operational order at five o'clock on Saturday evening.'

'And after that? Where was it garaged?'

'Usual place. The number one bay. The vehicle was double locked, and the bay door is coupled to an alarm.'

Paul climbed out of the back door and stood by the side, staring at the machine, perplexed, confronting the kind of mystery he did *not* like. 'But it still stands, doesn't it? We went to an accident today, and we took with us two empty Portogen kits and a built-in line system that didn't work. How?'

'I've no idea.' The man clearly did not regard the problem as his.

'Okay, thanks. And I'm sorry if I upset your guys. You can see the dilemma I'm in.'

'That's all right, doctor. But if it happens again, you'll know where not to come for explanations. My staff are good, they're very good. They don't make many mistakes—and they never blunder.'

A check with security administration confirmed what he guessed; the ambulance had rested undisturbed over the weekend, safely sealed up in the appropriate bay. Having drawn a sheaf of blanks, Paul had not option but to report what had happened. A cover-up would only add to his troubles.

Back in the casualty department, he met Mary Scott, wheeling a small boy to the treatment room. 'Broken toe,' she said.

He nodded and smiled briefly to the patient. 'Nurse, I want to apologise—'

'Save it, sir,' she muttered. 'I *should* learn to stay on my feet.'

'Yeah, but you've got special overbalance hazards.' He glanced pointedly at her prominent bosom in its starched white apron. 'Listen, this oxygen thing is kind of serious. Nobody appears to be at fault.'

'Somebody has to be.'

'Oh sure, logic dictates there has to be a human error. But whose? I've talked to everybody who touched that vehicle over the weekend. The mechanics couldn't get into the back, even if they'd wanted to, and the technicians, made a thorough routine maintenance and systems-check tour.'

Her eyes widened dramatically, 'Ghosts?'

'You're some help.' He crossed to sister's room and put his head inside. 'Anything for me?'

Sister Mclean, a Glasgow woman who had been in Westfield casualty for ten years, looked up from her papers and nodded. 'I'm afraid so, doctor. That old man you brought in earlier. He's died.'

An immediate image of the empty cylinders and disrupted pipe flushed in his consciousness. 'What's the verdict?'

'I don't know yet. They took the body over to pathology. The family doctor rang in, he said the man had chronic heart failure.'

Oxygen would have made a lot of difference in that case, he thought. 'And he was out driving around in the fog?' It was self-defence, he knew that.

'Aye, well, these things happen, don't they? Dr Grace has asked for consent to have a post mortem.'

'He takes a lot on himself, doesn't he?'

'Oh, doctor,' the round motherly face frowned, 'in a case like that, what else would you do?'

He put up a hand. 'Okay, I know, I'm sorry. I'm just sore about the way things went today. Look I'll work on the list for a while, shall I? Keep my mind occupied.'

On Monday evening Paul took Edith Roberts to dinner at a restaurant in the centre of Westfield. The town, smoky and disfigured by industrial overactivity in the thirties and forties, squatted midway between the hospital and Paul's house. From the air it looked like a grey smudge on an otherwise clean, green stretch of countryside. It depressed Paul, with its rows and rows of outdated, too-small houses crouching together and the periphery of factories and warehouses. Its people still carried the marks of the old days, days when most of the money earned from steel production, iron smelting and light engineering went into the well-padded pockets of the owners. The pinched faces of the older locals were reflected in their offspring and mean expressions that had once been a reaction to grinding poverty, overwork and poor nutrition were now set, genetical links with an era that had the power to stunt a person from the soul outwards. Forty thousand people lived in this town, served by the minimum in entertainment; one cinema, four Bingo halls, a football field with no barriers, a dog racing track, over a dozen bookmakers' shops and five middling restaurants. The inhabitants of Westfield seemed to exist to little purpose, moving around with fixed expressions for the greater part of the time, and there was more casual hostility than good humour. If they had one large purpose that Paul Avery could detect, it was to make him eternally grateful that he had not been born with the setback of such an environment.

His American self rebelled at their apathy. He longed to shake them, impress on them his knowledge that there were other ways to live. But he kept quiet, and as America receded he grew less moved. Constant indignation simply could not be sustained.

The Consort was the best restaurant of the town's five. To find anything better Paul would have had to drive another ten miles; the expression of truculent acceptance on Edith's face as she read the menu indicated that she might well have appreciated it if Paul had made that extra effort. They had come to the place on the recommendation of Ernie. That fact alone could be going some way towards Edith's dissatisfaction.

'Have they crossed out the caviar?'

Edith put down the plastic folder and regarded him blankly. 'No need to be sarcastic, Paul. You don't have to be a gourmet to know a pedestrian menu when you see one.'

He cast a dead-pan look around the place. Three waiters in scuffed dinner jackets and Borstal haircuts were gathered by the cash desk, picking their nails and yawning. The surroundings, Paul had to admit, did not inspire a lively appetite. Dark mauve flock wallpaper was the mainstay of the decor. The lighting came exclusively from opal glass wall-fittings, designed to look like sea shells. Music, delivered via a sound system that rattled on high notes and tinted the tunes with the quality of an early radio set, drifted around the room with the same sluggish persistence as the smells from the kitchen. Three other couples were present, huddled clandestinely in the darker corners. Paul had chosen a centre table for his usual instinctive reason; he liked variety, in angles of view as much as in anything else. Most other times he would have felt inclined to be in accord with Edith's distaste. Tonight, he was ready to oppose her on anything, anything at all.

'I don't think it's so bad. But then I don't have the same affluence in my background that you have.' He smiled, tightly, just to confuse her.

'Well really.' She stabbed a finger on the typed slip within the see-through pocket of the menu folder. '"Vegetables: chips, peas, cauliflower, cabbage." We could have dined like this at the canteen.'

'They don't have the atmosphere, though. That's important.' He lit a cigarette and beckoned a waiter.

A stooped individual, looking as if he had drawn a short straw, sidled up. 'You wished to order, sir?'

'Not yet. I was wondering if we could have a drink while we make up our minds. Oh, and could you bring the wine list?'

'Er, we don't have a list, sir. Very little call for it, you see. I can do you a nice carafe of red or white, however. Would that suit?'

Paul looked at Edith, who was holding the side of her bottom lip firmly between her teeth. She was going to say nothing, he felt. 'Make it a carafe of red, then. And a gin and tonic and a scotch meantime.'

The waiter shuffled away and Edith let out a small gasp. 'Unbelievable.'

'That's atmosphere, baby. If I half close my eyes, I can imagine I'm in a chowder house in the Bronx.'

'And whisky is hardly an aperitif,' she added, chiding him quietly for his affection, which was inclined to come and go, for scotch.

'Oh, relax, Edith. I've had a rotten day, just let me indulge myself.'

'What's the trouble?' She could have been asking a patient that, he thought.

He explained about the breakdown in efficiency and how there was no apparent clue to the source. Edith was sympathetic, but in the manner of a colleague. She cited remembered instances of loss, breakage and malfunction in wards where she had worked, as if the reminder that accidents had happened before might make him feel better. The drinks arrived and Paul swallowed his in two gulps.

'There's got to be an answer,' he continued, insisting on his main point. 'But I want to let it boil for a while. Let's talk about something else.' He tilted his head and measured her appearance. She was halfway between her relaxed, real-nice-girl self and the other, rule-observing, establishment worshipping side. It occurred to him how much more pleasant it would be to have Mary Scott with him, to sit there and talk to her, *really* talk to her. Since spending the night with his nurse—in consequence of which he was now quite tired—Paul had made an assessment that surprised him with its objectivity. Mary was great, a dynamic bundle, but she was not his sort of woman. They worked well together in bed, but that did not mean much in the long term. Although she would have been so much more fun on a date, she was the sort of person who would damage almost everything he was aiming for. She would cut through his public persona, the package of carefully balanced enigmas that he presented to the outside world. She would always talk right through all the dressing and touch the unclothed character at the centre, and people would notice—in time, Paul Avery would have a gap in his hedge that everyone could see through, opened and kept open by Mary. The double-sidedness, the cool, rule bending American on the surface who was a meticulous perfectionist underneath, would be gone. He needed a woman who would respond to whatever mood or political front he was using at any given time. Edith was the ideal candidate, of course. It was just sad that really she was not much fun and after a strong dose of the earthy, breathtaking Mary Scott, she was looking less like fun every minute. What a pity, he was thinking, that he was in a racket where appearances, even for a loner, were almost as important as ability.

Edith's strictures were showing badly tonight, and Paul wondered if it was perhaps more than the contrast effect; she was different. He recalled the mysterious Saturday-night appointment that had kept her, thankfully, from the party. 'Are you feeling okay, Edith? You don't seem to be on the ball tonight.'

'Just tired, I suppose.'

Her too. For the same reasons as he was? He scrapped the idea, it looked all wrong, however enticing. 'Order something with plenty of iron. You could be getting run down.'

'Paul—'

'Mm?'

'Do you think we're getting anywhere?'

The question was palpably loaded. 'Do you want us to get anywhere?'

'Of course I do. But I don't know, we seem to be in low gear just now. Always on the verge of bickering, doing nothing very interesting, you know what I mean. Everything's kind of flat.'

'We haven't been to bed for a while,' he reminded her.

'There's more to a relationship than—'

'Skip it. I was throwing out a possible answer. You could be pining for a little hay-threshing, it's not such a far-fetched theory, Edith.'

'I feel,' she said, drawing a fingernail across the table cloth and watching the course of the little valley it made, 'that we're at a spiritual low point. I think a lot of it is my fault. Maybe all of it.' She looked up, and the rectitude had fled, there was only the pretty, soft girl there. 'I just want to say that I've got a lot pressing on me at present. I don't feel any differently towards you. I'm simply weak on the demonstrative side. It'll pass. Does that help?'

'Honey, you worry too much.' He squeezed her knee under the table, a habit he was not at pains to shake off. He felt her recoil for an instant, then relax, though not fully, not with any of the openness that typified a Mary Scott. He remembered the feel of that girl's legs, the welcoming loosening in the muscles and the eagerness that went beyond willingness and became open incitement. The best he had ever had from Edith was permission to enter, with a hint of apprehension always a step ahead. And this, he thought, is the kind of woman for me.

'Let's order,' he said. 'I'm feeling very hungry.'

Katie watched Andy's expression carefully as he manipulated the small tubs and phials between his hands. They were in his car, parked well away from main roads.

'Are you pleased? I couldn't get any more, my uncle doesn't have a proper bag. They're all samples he keeps in a drawer in his desk. Some of them are on the list you gave me. Maybe you can find out what the others are.'

His face was very serious as he read the labels by the dash light. Then he slipped the containers into his jerkin pocket and pinched her cheek between a grubby finger and thumb. 'That's fine, chicken. You're a very good kid.' He kissed her and casually placed a hand under her skirt. 'Well done.'

He returned his hands to the wheel and pursed his lips, the look she knew, from experience, that meant he was considering something very important. It was raining heavily. Large drops struck the roof of the car in a regular beat that was echoed from the road and softly imitated on the leaves and branches surrounding the lay-by. The windscreen was covered in a steadily flowing skin of water, and through its gentle distortion of the weak light beyond, Katie saw the road, the trees and the lamp posts as a blurred, impressionist study of dark tints and winking spots of whiteness. She was warm, snug, in a state of physical and emotional well-being. She was in credit with Andy and they still had hours ahead of them, time to wallow and savour. She was aware that he did not attach as much romantic significance to their relationship as she did, but he was a man after all, and so much older, so much more immediate in his outlook. She laid her head on his shoulder and savoured the faint odour of oil, an earthy scent that held the comfort of something familiar. Katie often wondered if people lost this capacity when they grew older, this marvellous ability to enjoy every single component of the things that excited them. There were moments when she could become elated by simply watching his foot move within his boot. The barely audible rasping of his hair on the collar of his jacket, the tiny twitch of his cheek an instant before he spoke, even the dry clicking sound of his tongue against his palate when he had smoked too much—they were each exciting assertions of who he was and what he meant to her. One day she would write a poem, a long epic work in praise and celebration of the way this man moved her, of the storms he could create beneath her skull and her skin.

He was quite high. She could tell from the slowness of his actions, the loose movements of his hands and the easy way he slouched down behind the wheel. Katie wondered if he stuck to hash, or if there was more, an area of experiment and indulgence that he kept to himself. He was alert, there was no impression of sleepiness; it was only his body that appeared to be moving within some thick, transparent liquid.

'Do you fancy a lifter?' He glanced at her sideways.

'Like what?'

'Like a burn down the motorway.' He patted the wheel. 'I've had her souped, Katie. She can top a hundred.'

She thought of the rain, the slippery roads. 'I don't know.' His obsession with speed and the complex offshoots worried her. 'I hate the idea of anything going wrong.'

'Trust me.' He turned his head and smiled. 'It's all sensation, you know. That's what it's all about. Hurtling, rubber screaming on cement, pistons thumping, tearing you forward. It brings out the reality, chicken.' He touched her arm. 'Come on, huh?'

'Okay.' She sat back, still reluctant beneath her agreement. The depths in him that fascinated her were just those that made her worry.

They fastened their seat belts. Andy started the engine and pulled out smoothly from their parking place. A gust of wind drove the rain harder against the roof and Katie sank down, setting her feet firmly on the sloping support beneath the panel. She noticed that the engine did not sound different, it rumbled more and when he touched the accelerator it almost whined.

Andy sat upright, as if he had a stiff back, and he gripped the wheel with hands well apart, thumbs caressing the leather cover he had installed for extra sensuality. The roads were clear. They did not pass more than three other cars on the way across country to the motorway approach road. As the distant overhead lamps came into view he shifted in his seat, spreading his knees and setting his feet precisely over the pedals.

They took the high swinging turn along the overpass that brought them to the top of the slip road. Andy flipped the switch that put the wipers on double speed and turned his head once to look at her. His eyes were wide, tense, and his smile was tightly confident. In the gloom she smiled back.

The unexpected surge threw Katie's head back. He hugged the right side of the sloping approach and hit the motorway rising eighty miles an hour, shifting swiftly to the fast lane and pressing the accelerator pedal firmly towards the floor. The rain lashed the windshield and turbulent air striking the wing mirrors set up an urgent, unsettling squeal. The amber lights, high on concrete pillars, filled the inside of the car with a flickering strobe that etched the reddened areas of Andy's skin like black stigmata on his cheeks and nose. His knuckles stood up like bony extensions of the steering wheel, his eyes taking a line between them. Katie peered straight ahead, her hands clasped in a tight wad in her lap, praying and invoking every good-luck ritual she knew.

A car appeared ahead of them, tight over to the right, growing alarmingly larger as Andy stepped up his own speed another notch and began to lean on the horn. The car stayed where it was, and Andy switched his lights to full beam, illuminating the apprehensive face of a woman sitting in the back seat, her lips moving, complaining at his recklessness.

'God, Andy—' Katie's hands came up involuntarily and covered her mouth as the distance closed. 'You'll hit them!'

'Move over!' Andy took a hand from the wheel and banged it on the windshield, a threatening fist that had the belligerent power to do what it promised.

When the space between the two vehicles was no more than ten feet, the car in front slipped over into the centre lane and Andy passed it a moment later. Through the rain-distorted side window Katie saw the driver's face for a moment—white and outraged.

'My God, that was terrible!' Katie was breathless, frightened by what had almost happened, nervous of the speed that still seemed to be increasing.

'Relax,' Andy shouted above the noise of the engine. 'Enjoy it!'

The overhead lights stopped suddenly and they were on a dark stretch, a void of rain-soaked black highway, dotted to the right with the lights of the oncoming traffic across the reservation. Andy's tension was increasing, it was apparent in the way he shifted on his seat and pulled himself closer to the wheel. He stopped moving suddenly and sat quite still, motionless as the car rammed on, its lights turning the streaking rain to silver, tyres humming on their bed of water. 'Now,' he said, 'One ton plus.'

Amasingly the speed increased. Katie became aware that they were on a down gradient, and the car gave the impression of lifting as the wind buffeted with mounting pressure on the roof and sides. The total noise was deafening. The configuration of the ceiling, the fascia, the seats and the occupants combined with the vibration to set up a roar that dissolved every other sound. Katie spoke his name and could not hear herself, she cleared her throat nervously and could not hear that either.

She was startled by his hand on her leg. Shocked, she saw his other hand resting almost lightly on the upper curve of the wheel. The groping hand slid higher as the car propelled itself past a huddle of heavy lorries on the left and Andy's fingers began to knead at her groin as the slope of the road increased and the noise intensified.

He was slumped back now, legs spread. His fingers left her body and grasped her wrist, drawing her hand across to his stomach. Sensing his intention, scared by the idea but too frightened to resist, she unzipped him and drew out his penis. His mouth was hanging open as he returned his hand to the wheel. Katie wrapped her fingers around his stiffness and began to jerk him. The inverted holiness of the moment possessed her, she understood by a process as dark as the night that sucked them forward. By putting them so far from safety and, by identical means, bringing them to the brink of oblivion, Andy had moved to a point of awareness where the greatest imminence was that of death, a match for his stampeding lust. His hips began to lurch and she quickened the tempo of her hand and tightened her grip on him, conscious of the total import of the act but terrified by it, too close in her heart to the precious quality of safety. She turned her head and saw a jumble of lights ahead, cars and lorries spread across the road in a slower-moving barrier. Andy's eyes were so wide that the strain had drawn the skin flat across his cheeks and his chest heaved as he began to manipulate his car, aiming it for a frighteningly narrow gap between the centre and fast lanes. Katie began to cry, she felt the tears strike her hand as it continued to work on him, fearful of stopping, scared of precipitating a holocaust.

At a distance of no more than seven feet from the tailboard of a lorry carrying huge bales, its tarpaulins flapping like the wings of menacing black bats, Andy pulled the wheel down to the left and nosed into the gap. The car wobbled for an instant and his hands strove against each other to hold it. On the right an astonished driver took his car dangerously near the verge and Andy's foot hit the floor. His car shot through the space and on to clear road ahead as his hips arched and semen spattered the St Christopher medal soldered beneath the speedometer.

Gradually he decreased speed and moved by degrees to the slow lane. At the first service turn-off, he cut the speed to twenty and they rode into the forecourt in a silence that pressed on the ears.

Inside the self-service restaurant Katie sat with her hands clasped on the formica table while Andy bought coffee. Her fingers pressed hard against the cool plastic, drawing relief from its immobility. She was trembling and by the way people looked at her, she guessed it must be showing.

Andy came back and set a glass cup in front of her. The coffee was frothy, which she did not normally like, but she was grateful at that moment for anything. He sat down opposite and smiled weakly. 'That was a gasser.'

'I nearly died of fright. I don't want to do that again, Andy. Ever.'

'Ah—' he mocked her gently with a wave of his hand. 'You're too soft, that's your trouble.'

'Girls don't have to be seen to be tough. I'm too fond of staying alive.'

'It didn't turn you on at all?'

'I told you, I was scared. In my mind, I can make it enjoyable,

I can make a collision enjoyable. But the real thing—I don't know, I just kept thinking of pain and losing my legs or something. Make-believe's my thing, Andy.'

'That's fair enough,' he said generously. 'You're on the right wavelength, at least.'

They drank their coffee, and she ran the experience over in her mind again. She would have nightmares about it, she was sure. She had been certain that he intended, at one point, to let an accident happen, to involve them in a blood bath. Already she knew that the notion of such things turned him on and he had told her about the previous time when he nearly did it. The odd thing was that she was still not repelled by him. She felt like a living part of this man and the feeling grew despite—or because of?—the devious paths of his needs and behaviour.

Her uncle had made a remark a few days before when he had been reading in the newspaper about a student riot somewhere. He said, as she recalled it, that young people were open to every influence and it was the strongest, not necessarily the best, that predominated. Andy was the strongest influence she had ever encountered and he certainly held sway. What should she do? It was clear enough that she was involved with a man who was far from normal, even though she could find sympathy for every one of his odd impulses. Not ever, she swore to herself, would she let anything like this evening's near-disaster happen to her again. Not even if it meant losing Andy, she added, trying very hard not to visualise that loss.

10

A repair was made to the damaged oxygen line in the ambulance and a reinforced checking-schedule was grudgingly accepted by the technicians. Between Wednesday and Friday the unit answered twelve calls, and by Friday evening, the practical Mary Scott had decided that something was basically wrong with the concept of the service, while Dan McGoldrick, inclining more to an inherited streak of dark superstition, averred just as firmly that the ambulance was cursed. He could bring forward precedents for his belief. There was a wagon in London that the men had finally refused to handle, because of its ominously poor record of service. People had died wholesale and the vehicle had even tried, once, to wipe out its driver. There was another in Scotland and one in Dublin. The nature of the work, Dan hinted, imposed a spiritual quality on the ambulance, and some of them did not have the in-built harmony required to do the job.

Paul Avery was in agreement with Mary Scott, and he was pretty sure that Ellen Haxton, the other medically trained member of the team, felt the same way. Something fundamental was wrong. With all its fine trappings and its ready, eager operatives, the Avery Life-Support Unit was achieving no more, it seemed, than an average ambulance. Indeed, although the three day record might well be an untypical sampling, the tally suggested that the unit was less efficient than the ordinary wagons. At such a time, when the first figures were being compiled, it was important to show a positive, glaring benefit in the scheme.

It made little difference whether the figures were indicative of a trend or not, morale would be damaged all round, there was no avoiding that.

It had started with the second call on Wednesday. A tree had fallen across a road and smashed through the roof of a car, striking the driver and causing severe head injuries. The man was young and in good general health. On the trip back to the hospital, his injuries were carefully noted and the theatre warned to stand by. There was a suspected fracture to the frontal part of the skull, so the procedure on arrival would be to take an immediate x-ray. From that point, treatment would proceed. In the interim, the unit could do everything necessary to sustain life, and in the case of a head injury there was often a lot that could be accomplished. The very first thing was to protect the airway to ensure continued breathing. 'Even if a guy's brain is hanging out,' Paul Avery had emphasised to the team, 'that does not contra-indicate the direct measures necessary to keep the airway open. This measure takes precedence over *all* the others.' The principle was sound and backed by experience from injury teams throughout the world. Despite what might appear to be a dangerous move, the patient was placed on his side, with his head lower than his body, and his mouth and throat cleared with a gloved finger. Then an endotracheal tube was passed, giving continued access for the air. The performance of this task was treated by Paul Avery as important, in no way to be regarded too lightly. First, a laryngoscope—an instrument fitted with a six inch blade which draws forward the base of the tongue, in order to expose the entrance of the trachea—is placed in the patient's mouth and manipulated until the proper path is opened. The breathing tube is then passed via the laryngoscope; there can be mishaps at this point, and because they can lead to delay and because delay can be fatal, Paul had made a minor craft of getting the tube into position as quickly as possible. On this occasion it worked first time. Occasionally the tube would go down blind, into a throat obscurred by vomit or other fluid, or along a path littered with natural obstructions like soft tissue or a small, hard-to-discern larynx. Then it was quite possible that the end of the tube would enter the oesophagus, and if air or oxygen were passed along the tube, the patient's stomach, instead of his chest, would start to inflate.

With the airway established and the patient breathing satisfactorily, the next thing to do was make quick, incisive observations of the general condition; blood-pressure, pulse, respiration, skin colour, a check of chest and abdomen, to ensure that other injuries, if they were present, did not in any way reduce the patient's chances of survival. It seemed that the skull damage was the only injury of significant magnitude, and Paul proceeded to make some observations relating to the nervous system. He first recorded the level of consciousness. There had been a fair volume of argument surrounding the methods of doing this. So many terms used by doctors needed definition in themselves; 'stupor' and 'unconscious' were vague, unscientific words, lacking in subtlety and clarity, and they did not convey an accurate statement of the patient's condition. Similarly, grading systems were, in Paul's opinion, just as misleading, because for accuracy the exact definition of each grade of consciousness would have to be written down on the accompanying case card. He preferred to employ simple, clear language that avoided any pigeon-holing. Accordingly, he noted that the injured man appeared to be in a light sleep, moving his limbs freely in response to any painful stimulus. That would provide more information for a surgeon than any amount of chart-ticking or number-rating.

There followed a check of the pupils and a careful examination of the limbs to make sure that the reflexes were approximately normal. Finally the external wound was attended to. With a pair of electric veterinary clippers, hair was cleared from the site and the wound cleaned with saline solution. A sterile pad was applied and a four-inch crepe bandage was formed into a head dressing.

The patient arrived at Westfield General in a condition of full emergency support. A casualty officer and two nurses took over and Paul retired to make a proper report. Halfway through he was interrupted by sister; the patient had died.

An hour later, while he was still smarting from the blow, having been unable to learn much more than that the man was dead, Paul was approached by Mr Madison, who looked fittingly sour. 'You missed a few points of emergency treatment with that skull lesion case,' he said. He had a habit of looking along his nose at people, even those who were as tall as himself.

'What did I miss?' Paul rarely spoke to Madison. The casualty department was the cinderella corner, full for the greater part of each day with minor accidents and people with imaginary ailments. It did not properly come into the realm of surgery and as such was ignored by Madison. Since Paul had taken over, replacing the tide of coming-and-going surgical staff who only worked there under sufferance, the place had taken on some modest status. Even so, it was unusual to see Henry Madison condescending to set foot in the department. Used to him or not, Paul had a fixed attitude to the man; polite attention and vigilance. He would not let Madison get away with anything.

'The man was full of barbiturates.' Something like a surge of triumph accompanied the remark.

'But he was driving a car. He couldn't have been all that full.'

'The facts are the facts, doctor. I am simply conveying them to you, and I am advising you that my report will carry mention of the fact that no gastric lavage was instituted.' The case, having been passed to surgery, had been officially Madison's when the man died. 'I would have thought that your ambulance would have carried at least one person able to detect the presence of drugs in a patient.'

'He was mobile—he responded to needle pricks—'

'His skull was damaged, doctor. The fact alone can produce some behavioural pecularities.' Madison turned and walked away, leaving Paul to fume.

Mary Scott came by shortly after. 'Did you hear about that blood test—'

'I heard.' He slapped his forehead. 'Would *you* have said there was any dope in that man?'

'No,' she shook her head, looking sympathetically glum, 'I wouldn't. But he had a lot.'

'I want to see the post mortem report, Mary.'

'It'll only confirm the blood test.'

'Even so. I want to see it when it's available. Tell sister to arrange it.'

As a man specialising in casualty work, Paul had taken on a job with a fearfully high hazard rate. On top of responding to emergencies which were never the same on two consecutive occasions, he had to bear in mind that a medical condition might well be superimposed on the injuries. He felt himself to be equal to that sort of challenge. Yet he had missed a common one. Drugs and trauma. The signs of barbiturate poisoning were clear enough: giddiness, nausea, indistinct articulation, coma, slowing of the pulse, shallow breathing—there were a whole clutch of symptoms which, when they occurred together, gave a clear indication of poisoning by a drug. Even the head damage should not have masked the general picture. And what was a man doing driving around with a load of barbiturates inside him? It was an odd kind of suicide, although he had to admit that it was not unknown.

Poisoning featured in the next case the unit was called to attend. A young girl had swallowed a quantity of tablets—guessed at fifty or more—from an unmarked bottle. She was in a heavy coma when the unit arrived and Paul had her placed on the number one stretcher and made a rapid examination as the ambulance moved off again. Pupils down to pin-points, no reflexes, cold skin, livid features. 'Opium,' he said, a reasonable guess in the circumstances. 'What did her mother say?'

Mary Scott had spoken briefly to the distraught woman while the patient was being removed to the ambulance. 'Not much. She said the girl buys drugs, she's threatened to turn her over to the police lots of times, but it makes no difference. They had a fight today, and she ran upstairs and stayed in her room. The mother found her like this. She says she's seen the bottle before, her daughter told her they were just aspirins. I get the impression the old girl's a bit afraid of this one.' The girl, even in coma, had a surly look.

'Let's get her emptied.' The girl's head was drawn over the end of the stretcher and allowed to hang down, supported lightly by Mary Scott while Paul passed a rubber stomach tube. First, he attached a large syringe to the end and drew up some of the stomach contents, for examination at the hospital, then a funnel was attached to the tube and a litre of water was poured into the stomach. As the stained water returned through the tube, it was collected in a large jug. On arrival at casualty, the patient was rushed through to the treatment room, where oxygen therapy was commenced while the fluid from her stomach was being analysed. She died fifteen minutes later.

The depressing toll continued. On the motorway, a young

woman and her husband were picked up from the wreckage of a sports car. Despite intense emergency activity, the husband died in the ante-room of the theatre. This surprised everyone, as he was the one bearing the least serious injuries. From a shop in the centre of Westfield, a woman was brought in suffering from a coronary attack. She was in great pain, and after having her placed recumbent on the hard stretcher, Paul administered thirty milligrams of Fortral intravenously. He listened carefully to her labouring heart. The beat was down to less than sixty a minute.

'Arrythmia, Mary. Get me the atropine.' He injected .06 of a milligram cautiously, and waited. The irregularity of the condition called for constant monitoring, as the stress within the system could take any course without warning.

A mile from the hospital, the patient's heart arrested. Paul did not hesitate. While Mary inserted an airway and commenced mouth-to-mouth respiration, he clenched his right fist and punched the woman's chest six times, as hard as he could, remembering an old instructor's advice 'go to it like you want to crack a rib.' He then placed the palm of his hand over the woman's sternum and began to pump it up and down rapidly, using the other hand as a piston. Mary and Paul struggled together for three minutes, but still there was no response.

'Bill!'

The connecting door opened and the attendant came through.

'Set up the defibrillator. Quick.' Paul kept on pumping at the chest while the twin electric pads were connected to their special power source.

'What power, doctor?'

'Full on.'

Mary stopped blowing down the airway and held the pads while Paul opened the woman's dress and cleared all the other clothing from around her chest. He applied one pad over her sternum and the other to the side of the chest wall. 'Don't touch her, anybody, for Pete's sake.' To lay hands on a person about to receive the voltage from this equipment would mean a severe shock for the carless one, and Paul had seen it happen more than once. He pressed the button on the handle of one pad and the patient's body sprang rigid and arched upwards. He withdrew the pads and checked the heart. It was beating again, but very feebly. The ambulance lurched slightly and someone outside pulled open the doors. They were at the hospital.

There was a sadness settling on Paul as he watched the woman being raced to the Intensive Therapy Wing. The coronary care unit was splendidly equipped, but that heart had sounded to him as if it simply wanted to go to sleep. It did, ten minutes later, and it would not be revived.

Of the four motorway accidents, three industrial mishaps and two sudden collapses attended in the next two days, only eight of the fifteen people involved lived and showed signs of eventual full recovery. Gathered in the canteen late on Friday night, Dan, Bill, Mary and Paul were collectively in the running for heavy neurosis.

'Even the way these things are rated,' Paul pointed out gloomily, 'we're going to look bad, very bad.' The system of assessing the success rate was very fair. Emergencies were listed according to type, with previous survival averages printed alongside. On the sheets that would eventually be made up, the Life-Support Unit's figures would be split and divided along the appropriate columns. As it stood, halfway through the first crucial month, the figures indicated, if they indicated anything, that the new ambulance was actually hindering its primary purpose. 'It only takes a few fatalities in the wrong columns to do the trick. We've got four already that should never have gone, according to past experience. Four. That's a hell of a lot to lose, when they should have been among the reasonable certainties.'

'We must have figured everything out the wrong way round,' Mary said. 'All along, we've presumed that fast action, immediate care and speedy return to hospital would be the biggest boon to accident work since the splint. What if it turns out that bad accidents need to lie unaided for awhile, so the system can start to build its own defences? What if we're interfering with a healing process that isn't properly understood yet?'

'What if the top jumps off your head,' Paul suggested, 'and shows it's full of cement?' He rubbed both hands down over his eyes and groaned. 'I have a feeling we shouldn't be trying to work anything out while we're tired. Let's all to home, huh?'

'Aren't you on call tonight?' Mary asked the question with ill-concealed calculation.

'I should be,' Paul agreed, 'but I'm putting in a deputy. What harm can he do? It might even help the figures. I'm curling up in my own sack tonight and I'm going to forget everything until tomorrow. I shall be calm, I shall proceed in a scientific and analytical manner—and then I'll probably panic.'

Dan and Bill excused themselves, and as they went Mary leaned across and tapped the back of Paul's hand. 'Fancy doing some group forgetting?'

'You're too much.' He smiled, tired, worried beneath the calm. 'It would be a kindness, ma'am. I'll pick you up in half an hour, okay?'

She went and he lit another cigarette, idly watching the few late-night visitors to the canteen, doctors, nurses, porters, the democratic little line forming by the cash register. He had hoped to make a splash, he thought. Something to ride home on. Now, it looked as if he was caught up in a misjudged mess. Perhaps it was as well that it was happening in England, the facts would be easier to bury at this distance. The Board of Management was not going to be pleased, and detractors—Madison and whoever chose to get on his bandwagon now he looked like being proved right—would bring out the stakes to drive through the heart of the scheme. And the other venture, the one he kept the Polaroid around for, that hadn't even started yet. He proposed to create a lavish atlas of accidents, with hundreds of his own pictures and a carefully written commentary. So far he had not taken one picture. There was something very cold-blooded about pointing a camera at an injured person when you were trained to help him, not record his misery. All his intentions, at one stage or another, ran up against snags. Now though, the big snag looked like being the first one to offer heavy resistance. Something was wrong, but he had no idea what.

Edith remembered very few lessons or pieces of wisdom from her childhood which did not carry with them some reminder of her station, or some forthright instruction on moral conduct. Of the handful of simple single-meaning aphorisms she recalled, one was a particular favourite: a reliable luxury is something to cherish, for it compensates for a whole world of uncertainty.

For a time at least, it looked as if she had found her reliable luxury. If any work could be described as luxurious, the sessions of indexing at Mr Madison's home came easily under the banner. As a change from her ordinary work it was ideal; as a productive way of using leisure, it was perfect; as an experience filled with the civilised peace and rectitude she so admired, it was superb. The likelihood of the work continuing for a long time was strong, because it took a great deal of patient labour to achieve no more than a few accurate entries. The surroundings, the compatability of the company, the solidity and the total aesthetic pleasure was disproportionate to the simplicity of what she and Mr Madison actually did. She had learned, from other experiences, that such was the case with most of the deeper satisfactions.

The floor was littered with papers, and for over half an hour they had knelt in the midst of page proofs and reference sheets, looking for a mistake that she had spotted on her last visit, but had only now remembered.

'I suppose you're quite sure—' Madison smiled warmly as he voiced his growing doubt. The very mention of an error had been enough to startle him. A book, he had already said, was heavily flawed if it contained one little mistake; a book bearing his name on the spine and title page could not be allowed to go on the presses—it was unthinkable—with anything other than an immaculate text.

'I'm certain, sir. It's my fault for not mentioning it. I spotted it when I was looking for something else, and I made a mental note to tell you. Then something cropped up, and I forgot. It was just when I was looking at the section on the endocrine glands this evening that I remembered. But where it was, I've no idea.'

The error was a simple misspelling in the name of one of the thyroid hormones. Apart from the direct references in the appropriate section, mention of the secretion could appear in numerous other chapters. On the brink of deciding that they would never find it tonight, Edith suddenly found herself with the offending page in her hand. 'Got it!' She held it out to him and Madison took it, looking relieved and still wearing his friendship smile.

'Yes, indeed, you were right, my dear. Thyroxine. It's been spelt without the 'e' on the end.' He made an insertion mark on the text and a marginal note of the missing letter. 'I'm very grateful to you.'

She could see how much it meant. Finding a spelling blunder once the book was in print would give Henry Madison as much of a shock as he would experience from seeing a houseman in a dirty coat. Matters of detail were as important as major issues, for nothing of magnitude could be sound or relied upon if the secondary features were marred.

As he pushed himself to his feet and gingerly flexed his right knee, he was looking bemused. 'I cannot think of anyone I've known who would have displayed such care in this task, doctor. It gives me a lot of confidence to have you aiding me like this.'

Riches beyond value; he would have no way of knowing, she supposed, how much something like that, the ordinary bestowing of praise, could lift her. It had never been a part of her conversational style to mention the things which made her feel good, and even Paul Avery had no inkling of the ways she could be won round. To admire someone as much as she admired Henry Madison and to know that he found her—well, indispensable was not too much of an exaggeration—was a source of warmth and security. For days after the last little session in this beautiful study, she had carried his parting remark at the back of her mind. A most stimulating companion, he had called her. Her work had been sharper and more efficiently executed as a result, she was sure of that.

Restored to order, they resumed their close silence and gave their attention to the main work in hand. There was a clock somewhere in the room, and Edith worked to its muted rhythm. Opposite her, she heard Madison's pen scratching methodically at his pad, his steady breathing so clearly audible that it was almost an intimacy. A lot of this fine feeling was connected to her frequent desire to return to the days when she was a student. At that time, Edith had been a very serious and well-balanced person. There had been fewer tensions, a lot fewer pressures, and all that had been required of her was that she should work hard. Work was no problem, but nowadays there were side issues in a tiring and unsettling profusion. Politics, protocol, public relations, staff-counselling and, most disquieting of all, the private and social requirements. A husband, or the promise of one, was desirable. She did not want to become one of those lady surgeons who work out their days in theatres and clinics, then retire to a loneliness filled with every comfort but the most natural one of all. Making a proper marriage was terribly important. Her family had instilled that drive in her and while she had personally modified some of the specifications she adhered to the primary reasoning. Paul Avery, with his easy style and his fine skill—which he played down too much, she thought—was the man. She had no real doubts. Apart from his desirability, he represented quite an achievement, because alone, unapproached and forced to make the effort without open encouragement, she hated to think what sort of man she would end up choosing. She was not good at doing the things a girl was supposed to do when she put herself on the market. Paul had done all the work necessary in establishing their relationship so she was grateful and, despite the field of potholes they seemed to be crossing at present, she was determined to stick to him. Even with the reasonable chance of a good marriage in the offing, she would still, though, like to be in that wonderful student state again. Just work, no pitfalls or concealed traps.

'Excuse me, I'm sorry to interrupt, doctor . . .' She looked up and saw Madison with the tip of his pen pressing lightly on his chin, his eyes behind gold-rimmed reading spectacles seeming more familiar than they properly should, 'I'd like to hear your reaction to a short passage I intend to introduce at the beginning of the section on new growths.' He looked down at his notes and began to read: ' "The terminology surrounding tumour formation has caused regrettable confusion in recent years. Simple new growths are similar in substance to the tissues from which they appear, so their names are accordingly devised. The suffix 'oma' means a new growth, so, for example, a neuroma is a simple nerve growth. Malignant growths, on the other hand, derive their names from the cells from which they have arisen. The two principal forms of malignant new growths are squamous-celled carcinoma and adeno-carcinoma." ' He raised his eyes, awaiting her comment.

'That's splendid,' she replied. 'It certainly reduces some of the verbiage to an understandable outline.' She could see this had been the right thing so say. She had said what she meant for she was aware that many text-books, excellent though they were, filled a student nurse's head with long, winding explanations which added complication to a subject that was anyway becoming more complex every day. It was significant, she felt, that the clarification should have been added to the section dealing with tumours; Mr Madison's favourite area of surgery was the treatment of benign and malignant growths.

'Fine,' he grunted. 'I'll polish it a little and mark it for insertion.'

There was no doubt about it, Edith reflected, they were a team. He treated as an equal. If the other side of her emotional wall gave on to as smooth and pleasant a view as this one, everything would be marvellous. Through her small surprise, arising from the instinctive presumption that she had some kind of emotional relationship with Henry Madison, she felt a stab of warning. 'One thing, sir . . .'

He was already watching her, almost grinning. 'All right, I admit I was being childish,' he said. 'You spotted the omission?'

'Well, yes.'

'I am a man of habit, doctor. I have been in the habit for many years of trying to catch my colleagues out on every and any point I can. Will you believe me when I tell you that I was testing the degree of your excellence? I wanted to see if your could assess clarity and accuracy at the same time. Clearly you can, I had really no right to presume you couldn't. For your information, I have added mention of sarcoma and melanoma.' He bowed his head, still watching her, like a naughty schoolboy. 'Am I forgiven?

She blushed and muttered something about it being perfectly all right, and returned to her indexing. She would be very sorry indeed when the job was finally completed.

A variant to the parting scene this evening was coffee. A dark blue Russell Hobbs Wedgwood pot had been holding a French blend at the precisely correct temperature since she arrived, and as Madison poured her a cup he explained how the scientific facts of life could easily be turned to the service of superstition. 'I know several people who will not take coffee at night because it is thought to be an excessive stimulant. Yet the same people will happily accept a cup of tea. The voodoo word is caffeine. It is seen as an acid of some kind that will cause the nerves to jangle and the eyes to stay wide open. I don't contest the fact that caffeine is present in coffee, but people do not seem to realise that tea contains a good deal more. Now, I have no reports of sleeplessness from my wife when she takes late tea, but coffee, she insists, keeps her awake. The facts make no difference—the scientific facts. The falsehood has been planted, and no amount of reason will uproot it.'

'I sleep very well, whatever I drink.'

'Oh, I'm sure you do. You have a certain serenity, and that can count for a lot. Your stability, doctor, sits well on you. You are made for the life you have chosen. Not many people ever choose the work they were born to do, you are very fortunate.'

When it was time for her to leave, Madison became irregular in his movements, fussing with the handle of the study door, apologising for nearly bumping into her when there had been really little danger of it happening at all, then he took a deep breath as he was helping her into her coat, and grasped her arm quite firmly above the elbow. 'Would you bear with me, just for a moment?' He glanced across the hall, to the front door. 'There's something I want to say.'

He led her back to the study and pushed the door shut. Edith was at a loss. He looked very serious, he was tapping one lip on the other the way he did in the hospital when he was about to make an important pronouncement. 'I wouldn't be able to sleep tonight—and it has nothing to do with the coffee—if I left this in abeyance.' His hand came up again and rested on her forearm. 'Edith, I indicated to you when you were leaving last week that I found you pleasant company. That was true, but it was inadequate. These past few days I have had to be honest with myself. In truth, my admiration for you is very strong. It is stronger than mere professional respect. I know this may shock you, but it has never been my practice to side-step the responsibility of my inclinations. My regard for you is honourable, let me emphasise that. I am not the sort of man who would jeopardise his career or do anything foolish. I am too old and too well chastened by the example of others to add irresponsibility to my burdens. But there is great breadth to my intellect and my spirit. There is room to accommodate the warmth I feel for you. Do you reject this?'

Her blood was racing. She was overwhelmed, elated and quite astonished. 'No, I don't reject it. Not at all.'

'Dare I ask you, is there anything in your regard for me that could be called warmth . . . oh! I'm being stupid. I'm sorry. Forgive me, please.'

'There is nothing to forgive.' She was finding it easy to say. Liberated from any need for restraint, her feelings for him were surprisingly warm. 'I do have a very deep feeling for you. I would have been afraid to mention it before. I think I admire you, professionally and as a person, more than I've ever admired anyone in my life.' She felt as if a weight had been lifted. There was nothing disloyal in this, she thought. Admiration and respect combined to create something very much like love, but it was a pure thing, much finer than the usual state people called love, with its sexual overtones and possessive rules. It was easy, right then, to admit that she experienced more emotion for Madison than she did for Paul Avery. It was different, her feelings for the older man were spiritual, they arose from the parts of herself where the religious instincts lived. Relatively, she sensed, her affection for Paul was a practical thing, a surface need like money and property.

'Thank you.' He took her hand and squeezed it. 'Thank you for honouring me in this way.'

The correctness of it all was very appealing. They might have been living in the nineteenth century. In his way, Henry Madison epitomised the propriety and distinction that Edith's upbringing had conditioned her to seek. His feelings for her were a bequest, he was bestowing a sacred part of himself.

Surrounded by the symbols of Madison's learning and his stature, they made a halting pact. Edith could cherish the secret knowledge that she was adored by her hero, and Henry could be content that she shared his spiritual attachment.

After she had gone home, Henry sat by the fire, a glass of sherry in his hand, allowing the reality to dawn slowly on him. He had committed himself, an act that could have held dangerous consequences. But something in the girl made him confident; it was the same confidence he felt when he approached certain tasks that would have seemed, on the surface, to be dangerous. He was shaped for a particular quality of risk, and so long as he remained in character, there was little that could harm him. One of the benefits of authority was an immunity from the normal laws of chance. He could do and say things, within the contours of his personality and status, that ordinary people could not say or do. There was a great peace, now that his agitation over Edith Roberts had been stilled. She was his. His aesthetic waters were calm. It only remained to clear the threats that impinged on his authority, and he would be a most happy man. The way things were going it would not be long at all before his house was fully in order again.

11

Pemberton and Morris occupied offices on the top three floors of a Victorian block near Euston. Ernie had found the lift out of order and by the time he reached the reception desk he was breathless. The girl smiled cautiously and asked him to state his business. Publishers were habitually invaded by people whose views of their own merit came nowhere near their true commercial or artistic value, and a good receptionist was expected to repel the bulk of undertalented invaders who sought audience with the editor.

'My name's Hale,' Ernie panted, 'and I'd like to see Mr Miles, please, before my heart muscles finally give out.'

'Oh, is that *Doctor* Hale?' She had brightened, dropping the tentative rebuff.

'The one and only.' He sank back on to a chair and took a deep breath.

'Mr Miles is expecting you. I'll tell him you're here.'

It was a very plush reception room, Ernie observed. He had only been in the place once before, and the walls had been a different colour then. They were big, and they probably employed every advertising and promotional device of persuasion to ensure they stayed that way. The walls and the carpet were no doubt the colour combination of the month, the decorative equivalent of keeping-up. He could remember how, years before, he had been one of the frenetic followers of cultural fashion. It had been like walking on eggshells twenty-four hours a day. He attended parties where people said all the right things, dropping comments and quotes apt and apposite to the prevailing trends. Nowadays people were into the serious kick, appraising the roots of everything. The game was not really about knowing, it was about being in the right camp. The portals of Pemberton and Morris were no less honest than those of certain other more conservatively opulent publishers. The major difference was that Pemberton and Morris dealt with the public, the people in the street who kept the world moving. Catering to the mass market was still, sadly, the cultural bogey, the practice which horrified certain cliques of mutually-admiring misfits who preferred to cling to their rafts of drifting persuasion than join the crowd on the mainland.

Long ago, Ernie had faced the truth. He wanted distinction, but he wanted it among the real people, where it mattered. The gagged and bound intellectual in him insisted, weakly, that he should not dilute his talent, but Ernie found it easy to resist. He could spend years of his life struggling to produce a profound treatise that perhaps ten other people would understand. Big deal. Barring disasters, the book he had spent less than a year writing would entertain, inform and amuse tens of thousands of people, and the detractors would be few and pathetic enough to be ignored as easily as his conscience. Acceptance by this publisher had meant a good deal to him, even if a few fussy little shops *did* refuse to stock their books.

'Mr Miles will be free in a minute, Dr Hale.'

'Thank you.' He took the letter from his pocket and read it again. It had arrived on Saturday morning, and he had spent the best part of the weekend organising a couple of stand-ins so that he could get here on Monday as the editor requested. It was urgent, the letter said. Ernie had carefully kept his mind away from the speculations that had raced forward. Worrying would do no good. He had told that to enough patients in his time. The best thing was to wait and find out, then he could tackle the trouble with energy that had not been depleted by fretting.

Logan Miles appeared in the doorway and extended a confident hand. He was very tall, a man with the face of a highly polished winner, his grey hair immaculately brushed into wings over his ears, his smile perfected by practice and expensive dental work.

'Glad you could make it, Dr Hale. I appreciate the trouble you've taken.'

'No trouble,' Ernie said. 'The hardest part was getting up your stairs.'

In the small office, lined with books and posters advertising notable Pemberton and Morris successes, Miles ushered Ernie into a chair and sat down behind the desk. They lit cigarettes and after some preliminary discussion of the weather and the parking situation in London, Miles got down to business.

'It looks as if your book may be in trouble, I'm afraid. The authorities are being alerted by your Mr Madison.'

'What authorities?'

'You'll know that better than I do. Our directors have received a letter which states, in essence, that Madison will be prepared to go to the highest level to ensure that the proper authorities read *The Marshes of Despair* before it's published. He adds that they may well decide that a severe contravention of ethics has been committed. Now that is the kind of trouble we like to avoid, doctor. There are enough difficulties surrounding the production of a new book without some medical disciplinary committee coming down on us. Everybody in this business knows the financial nightmares caused by a book that gets printed and bound and advertised and then never sees the light of day. We don't know the strength of the medical policy-makers, doctor. I'm hoping you can hand me some practical reassurance that I can convey to the directors. We want to do the book, but we have to feel reasonably free from threat.'

Ernie scratched his chin. 'Well, I don't really know how any pressure could be placed on you. The case histories were all collected while I was doing voluntary work among convicts. Where the patients were thought to be responsible enough, they were asked for permission to print. Permission to use one or two of the cases was granted by senior psychiatrists. There's not one item of information in the book that has come from Westfield General. Now, the question of ethics, in an overall sense, doesn't really arise. I can do this book if I want to, nobody can stop me. I'm not breaking any laws. Madison hasn't got a leg to stand on.'

'But nobody can stop him shouting, right?'

'That's true. He's vindictive. I've stepped on his toes once or twice, and I daresay he sees the book as an opportunity to get his own back. Did you let him have any details of the contents?'

'None.' Miles tapped a letter on the desk which Ernie recognised as the one he had written recently, in reply to the first alarm call about Madison. 'We did just as you asked. We wrote and told him that the relevant detailed list would be available in due course, and that he'd get a copy when it was to hand.'

'So then he started to kick up the dust. Well, I don't know what other assurances I can give you, Mr Miles. Madison can start a stink, no doubt about that. But I can't see any harm, from your point of view—'

'I can. It only needs a few high-sounding medical types to write letters of protest and we'll find ourselves with an investigation, a boycott, a block on publication—all sorts of hold-ups and frights. There are a lot of booksellers in this country, doctor, who live in fear of a prosecution. Any book that comes out with a history of complaint and controversy at an official level is likely to get snubbed. We might well get a public demand on the strength of the publicity, but that can never be depended upon. You see,' he clasped his hands, obviously covering ground that was familiar to him, and frowned to convey the seriousness of the situation; 'your book deals with the mentally sick, an area that is dodgy at the best of times. Opposition arguments could be phrased to imply that you have exploited these poor creatures. There's no point in protesting that they're nutters and vicious maniacs, the old sentimental arguments can be hoisted and people will listen. You know how mawkish the tone can get when there's a so-called public outcry.' He sat back and folded his arms. I'll need a good argument to convince the directors that there's nothing to worry about. The official stand in this firm, doctor, is that we can show a profit easily enough without getting our balls in a snare.'

Given the immediate opportunity, Ernie Hale would have liked to kick a hole in something large and brittle. Of all the likelihoods that had occurred to him when he was beginning his book, the present cloud had been nowhere. He had used a deft series of strokes to make sure that he did not infringe the laws governing obscenity; he had protected his own image by adopting a fairly moral and cool tone throughout. The book would stand as a model of professional workmanship, and would be eminently commercial, yet it only took an old fart like Madison to undo everything. 'Look, can you hang fire on any decisions for a little while?'

'I suppose so. I must say, I was hoping we could thrash out something here and now. What kind of time do you need?'

'Three weeks, at the most. No, make it five. Can you do that?'

Miles looked uneasy. 'I suppose so. What are you planning to do?'

'The plan hasn't formed yet. What I want to achieve is clearance for my book. I have my own devious little ways, Mr Miles. If I don't get matters sorted out in five weeks, then we can talk about a change of policy. Fair enough?'

'Yes, I suppose so. I must say, I'd like to see this one go through. It would do well for you. I read Chapter Five last night. It nearly curled my hair. Is it all absolutely true?'

'Every word. The world is one great big psycho unit, Mr Miles. I'm afraid most of the really terrible cases are still on the outside of the hospitals and institutions. Take Mr Madison, for instance.'

Miles looked surprised. 'Do you think he's unbalanced?'

'I've thought that for ages. Maybe I'll find our salvation along that line of probability. I'm good at uncovering kinks in people.'

Miles saw Ernie to the door a few minutes later. 'I wish you luck, doctor. And I'm sorry if your journey has been wasted.'

'It won't be wasted,' Ernie assured him, shaking his hand warmly. 'This town has enough distractions to make my trip worthwhile.'

From Euston he travelled west towards Chelsea and within half an hour he was on the Fulham Palace Road. The new Charing Cross Hospital stood like a complex of offices, or perhaps interlocked hotels, he thought. The last thing it resembled was a hospital. He put his car in the park at the front and made his way to reception, where an extremely attractive young woman asked if she could help him.

'My name is Hale, and I'm looking for an old colleague of mine. I believe he works here now. His name is David Spence.'

'Is he a doctor?'

'Yes—a surgeon, actually.'

'One moment, please.' She consulted a woman at the opposite side of the desk, then came back with a slip of paper in her hand.

'Yes, sir, he works here. If you could write your name down here, I'll see if he can be contacted.'

It was almost an hour before Spence showed up. When he did, he came loping towards Ernie in a green gown and white rubber boots, He was in the mid-thirties, approximately Ernie's age, and he had unusually long hair for a professional man. The next most noticeable feature was his nose, which was long and hooked, making his eyes appear rather small. He had a cheerful face which grew brighter by degrees as he drew nearer.

'Ernie Hale. Of all people. How are you?'

Ernie slapped his arm, feeling as much pleasure as he displayed. 'I'm fine. I had to come to London for the day, so I thought I'd look you up. How long has it been?'

'Must be three years. Just before I got married.'

They brought each other up to date as they walked towards the cafeteria. David Spence had once been Ernie's closest friend. They had worked in the same hospitals for as long as it was practical, then the separating processes of promotion had intervened and they had lost touch. David had laboured under much the same handicap as Ernie. He had a sense of humour and an eye for humbug that did not make him supremely popular with authority. In Ernie's case the problem had never been so severe, as idiosyncracy was accepted among psychiatrists. David had to prove his ability against the opposition of stiff-necked authoritarians and traditionalists, and he had finally been accepted, for all his worldly faults. He was climbing.

They took cups of tea and, in the interests of nostalgia, cream doughnuts to a table in a quiet corner. As students, they had shared a passion for the sticky wads of dough that was matched by their spirited pursuit of women. 'I shouldn't really eat this,' Ernie complained, sinking his teeth into the edge of the confection and tearing off a piece. 'My weight's up again.'

'Poor old bugger.' David grinned and clasped his hands across his own flat abdomen. 'It's contentment that does it, you know. I'm still ambitious, Ernie. I haven't put on an ounce in years.'

'You can sit there, with an expensively acquired knowledge of the influences governing human metabolism, and talk like that?' Ernie's eyes were wide above his churning teeth and lips. He swallowed a lump of doughnut and washed it down with tea. 'I'm putting on weight because I spend too much time on my arse, David. I'm in a sedentary occupation. You stand on your feet all day, butchering people. Actually, it's a particular butcher that brings me here. I want some information.'

'I might have known. You wouldn't look me up out of simple friendship would you?'

'No.'

'Who are you investigating?'

'Henry Madison, consultant, sage, teacher and all round shit house.'

'I couldn't have described him better myself. Why do you want to know anything about that character? It's dangerous to dabble with disease, you know.'

'You worked for him once, you may have some clues, the kind I need. Before I go into detail, David, would you say that there's anything unbalanced about Madison?'

David chewed his doughnut thoughtfully for a minute before replying. 'Well, you know the way I used to go on about him. He's not the most normal person I've met. Yes, I think I'd say there's a bolt missing somewhere. But what's it all about?'

Ernie explained the book, which brought on some amusement, then he detailed Madison's interference. 'It's a pattern with him, David. He opposed the new Life-Support Unit we've got. He was the only one who didn't like the idea.'

'That's Avery's baby, isn't it? He's a bright boy. If he sticks at it, he'll get accident work a bit of real status in this country. Just like Madison to object to something like that.' For four years, David Spence had worked as a houseman, then a junior registrar under Madison at the Phoenix Memorial Hospital in Surrey. They had not been happy times, and David had often bored Ernie into the night with complaints about his superior. 'There were times when I thought he was going to crack up, Ernie. He used to go into rages, and he would be so petty that it went beyond anything funny. He terrorised his team.' David folded his paper napkin into a series of diminishing triangles as he recalled the period. 'One of the girls packed in because of him, you know. Nice girl, no hang-ups, perfectly balanced. But the old bastard reduced her to a nervous wreck. I was never quite sure why he did that, but I'm sure it was deliberate. She was so downright nice, the sort of person everyone liked, and yet he homed-in on her. It was the old petty technique, but intensified.

He would ignore her when she asked him a question on ward round, then when she was explaining a case he would start talking, as if she had finished. All the time, he left her in mid-air, accused of nothing but knowing just the same that she was being punished. Any time she made a mistake, he would inflate it, bawl her out, and if she offered an excuse he would listen with that superior, disbelieving smirk of his. On that count alone, somebody should have kicked him in the nuts. But we were all too scared ourselves. He had a lot of power, and he used it like a sledgehammer.'

Ernie understood the behaviour of certain men who picked on innocent women, usually very attractive women. It was a refinement of sadism, motivated by a desire to punish the woman for being so attractive to her torturer. It was a seam of possibility he had not considered before. Madison would fill the role of sexual cripple as well as anybody. 'Do you know of other instances? I'm playing a hell of a long shot, but it's the only one I've got. I have to know if there's anything I can stop him with. Did he break the rules at any time?'

David unfolded the napkin and inspected the satisfying matrix of geometrical shapes. 'It's hard to know. He could camouflage anything. We had a ward sister at the Phoenix who went over the top one night and actually let slip her belief that Madison had deliberately allowed a patient to die. She tightened up after that. I don't think anybody could pin anything on him, he created too much confusion around himself. But if you want my opinion, I'd say it would be unlikely that he *never* broke any big rules. He's full up to his ears with tradition and ethics, but he's got the kind of steamrolling style that likes to step outside of the ethical structure from time to time.'

'Power crazy?'

'Definitely. Power was the most important thing in his life when I was stuck under his hoof. He's a good surgeon, very, very clever. But you would have thought sometimes that the professional talent was only a tool to assist his ambition.'

Ernie got two more teas, promising not to detain his friend much longer. 'What about jealousy? Did you ever see traces of that?'

'Traces? You could hardly *see* him through the pile of jealousies and envy he carted around. Other surgeons, men with equal status, used to drive him hairy. I can remember him trying his hand at an emergency cardiac repair once. The heart specialist was on his way, but the patient was very low so Madison went ploughing in. He didn't do too badly, either. But when the expert turned up, the old lunatic wouldn't let him near the table. He said he could finish what he started. Then he did something wrong and there was a fountain of blood, and the specialist forcibly intervened. Madison was away for a couple of days after that.' David laughed suddenly. 'It was a scream, sometimes. One of the men on our team, I think he was a registrar, was very hot on suturing. You know how some people have a knack for a thing? Well, he was assisting Madison one day, performing a simple laparotomy, and when it came to closing the abdomen, this bloke says, "shall I attend to the stitches, sir?" all innocence, forgetting that Madison always liked to finish the job himself. The old man flew at him. He wanted to know if the registrar thought he wasn't capable, did he think he was so inadequate that the suturing was too much for him to handle . . . he went on and on, and by the time he'd stopped raving at the poor sod, his hands were shaking so badly that he nearly did make a bog of the stitches. And there were the letters he wrote. He was always writing to the journals about this and that, and he blew a gasket when they showed a picture in one of the magazines of a prize-winning nurse with a bikini on. He told the editor he thought it was disgusting, filling his pages with the cheap kind of titillation that was more at home in the gutter press.'

After relating a few more anecdotes, David said that he must go. Before they parted, Ernie asked for the names of any people David could recall from the time he had worked for Madison. There were four, all of them as unsympathetic to the consultant, David assured him, as he was. 'All we've done is talk about old Madison, Ernie. Not a word about my nice little son or your latest crumpet.'

'You'll have to forgive me for that. This book means a lot to me, and I have a feeling it'll take a lot of work on my part to rescue it. But we'll get together for a proper social evening soon, I promise.'

They crossed the broad entrance hall and David held the door while Ernie slipped into his overcoat. It's been nice to see you,

Ernie. I hope your campaign is a success. Don't give up too easily, anyway. Remember the old saying.'

'Which one?'

'Faint heart never fucked a pig.'

It was after eight o'clock when he finished checking through the mail. The drive back from London had given him plenty of time to frame a sketchy picture of Madison's private personality. His own experience, added to David Spence's, confirmed his earlier suspicion that the consultant was distant enough from the guidelines of sane behaviour to qualify for some psychotic label. That was hardly enough, though. Plenty of people held responsible jobs while they were tethered by some hefty mental illness. In a consultant, a great deal could be condoned and simply called eccentricity. The certainty that there was a defect was no more than a starting point, a reassurance that there *might* be something worth digging for.

Ernie bundled the important letters into his case and looked at his watch. Cynthia, if he remembered correctly, would be off at nine o'clock. He did not pause to consider whether he really wanted to see her tonight. Variety was a thing one forced on oneself; it was invariably beneficial. If he spent every minute jammed on this one frequency, he would lose his drive. He had noticed in many patients that obsession always affected their sense of direction, and he could not afford to lose that.

On his way through the short passage connecting the clinic with the main surgical corridor, he caught sight of Henry Madison for an instant, as he swept past the end, wearing his stiff white coat. On sheer impulse, Ernie quickened his step and followed the path the consultant had taken, towards the anteroom of the main theatre.

As Ernie entered, Madison had his back to him. He was reading a chart attached to a clipboard. There was no one else in sight.

'I'd like a word with you.' It was gratifying to notice that Madison jumped.

He turned his head and looked over his snowy shoulder. The annoyance in his eyes was quite open. 'I beg your pardon?'

'I won't detain you for long.' Ernie put down his bag and folded his arms, asserting his intention to have his say. 'I've just come back from London, where a publisher told me a very curious story.'

Madison performed a clinical intake of breath, the hissing, lopped-off little gasp that traditionally accompanied a diagnosis. 'I usually see people by appointment. I'm rather busy just now.'

Ernie pressed on. 'You wrote threatening to create some mischief around the forthcoming publication of my book. Can you tell me why you saw fit to do that?'

'I wrote because you are clearly violating a number of set procedures. No senior member of the staff at this hospital was aware, until I discovered it, that you had any intention to write a book, let alone publish one. Also, it is clear from the available advertising that your work has a sensational slant and it is in the interest of this hospital and its reputation that your book be examined before any further steps are taken to market it.' His face had turned red; he was still regarding Ernie obliquely, his chin touching the upturned collar of his surgical coat.

'I am free to write a book, Mr Madison, whether or not the senior staff of the hospital know of it. The book was prepared in my capacity as a psychiatrist, not as a member of the staff here. As for your antiquated moral judgments, I would have thought you'd be better occupied applying them to something more deserving, like a paper on the sad decline of the bustle.'

'How can you talk to me like that!'

'It's easy. Something about you invites it.'

'This will be reported—' Madison waved his clipboard, turning now to face Ernie.

'I know, I know. You'll go haring off to dig out your Victorian dictionary and rip off a real back-stabber. Go ahead. I'll deny it. And I'll tell you something else, while there are no witnesses. You're a very odd person. Remember, it's my business in the mumbo-jumbo branch of healing to detect the people who don't quite fit. You stand out like a diseased digit. You're after me because I've had the cheek in the past to cross you. You're a witch-hunter and I'm well up on your list. Well, get this through your head, Mr Madison. I'm after you, too. I'll pursue you twice as hard as you're hounding me. And I'm using reason as my weapon, not some trumped-up claptrap calling itself ethics and discipline. Go ahead and make trouble. You'll gather as much as you send out.'

The look on Madison's face, as Ernie turned away and made for the door, was a startling amalgam of hate, outrage and anger. His mouth was open and his teeth were bared, and his arms were moving up and down under tension.

'This is monstrous! You will be dismissed for this, do you hear?'

Ernie paused with the door half open. 'Fine. Then I can publish my book without you interfering.' He left, letting the door swing shut behind him.

Madison clenched his teeth. 'I *will* prevail,' he groaned, beginning to tremble violently.

12

An old man who regularly cleaned out the boiler room at Westfield General and who had been an odd job man on the works staff for nearly fifteen years, had been brought to casualty from the canteen. Paul Avery, Sister Mclean and Mary Scott were on duty until midnight, and with two hours to go they were working at a steady, agreeable pace set by a regular flow of minor accidents.

Paul approached the trolley and looked at the man. He was blue in the face, his eyes were congested and he appeared to be expiring rapidly. 'What happened?'

The two porters accompanying the patient began to speak at once and Paul pointed to the older one. 'You tell me.' Mary Scott was already opening the old man's mouth and pulling out his dentures.

'He was eating his supper. He just stood up from the table and started to walk a few steps, then he collapsed. We brought him straight round.'

'Did he make any sound?'

'No, he didn't. That was the odd bit. He was silent, didn't even groan.'

'Coronary,' Mary snapped efficiently, undoing the man's collar.

'No it isn't.' Paul pushed his index finger into the patient's mouth and hooked it down over the back of his tongue. 'Nurse, go to the locker above the washbasin in the treatment room and bring me the white plastic tweezers from the top shelf.' He continued to probe the man's throat, adding the tip of his thumb to the fumbling efforts of his finger. Mary Scott was back in a few seconds, bearing the tweezers. 'Choke Saver' was printed on the handle.

Paul pushed the curved points down into the patient's throat, until he was holding only the last half inch of the handle. After twisting and closing the jaws a few times, he slowly withdrew the instrument. One of the porters gasped. There was a piece of meat, the size of a golf ball, caught firmly between the toothed prongs of the tweezers. 'Ventilate him, nurse.'

Sister Mclean, who had just finished dressing a lacerated arm, came across and peered at the wad of beef. 'Good lord. Did he try to swallow that?'

'Yup.' Paul dropped the meat into the disposal bin and set to checking the patient's chest. The old man was reviving, his colour returning to normal as Mary Scott administered oxygen. Within twenty minutes he was fully conscious again. Paul had him admitted to a ward for the night, then wrote up a brief report.

'How did you know what it was?' Mary Scott was sitting on the edge of the desk, swinging one leg. When she was working in casualty, Paul noticed that she had a capacity for almost total relaxation between calls. A well-compartmented girl, he thought. He finished his report before answering her.

'What you mistook for a coronary attack was one of the most overlooked emergencies in the world. Between seven hundred and a thousand people are estimated to die from the café coronary in America every year. The picture is pretty regular. The victim is usually middle-aged or elderly, usually with false teeth, and he's quite often had a few drinks. He tries to swallow a chunk of solid food and he becomes aphonic—he can't make a sound. I've seen five cases that I know of, but there could have been more.'

'What do you mean?'

'Well, it's been shown that one heck of a lot of so-called heart attacks are in fact no more than choking emergencies. Dead men at postmortems have been found with chunks of meat the size of a cigarette packet locked in their airways. There are some tragic side-effects, socially. There must be a lot of men lying in their graves now with a piece of food lodged in their throats, and their poor widows will have received not a cent of the double-indemnity insurance money payable in the event of accidental death. So always check, Mary. If silence has been a notable feature of the attack, it's a safe bet you've got a café coronary on your hands.'

'There's so much to learn, isn't there?'

'It's the cross you have to bear, kiddo. You're a healer.'

Sister appeared in the doorway. 'One for you, doctor.'

A teenage boy was lying on a treatment trolley, his left thigh fractured. 'How did you manage that?' Paul put on the customary cheerful face, but the boy's pain was too severe for him to respond with anything but a groan.

At Paul's elbow, Sister McLean explained that he had been set upon by a gang of youths outside a cinema. 'They knew what they were doing,' she observed. 'There's not a mark anywhere else on the poor wee soul.'

Paul nodded as he began to cut away the trouser leg. 'Violence is a craft nowadays. I haven't seen the results of a random brawl in ages. It's always a piece of sadistic workmanship lately.' The upper leg was misshapen and the fracture gave every evidence of being transverse. 'I think we can reduce it here and now, sister. Give him a shot of pentothal first.'

As he turned away from the trolley, Mary Scott was helping a woman towards the nearest row of chairs. She was pale and appeared to be entering shock. Mary glanced up anxiously. 'Could you take a look, doctor?'

'What's the trouble?'

The woman pulled herself gently free of Mary's encircling arm and began to ease her coat off her shoulders. There was a strong smell, one that Paul recognised, but the woman's appearance, the stern alertness of her eyes and the deathly pallor of her cheeks did not seem to marry up with the recoil the odour produced. The coat fell to the floor and Mary clapped a hand over her mouth. The woman's right arm, from the elbow downwards and including the hand, was burned to a twisted cinder. Paul felt his stomach lurch. 'How did that happen?'

'It was God's will.'

Great, he thought, just great. A nut was all he wanted, a *burned* one at that. 'Did you do it yourself?'

'Oh yes.' The woman spoke like an automaton, observing him with unblinking eyes. 'But I was directed to do it, you understand.

I burned it over the gas ring. It began to hurt a while ago, so I thought I'd better come here and have it looked at.'

Mary had gone as white as the patient, and Paul was aware that if he began to show any signs of his own revulsion, the whole thing would break down. 'Why, tell me why you had to do it?'

'I smoked a cigarette, doctor. I smoked one this afternoon. When I joined the Fellowship they warned me that smoking was a sin and I gave it up. That was three weeks ago. But today I craved a cigarette very badly. God was testing me, you see. I was weak, I smoked a whole cigarette and afterwards I was filled with guilt. So I punished myself, twice.'

'Twice?' Paul stared at Mary, who was swallowing hard and looking at the blackened, withered travesty of an arm.

'Yes. I burned my arm, the one that held the cigarette, then I think I must have fainted. When I came round, I did it again, until I could see that I had completed the job. I don't feel guilty at all now. But I have a lot of pain.'

Paul crossed to the office and rang surgical. He explained to the duty surgeon what had happened, then returned to the patient. 'I want you to sit quite still, do you understand? Just stay where you are and a man who can help you will be right along.' He touched Mary's shoulder, squeezing it momentarily. 'Stay with her, will you? They'll take her up to theatre in a few minutes.'

He returned to the patient with the fractured thigh and began to reduce the fracture with the sister's help. While he worked, he tried to keep from smelling that charred skin, muscle and bone. But it was locked in his head as it always was, and the merest whiff triggered recollection of all the burnings he had seen. Every doctor had his queasy topics, of course. Paul knew of one who could not bear to watch an operation for the removal of an ingrown toe-nail. Another, a surgeon, always started to heave when he heard a patient vomiting. Always, at one point or another, kinship with the patient entered the picture and a sympathetic reaction set in. Paul knew, however, that his own reaction to severe burning went beyond the usual limits of freak sympathy. He could be immobilised by it, as he had been when the boy at the garage had been roasted by the petrol. At this very moment, he was fighting to remain within the limits of his professional pattern. Miraculously, he felt, the fracture was set without mishap and sister took the boy away for the application of a plaster cast. Mercifully, when he looked round, the burned patient had gone. Mary Scott was talking to an elderly man by the reception desk. She beckoned as Paul was deciding to slip off for a cigarette.

'What can I do for you?'

Mary stepped to one side. 'He insists on talking to a man. Must be something up with his willie.'

Paul took the old gentlemen into a cubicle, noting that he walked very stiffly. 'Sit down, sir, and tell me all about it.'

'I can't sit down.' He was a phlegmatic type, red-faced, mindful of his dignity. The body, Paul reflected, could be a terrible embarrassment to the pompous of the earth. Especially when it got old. 'I find that I can't pass water.'

'I see. Well, can you lie on this couch, and we'll have a look.'

It was a typical appearance. The lower part of the man's abdomen, from just under his naval, was distended and rounded like a large ball. 'We'll soon rectify that for you,' Paul assured him. 'Lie quite still, I'll be right back.'

He was in the medical store, looking for a Gibbon catheter, when Mary came in, blushing furiously. Paul held up the sterile packet he had been looking for. 'The old guy's a bladder-daddy,' he announced. Then he noticed Mary's confusion and asked her what was wrong.

'Do you remember a man called Rourke? He's a bricklayer, we put a leg bandage on him a few days ago.'

'I think I remember him, yes. What about him?'

'He's back. He said the bandage was too tight and he wanted the tension eased a bit. So I told him to take off his trousers and sit on the stool.'

'And?'

'He sat there and let me take the bandage off, and when I looked up, he was flashing a full seven inches of rigid gristle.'

'What did you do?' Paul was amused. It happened quite often.

'What could I do? I was at a disadvantage. I replaced the bandage and he's getting his trousers on again. Christ, some men . . . '

'And some women.'

'Really?' She was looking suddenly interested. 'In here?'

'Yes. But I can't stop here chit-chatting. I've got a distended bladder to put out of its agony. Just to whet your appetite, though, I'll ask you to cast your mind back a few weeks. There was a case brought in from an insurance office, a forty-year-old woman who had hurt her back when she was on a step ladder.'

'Oh, yes.' Mary puckered her lips and raised her eyebrows. 'What did she do?'

'Tell you later.'

He returned to the acute retention case and catheterised the man, then gave him a letter to take to his doctor. When he finished, Mary was waiting for him. 'Finishing up time,' she said. 'Doing anything important?'

'Funny you should ask that,' he said, and grinned.

'Diagnosis is my strong point,' she said.

By twelve-thirty they were back at Paul's house, drinking hot chocolate and unwinding together on the couch. He had his arm around her shoulder and she had her feet raised on a rickety foot stool. One lamp cast a warm, dim glow across them. The ritual was well on the way to becoming permanent, or as close to permanent as their liberal arrangement would permit.

'Right, tell me what that woman did.' She turned her head and rubbed her nose against the side of his face.

'I'm not so sure I can, now I come to think about it,' he said. 'Ethics don't really permit the dissemination of matters privy to the sacred—'

'Knickers. Tell me what she did.'

'Well, I must say, I think you have a really dirty little mind there.'

'Yes, I have, and it's lovely. I don't know how clean-minded people pass their time. What did the lady do? Huh?'

'She flashed. I had a nurse with me, but she spent most of the time looking for things. The woman was on the examination couch, and she kept lifting her knee. It was quite deliberate, I could tell the way she watched me. There was nothing wrong with her back, either.'

Mary mused. 'Flashing among females is not common. They're usually frustrated, aren't they?'

Paul shrugged. 'I don't know. Ask Ernie. He gets all the real kinks. If you ask me, I don't think I know one straightforward person, not one. We're all subject to the kink syndrome, somewhere along the line.'

She considered it. 'Yes, that's right. Listen, Paul, this work we do—don't you think we have to be a bit odd to do it? I mean, sorting out all those odds and ends in casualty, it's a funny kind of life, isn't it.'

'It's what you want to do, isn't it?'

'Oh yes, definitely. But it's not like any other branch of medicine or surgery. It's really like the rag yard. You specialised in casualty work in America, didn't you? Why did you do that?'

He drained his mug and looked at it thoughtfully. 'A lot of reasons. The main impulse, I think, came from the sense of urgency. And the sense of proportion some good teachers gave me.' He wriggled further down in the soft upholstery, glad that Mary, although not his type, although not at all the girl he could ever see himself settled with, was nevertheless here, asking genuine questions from a curiosity that was simple and honest. 'There are more people killed in accidents than there have ever been in all the major wars put together. The way I see it, an emergency is loaded with challenge. A perfectly healthy person, breathing air and functioning like a Swiss watch, can be changed, in the space of a second, to a damaged, disrupted entity close to death. Now although it looks to you like a jumbled, imprecise branch of medicine, it isn't really. It's a pure speciality. Trauma. A condition with a million symptoms and thousands of possible cures. The state of mind of any doctor dealing with people who have been injured must be the same as any surgeon's, but his terms of reference are different. He's dealing with the results of violence, he is fighting something man-made, not the natural phenomenon of disease. So the challenge is keener, I have to attack something which mankind has foisted upon itself. Also, between me and you, I stick to casualty because it's a different way to make a name for yourself.'

She craned her neck to look at him, checking to see if he was kidding. 'That's a big reason with you, is it?'

'Sure. Make no mistake about it. I'm ambitious. But I want to stand out, I don't care to be lumped with all the other fellows who just make it in the old established way. Does that shock you?' He had not told her about his individual route map before. The only reason he told her now—knowing that there was no harm in doing so—was to plant a subtle indication of how much he fundamentally differed from her. If she accepted it now, she would not be led into any sticky expectations later. It was all very well for her to lay down her own conditions at the start, no adhesions and so forth but he had seen that kind of cocky self-assertion go down the drain before.

'It doesn't shock me, no. I just thought, well, we're very much alike in a lot of ways, but I can't say I'm ambitious at all. I certainly don't want to be *distinguished.* Maybe that's because I'm a woman, of course.'

Paul did not like the way she had of rationalising awkward points. Before they got into a level of their affair where she could start identifying with him too strongly, she would have to be made to understand that, whatever pains it might bring on, his career was of primary importance to him. She did not fit the scheme. He knew it was neither gallant nor fair, but it was very much how he was. His nicer aspects, if he had any, were reserved for his work and for occasional spectacular display during his flashes of human sympathy. That was it in a tidy nutshell—the real Paul Avery was the doctor. The other man was Paul Avery switched off.

'I'll tell you something about yourself,' he said, massaging her shoulder with the palm of his hand. 'You're lacking in artifice. It's no crime, but it's the thing that'll keep you predictable. People without a lot of artifice don't have too much ambition.'

'Are you telling me I'll get nowhere?' She crossed one leg over the other, letting her short skirt fall back unheeded and simultaneously loosening Paul's grip on the flow of his spiel.

'No. You've got natural intelligence, you're smart, bold, courageous, skilled . . . all that can carry you a long way. What I'm saying is that you won't use your abilities and characteristics as any kind of lever. You couldn't, even if you tried. You're Mary Scott, State Registered Nurse, and you're all out in the open. When you say you're like me, you should realise that you're like one side of me.'

'Thanks for the lecture.' She blew a refined raspberry in his ear, but beneath the joking, he knew the message had landed home. 'I may not have ambition, but thank God I've got my sanity. Look at that poor woman tonight. A religious nutter. That was horrible.'

'I saw one once who put her hands in a mechanical press, just because she had touched a man, after taking a vow of chastity.'

'Chastity! That's another weird idea.' She suddenly snatched at his crotch, making him howl. 'Oh, I'm glad I'm not clean-minded, or ambitious or chaste!' She bit his neck. 'I'm just dirty little Mary Scott, who fancies having it off before the conversation turns us both frigid.' They rolled about on the couch, laughing and shouting, and Paul realised that not only had the message got home to her, but she was telling him that it was accepted. Now why couldn't Edith be as straightforward and down-to-earth as that?

Afterwards, when they had exhausted their glandular ambition and lay naked together on Paul's bed, Mary became quite serious. She usually did, Paul had noticed. A good part of her usual bounce and sparkle was probably accountable to her sexual drive. Like the Dead Sea, he mused; so full of salt that it would hold up any weight, but without the salt it simply would have allowed the lightest object to sink. That was Mary. Drained of her sex content—whatever *that* was—she ceased for a time to be any sort of support. She needed to be held until her cells recharged.

'What's going to happen to our ambulance, Paul?'

'You sound like you think it's threatened.'

'Well, isn't it?'

He raised one knee and plucked thoughtfully at the dark hairs. 'It might be, I don't really know. I'm in the dark, Mary. There's a flaw but I can't find the root. Troubles attend a lot of new schemes. It could just be some natural law, or an absence of deep-down skill on our part. It's like when you give an injection. At first, when you haven't done it very often, you know the mechanics and that's all. Later, it's an instinct, and you probably make a much better job of it. Maybe we're so green we just aren't doing our work as well as we do it in really familiar surroundings.'

'Do you really believe that?'

'No, I don't.' An impulse that was no more than a natural gesture, uninformed by any desire, made him put out his hand and brush her tight pubic curls. She lay with her knees slightly bent, her thighs turned outwards in an open attitude which Paul considered to be the equivalent of the open palms of patients who decided to level with the doctor. She was moist, warm, and his fingertips dipped within her, gently mashing the pliant flesh.

Mary put her head close to his and grunted deep down in her throat. She adored to be fondled after sex, unlike Edith, who could not bear to be touched once she was spent. Paul did not want to talk about the ambulance. He was going through the gestation period of a course of action. Left to simmer within his reasoning centres and his memory banks, the dilemma would re-shape itself to become a recognisable problem. Problems always had answers, and when he knew the precise nature of a hurdle, he would put on the appropriate jumping shoes.

'Let's not talk about the unit, Mary. Just let me say that I'm working on the trouble. All the facts have been put in my computer and it'll come up with a clear picture soon. I've even fed in that business with the fractured oxygen pipe and the empty cylinders.'

'Do you think that was sabotage?' She asked the question in a whisper, her breath rising and falling with the rhythm of her hips, which were now moving in response to the action of his hand. Her cells charged quickly when they were assisted and encouraged.

'I said let's not talk about it.' He kissed her forehead and reluctantly added sabotage to the programme of possible problems. He could not believe it, but there was no point in being a bigot. He rolled on to his side, permitting his hand more scope. Despite himself, he began to wonder where an answer might come from, from what portal the light would pour forth and spring the lid of his action box. Perhaps there would be no eureka, perhaps the fog would persist until the entire scheme died and his reputation developed the tarnished skin of professional error. He bit his lip and told himself to stop it. Work was work, bed was bed.

'I wonder if Ellen Haxton ever screws?' Mary's throaty speculation helped to bring him back to the present.

'I thought you girls knew all about each other?'

'Ellen isn't really one of the girls. She's quite a loner. Never goes out, doesn't drink, doesn't do anything but work, as far as anybody knows.' It was curious, and faintly amusing, that Mary could chat quietly about something while she lay back with her legs spread open, churning against Paul's busy fingers. Her speech, like the movements of her body, was slow and deliberate. It occurred to Paul that she was perhaps turning herself on by wondering about the sex life of the quietest nurse in the hospital. She had already admitted that her fantasies were unusual. So far, though, she had not been specific.

'Perhaps she sublimates her drives. Work, especially her kind of work, can soak up most of a person's urges, Mary. In your case of course, everything's in the right bag. Ellen's a religious girl, isn't she? That can be a big drain on the emotions.'

'Yes, she's secretary of the Catholic Nurses' Union in Westfield. I think there's only her and two or three others. Odd, though.' She paused and closed her thighs for a brief moment, trapping his hand and arching herself. 'If Ellen doesn't indulge, she's crazy.'

Cross infection, Paul suddenly thought. She *was* using talk and thought about an absent third party to spice her activity, and it was working on him now. Mary's hand had found his penis and she was stroking him with lightly encircling fingers, linked in their pace to her speech and body actions. He was hardening again. Removing his hand from between her legs, he rolled over, straddling her, placing the tip of his erection lightly on the damp entrance to her vagina. She was looking up at him, her mouth tightly shut, eyes expectant. Testing himself, he closed his eyes and pictured the demure Ellen, remembering the soft brushing of her knees against his at the party, then inventing a surprisingly vivid picture of her laid out under him, still in uniform, the crisp blue dress drawn up to reveal firm thighs and a gaping, eager crotch.

'Christ!' Mary gasped the word as he lurched into her and began to assault her with fierce short strokes. With limited, urgent caresses and pinched cries that sounded like pain, they strove together as if they were enclosed in some container that restricted their movement. When he came, Paul slammed against her so hard that Mary's head struck the board at the top of the bed. The accidental violence whipped her own climax to a higher curve and she emitted a hoarse scream, digging her nails into his buttocks and holding on until the spasm passed.

It was several minutes before they even moved. Paul disentangled himself gently and stepped clear of the bed, grinning at Mary as she curled into a ball and rolled her eyes upwards, as if she were deranged.

'There's a joke about that somewhere, isn't there?' she said.

'About what?'

'One hippy screwing another. He's grinding away for a minute, then he says, "Tell me who you're thinking about, and I'll tell you who I'm thinking about." '

He scratched his stomach and shook his head. 'Terrible. Poor Ellen, she's probably tucked up in bed with a prayer book under her pillow, and here we were using her for lust fodder.'

'My personal twist,' Mary said flatly. 'I've even used Dr Roberts from time to time.'

Adhering to the tactit taboo, on his side at least, concerning any mention of Edith, he stretched and announced that he was going to take a bath.

'I'd come with you,' Mary announced, reaching for the edge of the sheet and drawing it over her shoulder, 'but that would only put more ideas into my corrupt little head.'

In the tub, he lay back and soaked for a while, pleasantly detached, not thinking particularly hard about anything. Perhaps this was Ernie's secret. He was a man who could cut across the difficulties of life without collecting much guilt or confusion on the way. He was a constant fornicator and he had admitted that he occasionally feared for the security of his heart, such was the strain he placed on it. There was no doubt that a full release of the tensions seemed to be possible in bed. The equation, if it was accurate, was simple. Sexual excess equalled balanced living; the converse might be just as simple to pin down—repression equals confusion. He thought of Edith and the reasoning became a shade more convincing. Maybe this was the way to undo his knot about the Life-Support Unit. He smiled to himself and began to apply lather to his arms and legs. Even if frantic regular copulation was the answer to a person's confusions, Paul would never be able to find an acceptable way to publish his findings.

13

Beatrice Victoria Cowell was a fussy girl, the sort of person who would immediately empty an ashtray of one cigarette end, or finish a domestic polishing task by running the duster over the can from which she had applied the polish. She had been in service since she left school, because her mother had told her that there was no better occupation for a girl of her station. The lowly born, she had been constantly reminded, could be ennobled by devoting themselves to the service of the privileged. Beatrice was twenty-six now and the life, though hard and at times frustrating, gave her a strong sense of security. Her employer was a pleasant, absent-minded gentleman who was always working and his wife, also pleasant though she drank too much, was civil enough to give Beatrice an occasional extra day off if she had been ill, or put an extra pound note in her wages when it was a birthday or at Christmas. Beatrice supposed she was happy; she would probably never marry, because of her looks, but she had the compensation of being needed. Giving full satisfaction was her primary aim, so it was all the more irritating and embarrassing that she should have slipped on the tiles that morning and fallen on a glass table. The table was ruined, and worse, the blood that had leapt from her gashed side had marked the porous pseudo-Mexican wall for good. She did not suffer very much pain, but by the time the efficient-looking ambulance arrived, she was losing consciousness, aware of a feeling of lightness and cold.

The distracted, gin-smelling lady of the house tried to explain what had happened, pointing to the blood on the wall, trembling while she sucked on a cigarette and eyeing Ferdie Nesbitt's dark skin with as much hostility as her concentration would permit. Ellen Haxton and Lester Hill placed the stretcher beside the chalk-white girl where she lay on the hall floor and removed the blanket from her body. The sight was alarming. Beatrice was lying in a warm pool of her own blood, a seeping dark semi-circle that issued from a five-inch tear in the side of her black dress. Paul Avery, entering the house after the others, took one look and clapped his hands once, loudly, stilling the woman's chatter and turning the heads of his team.

'Get her into the wagon double quick. Ellen, set up the blood. Madam, could you come with us and give some details to the people at the hospital?' Before the woman had time to reply she was hustled out of the door behind the fast moving stretcher and helped into the cabin.

Paul followed, climbing into the back of the ambulance where Ellen Haxton had already set up a bottle of O-negative blood, the universal donor group. The patient was very still, the colour of ivory, her unpainted lips standing out against her pallor like a vermilion gash.

As the ambulance moved off, Paul had already determined that the girl had suffered a ruptured spleen. The flow of blood from the wound was reduced by now, but the very absence of blood in her system was placing her life in grave peril. It was necessary to arrest the loss and replace the blood at speed.

'Nobody should die from blood loss alone,' Paul announced, placing a sterile glove over his right hand and probing the wound. He was not an advocate of swashbuckling surgery, but there were times when it was the only course open. It would take fifteen minutes to get back to the hospital, and in that time a great deal of deterioration could occur if drastic steps were not taken.

He found that the splenic veins were bringing blood straight into the wound. It was an ironic situation, for the spleen acted as a store-house for blood, and during haemorrhage from any other part of the body it would pour blood into the circulation. Now it was acting as a major exit for Beatrice Cowell's life. 'I'm going to hang on to the artery, nurse. I want you to get as much blood as you can into her. Can you handle a large-bore catheter?'

Ellen Haxton nodded. For an instant he recollected his fantasy a couple of nights before and he felt a tremor of something very personal at the sight of her face. The moment passed and Ellen was busily preparing to pass the requisite catheter into the patient. A large needle had first to be inserted in a vein at the elbow, then through this was threaded the flexible catheter, which could then be passed along the vein until its tip entered the superior vena cava. It took her only a minute to accomplish the feat, and Paul, bent awkwardly over the patient with his fingers tightly clamping the splenic artery, smiled his appreciation as the blood started to flow into the patient. 'Swing across the other holder, will you nurse? I want another transfusion in to the external jugular vein.' The second blood inlet would act as a reserve, and drugs, should they be necessary, could be injected directly into the flow.

'Lester, go through into the cab and radio the hospital. Tell them it's a torn spleen, and we estimate she's lost four pints of blood. And you'd better stay in there for the rest of the trip. I don't think that woman likes the idea of being isolated with Ferdie.'

They arrived at casualty within ten minutes. En route, the only supplement to the blood transfusion had been an infusion of two hundred millilitres of ten per cent mannitol, a natural sugar that had once been used as a test agent but which nowadays was used therapeutically. It protected the kidneys from failure in cases of low blood pressure. In common with every other medical man, Paul had no clear idea why it worked, but it did and he was glad of any help he could have, explicable or not.

In casualty, Paul explained what measures had been taken and a junior surgical officer wrote down everything, then read it back for double accuracy. The patient had been given three pints of blood and probably stood in need of some more. From here on, it was the surgeon's job to follow up the efficient emergency care.

Thirty minutes later, while Paul was squatting in the ambulance, checking the list of equipment in the boxes, Ellen Haxton came forward and told him that Beatrice Cowell was dead.

'What?' For a moment his brain refused the data. He would not allow himself to connect the name to the patient with whom they had dealt so promptly and positively. She was young, there was every reason why she should live. He rose to his feet, the temper that he kept so well controlled beginning to push its way through his caution. 'What in the name of Jesus happened?'

'They didn't even get her on the operating table. I don't know the details, doctor.'

Before Ellen had finished speaking he had jumped down past her and was storming towards the theatre. He found the surgical officer to whom he had spoken earlier. He was a timid young man called Frazier, and he looked rather apprehensive as Paul strode in with his coat tails flying.

'So tell me what went on here.'

'The patient died from heart failure.' Frazier looked at his hands. 'I think it was overloading.'

'Holy shit! Overloading? Wasn't anybody monitoring her central venous pressure?' It was rare for a patient to be given too much blood, and in circumstances where expert attention was available it should not have happened at all. 'Who was in charge?'

'Mr Madison.'

'And how in hell did he let things get to that stage? What was done about the failure? Was there any rescue action at all?' In the heat of his outrage, Paul had grasped Frazier's lapel and was twisting it. His eyes were staring like a prophet's, and he gave every appearance of a man about to hit somebody.

'There was another haemorrhage,' Frazier yelped, trying to draw away. 'Things got very complicated.'

'They must have, friend. That patient should have been on the table five minutes after she got here.' He ran his tongue across his drying lips. 'Where is Madison?'

'I am here.' He was standing just inside the theatre door, glaring at the scene. 'Just what do you think you are doing Dr Avery?'

Paul released Frazier's coat and crossed to within three feet of Madison. 'Can you tell me why that girl died?'

'She died as a direct result of right heart failure.'

'Caused by overloading, as I understand.'

'Yes, that is so. It has happened before, doctor. This was an emergency, and a thousand complications can interfere with prompt surgical action.'

'But overloading, for God's sake.' Paul pushed his fingers through his hair, finding his anger increased by Madison's detached pose. 'Not even in the crummiest cottage hospital—'

'Are you implying some mismanagement doctor?' Madison's eyebrows had lifted a fraction, prepared to be shocked. 'Is that what you are saying?'

'Yes!'

'How dare you!'

'Mismanagement with a great big M! You've exterminated a patient who should have been okay! This—' he swept his hand around the green tiled room, 'this isn't an operating theatre, it's a goddamned slaughterhouse!'

Madison was trembling and for a moment he could not speak. As Paul made to push past him, he placed one slender hand on the door. 'I think you should consider an apology before you go.'

'Apology? I'll tell you what I'm going to do, and I've already had time to give it full consideration. I'm going to draft a report and it's going upstairs. I'm raising an objection, Mr Madison. And I'm apologising for nothing. If you spent more time looking after the patients and less on making sure the etiquette was up to scratch, you wouldn't find people like me coming in here and saying things that make you want an apology.'

For the second time within a week, Henry Madison found himself quaking in the sidewash of an outrage committed by one of the medical vermin who lay at the root of all his unrest. As Paul passed him and punched open the rubber door, the old man's cheek began to twitch, responding to an intense desire to speak, to exert authority with the sound of his voice, as he was used to doing and as he was fully entitled to do. Frazier, trying for a stealthy exit by the opposite door, froze as the consultant's voice ripped across the echoing theatre. 'In future, you will discuss nothing with that man. Nothing, do you understand?'

Frazier nodded. 'Very well, sir.'

'He is an undesirable who will not be in this hospital much longer. Bear that in mind, whenever you feel tempted to let your proper loyalties slip.' He turned and left, his jaw set and his eyes wide with boiling anger. Frazier stayed where he was for several minutes, before slipping out through the side room. He was finding it difficult to work under Mr Madison, and he was also unhappy about the man's sense of procedure. Avery might be a fireball with no sense of respect, but he was right; that girl shouldn't have died.

Paul's official complaint was in the hands of the Medical Superintendent by the following morning. He had stayed up all night to finish it. By carefully going the rounds of theatre personnel, and by applying a heavy dose of charm, he had managed to obtain a fairly detailed account of what had happened to Beatrice Cowell. It appeared that confusion had piled on confusion, and one act of repair had cancelled another, time after time. There had also been some very slipshod technique applied to the sick woman's body. A clamp had slipped out of position during transfusion; when the trolley was being wheeled towards the theatre the wheels had jammed, and it was found that a wad of paper had become lodged in the supporting pillar; a doctor appointed to check the patient's blood pressure had been harrassed by constant freak calls on his communicator; nurses had found that a tray of instruments required for a splenectomy had become contaminated with what looked like milky coffee. Not one person in theatre at the time of Beatrice's arrival had been able to function properly. In every case, although it was only admitted reluctantly by a few people, Mr Madison had issued conflicting orders, delaying the start of the operation and causing a measure of neglect that had resulted, in Paul Avery's opinion, in the death of the patient.

He phrased his complaint carefully. The heart of his argument was that he could not, in conscience, be responsible for an emergency service that was not able to rely on routine efficiency at the hospital. While he recognised that mistakes frequently occurred, the instance under consideration revealed a randomness and a fundamental absence of organisation that would have shamed a rioting mob. One mistake, he pointed out, was bad enough though probably unavoidable. Two, three and four hinted at something wrong somewhere; ten or more, as listed in his summary, was open anarchy. In summing up, Paul said that as leader of his own unit, he was responsible for every lapse, and he was fully prepared to shoulder the responsibility. In theatre that day, a senior consultant had presided over a series of disasters which, if they were to be subjected to public scrutiny, would result in a major inquiry. He hoped, in closing, that some notice would be taken of his complaint.

James Towers had been a physician for many years before entering administration. He had the bearing and, to a large extent, the outlook of a military commander. In the Royal Army Medical Corps he had learned the value as well as the shortcomings of proper discipline. As superintendent of a large hospital, he had often found that a dose of old-fashioned drilling mixed well with a modern, go-ahead policy. In the case of Henry Madison, he was faced with something unique. The consultant was the champion of a disciplinary code that made Dr Towers' own look childish. At every turn, at the least breeze across the old established principles, a memo would land on the desk, worded in Madison's terse style, demanding immediate repair to the breach in the traditional wall. Now, amazingly, the hospital's own American bright-boy, their very own man of the future, was complaining, from his modern and anti-establishment standpoint, about the old warhorse himself. It was a turn of events that held every feature of ironic comedy and serious precedent.

As a man, unconnected with his duties at the hospital, Towers could not bring himself to like Madison. The manner, the constant mindfulness of superiority and the disdain for other doctors was difficult to swallow. There were hints in Madison's make-up of a gentler soul beneath, a simple perfectionist who had been altered by a system that placed too much value on personalities and achievements. Even admitting that gentle undertow, Towers was still conscious of his essential dislike. Madison never agreed wholeheartedly with anything, however well it fitted-in with his own outlook. If he was not the originator of a scheme or a policy, he would either agree grudgingly or voice noisy dissent. Dr Avery's ambulance was an example; Madison had even alienated some fellow consultants by his heated resistance to the unit. It was not so much that his argument was faulty, it was the energy with which he supported it. Fanaticism lay along that very same road.

After careful consideration, Dr Towers decided to speak to a few of the theatre staff himself. One by one, they came into his office and delivered their individual versions of the matter. The stories, given with varying degrees of reluctance, all tallied. They painted a picture of bumbling inefficiency caused, though none of them actually said so, by Henry Madison. It could be, Towers decided, that the man was losing his grip. A sharp reprimand would be a kindness, it would remind him of his humanity and perhaps put him back on his toes for a few more years. He decided that a letter, carefully worded and shrouded in enough old-style pomposity, would do the trick. He did not allow himself to dwell on the tiny spark of pleasure that sprang up as soon as he had made his decision.

The letter was delivered to Henry Madison at his home, and he read it over breakfast. For the first time that Amy could remember, he did not finish his porridge. Excusing himself with a cursory wave of the hand and a mumbled few words about something urgent to attend to, he went, with the letter, to his study. Behind the closed door, he sat and read the typed page carefully three more times, making five readings in all, then he crumpled it and threw it in the waste basket.

It was difficult to cope with the surging emotions, or even to separate them. Like a creeping malignancy the enemies were invading the system and reaching corners where their effect would be permanent. Henry Madison knew the full import of an official reprimand. In his letter, Towers had indicated that the complaint by Dr Avery had been noted. That meant it would be passed on to the board, and a mark against Madison's professional conduct would forever stand in the records at Westfield General Hospital. They had been checking up on him, behind his back they had been running round like hooded Arabs and gathering their facts, so that they could be built into a spear to stick between his shoulder blades. It was a bleak sensation, to be on the receiving end of official admonishment. Many, many times in the past Henry had been the instrument of complaint and punishment, and he was well equipped to know just how far and for how long the effects of top-level action could be extended. He was stained now; opinion and rumour and all manner of bad reputation could not hurt him, not until some of it became flesh and took solid stature in the records. Then it was a different story. He could expect to find his latitude restricted, his professional opinions to be regarded with rather less automatic acceptance. The charge was negligence, and there was no way at all to reverse it. Even an appeal would not erase the details which Towers had outlined in his letter. They would be written down, remembered, held up as a mark of his fallibility. If one emotion crushed him worse than the others, it was despair. He had lost his good name, and he had known long before he had ever read it in Shakespeare that he had thereby lost everything.

He sat quite still for several minutes, giving way to the lapping agony, wistfully recalling the stature, so recently departed, that had sat on him like a mantle. Like wildfire, the tale would be transmitted around the hospital. Madison's been officially ticked off for negligence and disorganisation. The humiliation was all the more severe when it was viewed in detail. Routine, strict observance of rules and procedures had been the flags under which his consultancy had flourished. He was being rapped for disregarding the things he had always most loudly supported.

He walked to the fireplace and rested his hand on the mantelshelf, staring across at the solid wall of books, the emotions shifting now. Anger, that was the next candidate for his attention. In all his years of practice, he had never before had to put himself in the kind of jeopardy that had resulted in this blow. It was all the fault of Avery, and his friend Hale. No doubt, no doubt at all, the complaint had been pressed by Avery as a supporting gesture for the despicable psychiatrist. They were prevailing, taking power and using the appointed authorities to help their plotting. That woman, the one with the torn spleen, had been sacrificed for a principle that transcended mere considerations of life-saving. Henry knew that he was appointed to take life as well as give it. No one who studied a surgeon's place in society could deny that. Decisions that resulted in death were commonplace, now as much as ever before. Within the terms of his profession, his decision was always acceptable, whether it resulted in a life saved or lost. What he had done, all of the things he had done in order to discredit the abominable Life-Support Unit—the *Avery* Life-Support Unit, no less—were justifiable; not to the authorities, of course, who had to maintain the double standard, the issuing of permission to kill but simultaneously retaining the right to reprimand and even prosecute any surgeon who admitted that he had deliberately done so. Henry Madison had no pangs of conscience. In each instance, a patient had died who would have died anyway, deprived of his expert intervention. If he had hastened the inevitable in one or two instances, that did not matter either, the facts stood: dying patients could be saved only by an expert, and then only if he chose to apply his skill. He had never seen the view expressed by any medical man, but a Danish philosopher had made it very plain. The book containing the concept was one of Henry's favourites and he re-read it often. From memory, he sustained himself with the clearest passage of all:

> *The man of medicine, when presented with a fellow who may be close to death, is qualified to exercise choice. By the special insights gained from his experience and his training, he is enabled to decide, often for reasons going beyond the superficial consideration of his rôle as a healer, whether his powers should or should not be applied. The morality of such a judgment is not for the ordinary man to assess.*

It made no difference to Henry that the philosopher had been dismissed in his lifetime as a crank. That happened to many men of vision; it had happened to himself on a small scale. The picture was clearer now, the quiet of his study had helped him to crystallise the random elements into a unified, understandable whole. He had foreseen the drawbacks to the new ambulance. He had argued his points and he had lost. But the principles were too important for him to simply drop and try to forget. So he had pursued his mission, which was to retain his own sovereignty and safeguard the future of a medical system that he had worked to preserve and enrich. That certainly went beyond any consideration of simple rescue. The dying had been allowed to go ahead and die; it was no crime, it was the mere exercising of a privilege for the sake of a very large and precious principle.

He probably had been too careless in his handling of the spleen case. Delay was all that had been necessary, but so many people at that particular time had seemed willing to assist that delay had degenerated into confusion and, for the first time, Henry had left himself vulnerable. And now he was paying, with a blot on his reputation. An official blot.

The anger surfaced again as he thought of the way those two men had spoken to him. They had treated him like some news-vendor, a man on a street corner to be abused and reviled at will. His hatred of them now had an element of fear, he observed. They could hit back, as if it were not bad enough that they could sway the authorities with their disgraceful tactics of cheap, vulgar, showmanship. Hale no doubt, would have a few rubber-spined people in authority to back up his scurrilous book, just as the trick-laden ambulance had its fervent advocates.

'Damn them!' He shocked himself with the loudness of his cry, and listened for a moment to hear if Amy had responded. Then he heard the sound of dishes being washed and relaxed a little. Above all, her respect and admiration for him, which had spanned a lifetime, must not be injured. Then he thought of Edith Roberts and a pang of sweet warmth seized his heart. Her respect, her continuation of their pact, must be preserved. He must pull himself together and shrug off this setback. That was all it was, a simple setback.

So one instance, one item in the catalogue of steps he had taken to put that ambulance and its founder in the bracket of failure where they belonged, had been detected; not even that, for the event was being treated as a lapse, not a felony. He would swallow that, would make himself do it, for the far greater issue of continued assault. Avery and Hale, despite any effort they might muster in defence, would go down. In future, Henry would be more careful, he would reduce the success record of the unit by the most cautious and meticulous of means. Subtlety was the watchword. He recalled with a wince how his first efforts, so crude despite the trouble he had taken, had almost been the subject of an inquiry. He had gone to the risk of purloining the ambulance keys from the dispensary, he had entered a restricted office and switched off an alarm and he had gone into the ambulance bay, equipped with only a torch and the keys, to undertake his task. It reeked of crudity and risk when he thought of it now. Emptying the cylinders had been easy, but the pipe link had resisted his twisting and, he had to admit to himself, it was an act of brute ignorance to strike it with the torch. No, in future he would operate within the safe blanket of his own special ability.

They could assail him with their puny weaponry as much as they liked, he would still win. He straightened his shoulders and prepared to go to the hospital, determined to maintain his dignity and resolving to keep up his fight. Virtue, after all, was on his side.

People had no idea what beauty meant. Not many of them, anyway. Ellen Haxton, at the end of a long shift, could draw beauty from her tiredness, she could detect fine depths in the release from duty and the enjoyment of her mind when it no longer had to adhere to the ordinary details of the present. Beauty, to any one of her immediate colleagues, was something crude when compared to Ellen's own understanding of the quality. Any object or sense or thought could excite admirable pleasure, if it was simply viewed from within. In violent death, there was always a terrible beauty, a dark and breath-stopping attraction that found its response in Ellen's soul, in the place where her pity resided. Death was not an end, so horror was not appropriate. It only needed a little sensitivity, she knew, to spend a lifetime of wonderment. Sickness, even when she suffered it herself, had beauty, for there was a taste of poignancy in the exclusion from everyday life. Ellen's whole existence pleased her and even when she was embarrassed or hurt some aspect of the event would turn, in time, to something pleasurable. She had decided this was possible when she was eighteen, and had believed it ever since.

One of the most pleasing aspects of her life was her room in the nurses' home at Westfield General. As a senior nurse she was entitled to privacy, and she had turned the room into a small home that suited her every need. Tonight, as at the end of every shift, she locked the door behind her and took in the place quietly, letting it welcome her. Then she went to the small bathroom and turned on both taps, returned to the main room and undressed slowly by the side of her bed.

There was a picture of a saint on the wall above the bed and she looked at it as she prepared for the bath. She had found, by regular study of the benign face, that the eyes had been applied with a finer brush than the other features, and they consequently held more life. They were not the kind of eyes that followed the viewer around the room, they looked off to the left, upturned slightly and filled with great sensitivity. The kind of inspiration that had been behind the hand of the painter was something that

Ellen sometimes understood. She had moments, sometimes hours of elevation where she knew, if she had been blessed with the technical skill, she could have made pictures full of the sort of life that only a spiritual fulness can produce. When she was naked, she looked at the picture a little longer, then crossed to the bathroom and turned off the taps.

Her adherence to routine would please her old tutors, she thought as she lowered herself into the water. Within the walls of her sanctuary she moved with a regulated decisiveness, right up to the time when she climbed into her bed. That, like everything else, had its beauty; a programme had the attraction of familiarity.

She had spent the last hour of casualty duty revising her notes for a gynaecology certificate she had plans to obtain. Qualifications were a great comfort when they began to pile up, and already she had quite a few. Lying back with her head resting on the end of the tub, she projected her knowledge across the screen of her lowered eyelids. Anatomy: the Fallopian tube . . . three to four centimetres long, three to five millimetres thick at the thickest point . . . inner end of tube pierces uterine wall, joining the uterine cavity . . . the outer end has thin finger-like processes—fimbriae—lying close to the overy . . . Concentration on a particular area always led to recall of specialised knowledge of the region. Ellen could detail the statistics for cancer of the cervix, automatically and without any recollective strain. Factors believed to lead to the condition included laceration of the cervix, chronic inflammation, erosion and any form of irritation. The subject of carcinoma disturbed her a little. It was necessary when thinking about it or working with it to suspend her theories about beauty. Ellen did not believe that the presence of something like cancer would prove her ideas wrong, it was simply that, she had not yet gathered the necessary courage to locate its redeeming features. Her religious principles were wrapped up with cancer too. The God of love was also the God of malignancy. For that matter, He was the overlord of pain, of suffering in children, of maiming and war and murder . . . She forced her thoughts back to the safer sands of her learning. Theology was not her good topic. She practised her religion from habit, and needed it the way a smoker needs a cigarette.

'Back to the tubes.' She spoke aloud to discipline herself.

With her eyes still closed, she considered chronic salpingitis. It was funny, but the condition was largely described as a catarrhal discharge. How many women knew they could suffer from catarrh of the Fallopian tubes? For such a small part of the body, the egg-pipes could be attacked by a huge variety of disorders. There was hydro-salpinx, haemato-salpinx, suppurative salpingitis, tubo-ovarian disease, a number of different cysts and tumours that could arise, and even in an undiseased set of tubes, trouble could occur in pregnancy. An egg could wander from one tube across to the other, become fertilised, produce the condition of ectopic pregnancy with a baby developing right inside the tiny tube. The whole reproductive region of the woman, so tiny in its span that it could all be easily held between two hands, was capable of giving rise to misery on a scale out of all proportion to its slightness. Even when no illness arose in the region, it could be a source of depression and even despair.

Ellen sat up and opened her eyes. It was not like her to be so morbid. The reason, she guessed, was tiredness bordering on exhaustion. It had been a hard shift, on top she had tried to cram in some bookwork and overlaying every other strain, there was her constant nagging worry about the Life-Support Unit. She stood up and reached for the towel. It would be safest, she thought, to simply give her mind a rest. That usually brought back her optimism.

Dried and wrapped in her warm nightdress and bathrobe, she found that she was not at all tired. Another sign of overwork. From time to time she found this happening, she would work hard all day, arrive in her room feeling washed out and ready to do no more than rest, but when it came to the moment to get into bed, she was suddenly alert again. Insomnia, of all things, she abhorred. Tossing and turning between rumpled sheets did nothing but wear out the scanty reserves of nervous energy, and it meant that next day she was useless for the first two hours, until the natural rhythms of routine brought her round. There were cures, which varied according to the true cause of her agitation. If it was worry, she would fix one stable fact in her mind and attach herself to it: worry was no more than the result of mental confusion, so finding some firm point from which to attack the disorder usually brought on enough relaxation to allow her to sleep. This often enough cleared up the bulk of the worry by processes she did not even want to understand. If it was simple over-tiredness (which tonight it was not) she would drink some hot milk and sit in a chair reading a light, undemanding book until she felt herself become sleepy. If the problem was sex, which her busy life and higher scruples did not altogether eradicate as a source of unrest, she would masturbate, using the lubricated handle of a plastic hairbrush between her thighs while her fingers played on her clitoris as she sat spread-legged in a chair and thought of being raped by a muscular black man with an enormous penis. The fantasy was an efficient one, just taboo enough to excite her to a quick release, which she preferred. No guilt ever ensued, for she saw the private act as a preferable to the awkward debauchery practised by so many of her colleagues, and far more practical than abstinence which only disorganised the calm she held so precious. If the wakefulness was caused by any combination of factors, she had her bottle of Dettol. It sat on top of the medicine chest in the bathroom and contained, in fact, not Dettol but Dewar's White Label Whisky. Standing by the dressing table, looking at her tired eyes and feeling more awake than she had all day, she decided that she needed the bottle, plus some soul-searching.

She poured a large measure in a tumbler and took it to her easy chair where she settled down in the soft upholstery and fixed her eyes on the gently swaying curtains at the window. She sipped, rolling the vaporous fluid around her tongue so that her throat might be accustomed before the first swallow. As she let it slip down and felt the slight shock beside her heart, she remembered Dr Avery's party, and how he had slipped her a vodka and orange, thinking he was being very sly. In truth, she had once been a heavy drinker, a private imbiber so scared of her work that she had to deaden herself in the evenings. But that had been in the early days, when so much could shock and frighten her. A lot of nurses turned to drink in order to counteract the stresses of their demanding work, others became highly promiscuous, others left the profession. Ellen knew she was one of the winners, among those who came to terms and adjusted. There was so much about her, she thought, that would surprise her present colleagues, especially those on the ambulance. Her genuinely shy front, her inability to mix with people, would no doubt lead to speculation of a cloistered private life, full of holy beads and disapproval of the others. She did not disapprove of anyone, certainly not anyone on the team. She had enjoyed the party and it had given her a warm feeling to know that she was part of a lively and useful group of people. Her personal preference for the quiet life, her absence of any desire to share her life with anyone, did not make her any less responsive to the spirit of teamwork. And the team, its work and its leadership, was what nagged now, as it had done for several days.

If she had been as thorough and practical in her examinations of the troubles as she believed, then they were either cursed, as the driver Dan liked to think or, more likely, they were being deliberately obstructed somewhere. To her own practised eye, there were breaks with established pattern that could only point at an unfriendly hand in the machinery. She knew, as any other trained nurse knew, that certain emergencies—and levels of emergency—worked out in certain ways. Yet the Life-Support Unit had, time and time again, brought in cases of a known nature which turned out, alarmingly, to terminate in ways she could never have predicted. It was not simply that so many of them died, for death was always one of the predictable alternatives in a serious accident, it was the way they died, as if they had picked up some new disease or injury the moment they came to the hospital. A man with a flailing chest wall died, if he died, in a way and with an atmosphere that was easily recognised, yet one such case recently had died with all the signs of a person who had been shot, or who had suffered a massive heart attack. Ellen was aware of just how vague her reasoning was. She could not use her feelings, her professional portfolio of half-instincts, to form any conclusion. Now, with half of the glass of whisky inside her, she realised that her suspicions could at least dictate a course of action. Nobody, so far as she knew, was doing much to root out the trouble, even Dr Avery seemed oddly inactive. The unit meant a lot to her, she believed in its aims and its ability. To do nothing at a time when it looked as if the project was running into bad trouble would have been less than loyal.

If her instincts told her that odd changes of pattern were occurring in the hospital, she supposed that the answer would be found by watching the intake carefully and checking the procedure. It was possible to believe that because the patients were actually arriving with some assistance already applied, the theatre and surgical staff were knocked off balance and were being less efficient than usual. That would not explain all of the oddities, but it would be a start.

At last in possession of a stable objective, a solid plan, she felt herself begin to ease up and relax. Beauty began to enter the picture again and as she drained her glass and prepared for bed, the most solid object of beauty in her life, Paul Avery, began to dominate her thoughts. She had no ambitions in that direction, she would not pursue a romantic attachment even if this (ridiculous idea!) ever appeared to be possible. He was simply admirable, so much more believable as a doctor and far more genuine in his regard for his calling than a number of allegedly dedicated medicine men. He was so open, so honest, even when it came to the touches of self-interest in his enterprises. And he was such a beautiful man. Ellen had never been slow to spot the really superior people, the ones who were attractive from the way they looked to the way they thought and acted. To be associated with Dr Avery was a privilege, and she asked no more than that. Anything she could do to help his Life-Support unit in its crisis time, she would be happy to do, for he deserved to win.

As she drew the sheets up to her chin and snuggled into the pillow, she admitted that there was some self-interest in her motive. Above all, Paul Avery must not be discredited for a fault not his own, but it would also be nice to think that she could work demurely at his side for a long time to come without the fear of the arrangement being disrupted. Easing down the slope to a state of half-dream, she paused to wonder, just for a moment, if he ever thought about her in his own private moments.

14

The youth was eighteen, and belligerent. He had long matted hair and a face that reminded Ernie of something moulded from a faulty batch of plastic which had distorted when it cooled. The left eye socket was markedly out of alignment with the right, which prompted Ernie to mentally dub the lad Isaiah (a remembered music-hall joke—'I call him that because one eye's 'igher than the other') and the nose, in common with the mouth, was twisted to the border of caricature. He was wearing a denim jacket and jeans with holes in them, and his shirt had girls' names written all over it in ballpoint ink. He sat in the chair opposite Ernie's desk with a clumsily hand-rolled cigarette stuck in one corner of his mouth, staring narrow-eyed through the stream of smoke, his hands clenched side by side in his lap. He had been referred by a court for a psychiatric report, and Ernie tried hard to concentrate on the case details before applying any opening gambit. It was hard to remain objective in the glare of the patient's open dislike. The added possibility of physical violence did not help. Ernie had been punched on the top of his head once before by a patient while he was reading the notes and since then his scalp had become ultra-sensitive to the likelihood of attack.

As with many of the cultural geniuses, Mark Jordan's most impressive work seemed to be appearing before he was twenty. He had a tightly packed docket of offence summaries ranging from robbery with menaces to attempted murder. The record was consistently violent, showing, at first reading, eight instances of assault where Mark's victims had required hospital treatment. The charge which had put him in Ernie's office involved a girl who had been systematically tortured, and the evidence showed that it was only the chance interference of a neighbour that had saved the girl's life. Ernie made a quick guess as a basis for investigation that with those looks, his aggressive approach and record, Mark Jordan might well be a casebook mesomorphic somatotonic. That was a short if tongue-tying way of saying he could be a man whose body-build was mainly constructed of tissues derived from the middle layer of the egg where he began, and that his behaviour was dictated by a need for excessive physical, muscular activity. To make him a case worthy of study in abnormal terms, the adjective paranoid would probably be apt enough. Paranoia, in its simplest form, consisted of a set of well-organised delusions, of grandeur and persecution. Ernie had found in the past that a court would take heed of a diagnosis if it sounded gothic enough. To say that Mark was a paranoid mesomorphic somatotonic would get more sympathy on his side than the bland announcement that he was rather dim, very physical and given to imagining things.

Ernie looked up and smiled. 'I suppose you're annoyed they sent you to me, eh?'

Mark's expression did not alter. 'I'm not annoyed. I expected it, didn't I? If you're expecting something, waiting for it, it can't really annoy you when it happens, can it?' His voice was rough, scratchy, as if he spent most of his time shouting.

'Well, if I don't annoy you—'

'You don't yet.'

'We'll get on, then. Tell me why you tortured that girl. Don't give me the story you gave the court. I want to know what made you want to hurt her, why you thought it was necessary.'

Mark lifted a finger and looked at the nail. 'She'd shopped me, hadn't she? She turned me in to the law. She told them about a job I did. She did it because her little brother got worked over by a couple of my mates about a year ago. So I got my own back.'

Direct enough, Ernie thought. 'Yes, yes, but why did you decide to do it the way you did? You were about to kill her, weren't you? Why was it not enough just to thump her?'

'I don't know.' He frowned harder at the fingernail.

'Mark, unless you cough your reason, you'll go back to that court with nothing from me that can lighten your sentence.'

'How can you get me off?'

'I can't get you off. But if I can show that you're not completely in control of the things you do, you could be sent to a hospital instead of a prison.'

'Yeah?' Mark was concentrating on Ernie's face now.

'So let me hear about your urge to cause that girl all that pain.'

'I'm not sure. Straight, I'm not, I can't just put my finger on it. It kind of grew up from nothing. I went after the bird and I didn't have anything planned. Just getting my own back. Then it got all complicated.'

'Did you feel she was persecuting you, did you think she had it in for you?'

That hit a button and Ernie decided to let paranoia stand. Mark had dropped most of his aggressive facial tension, and he was straining, so far as Ernie could tell, to tack the suggestion to what had really happened. 'I think that's maybe it. I hit her once, on the mouth, and when I did that I thought this cow has been setting me up, she's one of the creeps that want to put me in the shit hole.'

'Are there a lot of people who want to do that to you, or do you just believe it, without thinking about it?'

'I believe it. There must be a load of them.'

'Why must there be?'

'Because I'm big, I'm better than the rest. I'm not some fucking little petty thief or something like that. I've got talent, and if I put my mind to it I could really be the top. I'm not pulling your pisser, it's a fact.' He tapped his forehead. 'I've got plans up here that'd make Scotland Yard go bloody bonkers. So there's bound to be a lot of jealous inferior bastards trying to carve me down to their size, right?'

Paranoia could definitely stand, Ernie decided. 'So you worked on that girl to teach the others a lesson?'

'Partly.'

'What was the rest of it?'

'Look, chief . . .' Mark gestured impatiently, looking about the room, as if he hoped to find a queue of others waiting for attention. 'I can't get it all together, just like that. It's complicated. I sort of wanted to do that to a bird for a long time.'

'How long?'

'Years.' His hands linked in his lap and he leaned forward a fraction. 'It's a bit of a turn-on, you know?'

Sadism. This could become complicated. Real sadism was not all that common among active criminals. It remained, for the majority of people suffering its influence, no more than a condition of mind, fed and satisfied by books, films and magazine stories. The typical sadist was a meek person, one who longed to be the kind of man or woman who could be in a position to inflict pain on others. Mark was quite obviously in a position to do that whenever he wanted. If he was a bone-deep sadist, he would need watching for the rest of his days. The interview would have to stop right now while special tests were set up.

'Mark, I'm going to call a halt. I know it looks as if we haven't started yet, but there are good reasons. I want to give you as strong a case as I can, and to do that, I need a lot of scientific-looking paperwork.' He hoped that did not sound too patronising. 'If you go back to the centre with the men who brought you, somebody will be along later to give you some little tests. They're simple things, but they're important. Okay?'

'Whatever you say.'

Ernie pressed his bell and two guards, who had been standing by the door all along, came in and took Mark away. When he had gone, Ernie turned his swivel chair and faced the window. He could see the dark van, and after a few moments he saw Mark being put inside and driven off. That was the richest territory of all, a young mind that held the seeds of every kind of evil. The amount that could be learned, if only some system of testing could be set up, was probably enormous. The possibility of cure would not come along for ages, but extensive testing would at least bring the time nearer. He would have tests conducted to estimate Mark Jordan's reservoirs of psychic energy and to measure the relative strengths of his life and death instincts. It would be possible to draw a graph showing energy tensions, another describing how much or how little the boy's Ego was in contact with his Id and his Superego. The effects of frustration on function would be judged, and a great deal would be made of the chart dealing with Mortido, the tensions of energy relieved by destruction and violence. Not many judges went along with the underlying purpose of Mortido, which Ernie believed to be self-preserving.

When he laid the scheme out flat in the light of his experience, all the work for Mark Jordan would probably do no more, at best, than ensure that he would be put away for the rest of his natural span. But there was hope in that kind of decision, and where the truly bedevilled person was concerned, Ernie wanted more than anything to offer him real hope. Without so far working out *how* he would do it, Ernie wanted, one day, to start working on a cure for the people he had seen who were locked up with their own private sets of devils. Perhaps it was because he identified with them to a great extent. Ernie Hale had devils of a different kind, but they were just as destructive as Mark's. They had pulled him off his true path, and he had no wish to let them be stopped—just like Mark, who probably drew comfort from his obsessions and urges.

That morning, Ernie had filled a briefcase with research, a lengthy study which, if connected with his work, would have won him an honorary fellowship or two for sheer energy. He had used friendship, authority, wheedling, veiled threats, personal magnetism and a gift for making people just talk, and now possessed a rundown on Henry Madison that had enough levers within its coils to make the consultant back down ten times over. Having done it and felt the flatness that follows every triumph, Ernie had sat in his car and wondered just where the hell he was taking himself. If he had heard about anyone else doing this his professional opinion would use words like neurotic, obsessed and ego-ridden. That was him all over. Like young Mark Jordan, Ernie was a demon when off the main track and after revenge. Also like Mark, he had been gleefully anticipating going further, becoming vindictive both because he thought Madison was a rat to try to ruin his book and because he wanted to get back through Madison at all those people who might want to persecute him for seeking popular fame. A clear cut case of paranoia or, as it was sometimes called, the instinct to win.

He felt better now, of course. He could point out all the differences in his disturbance compared to Mark's. His intention was primarily good, he wanted to see that he did well and that the public enjoyed a very entertaining book. Mark was anti-social, doing no good to himself or society. Where Mark's special urges produced hurt, Ernie's were aimed merely at stopping hurt—to himself, of course. Ernie Hale was no maladjusted, soul-sickened psychopath, he was a young man with a vigorous and laudable desire to get on. He felt better now. He had all he wanted on Henry Madison; he would forget how much he had enjoyed gathering the dirt.

There was one more patient to see, a playwright whose brilliance was turning his mind, then Ernie had the rest of the day free. He had talked Paul Avery into coming with him for a bite and a talk. The pleasure of sharing was only part of it for he felt that Paul might well be, as he had suspected, a candidate for Madison's virulence. He spun the chair back round to face the door. I'm feeling fine, he thought. Although I should be feeling better.

He pressed the button on his desk. Half a minute later a man in a flowing herringbone tweed coat and a floppy-brimmed velvet hat swept in and closed the door theatrically behind him. He waited with a wide, agonised smile across his hawklike features until Ernie indicated that he take a chair. 'How are we today, Mr Sheldon?'

'Not yet vacated, doctor,' the man said, his eyes furtive. 'We still bear the festering burden of dead hopes and seething ideals. Everything still teems from me, but there is no order or cleanliness. My brakes have gone, I'm afraid.'

'Have you tried doing what I suggested? Forcing just ten simple sentences out from the chaos?' Ernie regarded the man as a difficult case. His problem was in the region of breakdown, but dealing with it was hampered by the eccentricity which sometimes threw out false clues. When he was in complete control of himself, Sheldon was probably still a very odd person.

'Not possible!' He clapped his hands in emphasis and shook his head vigorously. 'Can't be done. A word cannot escape without its adherents. Words are sticky. The solitary word picks up some more, each of the additional words fetches out a few more, and so on and so on. The whole store-house must be exploded, blown up, so that we can re-stock with smooth, non-tacky language and ideas. God, my ideas . . . ' He fingered his chin, looking forlorn, like a father just bereaved. 'The best of them are diseased now, infected by the matter I rejected ages ago. The damned stuff won't be jettisoned though. It hangs around my head, like a sack of dung. Mind you, those tablets helped me a little.'

Ernie had prescribed Prothiaden, to cut back some of the anxiety. 'Did they help your work?'

'I think they were responsible for a wonderful idea I had, a scenario about a family struggle. I took a couple of the tablets and I was lying on my bed when it all started to form. The setting is a desert, you see. That symbolises the aridity of family life, the vast emptiness that typifies the state. Mother and father are always fighting, holding each other by the throat, even when they speak their quieter lines. The children are filthy, messy, eternally crying and hurting themselves and destroying what little property the family has. So one day a storm threatens, a dust storm that will blow them all away and split them up, divide them by distances that will make it impossible for them ever to communicate again.'

He was speaking more and more quickly, his hands flying from side to side to enclose the action of his deranged drama. 'By the time the storm arrives, the tension of the waiting has brought a great deal of truth to the surface. The father looks forward to the release from his responsibilities, the mother longs to be free and again become a single, desirable human being, while the children want desperately to be allowed to practise their savagery without hindrance. The storm comes, splits them up, and we see their new lives, dotted about the big desert. Now that they are not so wrapped up in the exhausting mess of their unity, each one notices that the desert is not so bare after all. Opportunities occur, advantages are seen and pursued, and each becomes a great success, but not in the ways they imagined.' He was out of the chair, leaning close to Ernie. 'You see, the point of the story is that the family state inflicts false horizons on people. They all think they know what they do if they had the freedom, but freedom has its own landscape, and it imposes its unique drives on people. I haven't been able to work it out on paper, though.' Sheldon sat down again, looking exhausted. 'Everything gets knotted up when I try to express it.' He sighed. 'It's a terrible business, doctor.'

Ernie had an idea. 'Have you ever tried dictation?' It was not an answer to the trouble, but it might bring the answer within reach.

'No. I presume it would be just as bad if I spoke my scripts. The ideas come from the same place, you know, whether I speak them or write them down.'

'But the sound of your voice might help to impose a balance. It could enforce order. I think it's worth a try. All you have to do is convince yourself that you can still do your stuff, Mr Sheldon. That would be a big step.'

'Very well, I'll try it. But as I see it, the problem is still one of accumulation and blockage at one of my sewage outlets. The matter which I wish to throw out stays put, and it winds itself around my good material.'

'Try my suggestion, anyway. Use a tape recorder, and when you've talked to it for an hour or so, play it back and try to detect the points where you're falling down. Stay vigilant, Mr Sheldon. Don't let the part of you that is anti-productive interfere with the productive quarter.'

Somewhere outside, birds were squabbling in a tree. A car engine coughed, refusing to start, and a girl could be heard laughing. Ernie wondered if Sheldon could hear any of that, or if he was so embroiled in the hubbub of his mind that he was lost to the stabilising sense of distance and personal insignificance. Ernie talked some more, explaining that disorder in the mind could become a hobby rather than an affliction. People who started out with a problem often moved to a point where they supported it and kept it alive long after it should have died a natural death. Often, hoping for an improvement and trying not to over-tax the mind was all a patient needed to do to bring about a recovery. Compared to Mark Jordan, Sheldon was lucky. He was not mad, he suffered no pathological disorder. His trouble was largely behavioural and arose from too much intellect and too easy avenues of self-expression. He needed to tie himself down to a murderously difficult plot, and stick with it for a year or two. His mind would then feel satisfied, there would be no rebellion at the end of the work because the intellect would not feel prostituted.

'Come and see me again in two weeks, Mr Sheldon. And remember, the answer is with you. I have no magic cures, just helpful suggestions.'

The playwright left as flamboyantly as he had entered. Ernie wrote a few lines in his record folder and stood up, anxious suddenly to be away from the hospital. The prospect of a break was always pleasant, but today it was a strong need he detected. The details of Jordan's and Sheldon's cases pointed up too many parallels in his own situation. Overwork was not advisable for a psychiatrist, it laid his mind open to infection. It could start with the recognition of a trait, and it could end, as it had with a lot of practitioners, in the brain being invaded. Ernie took all the precautions, but sometimes they were not enough. He knew exactly what was going on inside Sheldon's head, he had felt it himself, and he knew that worrying about it, even giving it too much consideration, could have terrible consequences. Human beings today, no longer in the sort of immediate physical danger their ancestors had known, tended to create their own threats. Mental war games usually resulted in the individual being blown up by his own bomb. When he had been examining the levels at which Madison could be attacked, Ernie had been surprised to find that he was examining the details of details, splitting atoms to invest every move with deeper and deeper effect. That was obsessive, and it was in the nature of Sheldon's affliction. Head up, shoulders square, mind programmed for simple responses and obvious stimuli. That was the formula for survival. Ernie Hale worked hard, put a good deal of himself into every case; it was all the more important that out of hours he should pursue a life of relaxation. Wine, women and a bit of singing. He may well be regarded as a clown, but that was his insurance.

They had decided to go to a pub. Paul stocked up with two ham rolls and a pint of bitter. Ernie asked the barmaid to put two barley wines in one tall glass and he had a chicken salad. They took a table by the bay window, where they could watch the miserable inhabitants of Westfield going about their business. The food was eaten in silence, or without speech—Ernie's chomping technique with anything tougher than soup had prompted one colleague to remark that the food sounded delicious.

Wiping his fingers on the edge of the table cloth, Ernie

observed that Paul was looking tired. 'Is the strain of being a saint beginning to tell, mate?'

'The strain of screwing Mary Scott is pulling down my blood sugar, and that's a professional confidence. My balls feel as if they've been through a wringer.'

'Lucky sod. Cynthia's got one of those periodic doses of chastity women produce from time to time. She wants to feel there's something more to our relationship than just humping.'

'And is there?'

'No, there isn't. I've tried to make it clear, I've put out the warning lights I don't know how often. But she's still trying for a more meaningful arrangement. It's a disease with them.'

'Not all of them.' Paul took a gulp of beer, his eyes following a dustman on the street who was struggling to throw a loaded bin on to the back of his truck. 'Mary's got no plans for ensnaring anyone.'

'That's nonsense. One of the best ways of hooking a man is to make him think you're not interested. It's all tactics, Paul. And they all do it. They can't help it. By the way, you're noticably lacking in reticence where your little nurse is concerned. That could be a sign that you're dropping your guard, you know. And whatever is Edith going to say when she finds out?'

Paul's eyes wrinkled at the sides, the mark of a suppressed laugh. 'It's fun contemplating that, Ernie. I thought about it last night. What if she came storming into the bedroom and saw nothing but Mary's ass in the air where my sleeping head should be? I tried hard, but I couldn't picture the reaction.'

Ernie swallowed half of the powerful barley wine. 'I *can* picture it, Paul. Just you watch out. Either that, or unload Edith.'

'That's an old song, Ernie.'

'The old ones are the best. I've told you before, I don't want to interfere—I've told you that but it's not true. I do want to stick my nose in, and I'm telling you that you should get shot of Edith Roberts. She'll neuter you.'

'I told you I don't want to talk about it.' The dustman had given up trying to heave the bin and he was now unpacking some of the rubbish to lighten the load, his mouth working in patterns that did not need the powers of a lip-reader to interpret. 'There are sides to my life that you wouldn't understand, Ernie. Too subtle for a hack psychiatrist. Just stick to your gang of addled weirdos at the hospital. You'll get by that way. Me, I'm beyond your stretch.'

'Cheeky bugger.' Ernie finished his drink and indicated to the girl that he would like another. She pointed out that there was no table service and he groaned. 'Right, dear, I'll come over there. Don't want you to strain anything you might need later.' He took his own glass and Paul's, and when he returned, he was grinning.

'What's the joke?'

'You,' he said, easing himself back into his chair. 'You've got suicidal tendencies, but you think they're smart moves.'

'As usual, I don't get you.'

'Edith. You think she's the sort of class you can trot back to the States with you and use like a coat of arms. But she isn't. That woman will turn sourer and sourer until her vinegar gets into your own blood stream. There isn't a genuine laugh in her, and most of her smiles are artificial. I just can't see you doing that, Paul. It's the worst mistake you could make. You have terrible patches of blindness for a hot shot.'

'My, my. Aren't we being candid this bright day. Listen, Edith doesn't like you, you know that, so you should know that she's not about to smile at you and laugh it up whenever you're around.'

'She doesn't laugh around you either. Admit it. She's part of a society that's on the way out. She's genteel. Do you know, I have difficulty believing she's got genitals. I picture her being made of plastic from the waist down. And you can hit me for that if you like. I make my observations with good intent.'

'Just skip it, will you? You can maybe get inside a lot of skulls around that hospital, but you don't have the key to mine.'

Ernie nodded, a slow acceptance, eyes dipped, head bowed. 'OK. So be it. But if she means so much to you, how come you're playing around with that little sexpot? I'd say, strictly from my position as hack shrinker, that you were deliberately trying for a bit of salvation in spite of yourself. You're hoping to cause a showdown, you're hoping Edith will go through the roof and walk out on you and your lofty ideals. You won't feel guilty about throwing her over if you do it that way.'

'What do I have to do, Ernie, to make you drop all this? Did you get me out here today just to make a play for my salvation?

'No. I wanted to talk about another one of your blind spots.'

'Which is?'

'Henry Madison. I've been checking on him. Very thoroughly.'

Paul had some more beer, then put down his glass and folded his arms. 'You tickle me, Ernie. You go on about other people and their obsessions and their weaknesses. You've got a very dangerous thing about Madison. Could be pathological.'

'Oh yes? And what about that cock-up you nailed him for a few days ago? Wouldn't you say that some of my early fears were showing signs of being on the ball?'

'I blew my top, Ernie. I'm having trouble with the unit, and it did me no good to find that Mr Establishment was fouling things at the other end. But I don't see that as being—'

'Then just listen to this.' Ernie hoisted his briefcase on to the table. He withdrew a thick folder and dumped it before him, returning the bag to the floor and shifting in his seat, like a man about to deliver a lecture. 'Make sure you've got plenty of beer, mate. I don't want any interruptions halfway through.'

Paul regarded the stack of papers with some surprise. They were closely written, and there appeared to be marginal notes and cross-reference asterisks all over the place. In the past, when he and Ernie had discussed professional matters, he had noticed that his friend's learning went much deeper than he usually allowed people to think. These notes had the bulk and density usually associated with the findings of an advanced research project. 'What did you do, hire a team of investigators?'

'When Ernie Hale decides to defend himself, my Yankee friend, he does not piddle about. This pile of paper is going to be turned into a cannonball, and it's going to make a hole right through old Madison's line of attack. Now shut up and listen.' He cleared his throat and started to talk, keeping his eyes on the pages before him, looking up briefly only when he wished to emphasise a point. 'A string of contacts all over the country in hospitals, clinics and in private practice have fed me most of this data. It's dovetailed, one source usually corroborated another. I saw a kid with paranoia in the office this morning, but he had nothing on this old man for organisation and tactics. There is a record, and it runs like a thread right through Madison's rise to success, of violent and sometimes unbalanced reaction to opposition—any kind of opposition. Dr Freeman, my worthy chief, was only too willing to spill some beans. I got the impression he was just waiting to be asked. He doesn't like Madison at all but he's a generous man and did say that he had never missed any opportunity to see something good in the man. He won't fault Madison as a surgeon, but as a person he finds him an absolute crap heap. They're about the same age though I think Dr Freeman's a few years older. Anyway, my boss remembers a chap losing an appointment in surgery at the Makepeace Institute. It was a big surprise to everyone because the fellow was supposed to be really good at his job and the ideal man for the post. But he went down, and it just so happened that he was the only other contender for the fair hand of Amy Madison. Madison was pally with one or two of the people on administration at the time and Freeman says that everybody realised, eventually, what had happened. When the appointment was withdrawn the surgeon emigrated. In those days it was the best thing to do, you were finished in this country if you lost out on a key job. So Madison was left unhampered and married Amy, the poor old dear. Now listen to this one. Twenty years ago, Madison slapped a nurse on the face. He was in a rage because of some presumed slight, and it took a lot of oil to calm the waters afterwards. I located the girl, who isn't a girl any more, and she told me the lot. Madison first tried to get her fired when she threatened to make a complaint. He told her he was a man with a lot of power and could ruin her career. She didn't swallow that so he gave her money and got her to promise to leave the area. Imagine. Money. He could have gone over the wall for laying hands on a member of staff, so I suppose he had to do something desperate. But hitting her was a peculiar piece of behaviour, wasn't it?'

'Yeah, it certainly was. How much did he pay her?'

'Two hundred pounds. A lot of money twenty years ago. I think that gives us a measure of the price he put on his career. She thinks now that he would have offered her more if she'd stuck out for it. But her story is tainted with the same thing Freeman mentioned. She says Madison was always a bit strange, as if he had one very tight set of rails and if he got jogged he started to blow steam in every direction.'

'What else did you find out?'

'I've got details, really meticulous details, of objections to ideas and proposals, all from Madison and all directed at younger men. I've got letters, or copies of letters, he sent out to nursing organisations, recommending that certain people be reprimanded or cautioned for little lapses and the usual bundle of shortcomings you get on any ward in any hospital. The word "disrespect" keeps cropping up all the time. He's got terrific delusions of grandeur. There's a ward sister in Kent who remembers him spending weeks hammering at the hospital board to have her removed because she had no idea of what he called proper decorum. She sometimes forgot to call him "sir", for Jesus' sake. But that's nothing. I can't hit him with any of that, apart from the business of bopping the nurse. There are some really vicious little bits, and I've taken the trouble to follow them up. For example'—he flicked through the sheets until he found the one he wanted 'a fourth year medical student found his notes in ruins once. They were details of an experiment he had been conducting privately to study the effects of Eusol on leg ulcers. All his documentation was ruined and he found he was blocked from trying the experiment again. All facilities were withdrawn. Madison did it, the man is sure, and so are one or two people who are big enough to shoot their mouths off now. They'd still need coaxing, but they would do it, I'm certain. And the burns unit. Boy oh boy.'

'Burns unit?' Paul's awareness rose sharply at the mention of his area of special sensitivity and sympathy.

'A fellow called Struthers had almost clinched approval for a semi-experimental burns department in Westfield General, twelve years ago. Do you know that work they're doing in Texas right now? Direct tissue sampling, antibiotics straight into the infected areas, study of the reduction of salt levels—and saving lives where a couple of years ago it would have been impossible? Well, Struthers was on that kind of approach. And Madison got the idea squashed.'

'My God. How?'

'Influence and some bending of the facts. He first of all put up some smokescreen arguments. Priorities. Burns cases were being treated quite adequately in the surgical wards. No more could be learned about burning without the expenditure of massive amounts of cash, possibly millions. An experimental unit would achieve very little and the space and money could be put to better use—meeting the needs of understaffed and under-accommodated existing units. He backed up the clinical picture by quoting some really obscure joker from France who claimed that years of research had proved that burning would always be one of the areas where medicine could do very little. The bloke had a lot of unusual qualifications printed after his name, so he would obviously impress the board. Then Madison got a gang of his old chums to sign a petition, deploring the unit. It worked. It was perhaps only a coincidence that the man proposing the unit, Dr Struthers, was young, talented and very far-sighted. He's got his own burns unit in Canada now. And it's doing a lot of good.'

'I think you can skip the rest, Ernie. I get the picture.'

'There's just one more item I should mention, Paul. It kind of caps everything. Plenty of people have told me that Madison is very nasty with women. I think he's got a block there, and it's one of the creepy areas to have blocks. He was responsible, in the opinion of three very balanced people, for the suicide of a young female on his team. It happened just after the suppression of the burns unit. I understand the girl was a good doctor, a hard worker and very, very bright. Not everybody liked her but it was nothing serious, she just had an over-intellectual manner. Madison used to hound her. He would give her every tricky job, half as much again to do as anyone else, and would find fault all over the place. She was working on a paper, a good paper according to a consultant who wishes to remain anonymous, but the paper refuted something in one of Madison's earlier published articles. She couldn't get it finished, he kept her so busy. But she held on, and eventually got time off to go away and complete the paper. She went to a quiet resort on the south-west coast, and killed herself the night she arrived.'

'That's rough. Christ, Ernie, he sounds like a maniac.'

'I reckon he is. That girl's belongings were collected by the chap who is now a consultant. He's a very open person, but he doesn't want any sweat nowadays. He said her notes were ruined. Not one page of her paper was legible when he picked it up.'

'Just like the student working on leg ulcers.'

'Right. I'm not saying I told you so, but he's definitely not an average citizen, is he? You should have seen his face when I had that run-in with him last week . . .'

'I saw it when I tackled him about the girl who died. Quite the Mephistopheles. What are you going to do, Ernie?'

'I'm going to wait to see how far he goes on the subject of my book. If he tries to go ahead after I confront him with his past—'

'You'll tell him about what you've got?'

'Yes, I will. I think it's enough to shut him up. But if he tries to brazen it out, boom! I'll drop the lot where it'll do most damage. All's fair in a dirty fight.' He tilted his head. 'What about you, Paul? Don't you think you should now consider it possible that he's nobbling your enterprise?'

'That's something else again, Ernie. Hell, we're talking about the hard currency of surgery now. Lives. People dying—'

'I think you're sticking your head in the sand. Last week you lost one patient you didn't expect to lose. Whose fault? What was the name of the villain you tracked down? Think about that, Paul, it might not be such custard as you want to make yourself think.'

'Okay, point taken. And I know also that mental aberration has been found among big men in medicine before now. But you can see why I want to resist the idea, can't you? The Life-Support Unit is my baby. I want to think that if something's damaging it, it's not something that'll blow the whole scheme up in our faces. I want the unit to go on, I want that white beast to go on roaring up and down the highways. It could get choked out in a scandal. I'm still going to box cautious, Ernie. Let's just say you've convinced me that Madison's up the loop. I'll adjust my responses accordingly.'

'Do you think you can live with the idea that patients are maybe being sacrificed?'

'That's part of the caution, Ernie, I'll have eyes in the back of my head in future.'

They drank until the pub closed, then they drove back to Westfield in Ernie's car. In Paul's mind, there was a picture of threads, all of them trailing from the fabric of Madison. Somewhere in the waving strands there might be a knot, some overt act in Madison's make-up that would point a clear finger at breach of ethics. Waiting was still better, he felt, than rummaging among the tendrils and possibly causing a few artificial knots. But what Ernie had told him had left a shock mark. It all sounded so consistent, so ugly.

When Paul called at casualty to see if there had been any calls for him, he found a note asking him to attend the Medical Superintendent's office at four o'clock. There was no explanation, but he could guess. It just had to be the forthcoming report on the Life-Support Unit's first month of service. As he made for his quarters to change into a suit, he felt the grey clouds gathering. If any blood was going to be spilled over the matter, it would just have to be his own.

Dr Towers had on his strictly-business face. Beside him, behind the long desk, sat the chairman of the Board of Management, Sir Albert Macauley, dressed in a black suit, white shirt and scarlet tie. The one touch of colour helped to put some confidence in Paul's smile as he took a seat and dutifully refused a cigarette.

'It's the figures for the ambulance, doctor.' Sir Albert had obviously elected to do the talking, and Towers was backing him with the stern countenance. 'They're not at all good, as you probably know. We wondered if you could tell us anything that might throw light on this surprising state of affairs.'

They waited, not looking at all hopeful, as Paul prepared an opener. 'There is a flaw in the system, gentlemen. I don't deny it. But I don't know what it is.'

The laws of political argument did not really permit a man to place his neck on the block like this. Sir Albert cast a glance at Dr Towers, who glanced back, but remained silent. They were both waiting, hoping for more than this. Paul tried.

'There is a glaring group of losses, six now, that defies any analysis. Statistically, it's all wrong. People are dead who would not be expected to die even if the oldest, bumpiest, most badly equipped ambulance had brought them in. Yet they're gone. People badly injured, the group who might have been expected to survive because of on-the-spot emergency care, have died too, far too many of them. The figures are slightly worse than those for a badly run conventional unit.'

Dr Towers broke his silence. 'You have told us nothing we do not already know, doctor. Before a storm breaks, we would like to know if there is any factor at all, besides inefficiency, that you think may be contributing to this lamentable record.'

'No. As I said, I am looking hard, but so far I've come up with nothing. I'm satisfied that the staff are doing just as they should. They are efficient. I'm sure that the theory of our unit is sound, too. On-site assistance is bound to be a good thing.'

'Except that it does not appear to be the case in practice,' Sir Albert observed drily. 'Are you aware, Dr Avery, that a number of people on the board who will be taking face-saving about-turn measures when they see this report? And on the hospital staff there are those who will do likewise. And need I mention Mr Madison, whose loud cries of disapproval will be vindicated by this document?'

Paul spread his hands. 'What more can I say to you?' He looked from one to the other, transmitting his earnestness and his inability to manufacture explanations from thin air. 'If I felt there was any point of procedure or management that needed tightening, I'd see to it. You know how much care went into the devising of this unit. Findings and recommendations from all over the world were incorporated into our thinking. We got the finest of equipment, the very best people for the job and the greatest vehicle to carry our service. We are still working at top efficiency. I cannot understand it, and I'm sure you don't want me to invent excuses.'

'So we simply go ahead and publish the figures, without opening one path of hope?' Sir Albert sounded as if the idea appalled him. As one of those solidly committed to support for the scheme from the beginning, he had a good deal to lose in terms of prestige.

Paul folded his arms. 'I can only go on doing my job and trying to locate the defect. The figures are accurate and they have to stand. I understand there is a policy meeting in two weeks time. I will face whatever decision is reached then, gentlemen, and I'll accept it. In the meantime, I hope you'll add your prayers to mine and hope that I come up with something.'

Sir Albert exhaled loudly and nodded. 'Very well, doctor. We may as well leave it there. No use sifting the ground if you've already done that.' He smiled faintly. 'Just remember that I've still got faith in you, and I'm sure Dr Towers has, too. But faith isn't enough. Results young man. Get us some results, or an answer to why we've had such poor ones so far.'

When he left them, Paul went to the nearest telephone and called Ernie, who responded well to the suggestion that they continue their drinking session that evening.

Well into the night, they talked and discussed, dissecting what they had learned over the years and tried, combining irony and humour, to explain why they still had not mastered the art of living without dilemma. Both potentially under fire, they reduced their tensions to harmless tappings outside the door of their euphoria, and ended the night happy at least in their continued friendship and mutual support. In that condition, they both felt that they could tackle anything, anything at all that might be thrown into the arena.

15

Edith had gone through the kind of morning she called fragmentary. Not one task has been carried to a conclusion, she had started some, continued others and finished one or two for other people. It did not please her to work like that. An operation was something she could always relish, because the start to finish continuity had a roundness that was in keeping with her habitual tidiness. Today, she was not on the theatre programme. Instead, she had taken care of out-patients and a few ward cases.

There had been some interesting moments. A man had been sent in by a general practitioner with an accompanying letter explaining that a mouth ulcer showed signs of resistance to cure. Edith's examination located a large, furl-edged ulcer along the side of the tongue. She had no doubt at all that it was a cancer, and the man was told that he should come into hospital very soon. No doubt Mr Madison would operate, which was always a pleasure to watch. He had a flair for dealing with malignancies. Another patient had a bile-duct complaint requiring surgery, and Edith made a mental note to follow this one through, for she was interested in disorders of that type. She also saw a lady with a foreign body lodged in her rectum, a boy with a plastic whistle in his throat and a grandmother who complained of lumps that came and went on her breasts. There was variety, Edith could not complain about that. What really irritated her, apart from the incomplete nature of the day's work, was that she lately felt a strong desire to be doing something more dramatic. She did not have to look far to locate the reason, of course. To be the adored one of a consultant was an inspiring thing, and she was becoming a little impatient to show Henry Madison just what she could do in an operating theatre. She had no desire to be his equal, but to be worthy of him, she felt, she should raise herself above the ordinary run of hospital work. She could comfort herself, just the same, by thinking that it was only a matter of time until he found some way of elevating her. Every time they met now, the electricity crackled between them. He looked at her differently, sometimes there was something like wistful pleading in his eyes as he spoke to another surgeon and watched Edith over his shoulder. He was a dear man and she counted herself extremely lucky.

Around mid-morning, she had decided that she would call up Paul. There had been something wrong lately, something more than the difficulty they had talked about recently. Edith never listened to hospital gossip, but she had caught snatches of talk linking Mr Madison and Dr Avery. It was probably the ambulance again. She liked to stay out of any consideration of that argument. Mr Madison did not know that she and Paul had an arrangement, and she saw no reason why he should find out. What she must be sure to do was keep clear of any matters involving the two men, for anything less than neutrality would be unworthy.

By the time she had finished and was in her car on the way back to her flat, she was feeling distinctly anxious to see Paul. They had been like strangers for a while; her fault, for she had long periods when she did not like being touched, and any length of time spent alone with Paul usually led to something physical. The relationship was very important, and she realised that she should learn to put up with some personal discomfort in the interests of supporting it. Today, she wanted to see Paul and there was no twinge of revulsion when she reminded herself that it might turn difficult. Her sexual sap must be rising again, she thought wryly.

At home she first went round the place with the vacuum cleaner and dusted the furniture. There was rarely anybody other than herself in the place, but she liked to keep cleaning at it, maintaining its bright charm. Her bits and pieces were all new, there was nothing of the fine antiquity of Henry Madison's possessions, and the flat itself announced its recent origins quite loudly. It was a comforting place, nevertheless. The large windows, bright walls and soft carpet were all hers, they were her solace and her alternative environment. Paul said the place reminded him of a fish tank, but he said things like that all the time. She looked at his picture on her writing bureau and smiled. She decided to telephone him right there and then.

When he answered the casualty department phone, there were busy noises in the background. 'Did I call at a bad time, Paul?'

'We just got a couple of kids in from a school playing field. A matched pair of bad acid trips. They're seeing the same horrors, believe it or not. What's the trouble, anyhow?'

'No trouble. Goodness, does there have to be trouble before I call you?'

'Sorry, Edith. I'll start again.'

'Don't bother. I just wondered if you'd like me to bring round some Chinese food this evening? You *are* off, aren't you?' She kept a copy of his rota and convinced herself that she was not keeping tabs. It was merely that she wanted to know where he might be at any given time, in case she wanted to speak to him.

'Sho 'nuff, honey. I'll be at my place from seven onwards.'

'What shall I bring?'

'Get yourself something, I'll just have some furburger.'

'Paul! I told you before, I don't think that's very funny.' She didn't, either. Crudity concerning her person or any private practices involving her body repelled her. He only did it to annoy her. 'I'll get you some sweet and sour pork and a portion of fried rice. I'll be there about eight. All right?'

'Sure, great. I have to rush now, Edith. One of my little freaks has just tried to bite his tongue off. See you tonight.'

She went to the bedroom next and took off all her clothes. Nakedness made her feel awkward. She found her robe and wrapped it around herself, then went to the bathroom and turned on the shower. A satisfying end to the working day could always be made with a good hot shower.

Edith's method of washing would have surprised a lot of people. She behaved like a surgeon, rooting out any possible harbours of infection, scouring like a demented housewife. There were certain parts of the female anatomy that could never be rendered germ-free, but there was no harm in trying. Whereas nakedness in the confines of a bedroom always made her uncomfortable, in a shower her body became an object for professional care. When she had finished soaping herself she leaned against one wall, her knees half-bent, letting the water pelt her and wash away any microscopic particles she may have missed. Finally, she douched herself with a dilute antiseptic, and sprayed an odourless anti-bacterial agent all over her body from a glass atomiser. Then she dried herself with a towel white enough to be sterile, and changed into fresh underwear.

Before the bathroom mirror, she paused for an instant and looked at herself. White bra and white pants. That was supposed to be erotic. She could see nothing at all enticing, even allowing that she was a thoroughly heterosexual woman. Men were born with some distorted instincts, she thought. Although some men were not. Henry Madison, she was sure, would have managed to adore her even if she had been deformed.

She put on tights, a white wool dress and beige knee boots. They were a concession to Paul's little distortions; she did not like boots very much, they made her perspire and perspiration was one thing she hated. The smell of it, from a man or woman, could make her feel ill. It was different from the smells of the theatre and the post-mortem room, it had a squalid, sinful tang. Since she had been a child, she had punctiliously avoided ever perspiring so much or so long that she produced any odour at all.

She arrived at Paul's just after eight. He was in a silk shirt and Levis and looked, she thought, like a stage cowboy. She handed him the containers of food and waited in his sitting room while he put everything on plates. Edith liked the way he made little gestures like that; it showed he had an underlying streak of gentility and consideration. It went well with his brilliance and his promising future.

They ate the food quickly and followed it with coffee. Paul said very little. He appeared to be tired, and she could sympathise. All that casualty work, plus responsibility for the ambulance; she was on the verge of asking him how the unit was going, then decided not to. More and more, fear of raising the name of Henry Madison made her bite back topics she would otherwise have raised as a matter of course.

'It's been a long time since we did this,' he observed eventually.

'I was beginning to wonder if we ever would again. I like it, Edith. It's homey.'

'I'm sorry, Paul.' She crossed the room and sat on the small stool beside his chair, placing her hand on his shoulder. 'I've been very distant, I suppose. It's work. It catches up and wraps you in its folds. You remember what I said the last time we had dinner, don't you?'

'Sure I do. You said you were running off with a Portuguese sailor who had offered you the run of his chicken farm.'

'For goodness sake, Paul. Have you no romance at all?' She was laughing, even though she did not really like the way he stopped her warm drift with his wisecracks. 'I said you were not to worry, pressures, tiredness, the way things were—oh, I don't know. I never felt any different about you, I promise you that. I just hadn't the capacity to be domonstrative.'

'You are forgiven.' He leaned forward and drew her head towards his own, and when she was close enough, he kissed her. Turned at a difficult angle on the stool, Edith slipped down and rested on one knee, maintaining the contact of their mouths. She drew away at last and gasped air in through her open lips.

'You've obviously been saving it up,' she murmured, missing the brief spark in his eyes. She stood up and edged herself on to his knees, letting her weight settle gently, turning so that the upper half of her body faced him. He deserved some pampering, she was thinking. When she was not in the mood, he was never unreasonable or demanding. Not like the other men she had known. Grasping, fretful, dirty-minded devils who had more regard for what she had in her pants than what she represented as a human being, as a woman. There had only been a few, and nothing very satisfactory had come of any of the liasions. Which was just fine, for otherwise she would not have found her Paul.

They embraced for several minutes, then he showed signs of agitation and his hand pressed hard on the firm mound of her breast. As he began to push upwards against her thighs, she smiled and stood up, waiting for him to lead the way to the bedroom, as she always did.

He undressed with no shame at all, while she sat on the bed and tried to slip out of her clothes with as much grace as possible. By the time he was naked, facing her, his legs spread and his long manhood pointing at her breasts, she was still in her underwear. Feeling rather uncomfortable, she unclipped her bra, dropped it on the rest of her clothes and stood up, hooking her thumbs in the waist of her pants. His habit of leaving on the light was something she would have to speak to him about. Edith found it highly distasteful. The business of sex, if it was to have any value other than animal coupling, had to be conducted in a situation that admitted a spiritual element. That meant darkness. Paul's bedroom was lit better than his sitting room. She did not like to see the marks of his arousal highlit and casting obscene shadows on the white walls, just as she hated to look at her own flesh in these circumstances. As she stepped clear of the pants he took her in his arms and bent her gently back on to the bed. By gentle shuffling, mingled with their embraces, they managed to move to the centre of the soft mattress, and then he began.

She always had to close her eyes at this point. It would have caused her actual harm, she was sure, to look down along the length of her body and watch his head between her spread legs, nuzzling and licking, biting, sucking. The sounds were bad enough. She simulated pleasure, and indeed there was some, but it was edgy, more of an itch and a nervous discomfort. Paul was groaning, then she stiffened as she realised that he was moving round, placing the lower part of his body above her face. As the tongue continued to work between her legs and she sensed the bulk of his loins above her, she opened her eyes for an instant and shut them tightly again. That thing, stiff and jerking, coming down to touch her mouth—it gave Edith the feeling of being in a medieval torture chamber, with a lethal pendulum about to close on her and tear her apart. More than once she had refused to do this, but tonight she felt she must; the matter of making him see that it was unpleasant, horrifying even, would come later. He still deserved some consideration, she reminded herself. She took the penis in her hand and drew it to the edge of her mouth, running her lips around it, using her tongue to stimulate the tip. Paul groaned more loudly now and began to buck forward. She found her mouth being assaulted, the rigid length of him sliding back over her palate, and she began to resist. Before she knew what she was doing, in a smothering panic of revulsion and choking, she bit him and heard him roar. In an instant he was off her, and slowly she opened her eyes. He was kneeling beside her, glaring at her, his face flushed. Edith felt a coldness between her legs, where he had just stopped administering his technique, and it spread, her whole body began to shiver. She felt dirty, degraded, ashamed.

'Why don't you just face it Edith?' His voice was a harsh whisper. 'You're as cold as a witch's tit. Frigid. Why take the trouble to humiliate yourself?'

'Don't, Paul—'

'It's obscene! There's more sense in fucking a corpse! At least the disgust would only be one-sided afterwards. You don't like it, do you? You've never liked it. You've got a block as big as a boulder. Your pussy's as dead as rock, too. Why pretend, Edith? I don't need the hardship, for Christ's sake.'

'I'm not frigid, Paul.' She was beginning to cry. 'I just find it hard to enjoy certain—'

'That's called frigidity, doctor. Go read up the texts.'

'And you read up on etiquette, sensitivity, respect!' She was bawling at him through a distorting screen of tears. 'I'm not some sidewalk whore, like you were used to back home. You treat me like meat!'

'Oh?' His cheeks were flaming. 'You want to be treated like a lady then? No eating, no trimmings, just straight screwing?' He put his hands on her shoulders. 'Happy to oblige, Edith. And I'm going to watch your face, baby. I want to see some sign that you're not the ice maiden I have you figured for.' He rose up above her, one hand by her shoulder, the other curling round his penis.

'Stop it! I don't want this! I don't want it!'

'You're getting it. Straight cock, no frills.'

He came down, forcing his erection beyond the saliva-moistened lips of her vulva, jamming hard past the soft inner flesh and immersing himself so far on the first stroke that his pubic hair scratched against hers. Edith howled and he drew back, his face distorted with anger, and plunged again, hearing her voice break with the jolt, seeing the tears spill out from her tightly-closed eyes. Paul emitted a cry that was half rage, half lust, and began to ride her hard, putting his face close to her breasts, drawing her hips up off the bed so that he could penetrate more deeply. As his climax approached, he dropped her flat down and put all of his weight on her, stabbing at her with his hips until he ejaculated, then he lay still, his head buried in the bedclothes beside hers.

He moved after a minute, rising and pulling on his clothes again. She lay still, an arm across her eyes. When he had on his shirt and jeans, he nudged her. 'Better get dressed, or have a bath or do something, Edith. It's indecent to lie there like that.'

He went to the kitchen and switched on the kettle. After a few moments he went to the hall and listened. She was in the bathroom, running taps and rattling the little cabinet where he kept the soaps and toothpaste and deodorant.

'Sterilising herself again,' he muttered, going back to the kitchen and putting instant coffee in two mugs. At the corner of his eye he saw the little washing-up sponge she had given him. All jolly and domestic and lovable. Then it could go like this, hideous, ugly.

The coffee was growing cold by the time Edith finally appeared. Paul pointed silently to the mug and she picked it up, sipped and suppressed a wince. 'Tastes just like the medicine my mother used to force down me,' she said.

Paul looked at her, almost shocked in his appearance. 'Edith, don't go burying things. We've just been through a grotesque experience together. You can't just hang it up in a closet and shut the door. It happened, we're both bruised by it. Now let's straighten this out.'

Despite the unpleasant taste, she drank some more of the coffee. 'I forgive you,' she said quietly.

He drew a hand across his mouth. 'Maybe I'm dreaming. You forgive me. Does nothing soak through to you?' He stretched out his arm and pointed in the direction of the bedroom. 'Do you have any idea what that was all about in there? You got raped, Edith. And you invited it, you're lucky I didn't beat you up. Have you any idea just what effect your—your *distaste* for sex has on me? Why don't you talk about it, tell me if there's something wrong? You've always been withdrawn, but now it's getting worse. And I can't take that kind of thing.'

'Oh, I explained before—'

'You explained nothing. You've said nothing about this coldness or the revulsion. Nothing at all.'

She wrapped her fingers around the cup and held it under her chin, like a well-dressed waif. 'It'll get better, Paul. I'm just not with it at the moment. I don't seem to be able to get aroused. Work, uncertainty, things like that pile up.'

He leaned his back against the door frame and hooked his thumbs in the pockets of the jeans. 'Uncertainty? About what?'

'Us, of course. I don't know what you plan.'

'Edith, half your trouble could be that you want to live in the future all the time. You're never content to enjoy the present. All the time, you want to know what plans I have for us. Can't you just leave it, let it all happen? Or are you afraid I only hang around with you for the sex?'

Her eyes showed keen hurt. 'That was unnecessary.'

'I'm sorry.' He moved away from the door and crossed to her, placing a hand on her arm. 'It's a mess, Edith. I'm convinced you think I'm some kind of pervert. What kind of life are we going to have if you go on like this?'

She said nothing. As always, she did not want to touch on any exposed nerves. Two topics always seemed to be taboo with Edith when it came to discussion, her sex problems and her brother. He was an engineer, a talented young man, pleasant in every way, yet on the three occasions that Paul had met him, Edith had treated him like a second-class citizen. She would never talk about him or his work, and Paul had the impression that it was only by accident that he had been allowed to meet the fellow at all.

Paul sighed softly and turned away from her. 'Let's try to pretend it didn't happen, Edith. That's obviously the way you want to play it. I don't think that kind of answer works, but I don't think you'll go for any alternative. I'm sorry if I treat you badly. I *am* kind of coarse, it's the way I'm built and it's the way I've always gone on. We'll give this bruise time to heal, though.'

She went to the hall and picked up her coat. 'Remember, Paul, what I feel for you goes beyond any harm that was done tonight.' She was going to say more, but changed her mind.

At the door he kissed her briefly and watched her until she was in her car. She had the resilience, somewhere below her stiffness, to withstand the shocks. Paul's own flexibility, he feared, was not so good. He did not want to turn into the hairy ape again, and contemplation of a future with Edith now held that very threat. As he shut the door he thought about Mary Scott and felt something like relief. Perhaps, despite the careful planning, he would have to re-think the whole future pattern. A dignified, qualified English wife just might prove too much of an expense for the spiritual currency to withstand. And there was no denying he wished Mary Scott was with him now.

Driving slowly home, Edith found it hard to keep from thinking about what had happened. Paul was entitled to explanations she supposed, just as she was entitled to more consideration. But the consideration would not be forthcoming while she behaved like a dumb-struck idiot. Then again, she wondered, what could she tell him? Could she turn to him and say 'I'm sorry Paul, but the mechanics of sex repel me and they always will to a greater or lesser extent, and besides, I feel much less inclined to submit myself to the brutish behaviour now that I have a beautiful spiritual relationship with Henry Madison'—could she really convey any of that to him; and still be assured of his respect, or even his attention?

Close to home she began to hum. She did not feel like doing it, but it usually helped to keep her mind off difficult matters. The point at which she used the mind-settling trick was dictated by one little factor—whenever thoughts of her brother Ted entered the mental scene, it was hum-a-tune-for-sanity time.

Henry always drove slowly. Certain levels of co-ordination did not work so well after a man passed fifty, and the results of careless driving were too well known to him. It has been a full day at the hospital, and there had even been a ray of sunshine through the encroaching gloom of his professional insularity. A letter from Sir Thomas Quilley, written in his own hand, had come by the second post. Would Henry Madison care to attend a little soirée in London in a week's time, Sir Thomas wondered? It was a gathering to celebrate the eminent neuro-surgeon's imminent retirement, and as Henry had once been a valued colleague, it was thought that perhaps he would like to join in for old times' sake. For all of ten years Henry had not heard a word from Quilley, and he had worked steadfastly at resisting the possibility that the great man thought of him nowadays as just another provincial. The letter could not have come at a better time. So many doors were trying to close against his pressure that it was a tonic to find one opening unasked. He would attend, of course. He had already written his acceptance of the invitation.

Westfield was a dreadful place at night. As he drove cautiously along the main thoroughfare, he could see groups of youths, and older people who should have known better, wandering about the pavements, calling at each other, engaging in mock fisticuffs and behaving generally in the fashion for which the word rabble had been coined. At a set of traffic lights, he stopped and watched a man coaxing a woman to enter his car. She was resisting, but with a vulgar coyness that made Henry shiver. In the main, people did not deserve the facilities they were granted. Education was thrown away on a populace who cared nothing for the value of finer things, and he had always been able to detect a strain of the jungle in the men and women who turned their backs on every fine thing their heritage offered them. With as much free time as they had, Henry thought, he would be cramming his mind with literature, music, visiting theatres and concerts halls and museums, imbuing himself with the quality of spirit that came from pursuit of the arts. He was careful, of course, never to be a dabbler. The arts was the most deadly region of all for the undisciplined mind; a person should first be educated in the sciences and should work for some good solid qualifications. Then he would be equipped with a hardy framework on which artistic appreciation could hang like a glorious mantle. But this lot, the herd beyond his windshield, they pursued chaos. Was it Hosea?—'For they have sown the wind, and they shall reap the whirlwind'. It was not at all lamentable to Henry that there should be those who were set in authority over others. The concept pleased him; it comforted him to know that he was of a class of mankind set apart. Nevertheless, disapproval was in order, it was part and parcel of social superiority.

As he drew away from the crossing he saw a brightly lit front that had the words ROCKLAND DISCO spelled out in yellow and red and green bulbs. It drew the eye, and he reflected on the possible hazard to driving of such a distraction. A car could easily go out of control as the driver turned his head to inspect the garish display. Then Henry's foot instinctively touched the brake pedal. Three young people were climbing into a car outside the place, and he could swear one of them was Katie. Ridiculous, he thought, still watching the trio, trying to see the face of the girl. His car had stopped now and he was no more than ten feet from them. The girl straightened up for a moment, laughing, pushing someone into the car ahead of her, and Henry's heart began to beat painfully against his ribs. It *was* Katie!

He waited until the car moved off then he followed it at a safe distance, all the time trying to settle the conflicting impressions that crowded out his reason. How could she possibly be in the company of people like that? His memory presented him with a picture of the other two; there was one man with dirty clothes, a long-haired type with the stupid, churlish look of the corner-boy about him. The other was dressed in what had seemed to be, in the fleeting glimpse Henry had taken, a dark-coloured velvet suit. His hair was long too, long and thick, a clear badge of the disorder that typified his kind. And Katie had been wearing the short dress of which he had mildly complained to his wife. There was no doubt that it was Katie, but to see her in those surroundings and in that company was as bad as finding a junior operating without gloves—it was unheard of, a most unlikely thing. He staved off speculation as he kept the car in sight. It was the essence of any investigation, surgical or social, that the facts should first be gathered and *then* the conclusions could be drawn.

They turned off along a quiet, low-class street, past groups of grey men in soiled raincoats and cloth caps, past children who should long ago have been in bed being carried or dragged along by surly parents, and past houses that spoke all too fluently of the drabness and lack of ambition that they had enclosed for entire generations. Eventually, beside a block of badly built council flats, the car stopped. Henry drew in to the kerb a few yards behind and watched. The youth wearing the velvet suit climbed out and waved to the other two as he slammed the door shut. They drove off again and Henry was aware that there was an increase in speed now, a sense of urgency. Just Katie and that nasty looking oaf. He could still barely believe it; it would have been a great relief to discover that it was not her. Henry would have been quite content to accept that he was capable of seeing things, it would be less painful to bear than the fact of his beloved niece tearing round in a car with a guttersnipe.

They drove for some distance beyond the town, taking a route through the factory area and out into the greener country that bordered Westfield. It was a clear night, with a bright moon, and the details of farm machinery and stacked fence posts in the fields stood out clearly as they sped along. Abruptly, Henry saw the other car's brake lights go on and he was suspended for a moment in indecision, then he replaced his foot on the accelerator and drove past as the car turned off the road and into a small, deep cul-de-sac. With pounding blood he drove on for another minute, then swung the car round in a complete circle at a roundabout and drove back along the road at fifteen miles an hour. His lights picked out the break in the hedgerow and he drove past, stopping at the next corner and leaving the car as quietly as he could.

Treading carefully and keeping to the grass verge, he found himself next to the other car sooner than he expected and he leaned back into the foliage. He held his breath, as if he might be heard, and crept right up to the nearside of the vehicle. It was quiet at first and there was no sign of a light from within, then he heard a hoarse laugh and Katie's voice came through the darkness, high and whimpering. Henry's hands acted of their own accord, wrenching open the door, flooding the interior with light. The man was on his knees, hunched in the small space between the seats, and his head was buried in Katie's lap. A grisley slow-motion took over for an extended moment as the greasy head came up, confusion and anger beginning to break the blankness, and Katie's hands flew forward, fast but in a movement that Henry's startled gaze analysed in every detail as she drew down her skirt.

'Get out of there! Get out this minute!' Henry stepped back, waiting for his command to be obeyed.

'Who the fuck—'

'Shut your foul mouth! Katie, come out, at once!'

It was the man who came out first, his hands travelling before him, fingers like hooks. He remained bent forward as his foot touched the ground and his head butted Henry's chest, sending him backwards against a gravel bin. The edge of the metal bin struck him just under the ribs and he gasped as the pain shot along his spine and chest.

'Bleedin' old git—' The man snatched at the front of Henry's overcoat, ripping off a button as he drew him forward and punched him twice on the edge of the mouth. Henry was dizzy, unsure whether he was standing upright or if he had already fallen. He could hear Katie howling beyond the terrible ringing in his ears, then the hand he put up to defend himself was in the grip of terrible pain as the other man sank his teeth into the flesh at the side. Hearing his own cry mingling with the unbearable din, Henry started to sink until the ground came up and jarred against his knees. He was aware that he was being kicked, blows were landing on his chin, his stomach and his side. He tried very hard to remain upright on his knees, but the illuminated image of the car started to slip over, as if it were on a pivot, and in a second or so the ground was touching the side of his face. Then it became very quiet, except for that noise in his head.

Later, perhaps a minute or perhaps only seconds, Katie's voice came through the silence, printing its familiar sound pattern on the thick, nauseating fog. The man was speaking too, arguing with her, then he sounded less sure of himself, then there was silence again until the sound of his engine split the air and a smell of carbon monoxide penetrated Henry's darkness. The engine noise receded and warm hands were drawing him up, propping him against the gravel bin. The change of position caused some alteration in his air intake; his ears began to hear more sharply and barbs of pain started to set up a rhythm across his shoulders, his legs and his abdomen. In a few more minutes, the cold could be felt, and Katie's huddled form was clearly visible, bending over him, wiping his face and patting his cheek.

Full consciousness came back with a surge of discomfort, pain and outrage. Henry looked up at Katie and extended an arm. 'Help me up.'

He rose to his feet unsteadily, aware that there was blood in his mouth, and sank his fingers firmly into Katie's shoulder. 'My car is along the road.' They started to walk, which brought on some minor pains and a recurrence of the pounding noise in his skull, but he was well beyond the point of unconsciousness now, he was alert and seething.

Katie sat against the far door as he positioned himself behind the wheel, and she remained there, sullen and silent, throughout the long, difficult journey to the house. In the driveway, Henry abandoned his habit of leaving the car at the side and instead drove it right up to the front steps. Amy, alerted by this change of habit, was at the window before Henry had closed his door.

In the hall, the startled woman looked from Katie to her

husband with dumb alarm. In all the years she had known him, Henry had never appeared to her in any condition less than tidy: now, here he was, his coat torn and covered in dirt, his hand bleeding, his hair standing on end and a bruise discolouring one cheek. He looked as if he had been in a fight, and that idea was as alien as his appearance. Katie was dishevelled, too. Her knees were grimy and tear tracks showed on her cheeks.

Henry turned to Katie and grasped her elbow with his injured hand. 'Go into the sitting room. And stay there.' The girl, obeyed. avoiding her aunt's eyes.

'Whatever happened?' Amy's hands were snatching at each other, her fingertips moving restlessly as if she were telling a rosary.

Henry put up a hand, stemming any flow of questions. 'I will explain everything in a few minutes. Will you get my small emergency case from the bedroom, and put it in the bathroom. Then lay out my night things.' Without another word he crossed the hall and took off his coat, moving stiffly and gasping as he reached up to hang it on a peg. He then entered his study and poured himself a large brandy, drank it, and made for the bathroom. He passed Amy on the way, and she asked him again what had happened to him. 'All in good time.'

From the case, which was styled to look like a wallet-size roll of soft leather, he took a sterile-packed syringe and a needle and a small ampoule of anti-tetanus vaccine. Stripping off his shirt, he swabbed his arm and injected the vaccine. He then undressed completely and stepped into the shower stall. Turning on the cold jet, he stood motionless under it for an estimated minute, then brought up the heat gradually and soaped himself. The shower completed, he dried himself, noting where the bruises were beginning to develop about his body. He then dressed the wound on his hand and examined his face in the mirror. Only one bruise was showing, but the inside of his mouth was raw, and his chin felt tense and very painful when he moved it. The assailant had been wearing rubber-soled boots, sponge rubber Henry guessed, and even his punches had a certain padded quality. There was, really, the minimum of disfigurement considering the viciousness of the assault. Had the man been a rugger player, or someone with a disciplined understanding of fighting, the story, Henry reflected, might have been very different. But as in all things that marked the inferior types, the brute had used a maximum of effort to minimal effect.

In the bedroom he changed into pyjamas, dressing gown and slippers, and combed his hair carefully before going back downstairs. Amy was in the hall, waiting, her hands now folded in front of her. Henry pointed to the sitting room door and she went in ahead of him. He closed the door quietly and stepped to the rug by the fireplace, keeping his eyes on Katie, who was standing by the opposite wall, staring at a picture of a snake being conquered by a burly knight.

'Sit down, Amy. I have something rather unpleasant to tell you. Katie, come over here and stand where your aunt can look at you.'

Katie tried for a flash of defiance, but there was no power behind the impulses and she crossed the room to stand by side of the long settee.

'It would seem that we have been giving food, shelter and an education, not to mention our affection and protection, to a person who deserves no more than the treatment meted out to the inmates of a corrective institution.' He paused while Amy struggled to register the mounting list of shocks. Her eyes were unsteady, like those of a person about to see something very unpleasant. 'Our niece here spent the evening in the company of a person I can only describe as an undesirable. When I interrupted them, they were engaged upon some act of carnal dissipation which takes the matter into the realm of lawbreaking. As I understand it, this girl has been spending evenings regularly with a girl of her own age, a girl whose family we know. That *was* how I understood it. It now seems that she is a dedicated slut who has deceived us both monstrously. Have you anything to say for yourself?'

'You don't understand.' She said it flatly, looking not at Henry but at Amy. 'You're doing what you always told me not to do, you're presuming too much.'

'Is that so? Don't you think my experience of life, my knowledge of people, has some part to play in my presumption? Would I be wrong in thinking that the man who attacked me tonight was no better than a savage, a hooligan, a mindless son of the gutter who belongs safely behind bars somewhere? Or am I wrong there, too? Did I allow his filthy appearance, his foul language and his animal behaviour to blind me to the fact that he is a gentleman, a man of breeding and sensitivity?'

'You don't know anything about it. You couldn't.' Katie was still holding her aunt's gaze, trying to show some righteousness in her jutting chin, but losing it all with her quavering voice.

'I do not need to experience certain things to know that they are true. The stink of corruption is something I can make an accurate guess at. I daresay you could give us a more graphic account, from your own active pursuit of the subject.' His voice broke on the last word, and he took a step forward, nearer his wife. He was losing his control suddenly, the delayed shock-wave was breaking over him. 'My stomach turns to think what you have been doing. You have shamed me, you have shamed your aunt and you have shamed the memory of your parents. I can never look at you again without knowing what you are and what you have done.' He drew in a shuddering breath and his hands clenched into fists at his sides. 'You are filth!'

'Stop it!' Katie slapped her hands over her ears and shut her eyes tightly, giving way to a long wailing sob, dropping down on the settee and burying her face in the soft cushions.

Henry turned to face his wife. She was white-faced, speechless, and she looked as if she, too, might begin to cry. 'From now on, Amy, that girl goes nowhere on her own in the evening. She will remain in this house, and any time that she goes out, she will be accompanied by you or some other responsible adult. I am treating her lightly. Were it not for the publicity it would provoke, I would take action against her pugnacious friend. I have been insulted, beaten and exposed to scandal. It is scant return for all you and I have done for her. See to it that she bathes before going to bed. God alone knows what depravity she's been involved in.'

Later that night, as Henry Madison sat alone in his study, a book open on his knees, the second, more powerful shock-wave hit him. His tiredness, the pain in his body, the strain of maintaining the simple entitlements of his authority, those and the new awareness of Katie's betrayal brought a sigh to his lips that began to flow forward and become a soft, anguished cry. Another surge of sadness caught his throat and all at once he was weeping, something he had not done since he was a child. With a handkerchief pressed to his mouth he sobbed and flinched under the agony of all the betrayals, every hand at every turn that was against him. The price of adhering to his principles was much higher than he had ever realised; the treachery of other people could come closer than he would have believed. In all the world, there was no place where he could safely turn his back and know that he would be permitted his authority. He must always defend himself, and the burden, at that moment, was too heavy.

The tears, when they subsided, left a wake of hollowness. So much work, so many years of hanging on to ideals, and he had come to this, with the seeds of chaos inside his own home. His mind recoiled from any thought of Katie, she was gone from his heart and the space she left was bleak, a wound that would never heal. There was little comfort. Amy was constant, but her kind of faith was no balance for what he had suffered. It was perhaps a greater fortune than he had realised that Edith Roberts had become a part of the dependable side, a fierce light in his darkness. That young woman, and what she represented, could sustain him and prompt him to keep up the war against the others, the wolves at his gate. But for the present, weary and all but broken, he could defend nothing, trust nothing. All he wanted to do was sleep.

16

The post-mortem room, which led directly off from the mortuary and was designed to give a view out over a sloping field behind Westfield General, was the most brightly lit Paul had ever seen. There was an abundance of striplighting, in addition to working lights over the two porcelain tables and low, directional lamps above the dissection blocks and the sinks around the walls. To see out of the place, it was necessary to stand on a stool and peer through the upper clear portions of the windows, but it was an effort recommended to students who found the bizarre purpose of the room too much to bear.

That morning an old man had died in a medical ward, peacefully and with the dignity that most people secretly hope for. By eleven o'clock, five minutes after Paul had arrived, the body was on the table nearest the door. The head was raised on a wooden L-shaped block, and the deceased's eyes were open in a convincing imitation of surprise at the extent science would go to in order to determine a cause of death. A long incision had been made from just under the larynx, extending down the middle of the body, skirting the navel and continuing to the pubis. The flesh had been retracted on either side and the breast bone, together with the front portions of the ribs, had been sawn out in a high triangle, exposing the dark tissues of the lungs and heart beneath. The stomach had been taken away, tied at top and bottom, so that the contents might be analysed, for it was suspected that the old gentleman had hastened his own death. In hospitals, hoarding could have disastrous effects. A patient pretending to take his medicine, but really secreting his tablets and capsules under his tongue, could build up a fatal collection that would serve, when the clouds enclosed his reason, to despatch him out of the world in peace and happiness. In the interests of thoroughness and the pathologist's unspoken desire to cheat death of its mystery, a detailed examination of practically every organ would be made. To do this, the organs would have to be chopped up; the resulting soft, formless pulp would be returned to the abdominal cavity where it would be covered with newspaper to stop seepage, and the body would be stitched shut again with tough string. In the case of the brain, which turned to near-slime when examined, there was no really practical way of replacing it in the open head. The grey matter would instead join the other reduced parts in the abdomen, and the kidneys, which always retained some rigidity, would be wrapped in wet newspaper, which would be moulded roughly to fit the inside of the skull. The head, when closed, would thereby have a weight close to the original, and the embarrassing business of a hollow skull bobbing about in a coffin would be avoided. Paul never found the procedures following post-mortem unpleasant, but they did strike him as faintly primitive.

The senior pathologist, Peter Lawrence, had a level, practical approach to his work. He invariably whistled while he dismantled a body, and in the brighter weather he would even sing. Today he had called Paul to the dissection room because the pressure of work prevented him from visiting casualty for any length of time.

'I'll be with you in just a few minutes, Paul.' With a long slender knife he was detaching the dead man's lungs from their moorings. 'I didn't expect to do this one so early. If you like to hang around later, I've got a beauty coming in. He died in the psychiatric wing last night. Swallowed fifteen nails. Then he rolled about the floor, just to make sure.'

'I don't think I'll have the time, thank God.' Paul puffed on a cigarette, which he always did in a post-mortem room. Some of the unique smells rising from severed bowel could hang around for a long time. He had never forgotten how the odour of boiled eggs had reminded him, for years, of the gas rising from a small intestine he had once been instructed to examine. 'I'm grateful to you for going to all the trouble, Peter. You probably think I'm cranky.'

Lawrence looked up, his big brown eyes wide with surprise. 'Me? Think anybody could be cranky? You can't have opinions like that in a job like this, you know. When my wife finally understood just exactly what I do for a living, she wouldn't speak properly to me for days. All peculiarity is relative, Paul. In here you're relatively normal.'

Having removed the lungs, Lawrence transferred them to a wire basket by the nearest sink, where a young technician, a girl who looked too pretty to be doing this kind of thing, began the initial dissection with hearty sweeps of a broad knife. 'Right, Paul, let's go through to the lab.'

On the way past the two miniature examination blocks, Paul noticed the tiny body of a child curled up in an enamel dish. 'Asphyxia, that one,' Lawrence remarked, shaking his head. 'Inhalation of regurgitated vomitus. If I had a quid for every one of those I've had to handle . . . ' An old train of thought started up as Paul took another glance at the child's remains. Cot deaths. Alongside his interest in emergency work, he had entertained a long-standing curiosity about babies who died in their sleep. He had a number of theories, and if he had been emotionally equipped to become a paediatrician, he would have pursued them. Babies should not have pillows, he knew that, but he also knew that some children just stopped breathing in the night, and although a little nudge would make them start again, without some outside prodding they just might not recover. The possibilities for study and research, and the promise of dramatic results had attracted Paul to such an extent that there had been a time when he seriously considered making children his speciality but the emotional factor had intervened. A lifetime spent among the suffering, innocent young would have crushed him. He shook himself and followed Lawrence into the neat, alcohol fragrant laboratory.

From a desk drawer the pathologist took out a heavy bundle of papers and handed them to Paul. 'That's what you asked for. They all died shortly after being brought in by your ambulance. Where there were peculiarities, I've added an appropriate note on the cover of each folder. Now remember,' he raised a warning finger, still white from the chalk in the glove he had just discarded, 'in every case I examine, there are some oddities, some unexplained factors. Don't go jumping over the rooftops when you think you've spotted something spectacular. Take that case you brought in, the chap who was injured in his car when a tree fell on it. His blood test indicated high levels of phenobarbitone and something else that we couldn't identify. Well, when we examined his stomach, we could find no trace of a drug. Logically, with the sort of concentration he was carrying, his stomach should have been full of the stuff, or at least there should have been clear traces. But there were none.

'It surprised me, but it's the kind of surprise I'm always coming up against. There are so many vagrant factors, Paul. You see, if you were doing forensic work, if there was some definite suspicion of foul play to make us believe that the body would hold some clue to a crime, then the follow-up would be clear. He might have been injected with the stuff. People have been murdered that way before. But I'm in the business of locating causes of death, most of the time. The side roads don't have any place in the job, unless something very glaring indeed turns up. Given the time and the financial aid, we could start to find out why the picture is so distorted sometimes. As things stand, I'm content to accept the anomalies as another part of life's rich tapestry.'

Paul was frowning. 'What if I wanted to take issue on something that didn't look right?'

'You would probably get nowhere. How would you proceed? In this kind of investigation, you would have to start with a suspicion outside the body itself. I couldn't put my hand on my heart and say that people haven't been killed in this hospital. Blunders are always happening. You know that. Separating blunders from deliberate criminal acts, or punishably negligent acts is a hard thing to do. I've never had to face the possibility that patients are being deliberately or negligently put to death. Death is death, a reason is a reason. Beyond that, I'm inoperative. Now, if somebody in authority comes to me and says "Look, I reckon Nurse Thingamajig is bumping off her patients just for kicks", then I've got a legitimate lead, a reason to stop thinking of the oddities as anything other than natural phenomena. I suspect that you're looking either for negligence or faulty procedure. If you find any, you'll have a hell of a time proving it from post-mortem records. You have to start with a real three-dimensional villain, you can't work back from the results of lapses and errors.' Lawrence folded his arms and smiled. 'Remember, in medicine there's a lot of permitted lee-way for the taking of life. It's part of the game.'

Paul had not really expected to be told anything different. The medical profession, for all its safeguarding devices and careful monitoring of the sick could not be expected to have anything better than a human record of fallibility. Nobody knew, until he injected it, if a drug was going to help or hinder a new patient. The best life-saving compounds had killed a few people, too. Chance lay at every turn, and he was setting himself the task of making a distinction between natural hazard and avoidable accident. He could not yet fully permit himself to think that he was looking for deliberate sabotage.

'Thanks for the paper work, anyway. I have to make some kind of case for myself, and I can't think of anywhere else to look right now. There's a policy meeting soon, and if the Life-Support Unit is to survive it, I've got to come forward with something good.'

'I appreciate that, and I hope you win. If my opinion's worth anything, I'd say that you've hit a long streak of bad luck. But the committee who handle the cash don't listen to stories like that. They want facts and figures.'

As they walked to the door, Lawrence asked Paul if he was quite sure that his own team was up to the mark.

'I'd stake everything on that,' Paul assured him, 'but I'll tell you this. If morale goes on sinking, they'll start showing signs of carelessness. I've seen it before, so have you. My people like their work, and they're not likely to be cheerful at the idea of giving it up. It can't be easy to work like they do and feel it's doing no good, either. We're supposed to be making a dramatic contribution to life-saving. So far, it looks like we're a hazard to health.'

Later that day, Paul spent three hours carefully reading Lawrence's notes. His post-mortem reports were meticulously prepared, and when any statement became involved, he usually added a small drawing or two to clarify his point. At the end of the first two hours, Paul had isolated four cases, in addition to the six that he already thought to be strange, as worthy of detailed examination.

Each case carried tell-tale features in the pre-examination notes. It was fortunate, from the standpoint of gathering material, that Peter Lawrence always gave a brief summary of the events leading up to death. The first history showed that a long delay had been caused, prior to intended surgery, because the x-ray films were spoiled. A small note, which Paul had to examine for a long time before he could read it, explained that the cause of the breakdown was contamination of the developer bath with fixing solution. Anybody with even a passing knowledge of processing would realise that the contamination would have to be very heavy in order to ruin a plate. Accident? If so, how did such a big accident, the transfer of a good quantity of liquid from one vessel to another, go unnoticed until the time came to develop the films? Paul made a note of this query in the pad he had set aside for his investigation. The delay in obtaining good x-rays had clearly resulted in the patient dying. It was perhaps not a case for the fiery sword approach and Paul could not believe that it would excuse much from his position as defendant of the ambulance, but it was something.

The second account was harrowing, Paul read over the statement two or three times, picturing the event.

> This was the body of a young boy. He had obviously suffered severe multiple injuries, and there was evidence of recent surgical interference.

Paul remembered the case. The child had run into the road, chasing a ball, and a saloon car had struck him, throwing his body over a low wall, into a garden littered with broken bricks and sharp scraps of wood. He had been nine years old, and three weeks before he had been allowed home from hospital following an operation for the removal of his appendix. The details of the matter were overlaid by the grief of his mother, who had only recently lost her husband. The boy was her only child. He had been taken to the hospital with great speed, and en route Ellen Haxton had worked like a demon, splinting and dressing, while Paul had opened the airway and administered aid to the laboured breathing. He was a sweet-looking child, Paul remembered, and although that should have made no difference to the atmosphere within the ambulance, it did. There was a suspicion of serious head damage, in addition to the other grave injuries. Back at the hospital, the boy was raced to theatre for the immediate attention that sort of case required. All that Paul had heard, in the course of a busy day subsequent to the accident, was that the boy had died.

> Upon examination and superficial dissection, the following were the findings:
> The head was shaven, with eight surgical incisions, corresponding with eight burr-holes. There was extensive bruising to the scalp above the occiput. There was evidence of burning, and the presence of brain tissue, around the perimeter of one burr-hole.

That was the gruesome part. The holes had been tapped in the skull, with an electric drill, to relieve pressure on the swollen brain. But something had gone wrong, the drill had rotated too fast perhaps, and the boy's brain had been cauterised and welded to the edge of one drill hole.

The careful, dispassionate account went on in detail. Bruising was noted all over the body, on the eyelids, the small of the back, the arms and the legs. There were abrasions on the abdomen, and the right tibia and fibula had suffered a compound fracture.

Although he must have guessed the cause of death long before, Lawrence pursued his scientific examination at a steady pace.

> CARDIO VASCULAR SYSTEM:
> The heart was virtually empty. The myocardium was very pale. There was no evidence of disease of the heart valves, muscle, coronary vessels or great blood vessels.
> ABDOMEN:
> This was distended. There was a large retro peritoneal haemorrhage which extended from the diaphragm to the right iliac fossa. The haemorrhage seemed to arise from a rupture of the left renal artery.

The pelvis, miraculously Paul thought, had escaped fracture, and the spleen showed only a small tear. The stomach and intestines were normal, as were the pancreas and supra-renal glands.

SKULL AND BRAIN:
There was no fracture of the skull. The brain was swollen, soft and cyanosed; it was peppered with petechial haemorrhages. A portion of the left frontal lobe was found to be damaged, possibly by friction, and two thirds of the perimeter of the tear was adhering firmly to the scorched edge of the connecting burr-hole.

It made Paul feel ill. He could see it, he could see the surgical officer applying the drill, opening the head to ease the enlarging brain, and suddenly, on the eighth hole, the drill malfunctioned and began to race (that could be one reason there could be many) and smoke began to rise from the already outraged little head. Disasters that occurred under clinically controlled conditions were always somehow more hideous than those that happened on the random open roads.

CONCLUSION:
The deceased appears to have been struck by a fast-moving vehicle, with resultant heavy injuries to the head and abdomen. Further trauma would appear to have been caused by the accidental tearing and burning caused by the surgical drill used to alleviate pressure on the brain.
CAUSE OF DEATH:
Head injury and traumatic rupture of the left renal artery.

It was significant that Peter Lawrence had put the head injury first, thus placing primary responsibility for the boy's death on that particular piece of damage. Without the accident with the drill the patient would still, probably, have stood very little chance of survival. But that business with the drill should not have happened. An additional brief note went on the investigation pad.

The third case showed another malfunction to be a contributing factor in the patient's death. In his brief advance notes, Lawrence mentioned that the defibrillator machine had been the apparent culprit. First, there had been delay in finding one of the pads, which in itself was curious, and then when it was set up, the machine would not work. The patient's heart trembled on, and he died before any shock treatment could be applied.

Case four related the findings on a lady who had simply died on the trolley in the theatre ante-room. At the post-mortem examination, a massive pulmonary embolism was found to be the cause. In his additional note, clipped to the cover of the folder, Peter Lawrence expressed surprise. The embolism had been very large and not at all consistent with the level of the woman's injuries.

Then there were the six who should never, under any circumstances, have died at all. The pathologist's extra notes on these were longer than on any others. He could not understand a lot of things: why, for instance, a man with compound fractures to both legs should arrest suddenly, when before that moment he had been awake and in relatively good spirits. Cardiac arrest was the cause, but the reason for the arrest, that was a mystery. Other mysteries surrounded the demise of a man who, it seemed, had developed an extra wound on entering hospital, a fatal laceration of an artery at his elbow, which had gone unnoticed while he lay under sedation in the treatment room, waiting his turn for attention to the superficial injuries which did not merit emergency action. No mention of the lethal wound appeared on the notes made at the scene of the accident, notes tape-recorded by Paul Avery himself. It was all mystery, the emerging picture was of some dark force invading the hospital and inflicting untypical wounds and emergencies on people who would not, even in the most experienced eyes, have died the way they did. Many cases, of course, had been hopeless from the start. But they did not really count, they did not attach any damaging features to the Life-Support Unit's statistics. It was these others, the freak list, that could do so much harm. Paul filled his note pad with guesses and half-notions, trying to arrive at a viewpoint that would show some common factor. The only one he had located, so far, was delay; there had been delay at some stage or another of most cases involving unexpected death. Delay and, just perhaps, accident. Despite the shock-value of the reading, nothing looked clear yet. There were no conclusions that would put a committee on Paul's side.

He was interrupted by an emergency call on his communicator.

In the ambulance bay, Ferdie, Bill and Mary Scott were standing by.

'It's an attempted suicide,' Mary told him. 'And it sounds like a beauty.'

They drove quickly to the address given by the police. As ever, the details had not been given very clearly (a point, Paul decided, he would have to clear up, then he thought, if only it were things like *that* which caused all the trouble) but bleeding was a problem and they had several pints of O-negative on board. To call the emergency service, a policeman had to be reasonably sure that a life was at stake. Often the unit would attend an accident where perhaps four people had minor injuries but only one was critically hurt. That did not matter, figures were of no consequence. One jeopardised life was enough to put the team on the road. A bleeding patient, especially an attempted suicide, was something that always drove Ferdie's foot close to the floor boards. He had absorbed some stories in his childhood, stories he had told the others on occasion, and they were hard to shake. He earnestly believed that suicide meant an after-life of terrible, continuous pain. He was a charitable man, and he would not wish that on anyone. They were outside the house within five minutes.

The scene inside was reminiscent of a technicolour gangster film. The patient, a man, lay naked on the bathroom floor, his head and shoulders resting in a clotting puddle of blood. There were skidmarks all over the linoleum, starting pink at one end and merging to scarlet, where he had stumbled around as the police had drawn him from the bathtub. Ferdie, standing behind the others, turned away suddenly and started taking deep breaths. Bill, who had not yet seen the patient, grasped his arm. 'What's up?'

Ferdie's eyes were wide, reflective, as he moved to the bannister and rested his hands on it. 'He's cut his balls off.'

The two blood-stained constables stepped outside while Paul and Mary Scott knelt beside the groaning man on the floor. Paul lifted one leg gently and looked at the damage. The spermatic cords hung down, from the remains of the man's scrotum, and blood pulsed steadily from the mangled bunch of ducts and vessels beyond. He had made several attempts, apparently. There were slash marks on his thighs and when he had finally succeeded in slicing away the testicles he had been obliged to pull the edge of the scrotal sac free, as was clearly indicated by the jagged line of tissue beside the cleaner, cut edge.

Paul glanced into the tub. There was about a pint of blood in there, perhaps two more pints on the floor. The rate of loss was hard to determine, and it would probably undergo change when he was moved. Most of the haemorrhage, it was safe to guess, had occurred when he had been lifted out of the tub.

'The rent man found him,' one of the constables volunteered. 'He heard him screaming.'

Paul nodded. 'We'll have to stop the bleeding, Mary.'

She had anticipated him. From the bag she had taken some small artery clamps and was removing them from the sterile packings. Paul turned the man on his back and groped for one of the seeping outlets. The man howled and opened his eyes. Beside him, Paul heard Mary gasp.

'What is it.'

'Look at his face,' she hissed. 'Remember him?'

Paul took in the line of scar tissue along the man's cheek. He was the one they had picked up from the collision where his married girl-friend had died, the same man who had been attacked by her enraged husband.

The procedure was difficult for Paul and agonising for the patient. Clamps were applied to those loose ends which could be located, then a thick sterile dressing was strapped into position. With a coolness that caused one of the constables to grit his teeth audibly, Mary took a piece of gauze between her fingers and lifted the amputated organs from the congealing mess in the bathtub. Within ten minutes of arriving, they had the man on a stretcher, three minutes later he was in the ambulance and about to receive blood.

On the return journey, Paul found himself constantly looking at the tortured face, remembering the night that ugly scar had been received. How far did penance go before the sinner became a victim himself? Only that man could know what hell he had faced. He had lost his woman in the ugliest of circumstances, the kind that would be a joke to anyone hearing the story. He had been mutilated immediately afterwards, then had spent weeks in pain and remorse, depression and grief. A terrible peak of guilt must have built up in him to make him do what he had just accomplished. And this one would live, Paul thought. That kind of grim social tragedy always worked itself out, there were rarely any blessed abrupt endings. This man's memories would all be overshadowed save one, the excruciating drama of his loss, guilt and terrible self-punishment. Another gag for the neighbours to exchange. They should just take a look, or experience a tenth of the physical pain or a hundredth part of the mental anguish that marked the event. People in general did not respond very kindly, even to a tragedy, if there was scope in it for laughter. In the past Paul had heard men joking over an injury such as this man had sustained, yet if they could understand the subjective side, they would not be able to sleep for a week. It was like the old saying: If fish could scream, there would be no more fishermen.

The most sinister part, Paul realised as they drove up the steep path towards the casualty department, was that an act of this kind produced beneficial effects for others. Even he, for all his charity, was feeling measurably better about his own problems. This patient was condemned to a life of awful remorse and unhappiness; compared to that, the difficulties of a doctor and his ambulance were nothing.

17

It was almost a week since Henry Madison had spoken to Katie. When they were near each other in the house he ignored her completely, and on the one occasion when she had asked him something he behaved as if nothing had been said. His rejection of her was total. It was quite clear to Katie that he would have thrown her out if she had been at an age where that was permitted. As it was, probably the only thing that kept him from having her transferred to an institution was, as he had indicated, the fear of adverse publicity. Looked at from a slightly different angle, the only thing that kept a family roof over Katie's head was her uncle's pride.

She had adopted a regime of passiveness. Her aunt had not asked her anything about the terrible business the week before. In that quarter, things were very nearly as normal. Aunt Amy still served up breakfast and dinner, she still ironed Katie's clothes, she looked after the girl as a mother would and she still showed her kindness. She probably displayed no curiosity about the ghastly night of the showdown because she did not want anything to interfere with her love for Katie. There were, here and there, some sound arguments for ignorance. It was obvious, too, that Aunt Amy disapproved of the way her husband was treating Katie. She was the kind of woman who would be unable to condone harshness to any child, whatever the misdemeanour. Katie did not really think of herself as a child, but she appreciated the muted support of her aunt just the same.

She was missing Andy terribly. He had shown up at the school, lurking near the rear gate. Hurriedly, she had explained what had happened, and he had accepted the possibility of a long separation, or appeared to accept it. He had passed notes to her, through a devious channel of acquaintances, and they were filled, in stiff, inarticulate prose, with his longing and sorrow. They were touching things to possess and did provide a measure of comfort. But the wildness he generated in her, the abandon he nurtured, *that* had to be fed, and it could only work when he was actually present. On the day her Uncle Henry was due to go to the reception in London, she decided that she would get out to see her man.

Aunt Amy resisted at first. Sitting in the kitchen with a bowl of potatoes on her lap, she absently peeled off the skins while Katie exercised her talent for acting.

'Uncle Henry didn't give me a chance to explain,' she moaned. Dressed in a wholesome grey skirt and a grey woolly cardigan, she gave every outward sign of a girl whose case deserved to be heard. She had put her hair in a low coil at the nape of her neck, which added a demure touch, and she was fairly confident that the weight of her cajolery, reinforced by her no-nonsense appearance, would succeed. 'That was nothing, nothing at all. That man is somebody I hardly know, and there was nothing happening between us. Uncle Henry imagined that. I was doing a favour for a friend—oh, Aunt Amy, I don't want to talk about it. Can't you see that I'm telling you the truth? Anna is broken up, she never gets to see me now and thinks I'm deliberately avoiding her. At school she's always at me, asking me to tell her the truth. What can I do?' She flopped on to a stool and stared at the floor. 'Now she's down with 'flu, and I can't even visit her. It's very unfair. In fact, I think Uncle Henry is being cruel. I don't mind doing as I'm told, but surely, just once, I can go and see a friend?'

'You know what he said, dear.' Amy paused in her peeling and pointed the potato knife towards the front door. 'I'm supposed to keep you from stepping over that threshold. Now I've always found it's best to do as Uncle Henry asks. I know he can be difficult and I admit that this time he seems to be making a very harsh ruling. But look at it from his point of view. He was beaten! I don't want to know the details, but I saw the evidence myself and know how much pain and discomfort he has suffered these past few days. You have upset him terribly, and I think, for the meantime, that you should just do as he wishes.' She lowered her head and returned to her chore. Katie let the silence build up, growing into a tension between them.

'Aunt Amy, I know that all you say is correct, but do you think I'd deliberately lie to you or hurt you?' It was a key question, in view of the fact that she was fostering a lie and anticipating something which, if exposed, could hurt a good deal. 'I only want to go round and see Anna. That's all. Uncle Henry's away, he would never know. And it would do both Anna and me a lot of good.' She sighed deeply. 'It's bad enough being made to stay in all the time, but to know she's lying round there, thinking goodness knows what—'

The change probably occurred at that point. Aunt Amy's paring was taking an irregular turn, she had reduced one potato to the size of a large marble and she was still working on it. That would be her way of biting her nails, Katie supposed, waiting expectantly to see if it had worked.

'Very well.' Amy's voice was doubtful, despite the acquies. cence. 'For goodness sake don't say anything about it, though. Your Uncle Henry would never forgive me. And don't be late back.'

Inside half an hour Katie was changed, lightly made-up and ready to go. The make-up was something her aunt had given in to, all the young girls seemed to be wearing it nowadays, and she could not see that it hurt. Just like that rather daring underwear Katie insisted on having. A sign of the times. In the kitchen Katie placed an affectionate kiss on Amy's soft cheek and promised not to be late.

After she had gone, Amy finished preparing the vegetables and covered the bowls with metal foil. Always a realist in domestic matters, she frequently prepared the food for one day on the evening before, leaving herself time for any unexpected visits or readjustments by Henry of the eating schedules. She tidied the kitchen, then looked at the list of television programmes in the paper. She had a clear hour before there was anything worth watching. That would be time enough to go round the place with a duster and the carpet sweeper.

As she moved about her beautiful, already-clean home she

thought about Katie, trying to superimpose her own feelings at that age. Her childhood had been pleasant, a sunny time full of warmth and security. Katie, on the other hand, had not really had much of a life so far. The girl had put up very well with being an orphan, without demonstrating any of the difficulties alleged to attend youngsters who had lost their parents. She was level-tempered, sweet-natured, thoughtful and at times full of a refreshing sense of fun. Really, she was no less than a blessing. Without her about the place, Amy would have aged a good deal more rapidly, she felt.

Amy's hand began to move in a monotonous circle, dusting a table in the hall, as she moved to thoughts of her own loneliness. If Katie was obliged to handle that kind of isolation—and because of her age and her outlook, she probably did—then all the more sympathy was due. Amy was the servant, no more, of a man who showed her the minimum of affection and who gave her very little of his time. That, coupled with her day-to-day existence in a house large enough for ten people, made her a very solitary figure indeed. Five years before she had gone through a phase of resentment, determined to be more selfish, to create ventures for herself, to get out and do things. But the steady, unyielding drive of Henry's routine and his complete assumption of authority, soon brought her back to the old steady round of service and silence. She had no doubt that the man loved her, but his capacity for open affection had disappeared with his sense of humour, years ago, when his dignity began to matter more than anything else to him.

She was a trophy, Amy thought, he had won her and nowadays she was like any other prize, on a pedestal of sorts where only occasional dusting was called for—the equivalent in this case being the odd bunch of flowers or a rare visit to a concert. It was obvious too that she was not Henry's intellectual match, and that must be as saddening for him as it was for Amy, but nothing could be done to change the position. Perhaps that was his reason for having the young lady surgeon round to the house, he was compensating, Amy could not blame him for that. What she *could* find remiss was his arrogant treatment of poor Katie for whatever the facts of that night, however terrible, that girl did not deserve to be treated like an unwanted dog.

Amy crossed to the window and looked out. It was dark.

Whatever perils lay out there in wait for young girls, the risks were probably preferable to the grim, predictable certainties of her own existence. If Katie was taking chances on the quiet, it was only in the nature of womankind that she should. Inadequate now, able only to play the minor rôle into which she had descended from the great promise at the start of her marriage, Amy knew in her heart that she had only her devotion to Henry to keep her going—that and her pleasure in Katie. She wiped the window pane absently with her duster, seeing the still-smooth reflection of her face, a handsome middle-aged countenance that had very little holding it to reality. Whatever risks Katie faced, her aunt could only hope that something good would come of them. She should have taken a few more herself, long ago.

Andy was astonished to see her. It was easy to see that. It was harder to tell if he was pleased. The noise in the disco made it difficult to talk, and Katie had to wait until he had a few minutes' break until she could make herself heard in the slightly quieter bar at the rear of the place.

'It took some doing,' she told him. 'But I'm here. I brought you a present.' She handed him the key ring she had bought a few days earlier. It had a metal disc on the tab, and a silver skull and crossbones was etched into the green enamelling.

He looked as if that had pleased him. He pecked her cheek.

'Quite a surprise for you, huh?' After only a minute close to him she knew that something was amiss. She squeezed his arm and smiled warmly, trying to dispel the awkwardness between them. 'I've read your little letters so often these past few days, I've nearly worn them out.'

He smiled back, not meeting her eyes, fondling the keyring. 'It's been a long time.' It had been only a week, but they both knew how they had talked of separations being ages long, even when they spanned no more than twenty-four hours.

It occurred to Katie that he was feeling some discomfort because of what had happened at their last proper meeting. 'You know it's you I care about, don't you Andy? My uncle's just a silly old man. I'm sorry about what happened.'

'Yeah, sure.' He made a brave face and eased closer to the wall. 'You already told me. Let's forget all that.'

'What time do you finish? I can't stay out too late tonight.'

'Well that's going to be difficult.' He eyed the door to the main dancing area, and his glance was almost furtive. Katie tried to smother the tiny suspicion that began to gnaw at her. 'You see, I didn't know you were coming, did I? And I promised this mate I'd drop round his place after I got wound up here . . . '

'Couldn't you put if off?' She was aware of his distraction now, he was not telling her the truth and there was something close at hand bothering him. 'I mean, it *is* kind of special, isn't it?'

Andy shrugged and looked at the door again, just for the merest fraction of a second. He would still not look at her. She was finding that half of his power, the mesmeric quality he held for her, was wrapped up in his eyes. He was not nearly so impressive when he avoided her eyes, and his defects tended to stand out. She noticed, as she had noticed before, that the end of his hair did not turn in, as most long-haired blokes made theirs do, but they stuck out and looked untidy, messy. That would not have mattered if his marvellous eyes had been on her, if the man inside was shining on to her and warming her. 'It's awkward, chicken . . . '

'There's somebody else waiting for you, isn't there?'

'What are you talking about?' His eyes came up now, hard and tightly self-defensive. 'What do you mean?'

Katie watched the door and through the general movement outside she could see one static figure, pensively sucking on a straw stuck through the top of a Coke can. She was older than Katie, and her make-up was crude. She was wearing a dress that was a fashionable parody of a gym slip. That clinched it. How long had it being going on? Long enough, Katie thought, for the bird to be wearing the kind of clothes Andy fancied. 'It that her?' She pointed at the girl and Andy shrugged again, not looking. 'How long have you known her?'

He stiffened, elaborately, as if he had been struck. 'Don't start talking as if you own me, chicken.' He pushed the hair back from one side of his face, cautiously watching the people around them. 'Am I supposed to be a saint, is that the way you think of me? Do you expect me to live on an idea? For all I knew, you were locked up at home, for a long time. I need somebody alive, somebody near me.' He jerked his head in the direction of the other room. 'So she's waiting for me. She's maybe no great shakes, Katie, but she's available, a human being. I need a human being, not the memory of somebody shut behind a big door somewhere.'

She was feeling lost. Without Andy as an anchor, the whole place felt alien to her. The anger she had kick-started blew away suddenly. It's me he wants, she thought; she made herself think it hard, believing in it. The other girls was only an outlet, a poor substitute. 'Do you really prefer me? Andy, tell me. Please.'

He nodded briskly. 'Sure. You know that. You know what we've got between us, you know how you churn me when we're together. But I can't start living like a monk or something, can I?'

The space between the fear of loss and desperation to hold on is often very slight. Katie found herself momentarily at a distance from her situation, looking at herself with the enforced propriety of her home life on one side, and Andy at the other end of a long tunnel, surrounded by the spangled highlights and velvet shadows of the life he had taught her to enjoy, to want. The tunnel was in danger of being shut off. She moved closer to him, invading him with her scent and her clean, attractive presence. 'If I started seeing you regularly again, would that make it all right? You haven't really gone off me?' Never throw yourself at a man. She had heard that, read it in teenage magazines and seen the lesson laid out for her on television. Academically the advice had great merit, but in a position like this, it was as appropriate as a leg iron at a beauty show. This was a desperate moment, the niceties of caution and the need to preserve the feminine mystique did not enter into it.

He looked hard at her, reviving memories of closeness for her, and frightening her with the possibility that this was the thin edge of the wedge that would lock the door for good. Then he nodded, and a flood of gratitude welled in her and her eyes became moist. 'But how would you get away? You said your uncle—'

'Never mind that. I know what's most important.'

'It could be tricky . . .' He voiced the warning with the clear intention of hearing some solid plan to back up her earnest wish.

'Take my word for it. It will be all right. And there's more. I can get you some more tablets and things. And I still have money, I have a lot of things, I can get all sorts of things. Anything I have you're welcome to. It's the way it was, Andy, and I want it to go on like that.'

The effect on his ego was visible. In the push and shove of male-female relationships a man like Andy could never have hoped in average times to do better than the slag who was still watching from the other room. Even then, he would have to contend with a measure of coyness, the dead rind of femininity that clung to the worst of them. Yet here was Katie Madison, class, beautiful looks, a doll with the potential to make if where-ever she wanted even at the age of sixteen-minus, and she was laying it all on him, begging him to have it. 'You're an angel.' His face broke in the first open smile of the evening. 'I don't deserve you.'

In short order, he proceeded to set matters in balance again. He approached the girl with the can of Coke and exchanged a few words with her. She appeared, from where Katie stood, to be taking things rather badly. Her mouth moved in a series of wide ovals, vertical and horizontal, revealing teeth that were mis-aligned and a tongue that was long and pointed and comfortingly ugly. After a minute she clunked her Coke down on a table and stamped away. Andy turned and winked at Katie from where he was, then indicated with hand movements that he was going to take steps to get away early. She bought herself a glass of bitter lemon and sat down, feeling very relieved, a girl who had just won back her future. The details of holding on, maintaining the position, did not concern her now. That would come later, the plotting and scheming, in the quiet of her head, in the darkness of her room.

Andy took her back to his digs. The landlady, he explained, had gone into hospital, so there was no problem. Katie quickly dropped the thought that if she had not gone with him tonight, the other girl would.

He had changed the place since her last visit. There were fewer pictures now, even the black girl with her chicken had gone, but in a sense there was more to look at. He had obtained some very large posters and stuck them in a row along the wall opposite the couch. One showed a wrecked car with a cowboy standing on top, waving his hat. Another depicted a huge sun-flower in fluorescent colours, beside it a hand stuck up from a snowdrift, and to the right of that there was a nude girl, holding a grenade between her legs. The light was different too. He had put a blue shade round the bulb in the ceiling, and it made the place look cold, even though an oil heater had raised the temperature to a point that reminded Katie of the inside of a car in hot sunlight.

Andy made drinks, lemon flavoured this time, and produced a joint. They sat side by side and smoked quietly for fifteen minutes, saying nothing, both engrossed in whatever real or imagined vibrations were given off by the room and their presence within it.

'I think it's time for me to split,' Katie said at last.

He misunderstood. 'Right now?'

'From home, I mean.'

'But what would you do? You're not sixteen yet. You couldn't get a job . . .'

She turned her head, peering at him through the smoke that trickled upwards from her lips. 'That doesn't sound like you, Andy. You said yourself, the square rules are for the square people. We'd make it. And when I'm eighteen, I've got a lot of money coming. I could surely hang on for two years?'

'Yeah—well, I was just trying to put it on the line for you. I mean, I don't think you should do a thing without checking to make sure it's what you want. With your background—'

She leaned closer to him and moistened her lips slowly, smiling dreamily. 'Piss on my background.'

'You feel it all the way through, chicken? You think you could make it?' From a stance of practical counselling, he had shifted to the angle of acceptance, almost encouragement, in a matter of seconds. Katie was too taken up with her determination to wonder if mention of her forthcoming legacy had been responsible for the shift.

'It's what I want, Andy. I want out and I want you. I'm older inside than I am outside, right?'

'Right.' He took the joint from her and finished it with two deep puffs. He tapped the roach in the ashtray and turned to her, putting a hand on her breast, squeezing, making her open her mouth wide and gasp softly. 'We'll make it baby.'

She was suddenly so happy that she felt she might cry. Any difficulty, any price was worth spending the days as well as the evenings with Andy. And the nights . . . that was something she had often dreamed about. With a wave of generosity replacing the tears she had suppressed, she bent forward and slid gently to the floor, turning elegantly to face him. This was one of the things he loved, to be led, to have the initiative taken from him at certain times. She pushed his knees apart and slipped between them. She rubbed his fly, squeezed it, nuzzled it with her face, letting her hair fall on either side of his legs. Then she opened the trousers and took out his erect penis, looking at it, stroking it for almost a minute before she brought down her lips to enclose it. A thought flashed across her contented mind and she would have laughed if it had been possible. Was this what they called lip service?

They worked on each other for an hour. By the end, when they had exhausted the old repertoire and even tried some new variations, Katie had been changed by degrees from a wholesomely sexy girl to a naked, perspiring woman with a growing taste for the bizarre. All along, in her relationship with Andy, she had responded to the touch he possessed, the precise ability to activate those parts of her mind housing the components of madness. For the greater part of the preceding hour she had been out on a point, using her body and his to create sensations, shades of lust and varieties of climax that acted like explosions in her, knocking down the trends set by her background, revealing new seams and caves of electrifying sensation. Nothing would be the same—nothing ever was, after a few hours with Andy. Once, back when she first knew him, she had spent an entire morning at school wondering if perhaps she *was* going mad. She had indulged in things never even clearly dreamt of before. She looked up the definition of madness in her uncle's big dictionary: 'Disordered in intellect'. In time, a very short time, she came to like the idea. Disorder, according to one of her teachers, was possibly a re-ordering, making something from something else. Losing its image of confusion and destruction, her disorder became a very attractive thing her madness was no more than a reversal of the rules other people sought to impose on her. Tonight, she had gone further towards the reversal than she had done before, and the change would sustain her through the difficult business of leaving home.

Andy appeared to be more satisfied and more content than she had ever seen him. Before she left, unaccompanied as usual, he told her that he would be waiting patiently; she was not to worry. He managed to rally himself from his sleepy condition long enough to ask Katie if she was sure, *really sure*, that she would have enough cash to see her through at least the first few weeks on the loose. They would have to move somewhere else, after all, they couldn't live in this room, and the authorities would be looking for her for a while, so they would have to be careful where they went . . . She smiled throughout the litany of his touching concern and told him she would make it work out.

On the way home, with the cold air blowing through an open window of the bus, Katie began to come right down from her cannabis lift. At first she was frightened when she thought of the enormity of the thing she had decided. It deflated a little when she pictured the alternative life for years to come with Uncle and Auntie, and no Andy ever again. Her drug; the thought returned and teased her with its good and its bad, he was her drug. Very well, she accepted that. There would be trouble, terrible trouble. The school people would be after her, maybe even the police. But that would pass. Girls went missing every day, it was a common thing really. And soon, she would be sixteen, relatively free to do as she pleased. And there was Andy, she had to remember that all the time, there was her man, and there was the amazing, tingling, starburst and shadow world he had taken her into, made her part of, and allowed her to grow in. Oh, it would work out. Money answered most problems, and she knew where she could lay her hands on a lot of it in the house. Aunt Amy wouldn't say anything, she would cover up. All she had to do, Katie decided, was keep up the strength and the will to go through with the whole plan. Now, even if it became necessary for some unimaginable reason, she could not change her mind. What she planned was for her own good, so it was bound to work out right.

18

Ernie was surprised to encounter no resistance from Mr Madison's secretary. He announced that he would like to speak to the consultant, the woman went through to the office, and a moment later she returned, smiling sourly. 'Just go in, would you, Dr Hale.'

Madison was behind his desk, wearing his white coat, and for a moment Ernie felt the quiet power the man probably exercised over those timid enough to give him his place. He was resting his elbows on the leather top, his head was bowed forward slightly and his eyes looked straight ahead. A perfect front for any surgeon who wanted to establish his authority from the start.

Ernie closed the door and crossed to the desk, setting his case by the chair that waited. 'Good morning, Mr Madison.' Although the memory of their slanging match hung thick in the air, Ernie had thought it best to start on a civilised note.

'Sit down, doctor, and state your business briefly. I am very busy this morning.'

'Very well.' Ernie crossed his legs and rested his spine on the upright back of the chair. He was glad he had taken off his own white coat before coming across to the surgical outpatients department. When two doctors confronted each other it was usually the one in the suit who commanded authority. In this interview the edge would be slight, but it was there, if only as an irritant to Madison's composure. 'I've come to ask you, formally, if you will cancel any efforts you intended to make towards interference with publication of my book on mental illness.'

Madison's head rose a few inches, but he continued to use his forehead as threatening buttress. His eyes widened. 'Doctor, may I say that there is a measure of mental illness in what you are asking. What possible reason could I have for going back on my intention? I know of no new information, no redeeming circumstance that would make such a move likely. I am acting in the interests of my profession—*your* profession, too.' There was a curl to his lips when he had finished speaking. Amusement, mild but positive.

'Well, I did ask. I promised my conscience I would try to do the decent thing first.' Ernie smiled now, rather more broadly than Madison.

'I'm afraid I don't understand you. Now I did mention that I have a busy morning, doctor—'

'I won't take up much more of your time. My conscience placed one more condition on me, and I want to fufil it before I proceed with my own plans. Mr Madison, I presume I'll have to answer some select committee or other when your objections have been raised?'

'That is highly probable.'

'Then I must give you a foretaste of my defence.'

Madison sat back, shaking his head. 'I have no time to listen to your argument, doctor. I can guess most of it, anyway. I would remind you that spurious remarks about the freedom to speak and the dangers of censorship will cut very little ice with a panel of men who have their feet on the ground.'

'I wasn't intending to defend the book directly. I plan, in fact, to counter with an attack on you.'

'Me?' The low flashpoint of Madison's anger was something to be seen. 'What the devil do you mean? What impudence is this?'

Ernie held up his bag by the handle and waggled it. 'It's all in here. I have certain facts concerning you that I'm sure the committee will enjoy hearing. You know how one professional loves to stick a skewer through another. When I go before the panel, I'll argue first of all that it is unfair that I should be picked upon for a public act, when so many semi-private acts are condoned or simply hushed up.'

'You had better come to the point quickly, Hale. My patience is under great strain,' Madison's eyes followed the bag as it was returned to the floor. There was suspicion in his eyes and far less firmness than his voice implied.

'Of course. I shall go on to say that, although you have been the subject of rumour and accusation over a period of years, you are still in a safe enough position, it would seem, to exercise punitive measures against junior practitioners.'

'Say what you mean, Hale.' The consultant's face was growing red. The bruised area on his cheek began to merge with the surrounding skin.

'Right. I know about the nurse you bribed to shut up and move off after you'd slapped her. I know about the way a certain student found himself without any proof of the research he had done and without the opportunity to carry out more. I know about a girl who committed suicide—'

'This is the most—'

'—I have evidence, I have names, and I have a few people, one or two of them influential, who might very well back me up, if it became necessary. But I don't think it'll be necessary, do you?'

'You wretched little upstart! You scum! How dare you come into my office and threaten me with your bag of blackmail . . . '

'Mud,' Ernie said, maintaining his calm approach. 'It's mud, and if I throw it, some of it's bound to stick. Remember, a lot of people, individually, have one or maybe even two grouses about you, and here and there you'll find a man or woman who knows some dark thing in your past. But *me*,' he prodded his own breast bone, 'I've got the lot, I've collated and co-ordinated it, I have a case that could put pock-marks all over your reputation. And there's so much of it, you see. Goodness knows where it might lead.'

When Madison spoke, after a long moment of jaw-grinding and apoplectic fuming, his voice was very low. 'In all my years as a practising surgeon, I have never come across your like. It pains me, it sickens me to my stomach to think that I am in a profession that can permit charlatans and confidence tricksters into its ranks. You are despicable, and if you have done me one favour, it is that you have lived fully up to expectation. I despise you.'

'I'll learn to live with that, Mr Madison. May I say, in passing, that my little research venture hasn't exactly added any gilding to your own portrait. Now, do I have to put my original request again, or do you remember what it was.'

'Get out of here.'

'I want your answer, Mr Madison. I told you before, I'll go after you harder than you'll pursue me. And I've got superior ammunition, as well as a good deal less to lose.' Ernie stayed where he was, showing no sign of leaving until he was answered.

'I will not be involved in any business that is tainted by your filthy tactics and your brawling demeanour. I have no fear of your accusations, be sure of that, but I have enough personal reserve and dignity to avoid the ugliness of being maligned publicly.'

'Is that your way of saying that you won't do anything about my book?'

'No action will stem from me.'

'And from anybody else?' Ernie was still firmly clamped to his chair.

'I have no control over other people, not in matters of this kind. You have my assurance that, as far as I am concerned, the business is at an end. And I trust that you will leave your so-called facts about me unexposed, too.' He did not look at Ernie now, but watched a spot high on the wall instead. He looked quite shaken.

'Thank you.' Ernie stood up and walked to the door. Before he left, he raised the bag again and waved it as before. 'You can rely on my discretion.'

Madison sat in silence for several minutes, grappling with the chaos in his mind. His heart had begun to flutter with the raging frustration as he viewed the insult and the undeniable shame and realised that there was nothing he could do. What did a man come to when every effort of his life and every sacrifice of personal pleasure, directed towards a safe authority, was reduced to a waste of years by another man unfit to bear the qualifications he disgraced with his name? How many men stood to lose so much as Henry Madison, by the simple exposure of a past life measurably cleaner than most? Natural justice was a myth. If there had been any such thing, Hale would have remained the nonentity his character betrayed, and Henry would be allowed the simple, *deserved* seniority that was his modest grail.

He rose and poured a drink from the sherry bottle he kept in a cabinet by the door. The liquid warmed him, sent a column of heat down through the chill at his centre. He must bear up. The worst troubles always tended to come in a group. He must not allow his eyes to be blinded to the facts. Hale had a bag full of gossip, which Henry should and would put from his mind. It did not exist. The small battle had been lost, he must swallow that. The major war, the main line of attack, was still active, and soon he would win. There would be no evil fingers pointed in his direction when that ambulance was declared a failure, for the condemnation had already come from within, from the unit's own performance record. The figures would be seen by those entitled to see them, and the others, the herd, would see the clothed bones, the announcement that Avery's scheme had been abandoned. There was every cause for self-congratulation there. All other setbacks and annoyances were no more than a smoke-screen, and he must remember to keep looking beyond. He was winning, he was striking a blow for the established order.

After another sherry and five more minutes asserting the positive side of events, he felt calm enough to speak to the next patient. Dignity was everything, and true dignity, however dented, remained upright in every adversity.

The weather had turned warmer, warm enough for people to wear lighter coats, warm enough for them to smile a little more and be less abrupt in their dealings with each other. Even in Westfield, where the grime from the factories put a permanent filter of pale yellow between the sun and the inhabitants of the town, there was a premature feeling of spring and a cautious acknowledgement of the change among shopkeepers, bus conductors and the ladies who carried shopping back and forth along the streets.

Mary Scott had been in the park for almost an hour, just sitting. The sun had warmed the ancient, flaking wood of the bench and it was pleasant to remain there, motionless, watching the movements of people and animals and children without having to make any decisions or form any conclusions. One or two men, in passing, had given her hard, significant glances, and once or twice, just to upset the more timid ones, she had smiled openly. Nine times out of ten that sent them packing. She never underestimated her appeal, and sitting there in a short leather skirt, white sweater and leather jacket, she was fully aware that she presented an unusual focus for the attentions of wanderers and shirkers.

Mary had an appointment to keep in the park, and had arrived an hour early, so that she could take in some air and sunshine beforehand. For two years she had worked steadily without a holiday, in order to give herself the lead she now had on the promotion scale at Westfield General. Although she rarely felt fatigue, she had been conscious for some weeks that she was growing jaded, and the upsurge of work with the Life-Support Unit had intensified the feeling. Soon, she would have to take time off, or she would suddenly find herself in the rut of so many senior nursing personnel, working hard from habit and unable—even unwilling—to hand over the controls for a week or two.

The person who had asked her to come to the park was now approaching, striding across the grass from the direction of the main road. He was tall, broad and good-looking in the fashion of the late nineteen fifties, with short brown hair and a face rendered curiously blank by the high setting of his small eyes and his short nose. He was smiling lopsidedly, a mannerism that was second nature, part of his working approach. He was Detective Sergeant Kevin Morris, forty-three years old, married and successful in his job. For a period of eighteen months, he and Mary Scott had been intermittent lovers.

He walked right up to the bench and stopped in front of Mary. 'On time, as usual,' he said. She did not know whether he meant her or himself. 'You look very appetising from the road. I could hardly keep from breaking into a gallop.'

She smiled, showing her teeth, and patted the warm bench beside her. 'Sit down. It's very pleasant here.'

He remained standing. 'Well, I thought we could go for a drive, if you didn't mind.' He turned and looked across to where he had parked his car by the gates. 'It'll be very nice up round the farms on a day like this.'

Her smile faded. 'And it'll be secluded. Look, just sit down, Kevin. Let's have a bit of simple conversation and fresh air.'

He hesitated for a moment, then lowered himself to the bench, being careful to raise the back of his maroon jacket, so that he did not sit on it and cause wrinkles. He was very fussy about his clothing. The first time he had told Mary that, the evening they met at a hospital dance, she had replied, acidly, that it was understandable in view of the fact that his particular style must be hard to find nowadays. Things had changed after that, of course, they had found a mutual vibration, buried among the discord, and had exploited it. Lately, however, Mary had not been seeing him, and she guessed that was the reason for today's little meeting.

'I'd been wondering if you were ill or something,' he said.

'No, just busy. The new ambulance, the revised work schedule, things like that. Life's been very full.'

'Yes, work does get in the way of living, sometimes.'

'You sound like a lonely hearts columnist, Kevin. How's the wife and kids?' He did not like being asked things like that, by Mary anyway.

'Fine, fine. Same old grind. Nag, nag, nag and pay, pay, pay. If I'd stayed single, I'd be well-off by now.' He was uneasy, she could see it in the way he kept looking around. Too many eyes in a public place like this, she supposed. He was well-known, and rumours surrounding a policeman were more lively than most, and could do more harm. Mary did not really care about his discomfort. More than once she had felt a stab of annoyance when she realised how hole-in-the-corner their meetings had always been, how elaborate the measures were he took to ensure they were not seen. Knowing the reasons made little difference, even if she *was* being used and even if she *did* accept that idea, she objected to the absence of the token public exposure that even the scruffiest old bags were entitled to, and usually got.

'Why did you want to see me today, Kevin?'

'I've missed you.'

'You don't often miss me in daylight.'

'Now, Mary—'

'No use kidding ourselves, in there? I know it's cheaper to meet me in a public park than in a restaurant, of course.'

He was looking upset now. He was even forgetting to look around every couple of seconds. 'What's the matter? Bad mood?'

She opened her bag and took out a cigarette packet. 'Maybe my pride's rearing it's under-developed head.' She lit a cigarette and puffed on it reflectively. Now that he was here, she was forced to look at their arrangement in the light of recent events, the events involving Paul Avery. It was odd, she thought, how practical she could be about other things, yet in personal matters she always put off her decisions and evaluations until the very last minute. Soaked in the echoes of Paul and consequently changed in her attitude to previous or currently running affairs, her protracted fling with the detective struck her as rather tawdry now. Turning her head and gazing at him, she could not imagine what had induced her to go to bed with him in the first place. He was a boor of the old school, sex-centred and not at all interested in conversation or companionship. If she had ever asked him to give up anything for her, he would have run a mile.

'Are you trying to tell me anything, Mary?'

That was the policeman speaking, she thought. Out with it, no beating about the bush, gimme the facts, ma'am. 'I'm not sure. I feel a strong urge to tell you that I'm needled at the thought of you getting me out in the daylight so you can whip me across country to some isolated field and hump me in the grass for a change. I shouldn't be so silly, I suppose, I should think positively. I should remember that this thing has always been two-sided, and I should remember that I like getting laid as much if not more than the next woman. But just now, right this very minute, I feel like some kind of walking cunt, with no other function in my life but to be stuffed by you and the likes of you.' She dragged on her cigarette, experiencing some amazement at the sudden strength of her feelings.

He tried to placate her. 'You *are* being silly. You're a very bright, very clever girl. I mean, look at the qualifications you've got. You're as knowledgable as a doctor, and you're trusted every day of your life with the care of people who need expert attention. I know all that, I'm not blind to any of it. I don't just think of you as a body, for heaven's sake.'

'No, but that's how you treat me.' She threw away the cigarette end and crossed her legs, catching the dip of his eye as more of her thigh came into view.

'I'm sorry you feel that way.'

'I'm sorry I do too. I should be able to accept myself for what

I am. Instead of that, I'm acting up, I'm looking at you in a cold light. It must be the fresh air that's doing it. You're just a horny married man who can have it on the side, and I bet you brag about it.'

'Now listen—'

'I know what men are like, Kevin. With a bird like me tucked away somewhere, they can't stop shooting off their mouths.'

He looked about him for a few seconds. The fear of exposure was back, aggravating his growing defensiveness. 'You're starting to get big ideas. What is it you want? Do you want me to set you up in a fancy pad and send you flowers every day?'

'Big ideas? You just said I was the sort of person that could be respected. I don't want to be anybody's pampered mistress, but it would be a great change if people like you could see beyond the business of doing press-ups on me.'

His eyes narrowed to tiny slits. 'It's another bloke, isn't it? This is just a big show to make an excuse for a break.'

She stared at him, her head high, chin forward. 'Yes, there is another man. But there have always been other men. I'm not a tart, Kevin, but I don't go on exclusive diets, either. There's something happening to me, something I'm not altogether happy about. I'm losing my solo outlook. I'm getting emotionally wrapped up in somebody, and from where I'm standing now, the time I've spent with you has just been a sordid waste.' She only knew it when she said it. Her feelings for Paul Avery were growing deeper all the time and she had already passed the point where she could make herself believe that it was just another fun thing, just another groovy spare-time activity.

'You didn't think that way before.'

'That's what I just said, Kevin.'

'You didn't talk about sordidness when you were lying on your face with your finger up one hole and me—'

'Oh! For God's sake!' Her mouth was twisted with revulsion. She stood up and began to walk away from the bench. She had gone a few steps when she heard him coming after her. He grasped her arm and stopped her.

'You're not going to just walk out, not as easy as that, you're not.' His face was red, ugly.

'This is exactly how I'm going, Kevin. You've obviously got

some very clear memories, just live on them until you find another easy mark.'

The grip of his fingers tightened. 'I can make it tough for you, Mary. Don't think you're dealing with just some slob who'll let it go and forget everything. I can—'

'And I can make it tough for you, if you want it that way. I've stored up a few details of my own that your wife might like to hear.'

His hand dropped away. 'You rotten cow.'

'Goodbye, Kevin.' She straightened the sleeve of her jacket and walked off steadily in the direction of the nearest bus stop.

In her room at the nurses' home, she made herself a pot of tea and slumped into a chair with a cup in her hand. There was a dull pain in her stomach. She had noticed it quite a lot recently, and it always seemed to come on when she was agitated, overworked or tired. Her objective talent for diagnosis was nowhere when she tried to divine what troubled her own body. It had to be something extreme, she could never bring herself to believe anything else. Cancer, she thought, not really believing it but aware, nevertheless, that the pain could well be the first notes of a fanfare that would herald a fatal growth. It has been the same when her fingers had gone numb one day. It was cold, nothing more, and it had reduced her circulation to the stage where nerve-sensation was affected. But in her own mind she foresaw a growing paralysis. None of the answers she came up with were to be believed, she knew that, but it only took one twinge to set her mind on a short-cut course to malignancy.

Indigestion was hardly the thing for a bouncy blonde, she thought. Or an ulcer. Ailments like that were open acknowledgements that she possessed a stomach, a stomach that had gastric juices flowing through it, leading to—horrors!—a bowel. The oddness of the standard female mystique amused her. Women, particularly attractive women, could believably pass water, but the processes of basic excretion stopped there. For any woman to acknowledge, or any man to consider, that the distasteful business of solid waste disposal applied to the female of the species, was to reduce the whole concept of femininity to a painful reality that was unsupported by the greater body of culture.

Mary laughed quietly to herself for a moment. She could see the oddness of the persistent delusion surrounding women, but she knew, too, that it was necessary. It operated on several levels. To some men, the sight of a naked woman immediately removed much of the woman's charm. To others, a girl who flailed about enthusiastically in bed, but who never talked about sex at other times, was a proper, upright sort of person. And so it went on. The greater the intellectual freedom, the greater the scope for facing facts but even then, even among the liberated, there had to be something sacred. As she sipped her tea she thought about Paul. She had no clear idea for how long her feelings in that direction had been on the side of attachment. There was an easiness between them that had helped the process along, imperceptibly. Mary had no idea if he felt anything of an involved nature or not. Perhaps her mystique, low-grade by many standards, had gone down past the level where he could regard her as any more than a particularly unselfconscious, over-sexed bird. It was not pleasant to reflect that the carefree abandon could stand in the way of her being accepted as much other than a lay. Perhaps Kevin was not so much to blame. It was believable enough that she had over-emphasised one aspect of herself at the expense of all the other facets and depths.

But chiding herself did not remove the annoyance. Paul used her too. It was a fuller relationship, they made and ate food together, they shared jokes, and it spilled over into their work in casualty and on the ambulance. But everything stemmed from the fact that she remained willing to go to bed with him. Maybe that was unfair; all of their bed-dates, every one, had been lined up by Mary herself. She was always the instigator.

Impatient with all the theory, she drained her cup and decided to do some reading. Before she did, she determined to bring matters to a head with Paul Avery. She was getting attached to the man so she would either have to find out if he felt that way too, and if he did not, she would have to tear herself out of the relationship. She had no idea how deeply things went between Paul and Dr Roberts as he never mentioned that department. Drawing away would be painful, and she hoped quietly that it would not be necessary.

'I'm getting too old for the game,' she murmured, clearing the tea things away. Too old to exist much longer without sharing on a wider and more permanent basis. She settled down again with a text book, still wondering how he would respond. After drifting into reverie for a few more minutes, she brought herself back to the moment and the work in hand. She was good at her job, but constant study was essential. There was no room for complacency, whatever the case on hand.

19

Matron's party was an annual event, usually occurring in the flat part of the year when people were tired of the winter and there were few other functions on the hospital's social calendar. This could be the last time, people had been told. A re-organisation was afoot, the matron would soon lose that title and become, instead, the senior nursing officer, while all the other ranks and grades would be labelled with similarly characterless names. Along with the change would come a tightening of control, and events of such a whimsical nature as the party would be either abolished or regulated into some series that would run throughout the traditionally quiet summer months. There was a consequently higher attendance than usual, many people being prompted to come simply for the poignant sadness of doing something for the last time.

Miss Merchant, the matron, was a lady in her middle fifties who shared the medical superintendent's capacity for politics. She was surrounded at the party by three assistants, any one of whom could become her successor one day. Their mutual, veiled hatred and fawning attention on Miss Merchant gave the little group an outward appearance of solidarity. As they moved around the assembly hall, which also served as a church at weekends and a physiotherapy clinic every weekday afternoon, it was clear to careful observers that different faces and approaches were being used for different clusters of people.

Paul was playing careful observer. He had not wanted to come to the party. He had already promised Bill Davis and Lester Hill, the attendants, that he would drop in at their local pub in the town. But Edith had taken issue with him on two counts. One, he had said weeks before that he would take her to the party, and two, it would do his professional standing and his position of authority no good at all if he went into a public bar and started swilling beer and playing darts with two of his subordinates. On the second count Paul had been ready to put up a fight. Attendance at the party was the traditional thing to do, and going along the traditional, predictable routes was not his style; going into a pub was, for someone in his position, pretty unusual, which *was* his style, and besides, the idea appealed to him. He had not put up the fight, however. There was too much raw flesh between himself and Edith that still waited to be healed, without adding the complication of bruises. So he had put on his tuxedo, combed his hair, and gone along on the arm of his lady, prepared to be bored out of his mind.

The evening held every promise of doing just that. Far from bringing everyone together in a festive atmosphere, the party only served, as far as Paul could see, to replace the uniformed and white-coated cliques of the hospital staff with dinner-jacketed and evening-gowned cliques. The same old huddles were in evidence all over the place. Even though he tried to be different and really mix with everyone, he found himself constantly veering towards the younger men and women, those in surgery of course, for the medical people were too busy sub-dividing their hierarchy in other parts of the hall.

'This is a big waste of good time, Edith.' He made the announcement as he brought her a drink from the buffet table at the end of the shiny oak floor. 'All they're doing is talking about work. The band could have stayed home. Nobody's dancing. Nobody's even laughing much.'

'Give it time, Paul.' She was wearing a coffee-lace dress with a long skirt and a high, frilled collar. Her hair was swept up and she had attached a clip of dark amber stones one inch above the hairline. She looked very pretty, Paul thought. Good enough to woo and carry off somewhere—which would be when the trouble started, of course.

'There's been plenty of time. One hour and fifteen minutes. A morgue is a morgue, nothing will change that. Come on, let's dance.'

She drew her elbow from his light grasp. 'No, not on our own. I don't like making an exhibition of myself.'

He groaned. 'Well, let's talk to somebody.' He looked around, seeing a knot of senior surgical officers nearby, with whom they had already spent some time, and beside them a bunch of people from the maternity wing. He knew only one of them, a registrar who maintained he never remembered a face but on the other hand he could recognise a patient's backside at a glance, even putting a name to it. Then Ernie Hale came into view, flushed, looking as if he had been running. His dinner jacket was open, revealing as he crossed the floor that it had a pale blue lining. Paul smiled a welcome, hearing Edith's pained intake of breath at the same time.

'Hello, Paul. Edith.' He patted Edith's arm, which she immediately withdrew. 'I had to stop by the breakdown ward on my way here. One of my charges tried to eat a window pane.' He took a deep breath and looked around him. 'Some collection of moribund monuments,' he remarked. 'No sign of the patriarch himself, though.'

'I understand he never comes to these shindigs,' Paul said. 'Not enough dignity, I suppose. And red carpet's kind of expensive just for a party.'

'Who are you talking about?' Edith's forehead was gathered, indicating that she knew perfectly well.

'Henry Madison, my dear. Last of the divinely ordained knife men.'

'I knew he wasn't coming.' she said coldly. 'And I wish you'd leave him alone.'

Ernie tapped Paul's shoulder. 'I've been saving the news.'

'You've been to see him?'

Edith looked from one to the other, mystified.

'Yes,' Ernie said, smiling broadly. 'And it worked. No action. He promised. So you see, it pays to follow your nose. He looked as if he might have pups, right on the floor, but he had to back down. I've already told the publishers.'

There was still incomprehension on Edith's face. 'Am I to be let in on the secret?'

'No secret,' Paul said. 'Madison tried to block Ernie's book, but Ernie used a bigger block. The old man's decided not to proceed.'

She said nothing. Her heightened colour showed her feelings clearly enough.

Ernie excused himself. His superior, Dr Freeman, was by the door, talking to the matron. 'I have to tell him about a couple of new admissions. Now's as good a time as any.' He looked around the hall again before moving off. 'I don't think I'll be spoiling anyone's fun. There's more action over in the violent ward.'

'That man makes me *boil.*' Edith glared after Ernie's confidently striding figure. 'He's so smug. He thinks he's special, doesn't he? Taking on a consultant's just another piece of work for him. He doesn't stop to think that people's objections might be valid. They're just obstacles and targets to be knocked down.'

'He's my friend, Edith.' Paul laid it down clearly, straight-faced, with glinting emphasis from his eyes. 'I know your views on Ernie and his vulgar, wicked ways. Just keep them to yourself for now, okay?'

'But I'm right.' She could be such an enemy to herself, Paul reflected. At times when she knew that keeping the peace was very important, she would pursue a point just for the sake of having her say. 'If Mr Madison raised an objection to his book, there must have been a very good reason. But he didn't think to try sensible argument, did he? Oh no, not bright-eyed Dr Hale. He "blocked" the objection, whatever that means.'

'Maybe Madison's objections to the ambulance were valid too.'

'I didn't say that. He raised points and you answered them. Your view was upheld. That was fair, it was the right way to do the thing. I simply cannot accept that the sort of tactics employed by that little man have any place in a dignified profession.'

'You sound like a female Madison.'

'Maybe I am.' She blushed, and Paul remembered how that same blush had accompanied the mystery of her Saturday date, weeks before. 'I happen to believe that medicine has to be conducted with more decorum than bookmaking. If that makes me like Mr Madison, I don't see any call for an apology.'

Paul turned to face her squarely, deterring a tentative approach by one of the older sisters from men's surgical. 'Listen, Edith, you may not be aware of it, but Madison has the kind of past that you'd associate more readily with a Mafia leader than a consultant surgeon. I don't mind having my inadequacies and those of my friends held up to ridicule against the virtues of a genuine straight dealer. But compared to Madison, Ernie Hale and yours truly are a pair of Olympians.'

'Rubbish!'

'You won't listen, will you? Where's your reasoned argument now, where's the civilised approach?'

'I won't stand here and listen to you blackening the man's name. If you think he's so bad, accuse him to his face.'

'Ernie did. And Madison climbed down.'

'Lies!' She turned on her heel and moved over to join one of the assistant matrons, who had been temporarily isolated. With a talent for face-changing that surprised Paul, she began a hearty, spirited conversation. He looked at his watch, looked at Edith again, then made his decision. He walked over, touching her shoulder and apologising to the executive lady.

'I'm going now. Hope you have a nice time.'

He walked off towards the doors, waving to Ernie as he passed. In the small foyer, Edith caught up with him.

'What on earth do you think you're doing?'

'I'm leaving. I didn't want to come to this wake in the first place. It was your idea. Well, you go ahead and derive whatever you get from this kind of set-up. It's not for me, and I don't like to waste my evenings arguing with you, either.' He moved away again, taking his overcoat from a peg in passing, and made for the car park.

She was following him, he realised. He could hear her feet clopping across the tarmac behind him. He reached his car and started to unlock the door.

'Paul—' she was breathless, 'listen to me . . . '

'I've heard it all,' he said, pulling open the car door.

'You're behaving like a child!'

'Well, it's just the way I am. Sorry about that, but I can't really change. Now will you take your hands off the bonnet and let me sail away to work out my own inferior destiny?'

She stepped back, her hair blowing loose in the cold breeze. In the light from the main building, Paul thought he could see tears in her eyes. 'Is that all I mean to you?'

He paused and stared at her. 'I'll tell you what you mean to me, Edith. You mean a lot of discomfort, you mean someone who doesn't see eye-to-eye with me on anything. You represent a girl who used to be able, occasionally, to act naturally, to get out from under the big cloak of dignity and higher principles. You're now an example of a view that is old and worn out, as far as I'm concerned.' He stopped to catch his breath, not caring that she was openly crying, but recalling instead how she wanted to re-organise him, pick his friends, shape his future to fit her ideals. 'You're a cold traditionalist with a refrigeration unit smack in the centre of your brain, and there's a very special nerve connecting it directly to your pussy. There. I'm crude and I'm vulgar and I'm bad company. Just let me alone, and I promise I'll do the same for you.'

He got into the car and started the engine. Edith stood aside and he drove away, the sound of his engine diminishing rapidly, leaving the place quiet again, except for the faint trills of music from the assembly hall and the sound of Edith's whimpering.

'Mary?'

Her voice at the other end was faint, sleepy. 'Paul, is that you?'

'Yes. Listen, do you want to come out for a drink? I'm going to the Flag and Gatepost. I promised Lester and Bill I'd join them for a pint or two.'

'Uh, yes, I'd like to. I fell asleep, I'm still a bit woozy. Where will I see you?'

'Get a cab to pick you up. I'll be in the public bar three minutes from now. Okay?'

'You're a real smooth talker. Right, I'll see you in a few minutes.'

He put down the receiver and walked the distance from the call box to the pub. On the pavement he stopped and listened. Recorded music from the smoke room joined somewhere in the air above his head with off-key singing from the bar. A dozen levels of speech could be heard, plus the sounds of glasses clinking, money falling in the tills and the steady explosions of coughing and laughter. That was the sound of enjoyment, people doing what they wanted to do, unhindered by any need for show or stylised dignity. He pushed open the door to the bar and stepped inside.

The noise dropped back a few decibels, as people paused to look at him. Very few tuxedos could have walked into this place in the eighty-odd years of its existence. Very few Americans for that matter, although he doubted that his nationality showed. After a few seconds he was accepted, a part of the throng. He pushed past two men who were trying to balance twopenny pieces around the rim of a glass, past a fat woman who was singing *Love's Old Sweet Song* to a glazed diminutive male companion, and reached the bar by edging past a silent man who stood with his glass clutched to his chest, staring at his distorted reflection in the mirrored fitting behind the optics.

'A pint of bitter, please.' The barmaid, traditionally busty though rather more pasty-faced than the buxom girls on the beer advertisements, coyly accepted his order and applied her fingers lasciviously to the pump handle.

'I'll pay for that!'

Paul turned and saw Bill Davis waving from the other end of the bar. 'Thought you were going to let us down,' he called.

'So did I,' Paul muttered, so quietly that only he heard it. He took the glass from the bar and hoisted it aloft, making his way to the corner table indicated by Bill. Lester, looking more like Brando than ever in the artificial lighting and smoke-saturated air, was sitting there, examining a pack of cards. As Paul sat down he looked up and grinned. 'Welcome to the Ritz, but you needn't have dressed.' He held up the cards and nodded his head towards Bill, who was fitting himself into a chair. 'He thinks they're marked. A bloke just took two quid apiece off us at brag. I think he was just lucky, myself.'

Paul put out his hand and took the cards from Lester. He squared them carefully, then riffled the deck from top to bottom. He did it again, staring at the backs as they flew past, then he looked up, smiling. 'They *are* marked.'

'What?' Bill stared at Lester. 'I told you that bastard was a con man. Good thing I nicked his bloody cards, isn't it?'

'Good job?' Lester was looking very morose. 'It doesn't get us our money back, does it?'

'No,' Bill agreed. 'But he won't do it on anybody else tonight, will he?'

'Fat lot of bleedin' good that does me!' Lester switched his attention to Paul. 'How can you tell they're marked?'

Paul demonstrated. As each card mark had to occupy a different position, it was easy to detect the fakery by riffling. The back design stayed constant, but a little white dot appeared to be flying about the geometrical pattern. 'See? That's the mark.'

'That's amazing!' Bill was delighted, despite the loss of his two pounds.

Lester was less enthusiastic. 'The next time a stranger wants to play cards, you give him a game. I think you enjoy getting swindled.'

Bill, who had obviously drunk a lot of beer, pointed to Paul's open coat. 'Why the fancy suit, doc? This isn't formal night, y'know.'

'I'm expecting a lady,' Paul cracked. 'I always try to look my best.'

'Better not bring any ladies in here,' Lester warned. 'The language would curl their hair. Drink up, the beer's great. That's what we come in for. It takes our minds off the stresses and strains of the medical life.' He laughed and sank half of his own pint.

The talk and the drink ran freely for several minutes. Lester told two thirds of a joke and forgot the ending, Bill briefly propounded his theory concerning the effects of alcohol on the brain cells (beer widened them and made them muscular, whisky and gin took away the substance and reduced the mind to an automatic thing, a mere mechanism for controlling the body). In the middle of an escalating laugh, resulting from Paul's attempt to handroll a cigarette from Lester's pouch, the door swung open and Mary Scott entered, wearing a dark blue mac and a yellow silk scarf round her head. Lester saw her first and nudged Bill so violently that he almost fell off his chair.

'She must fancy one of us after all,' Lester said.

'Bound to be you,' Bill replied. 'You're the suave one.'

She fought her way to the table and waved her hand to disperse the smoke. 'It's not often you see fifty people getting lung cancer at once.' She took the chair Paul had found for her and sat down, smiling warmly at the trio. 'This is certainly different from what I'm used to. I didn't know Quaglino's had a Westfield branch. What's the beer like?'

'It's great,' Paul assured her. 'A pint of this stuff and I'm anybody's.'

'A tablespoonful should do me, then.'

'Seriously now,' Paul said, 'what do you want to drink?'

'A pint, please'

'You're kidding.'

'Just you set me up a pint and see if I'm kidding.'

Ten minutes later Paul was marvelling at the beauty of it all, at the way people could just have a good time without hang-ups. He would have liked Edith Roberts to see this. The distance between her formalised ideas of what was the done thing and this group's instinctive exercise of their capacity for fun was too much, too great a chasm ever to be bridged, but she should at least know what she was missing.

While Bill and Lester were arguing with another regular about their contribution status in the weekly sweepstake, Mary leaned close to Paul and said, 'Thanks.'

'What did I do?'

'You asked me out. I haven't had a knees-up in a pub for ages. It's one of the best ways I know of relaxing.' She sipped some beer and then added, 'Are we in separate beds tonight?'

Paul drew a limp forefinger down one temple. 'Well, I *do* have a bit of a headache . . . '

'Twit!' She shoved him playfully and drank some more. 'I should be a regular ball of fire on this stuff.'

He grinned. 'I may not be around to see the action. Beer goes to my bladder the way iron goes to a magnet.'

'No need to waste it,' she said darkly, trying for a wicked droop of the eyelids 'I've been reading up on urolagnia.'

'Yeah!'

'Incidentally, Paul why the fancy clothes? I was hoping you would volunteer an explanation.'

'I went to Matron's orgy. I had to come away when they started playing hunt the slipper. Too rich for my palate.'

'Did you go alone?' She was watching his eyes, perhaps expecting a small deception.

'I went with Edith Roberts.'

'What happened? Did she have to be in bed by nine?'

'Now, now. No claws, please.' He waved a cautionary finger. 'Seriously, it was a mess. I don't want to talk about it. Let's just say I left the party because I wanted to. And for the record, I'm very glad that I did.'

For the remaining hour until closing time they drank, played a quickly abandoned game of pontoon with the marked cards, joined in the singing and reached a state of inebriation that was nowhere near stupor.

On the road outside, Bill and Lester said goodnight, expressing their joint pleasure in having the company of the doctor and his nurse. Paul and Mary both said they had enjoyed it too, and the two men trotted off towards their homes. On the way to the car, Mary caught Paul's arm suddenly. 'Hey, just kiss me once, will you?'

He did as asked, and she growled like a contented cat. 'There's something about a kiss out in the night air, when you've had a belly full of beer,' she whispered.

They were at his house inside ten minutes. While Paul garaged the car, Mary went inside and switched on the kettle. A long standing habit with medical personnel the world over was to have a hot drink at bedtime, no matter what they had taken beforehand.

It was almost half an hour after he had come in from the garage before Paul noticed that Mary was still wearing her coat and head scarf. 'Are you cold?'

She shook her head slowly and unwound the scarf, dropping it on the settee. 'I was waiting until I could be sure I would get some attention.' She kicked off her shoes and he noticed that her feet were bare. Then she undid the buttons and opened the coat, and he almost dropped his cup of hot chocolate. Mary was wearing, in addition to the coat, no more than a black lacy bra and black nylon panties. She stood holding the coat open, gauging his reaction.

'You've been like that all evening?'

'Yes. All the time. What I really meant, when you kissed me, was that it's great to have a kiss out in the cold when you're standing in practically nothing but your knickers.'

He was on the verge of asking why, automatically, then he stopped himself. He knew why. He knew why she did that just as he knew why she did all the other erotically inventive things. It was only partly to do with a personal drive; much of it was directed at eliciting something from him, and making him feel gifted. Mary had the decency of intent to ensure that she did not simply offer her body, which was an easy thing to do. She worked at everything, even turning him on.

She took off the coat and stepped up close to him, moving to the side of the chair, allowing him to place his lips against the small navel, pressing forward gently so that his face became softly embedded in her flesh.

He put down the cup and let her draw him up from the chair. She tiptoed ahead of him, holding one hand, an enticing blonde imp who could fulfil every promise implicit in the gliding hips and smoothly brushing thighs.

She made love to him that night as he had never known it before, with her or anybody else. In turn, he found himself labouring to please her and drawing enormous secondary satisfaction from his success. When it was over, when they had both used up the available quota of invention and need, she lay beside him, smoking and talking.

'You have to know this, Paul. What I said at the start, about there being no adhesions, no mutual responsibilities or barriers, it's all evaporating for me. I'm getting to need you, and not just for this . . . ' She touched her moist groin, stroking it with the respect and affection naturally applied to anything cherished, 'I've got myself to a state of affairs where I feel possessive. That's not like me, I'm not possessive about anything, or I never was before. You know what I'm like, there's nothing you don't know, nothing important. You know and I know that I'm easy to fathom, you told me that very clearly one night, in this house. You put me in the picture. I accepted that. But I can't now. I want you. And if I can't have you, I'll have to keep away. Don't think I'm blackmailing you, I'm not, you know I don't have that in me.' She lay quietly then, waiting and breathing softly, her side soft and warm against his.

What do I say, he was thinking, what is it I want? He sensed the clear lines of an ultimatum, and in the circumstances she was doing the right thing, raising it now—now that she could still pull out, and now when they were both drained and in a better condition to know how they really felt about each other. There were influences on him that he could not trust too heavily, the row with Edith still produced a heat that would die down—he would not think so badly of her in the morning. There was his underlying desire, which had been hanging around for days, to alter his plans. Should he do that now, and perhaps face the uncomfortable—perhaps agonising—consequences? He sighed and tried to think clearly. What he wanted was still the same, he wanted success on his own terms, and he had *thought* he knew how to have that, sure he knew the trappings and trimmings necessary. But one of his old rules was that he should always be ready to revise his views on anything, for people and trends changed. That applied even when you avoided the trends.

He shook himself, his head, shoulders and arms, a rippling movement that made Mary lift her head and look at him. What was all this, he wondered? What am I thinking about, what have I been pissing around for all this time? I am Paul Avery, self-styled self-stylist. I make my own opportunities, I do not lie about trying to guess how the planets will move me. This girl, this Mary Scott who can openly admit to freaky fantasies and who is ready to calmly face the return journey to the hospital in nothing but her underwear and a raincoat, is possibly the most interesting, most exhilarating girl I have ever known. *There* were his facts, without the ifs and buts. The objections were all tied up with the kind of attitude Edith represented. Propriety, he had been screwing about because of that old walrus. To be the man he wanted to be, to have his consultancy back in the United States, the only thing required was to keep on doing his own thing, following his nose like Ernie said. His nose, eyes, skin, nerves and glands told him this woman was right for him, she was open, honest, amoral and a delight. He felt like blushing now, thinking about how he had clung to Edith, the girl so wrong for him, just because she had the correct front. The experience in the pub was the clincher, when he thought about it again. Simple fun, the enjoyment of as many of a man's hours as were free for the purpose—*that* was the route, and Mary Scott was the companion. She had intelligence, she had looks, she had sex in dazzling quantity, but above all, she had honesty. He recalled how he had seen her as different from himself, not realising that those very differences were the ideal qualifications for the person who would be his partner. He wanted a wife, a companion—not daily opposition. He was an idiot for not having seen that before.

'Mary?'

'Uhuh?'

'Do you think you'll like America?'

She wept and laughed and wrapped herself about him, and much later she slept, leaving him awake and feeling better than he had for months. Like every major decision of his life, this one had been made after concentrated inner debate, and like the others, it would stick. He was thankful, breathlessly so, that he had never settled to actually making up his mind about Edith Roberts before. So much would have been lost.

Paul began to fall asleep, realising as he drifted that for a man whose professional sheen was in danger of being rubbed off, he felt mighty like a winner.

20

A disaster, like any other surprise event, often provides clues that it is coming, warnings which can touch the nerves of those with sufficient intuition. On Friday morning Ernie Hale had a feeling that something was disturbing the air around him. Unable to shake it, he decided that he must be about to catch a cold; he could not even consider the possibility of a premonition for Ernie did not believe that a day could be foreseen. A man imposed his own pattern on events and the future, to a large extent, was for him to decide. If he had not been so busy, he might possibly have realised that a chain of past events could lead towards an outcome already calculated by his unconscious mind. But Ernie was extremely busy that day, and he took a couple of aspirins and hoped the cold would not be too severe.

He had promised to make a ward round on behalf of Dr Freeman, who was lecturing at a teaching hospital all morning. Accompanied by Sister Muir, who knew as much about mental illness as any doctor, he set out at nine o'clock to examine the wounded minds that his craft tried gamely to help.

A man called Rutter, who had been in the hospital for three weeks, refused to answer any questions. There had been a time when he could not be silenced, but now he appeared to be withdrawing. Ernie read the case notes briefly. Rutter had thrown an electric iron at his wife which missed her, and had then gone into the street and heaved a stone at a passing policeman, which did not miss. Prior to that he had been a very reliable and hard working clerk in a bank. He had not been violent since coming to Westfield General, but displayed symptoms of general confusion and derangement. In Ernie's opinion, Mr Rutter's mind had torn itself free from the monotony of his job, but it was now in alien territory, out in a world where Rutter had no experience. The patient hated his work, and would never face it again, but the alternative was confusion and fright. Security was not always a good thing, and in Rutter's case it had absorbed his santity.

'He's got to get attached to something else,' Ernie told the sister. 'There's bound to be one thing that will attract him. How did he get on at the occupational therapy class?'

'He upset a lot of the others,' she replied. 'He just sat with a tray and some canes on his lap, staring out of the window. He makes a lot of people feel that he's going to explode any minute. They get very touchy about him.'

Ernie made a note to discuss the case at length with Dr Freeman. 'Keep him on the same medication, sister. We don't want him to start noticing the attractions of suicide.'

The next patient was relatively normal in his behaviour. His trouble was depression, which could reduce him to tears right in the middle of a conversation. The treatment, with which Ernie did not entirely agree, was drug therapy and regular applications of electro-convulsive therapy. It was all wrong, in Ernie's view, to get at depression in that way. The cause had to be located, so that the beast could be killed at its source. That, however, would need a complete revision of the system, and several thousand new psychiatrists would have to be found. So in the meantime this patient and all the others like him would be doped and shocked by turns until they did not dare become depressed.

A young married man with a promising future in school teaching lay in the next bed, convinced that he had a brain tumour. It was a very special tumour, it talked to him and told him what it was doing to him, how it was slowly taking possession of his entire brain, and how it was able to render itself invisible to surgeons or radiologists. The problem was that the patient had encouraged the madness, he had found his life too easy and had created a problem for himself. He had done the job too thoroughly, and the problem was stronger than his will to fight it. Ernie talked to him for a few minutes.

'I soon won't be able to walk backwards,' he said. 'It's getting its tendrils right through the cortex now, and my motor functions will be thrown into chaos.'

'You know a lot about the brain, don't you?' Ernie's major sympathy was for the man's wife, who was a quiet little mouse, quite unable to cope with the peculiarities of her husband's condition.

'I've read about it a good deal,' the man agreed. 'And I know there are things that medicine doesn't yet know. Thousands of things. This growth of mine, it's a separate intelligence that's sprung from a few thousand renegade cells. It wants to immobilise me. And it will, unless you people do as I ask.'

'What you ask is not possible. You would die.' The patient had repeatedly begged that his brain be exposed and that a weak solution of iodine be poured over it.

'But that's the only cure!' Ernie still found it hard to tie up the natural behaviour of this man with the bizarre lunacy of his obsession. He looked and sounded like a very reasonable person, and if he had simply been arguing that he had a pain where no one else could locate it, he would be classified as perfectly sane. 'I'm able to read this thing's mind, you know. It knows that iodine would melt it and evaporate it into the atmosphere. Can't the surgeons take my word for that? This is something that hasn't been dealt with before, they should remember that experimentation is the basis of all progress.

The sickness was going forward unchecked. Ernie had already discussed it with Dr Freeman, and they were both of the opinion that this man would enter the horror-chamber of total insanity quite soon. After a few more words and a reassurance that he would try to do everything in his power to reduce the threat to the patient's brain, Ernie walked away, feeling the same futility that hit him, on average, ten times a day. 'What a mess,' he muttered to Sister Muir. 'A young man with everything going for him. Terrible.'

'He may come out of it,' the sister ventured. 'I've seen one or two like him go right up to the brink, then the symptoms vanished.'

'I'd like to think so, sister. But he gives me the creepy feeling that he's accelerating. I don't think he can stop.'

'It would be nice to think there was something we could do.'

Ernie flicked a glance back at the patient. '*He* could have done it. He doesn't give a damn for anybody but himself. His wife is just a thing he owns. If he was anxious to be re-united with someone, or if he was terrified that he might lose something precious outside, he would be able to use it as a life-line. But he's completely self-absorbed, and so far as we can learn, he's always been that way. The only precious thing he's got is his brain, and losing that is the whole bother in the first place.' He sniffed loudly. 'Let's press on. I've got a clinic in an hour.'

There was a compulsion-neurosis in the bed at the top of the ward. He was quite old and rather effeminate, and Ernie drew an immediate comparison between this man's symptoms and those of the young married woman he had seen, the girl who could not face the fact that her husband was a homosexual. She had been an easy case because her obsessions and phobias were not so strong that they altered her personality. They were just irritating habits. In the main though this kind of condition, when deeply seated, was hard to cure. The old man was a compulsive washer and memoriser. He could not read a newspaper in anything less than four hours, and then he only read short pieces, because he had to memorise each section before he went on to the next. After reading, he would wash and dry his hands five times. If, part-way through the washing process, he forgot how many times he had already performed the task, he would start all over again. He had been brought into hospital because he had lately developed an alarming need to shout at the top of his voice every ten-minutes in order, as he put it, to punctuate the day. On retiring at night, he would emit the loudest whoop of all, a resounding full stop.

Ernie spoke to him only briefly, for the case depended on the patient regarding Dr Freeman as the ultimate authority. If his faith in the senior psychiatrist could be brought to a strong enough pitch, he would believe that it was in someone else's power to rid him of his obsessions. Dr Freeman had done it before, and he had hopes of doing it again.

'How are you today, Mr Lowry?'

'Just fine, doctor. But I can't talk to you just now. Forgive me, won't you?' Ernie looked down and saw that the man had a book open on his knees.

'Are you memorising *that*?'

'Trying. Shh.'

The round was finished a few minutes later. Ernie had a cup of coffee with Sister Muir while he summarised the morning's findings. 'No emergencies, sister. Just step up the transquilisers for Lowry and keep an eye on our self-inflicted brain tumour. Maybe he'll try opening his skull by himself.' He looked around the tidy office and smiled. 'You've got a good ward here. It has a happier feeling than some of the others. I feel more like a psychiatrist in here.'

'What do you mean?'

'Well you know the stance, sympathy and sane detachment. It's easier to make it work with the level of illness in here. Over in breakdown and up in the violent ward, I feel more like an inadequate exorcist. You know what I mean? I often feel that I'd get on better if I went round in an ankle-length cloak and carried some beads and a rattle.'

'Faith is what an awful lot of the patients need, doctor. A juju man might be the answer.'

'I'll raise it at the next staff meeting.' He looked at his watch. 'I have to get moving. Can I use your phone, sister?'

She nodded and slipped out of the room while he dialled the number of the nurses' home. After some searching by colleagues, Cynthia was found and came to the telephone.

'Hi,' he said. 'This is your saviour speaking. What do you want to do tonight?'

'Same old thing, I suppose,' she replied, giggling.

Why do I like the dizzy ones, he wondered. 'I meant early in the evening. There's a Scandinavian movie on in town. *Confessions of a Surgical Boot Fetishist* or something like that. Or we could eat.'

'Let's eat.'

That was so like her. Eating and screwing, a simple regimen that kept her body fit and her mind safely numb. 'Right, I'll pick you up about eight. Have a good day.'

As he crossed the open ground between the wards and the psychiatric outpatients' clinic, Ernie reflected on the way his pattern was developing in some parts and remaining static in others. His career would take a dramatic change when the book came out, he was sure of that. Change would bring him into contact with different opportunities and his abilities could be shunted along different lines. But his private life did not alter very much at all, and he could see no prospect of it ever being much different. He did not want to marry, and apart from Cynthia's occasional flushes of chastity and romance, the arrangement there would suit him until an almost identical alternative came along. In a cockeyed way, he thought, he was stable where it mattered.

Dealing with the people whose minds were off-tune was getting no easier. As Ernie stepped into the consulting room and looked at the list, he felt, just for a moment, that he would like to run into the waiting room and yell at them all to go home and get some hard work done and stop imagining they were ill. Patience was the primary requirement, but it had to run thin sometimes.

The nurse tapped the door and put her head round the side. 'Mark Jordan is here,' she said.

Ernie looked up. 'I'll see him first. It must be embarrassing to sit out there with a guard on either side. Send him in when I buzz you.'

As he had suspected at the previous interview, this case was one for permanent committal. The boy's desire to cause pain and his fantasies of persecution had been shown in a fiercer light by the results of the tests carried out two days before. Ernie wanted to see the youth one more time to instil some feeling of his personality into the report he would prepare for the court. There was so much that could be done, he was still sure of that, but as yet the mechanics of simply starting treatment—*meaningful* treatment—were not even down on paper. Ernie read the notes again, wincing at the details of Mark's attack on the girl who had shopped him. If that kind of ingenuity could only be diverted along a productive route . . .

He pressed the button on the desk and Mark Jordan came in. He was dressed as before and looked a shade more sullen. He sat down and clenched his fists on his knees, observing Ernie through half-lidded eyes.

'Nice to see you again, Mark. How did you like the tests?'

'They were all right. Bit stupid, I thought. But they weren't difficult.'

'Good. Well, I wanted to see you today just so we could be a little better acquainted. I'm going to write my report tomorrow, and I want it to convey plenty about you as a person, just to balance all the facts and figures that came out of the tests.'

Mark cleared his throat. 'I wanted to see you, too. They don't tell you much at the centre, and I want to know what was happening. Is it true I can get put away for good?'

Ernie tried to keep his cheeks from colouring. 'Who told you that?'

'I just heard it. You pick up a lot if you keep your ears open and your mouth shut. Is it true?'

'It's up to the judge. You haven't killed anybody, Mark, but your record shows that you might one day, if things went on as they are. So you could be sent to a hospital, as I said last time. My report will recommend that you have treatment, so you might well avoid having to go to prison.'

'But *can* they put me inside for good?' His voice was flat, the only emphasis coming from the occasional lengthening of some words. It was an unpleasant effect, and Ernie could easily imagine this lad frightening someone half to death with simple threats.

'It'll be up to the judge.' Ernie knew he was being cowardly on this point, but he could not see any way of enlarging on the facts. He could not tell Mark that he was considered to be dangerously unstable. For one thing, he might feel flattered.

'I know about other people,' Mark grunted. 'I know there was a bloke in London who did what I did, or something much the same, and they stuck him in Broadmoor. For keeps. And I know some of the words they hang on you when they want to put you in there. Sociopath. I know that one. I know what it means.' He tapped his forehead as he had done before. 'I've got a lot of learning up here, doc. And I reckon you're using words like sociopath on my report, because you're one of the people that have to put me down.'

'I'm the one who wants to help you, Mark.'

'That's not true.' There were no signs of increased life in the unattractive face, but the voice was filling out. Mark used his body, Ernie thought, like a machine that had only a limited supply of fuel, he did not move one muscle unnecessarily. Even his eyes remained fixed. His resentment was typical of his condition, and Ernie was fascinated to see how it could grow, like fire on dry twigs, from a tiny spark. 'There are people all over the place, law-makers and law-breakers, and they all want me put down or put away. I've got talent, remember, and when people find out just how good I am, they always start putting the blocks on me. Now you're ganging up with the judge to sling me inside for the rest of my life.' He blinked, slowly, and when his eyes opened again they were wider. 'It isn't fair. You don't know anything about me.'

'The tests tell us that you need help, Mark. If you were allowed to go round doing what you want, you'd really go down. There are things you don't know about yourself. You have to be assisted over some hurdles. Others will always be there. But you can make a go of your life.' Ernie's heart was nowhere near the sunshine-and-hope of his message. The best that could be hoped for, as things stood at present, was a form of imprisonment that would show Mark some new angles of conduct, and keep him under enough discipline to prevent him degenerating into a raving animal.

'Nobody wants my talent to get up above the surface. That's all there is to it. That's the real truth. I'm not to get a chance, because every bastard wants to keep my sort out of circulation.'

He leaned forward, and it was the movement of a concentrated force. Ernie could see the shadow of the guards outside, standing close to the glass panel in the door. The button was within reach of his fingertips, So long as he was able to feel safe, Ernie liked to study a violent patient when anger was moving him. Growing detached, he watched Mark's fingers as they began to squirm around each other. There was a geared, massive energy rippling across Mark's shoulders, something that could not be seen but which could be felt very easily.

'I'm bigger than anybody knows, doc. They think because I don't talk much that I'm thick, but I'm not, you should know that. You won't let yourself believe it, will you? Because you and that judge and the police—'

'Mark, I told you already, I don't want to harm you.'

'You?' The gears were shifting, his hands came away from each other and hung loose, ready, at his sides. 'You couldn't hurt me, even if you wanted. You have to do it in gangs!'

Ernie shifted in his seat, keeping his hand within reach of the button. There was a war in him, one he did not often think about, but it was active now and he flowed with it, moving from one viewpoint to another. There was the man of sympathy, the good psychiatrist, but there was also the scientist. They were so different, like separate people. The one wanted to offer help and support, but the other would stand by, a dissector of events, a prober of meanings, and that one would let harm come to a patient, just in the interests of learning more. He was still anxious to give Mark some reassurance, but he wanted to see this kind of anger at its peak, too. The psychiatrist should be stopping the boy's growing fury, Ernie knew that, but the other side of him held back, just for a few more seconds. Just a few more.

Mark stood up, pointing a finger straight at Ernie's forehead. 'Every time I get near some bloke behind a desk, it's trouble for me. I've a right to work out things for myself. I haven't had a hearing, they wouldn't let me speak up in court. I told you one or two things and you're using them to put me away. That's all wrong.' His eyes were moving now, they looked hard at Ernie while he spoke, then they shifted off to the side, fluttering as if he was reading the signs of some terrible inner revelation. Ernie sat still, watching, noting.

'Let me tell you something, doc. When they brought me out of that centre today, I told myself I wasn't going back. If I don't stop all this now, they'll have me where they want me. Tied down, for life. If people want to go on trying to ruin me, they're going to find out just how big I can be.'

'But how are you going to keep from going back? You'll only make more trouble for yourself—'

'No, *you* make the trouble, with your bits of paper and your tests. That's where my trouble always comes from. If I keep away from the men with pens and the law on their side, I'm safe.'

'But Mark, you're in custody.'

He came close now, leaning right across the desk, his chin only a few inches above Ernie's hand where it lay, close to the button. 'Custody's just a word, doc. A fuckin' word. I'm in here and I'm free as a bird. I'm only trapped when I let you and your mod get your heads together and bundle me into a nut house.' He shook his head slowly from side to side, and in the quietness and closeness Ernie could hear Mark's breath, sharp and trembling. 'I'm not going back. That's a fact. Nobody's going to touch me.'

An urgent sense of responsibility broke through Ernie's fascination. 'Sit down, Mark. This is getting you nowhere.'

'Don't order me about!' He remained bent across the desk, his teeth bared. 'You're still putting up your front, aren't you? You pretend I'm somebody you want to help, but you know bleedin' well you're just waiting to ship me out.'

'Sit down, Mark.'

'Don't talk to me like that!' His eyes were growing moist, anguish tugging at his coarse features. 'Fuckin' laws! You bastards are the bad ones, you're the lice that tramp on people if they step out of line.' He stepped away from the desk suddenly and Ernie's hand shot to the bell. In an instant Mark saw the move and his own hand swiped out, knocking Ernie's aside. 'See?' His eyes were glaring, accusing. 'You were going to do it, you were going to get them to drag me away. Bastard!' His hand slipped into his jacket and emerged holding a screwdriver, a large one with a razor-honed tip. 'You won't touch me—'

Ernie was half out of his chair, keeping his eyes on the weapon, thinking a thousand things about personal safety and the rotten security in remand centres. 'Give me that, for God's sake!'

Mark drew the glinting shaft upwards, his fingers clamped around the handle. 'Take it! Take it!' he drove his arm down and Ernie's hand slammed on to the desk button. He could hear the buzzer going outside an instant before he felt the point of the spike go through his skull, and though the guards were in the room within the second it was too late. Mark Jordan had frantically raised and lowered the screwdriver five more times and Ernie Hale's brain was showing through the torn scalp, pieces of bone littering his brow and flecking the vacant socket where his left eye had just been jabbed out. One guard grabbed Mark by the hair and drew him backwards, sinking the end of his truncheon into the boy's stomach and following through with a blow across the teeth. The other guard stood quite still, staring at the disfigured pulp that had been Ernie's head. The body was slumped over the desk, blood leaking across papers and dripping on to the carpet.

Mark Jordan was unconscious, and if he had resisted at all he would have been clubbed to death. The nurse was standing in the doorway, chewing the back of her hand. Without turning his gaze from the desk, the guard released a trembling breath.

'Better get somebody over here quick. There's going to be trouble.'

His partner, still bent over Mark's body, nodded and looked at the nurse. 'Do something, love. Don't keep staring at the doctor. That won't bring him back to life.'

She turned and started to run, and as she hit the open air she began to cry. In the main office it took them over a minute to understand what she was saying. When it got through an assistant matron and a secretary began to activate the proper procedures. Within ten minutes of Ernie's death, almost a hundred people knew of it. Among the last to learn was Paul Avery, who had been out on an emergency call.

He sat in the canteen for an hour afterwards, trying to cope with his shock. He had been bluntly told that a large part of the background to his present life was gone. Ernie Hale was dead. That meant a whole area of humour, kinship, underlying love and dependence was, for the American, at an end. For all the death Paul saw, all the futures abruptly cancelled, nothing had prepared him for this kind of loss. Every few minutes his mind returned to the basic fact, the jolting truth. Dead, gone. It seemed impossible. Ernie was so lively, so positive. Death did not fit him. He was one of the people who joked about dying. He had a sign hanging in his study at home: *Death Is Nature's Way Of Telling You To Slow Down*. And now he was over the void himself, so completely absent that Paul Avery was losing control of himself, refusing to look at the aching wound that would never completely heal.

Mary Scott came in, carrying her cloak over one arm, looking pale and haggard. She sat down opposite Paul and touched his hand. 'It's crazy,' she said, her lips barely moving. 'I saw him just before we went out on the call. He was crossing the grass behind the clinic.'

'Striding out to meet his fate.' Paul tried to smile, aware that only some kind of cheap irony was going to make the horror bearable. 'My mind's going round and round. I always took him for granted. He was around all the time. Ernie. Christ.' He shook his head. 'I'm behaving like one of those people we're always telling to get a grip on themselves. But I want him to walk through that door. I've been wishing that since I came in here.'

'He won't, Paul.'

He looked at her and felt some of his bereaved dependence move over and rest on her. One loss can intensify the terror of another. 'Everything's going to pieces, Mary. These past few weeks have been hellish, when you look at them coldly. And just when Ernie had it all rolling for him. The book, that was going to be his ladder.'

'The kid who did it is in men's surgical. He's got a broken jaw and cracked ribs.' Mary offered the information perhaps as some consolation.

'I don't want to think about the details. The fact is bad enough. It's done, nobody can undo it. No amount of busted ribs and scattered teeth can change anything.' He put his hands on the table and pushed himself up. 'I'm going for a walk.'

'Can I come?'

'Sure. I'd be glad if you did.'

They strolled around the open area flanking the hospital, taking a detour to avoid passing the mortuary. Mary held his arm and he let her, not caring at all if they were breaching some code of hospital ethics. Neither one spoke. Mary had nothing to offer that could fill the need for comfort, and Paul was concentrating tightly on accepting, believing. However successful he might be, the thought of Ernie Hale's absence would be the first to hit him for many mornings to come.

Passing the rear of the administration block, Paul caught sight of Henry Madison, standing by a window, staring out at him. Even at a distance of yards, the etched lines of his face showed clearly. He looked faintly mystified, and Paul was prompted to wonder if the old consultant was on the verge of believing that dreams could come true. Just how deep Madison's feelings of dislike went, Paul did not really know. It was no more than simple charity to presume that he was as shocked as everyone else. The triumphs were piling up for the senior surgeon. Tomorrow the official report on the Life-Support Unit would be released, a death-knell of firm proportions. Some kind of miracle was going to be needed to rescue the scheme. And this, Paul almost said aloud, is not a season for miracles.

21

'I think it is important that we don't weigh down the reader's absorption capacity, Edith.' He still used her christian name with difficulty, and she noticed that he looked away each time he said it. 'A general description of Acute Circulatory Failure should occupy no more than ten pages of the text. I have decided to cut down the length of the Clinical Management passage, so if you could perhaps make the appropriate deletions in the index . . .'

When she had arrived at the house, less than an hour earlier, he seemed different, much less enthusiastic than usual. Edith had her own degree of upset, and for a time she thought she might be imagining the change in him. But now she was sure that he was definitely disturbed. He was working at a more intense pitch, and the easy confidence he had previously shown in the book was not there now. So far, he had decided on five major changes in thirty minutes.

'Electrolyte balance has to be given more space, and I think we need another drawing.'

'Isn't that going to be rather expensive at this stage of production? She had almost called him 'sir', but stopped herself in time. He had not actually asked her to use his first name, but she felt that in view of their special relationship, the cold-sounding subservience of the official address would be inappropriate.

'I don't really care about that.' He smiled, with an effort. 'The book itself is the important thing. Too many texts are rushed on to the shelves before they have been properly finished. This one will be as close to immaculacy as you and I can make it.' He went on pencilling at his page proofs.

Edith wondered why he had shown no warmth when she came in. She had been wondering that every few minutes and was aware that she stood in need of some comfort, so perhaps she was over-emphasising the significance of his stiffness. They worked on until ten o'clock. Edith had to make so many changes in the index that a new set of corrected sheets would be required, and Henry had already made his notes and revisions into a small booklet, stapled and clipped. The bulk of work was impressive, but it represented an actual setback. When they finished, Henry appeared to be more edgy than ever.

'Well,' Edith rose after packing the papers into their sectioned wallets, 'I'd better be going, I suppose—'

'Wait . . . ' He stopped halfway through packing a desk drawer with printed sheets. The strain had left his features now, and what was left looked like desolation. Edith had the alarming sensation that he had become ill. 'Please wait, Edith.' He came across and tentatively put a hand on her shoulder. 'I'm sorry if I've been difficult this evening. I should learn to confide in you.'

'Is something wrong?'

'I must confess that I'm feeling very low.' He removed his hand and moved back to the chair opposite Edith's. He sat down slowly, an old man fearful of distressing his joints. 'Matters have accumulated around me—I know we don't talk about our work when we are here, but today . . . '

'Dr Hale's death?' Edith had entertained her own mixed feelings, most of them guilty. Nevertheless, the one pain uppermost in her was the loss—she was sure now that it was a loss—of Paul. In Ernie Hale's going she saw no call for sadness on her part, although the shock had been formidable.

'That, and less obvious things. I can usually talk to myself and regulate my troubles, but I feel as if I've lost my resistance.'

'Has it anything to do with your accident?' He had told Edith briefly, the previous week, that the bruising on his face and the cut on his hand had occurred as a result of a fall.

'Oh, the rattle my body took may have contributed. I don't really know about that.' He removed the glasses he wore when working and folded them, tucking them carefully into a leather case. 'When I came home this evening, my wife told me that my niece had run away. She took most of her clothing and she helped herself to a quantity of money.'

'Oh, that's terrible.'

'Yes, it is. What makes it so hard to bear is that the girl has been given everything, every facility I would have offered my own child. Materially she lacked for nothing, and her moral welfare, her education, her grasp of the cultural necessities . . . we attended to it all. Yet she has seen fit to leave.'

'Young people can be very cruel,' Edith murmured.

'Yes, cruelty and disregard for authority seem to be the flags today's generation marches under. Her leaving, on top of the other strains . . . ' He stood up again, a hand on his forehead; 'I don't know, I just don't know.'

She rose and moved over beside him. 'You have to withstand so much.' Before she realised what she was doing, she had put a hand on his shoulder, the first time she had ever indulged in any act with him that approached a spontaneous intimacy. Her own sadness was suddenly at his disposal. Henry Madison, above all other men, was the one who cherished her spiritually. He was, for all she knew, the only man in the world who cared for her at all. He was looking at her, his face softening, some warmth reviving him. His own hand came up and rested lightly on her waist, above the hip, the fingers barely touching her. 'I'm truly sorry, Henry.' She had said it, his name, and the bond between them was elevated, like some golden chalice. Tears came to her eyes.

'Thank God you are part of me, my dear.' He spoke so quietly she could barely hear him. 'Those people, all those enemies, they work against me, they will not leave me or my standing alone. It is so lonely, sometimes.' His other hand moved up and settled on her waist at the other side. 'If I have done anything wrong, it has only been to right the worst wrong of all.'

Edith felt his fingers close slightly, and the pressure brought a wave of response from her. She swayed closer, and found her head going to his shoulder, turning and resting against the rough material of his jacket. Something rankled through the misty softness of the moment: wrong? What wrong had he done?

'Hale treated me like a common workman. The presumption

of the man . . . Avery put shame on my name. There is a hard justice in Hale's death. I would not have wanted that, even though I did despise him. But it is just. My end has been accomplished. Some kinds of providence are shocking.' He turned his head and spoke against her hair. 'If nothing else, I have been shown that my own efforts against the American have not been at all extreme. It is just that the negative quality of everything just now . . . it presses on me. At the hospital I have to fight, I have to take dangerous steps to preserve my rightful place and the tradition I represent. At home, the child I protected has treated me with the kind of shameful ingratitude I would expect from no one.'

Edith began to stiffen. What was that he said about efforts against the American? The soothing rhythm of the tableau began to diminish. Dangerous steps? And what *was* the wrong he had done?

His mouth moved closer to her neck, and she realised that he was kissing her. With a shock that made her catch her breath, she felt his hand move round and down, clasping her buttock. The spiritual union was suddenly transforming, the discomfort of physical need was being inflicted on her. She stood still, confused, uneasy. He was mumbling, half of his words lost. 'You help me . . . sustaining myself . . . a man often needs the warmth . . . the wholeness . . . tender . . . want you . . . finest woman . . . the very finest . . . '

Now Edith was growing panicky. The spiritual filigree was gone. Henry Madison was squeezing her backside, pushing himself at her, and with a sensation close to nausea she realised that he had an erection. 'Don't . . .' She started to move away and his head rose from her shoulder and he looked directly into her eyes. She would never forget that. In his face she read every kind of squalor, and she searched vainly for a trace of anything that would remind her of what she had held sacred. This was Henry Madison, her idol, the holy man of surgery, the god who had chosen to illuminate her with his chaste adoration. It was awful. He was groaning, drawing her to him with hooked fingers, making the actions and movements of sex against her. Edith twisted free and stood back from him.

'Please, Edith . . . ' He looked pathetic, without dignity or self-control. Just another man, and an old one at that, obscenely in the grip of the base need that always came along, sooner or later.

'I'm going,' she said, smoothing her dress, patting her hair, trying not to stare at the pathetic, bent-kneed stance, the reaching arms with their grasping hands.

'For pity's sake . . .'

She turned to the door, feeling hurt, offended, then spun back to face him. 'Did you know that I was having an affair with Paul Avery?' She had never wanted to hurt someone back so much in her life. She could almost believe that this creature had been planted in the room as a corrupt substitute for Henry Madison. With only a small effort, she could make herself hate him. 'We were lovers. The man you hate, the man you've been opposing, he and I have been together. Did you know?'

Slowly her words seeped through his confusion and he began to change again. He straightened, his hands dropped at his sides, his jaw set hard and he glared at her. 'This is true?'

'It's true.'

He started to shake his head, and it went on and on, shaking from side to side, set in motion by ungovernable outrage. 'Treacherous whore.' His voice could barely emerge. 'You foul—'

Edith was into the hall before he said any more. She snatched down her coat and let herself out, running the short distance to her car, scratching the lock with the key as she tried three times to insert it, managing on the fourth attempt and wrenching the door open.

As she drove away from the house, her heart was pounding, and the nausea returned as a physical playback imprinted itself on her body, the clutch and thrust of his sickening, degrading need.

Neither humming nor anything else could deaden the sensations that began to crowd in her. As she thought of the man he had been, the loving, kind, wise and respectful senior, she felt the way Paul probably did, the sense of terrible loss, tainted by ugly shock. The image of her brother jumped up again, the image she always fought, but tonight she was not strong or determined enough to resist. Paul was one kind of loss, but Madison was a worse kind, for he had destroyed her faith. And brother Ted stood behind the whole mess of unsatisfactory romance and incomplete womanhood. Maybe if she *had* been a little promiscuous, a great deal more interested in sex, a balance would have worked itself out. She might even have been able to withstand the idea of Henry Madison laying hands on her and touching her with his body. Maybe. She thought of his lusting face and felt the hooking fingers again, the revolting stiffness against her groin . . .

She almost hit a dog beside a crossing. Shaken, she drove on more slowly. Ted, that swine. Almost twenty times, between her fifteenth birthday and the day she left home four years later, he had forced himself on her, used her as if she were a prostitute. The implications of the situation had always been clear to her. Incest was an evil thing, and the most evil thing about Ted and her doing it together had been that, almost half the time, she enjoyed it. Then it had happened, something snapped and she was two people, the one who preferred mannered, cool-living safety and the other, the one who had grown smaller and smaller until she was now practically gone, the girl who enjoyed being used. The morass of shame and guilt she had lived with gave way, eventually, to what Paul called her coldness, her automatic rejection of sex. For all she sknew, things would have been a considerably different if Ted had left her alone. She hated him now, she could scarcely seriously believe that he was her brother. To acknowledge that would be to revive her tortured self-disgust.

And Paul. He was under some threat from Madison. The old man was abnormal, there was more than simple spite at work there. Edith could still feel a responsibility towards her handsome American, even though he was no longer hers, even though he had forced on her the fearsome, terrifying necessity to re-place herself on the market, to find that good marriage which, in spite of herself, she wanted so very much.

Work at Westfield General would be impossible now. She would not be able to face Henry Madison. She needed time to think. There were appointments which she passed up regularly, simply because she had enjoyed being on Madison's team. Now, with the idol fallen, she could look around. A few days off work, she decided, and some ringing round. That would be a start.

The sum total of events in the past few days did not show any encouraging trends. She had lost her great, shining, pure relationship, she had lost all respect for her boss in the same stroke, and had lost the man she had wanted to marry. In the death of Ernie Hale, she had lost a focus for some of her frustrated anger and annoyance. Loss all the way. If nothing else, a change would take her out of that morbid stream. And perhaps she could become happy again; anything would be better than the familiar deadness that was creeping over her now, protecting her from life.

The following Thursday, the day after Ernie Hale's funeral, Paul decided to work a double shift in casualty. The shock had mellowed to a steady sadness, and work was the only thing to cure that. By the afternoon, he was tired, but his spirits were much higher. His awareness of other people started to rise, too, and his attention was drawn to Ellen Haxton, who was performing well below par. During a short lull, he spoke to her.

'Not feeling well, nurse?'

'I'm fine thank you, doctor.' There was obviously something wrong, he thought. She hadn't even bothered to blush.

'This isn't a complaint,' he assured her, 'but you've dropped practically everything you've picked up today, you've walked into the trolleys so many times I think you're getting to like it, and you missed half of the splinters on the old farmer's back. Come on, tell me about it.'

She frowned. 'Perhaps I'm just feeling tired, doctor. I've had a long week. My last day off was over ten days ago.' She did not sound as if she believed it herself.

A patient was brought along on a trolley. 'Stepped into a cold frame,' Sister Maclean announced. It was a small girl, no more than four or five years old. She looked huffy.

'Why did you do that?' Paul made his dependable-uncle face and drew back the cover to have a look. There were two lacerations, one on either side of the calf. They were deep, but no essential vessels had been damaged. The problem would be removing the pieces of glass that still lay around in the wounds.

'I was chasing the cat,' the girl explained. 'He wouldn't eat his teatime treat.'

'What was it?'

'Salad. I made it myself.'

Between them, Paul and Ellen Haxton managed to remove the glass and stitch up the leg without causing the girl too much discomfort. All the time, Paul watched Ellen's hands. They were not co-ordinated in their action. She was applying skill to the work with forceps and folded gauze, she picked and dabbed and took care not to pinch sensitive tissue, but she had lost her elegance. It was the difference between a ballet dancer crossing a stage and a lame charwoman doing the same thing; both managed the task, but one made it an art. Always, before, Paul had observed how well geared Ellen's actions were. She understood not only technique, but rhythm, too. She had the kind of flowing efficiency that transmitted itself to a patient, giving him enough confidence to relax while she worked. Now, she was just another nurse who got by on the bare essentials.

When the child had gone, Paul asked Ellen to accompany him to one of the empty treatment cubicles.

'Okay,' he said, sitting himself on the edge of the examination couch. 'I won't stop pestering you till you tell me what it is.'

The intimacy of their surroundings, alone with the curtain drawn, had brought on her customary blush. 'I'm just tired—'

'You're preoccupied. It's happening to people all over the hospital lately. What's causing *your* bout?'

For the first time he could remember, she looked squarely at him. 'I'm worried.'

'You can tell me.'

'It's you I'm worried about, doctor.'

That stopped him. Nowhere in his speculation had he expected to find himself as a component of her unusual behaviour. 'How come?'

'I've been convinced for some time that the unit, the whole life-support scheme, was being tampered with. So I've been investigating. I felt that your work should not be cancelled out so easily.'

He was rather moved, and together with his realisation that she was a more human creature than he had supposed, there came a tiny pinprick of guilt. The only time he had really concentrated hard on this girl was when he had used her as a sexual fantasy. 'And your investigation has been getting you down?'

'It's depressing.' She fumbled beneath her apron and brought out three folded slips of paper.

'What are those?'

'They're requisitions.' She unfolded them and showed them to Paul. 'You'll see that the first one is for blood. Five pints of group AB. The patient's name is Morfield. If you check the records, you'll find his group was B.'

Paul was staring at the bottom of the slip. A very fine replica of his signature was scrawled across the paper. 'But I didn't sign this.' He looked at her, surprise jostling with disquiet.

'You didn't sign any of them, doctor. But they all have your name on them. I shouldn't have these, I'm afraid, but my curiosity has led me to break quite a few rules in the past ten days.'

He examined the other slips. One was for insulin, the other for morphine. He did not recall the patients whose names were at the top. But he was sure, as Ellen was, that he had not made out the slips. The signature looked like this, but the rest of the writing, even though it was block capitals, was nowhere near his style.

'I don't know if it's mischief or a deliberate attempt to have patients damaged,' Ellen said. 'The insulin wasn't given to that patient, in fact I don't remember any injections being given at all. And the morphine would certainly have killed that Bratby child, if it was administered.'

Paul was beginning to sweat. At last, crushingly, he could see evidence, clear and hard, that he was being sabotaged. 'Did these three patients die?'

'Yes. Only one had a post-mortem. I think these slips were placed on file to discredit you, if the need arose. I found them by accident, really. I was looking for something else. It was the ink that drew my attention.'

'The ink?'

'You've always used your own pen as long as I've known you, and it's got a black refill.'

He gaped at the blue ink. 'That's right. Yeah, that's dead right. I haven't used anything but black for years. Habit.' He touched his chin, at a momentary loss. 'Who did this?'

Ellen turned down the corners of her mouth, an uncharacteristic gesture. 'Would you like to see some more?'

'There's more?'

'A good deal.'

Paul made arrangements with Sister Maclean to excuse himself and Nurse Haxton and put on a substitute team from surgical, just for one hour, he promised. He went with Ellen to the side door of the nurses' home and waited impatiently until she fetched her briefcase. Then they went to the canteen. Fortified by large cups of coffee, they slowly went over Ellen's findings.

'I got this by bribing a porter,' she said, smiling briefly.

Paul could not imagine her bribing anybody. The investigation must have been important to her. 'What did you give him?'

'Six months' supply of vitamin tablets.' She caught his little frown and added, hastily, 'They were my own. I buy them in bulk. He didn't know exactly what he was borrowing for me, I told him I needed the technical details for a paper I was doing.'

'Did he believe you?'

'People always believe me.' She unfolded the paper. It was a service report on an electrical drill. Paul remembered the case of the boy whose brain had been cooked by a drill. Ellen outlined her reason for wanting the report. She was familiar with the drill, she had spent over a year's duty in a theatre where one had been in steady use. Another nurse had told her what happened in the case of the little boy, and Ellen had added the incident to her suspicion list. 'If you look there, you'll see the electrician's remarks.'

Paul read it. According to the man who had completed the repair, there were traces of graphite powder inside the motor casing. Shorting had occurred, and before burning out, the motor had started to race. Just as Paul had thought. Further down, the senior electrician had added his observation that he had never come across this kind of fault previously. The drill was enclosed in an insulated cover. Graphite, or anything else for that matter, should not have been able to get in.

'Sabotage,' Ellen said firmly, more firmly than she normally said anything. 'And these . . .' She put some other workshop slips on the table. 'I had to get them from the other repair room by myself. Please don't ask me how I did it. I get frightened when I remember how close I came to getting caught.'

Paul was thinking, as he began to look at the papers, that he had never realised just what a great team he had. 'This is the defibrillator that wouldn't work, right?'

'Yes. You remember the chaos it caused. Look what the technician wrote.'

Paul read aloud, ' "Supply leads pierced in three places. If this instrument had not refused to function, it might well have electrocuted someone." '

'The other sheets are on much the same lines. I just went right through the files for the past month and extracted repair reports that rang bells for me.'

In addition to the suspicious electrical failures, Mary had the sworn word of a junior theatre nurse that a patient had suffered a wound in his neck between the time he entered the pre-medication room and the theatre. 'She was gossiping in the common room. Nobody would listen to her, but I know the case. It was one of ours, and there's no mention of a neck wound in your notes.'

Paul drank his coffee and considered the picture that was building up. On the one hand equipment and possibly patients were being sabotaged, and on the other there was some forged evidence to suggest that he had been less than efficient in making casualty requisitions. So his unit and his skill were both under fire. His mind would not take the next step. He knew where it led, people and events had been pushing him that way, but without evidence of actual villainy he had not wanted to embark on the grisly journey towards uncovering a felon. There was no excuse to shade his eyes any longer, but a fragment of distaste, a professional hope that all was really natural and above board, kept him clinging to the receding edge of his ignorance. 'Anything else?'

'Delays,' Ellen said. 'A terrifying amount of delays and confusion. You took action about one of them, but it wasn't the worst. It was just handled less cunningly than the others. You know that I'm the sort of organiser for the Catholic Nurses' Union? Well, one of the girls told me she had been warned never to mention something she saw over on men's surgical. She told me because she felt it was a sin not to reveal possible wickedness. She's scared of losing her job. I warned her that was not the way to look at things. If she does the right thing she'll be all right. But she says she'll never admit this to anyone else.'

'What is it, Ellen?' Paul was becoming impatient, knowing the naming of names was at hand, anxious to have it done with.

'She saw a patient being given a straight whiff from a toxic gas cylinder.'

'What?' This was savagery, murder.

'She was told that she had no right to be in there, and warned that the treatment was still experimental and that she must not ever say what she saw. She's a very bashful girl, and she gives the impression of being rather stupid. But she's not. She knows what happens if the wrong mixture or only part of it is given to certain patients.'

'You've really worked at this, haven't you, Ellen?'

A faint tint of pink suffused her cheeks. 'I thought it was necessary, doctor.' She paused, then said, 'I happen to admire you.' The colour deepened and Paul felt a surge of warmth for her. 'Of course,' she went on, 'you probably have your own suspicions.'

'Yes. I've been looking for something wrong on my own, but I don't have your talent for organised snooping. I've read some post-mortem reports, and I've found some discrepancies, but nothing you could call dynamite.'

'What I really meant, doctor, was that you've had suspicions about who might be behind it all.'

'I've tried not to. But I don't think your suspicion is going to surprise me.'

Mr Madison?

'Did he warn the nurse not to say anything?'

Ellen nodded. 'It was him.'

'Oh, Jesus.' He propped his elbows on the table and scanned the sheaf of papers. 'What were you going to do with all this, Ellen? I presume you had some finale planned?'

'I was hoping to get some firm evidence. Something conclusive. This reeks of criminal activity, but it doesn't actually point at anyone. The little nurse would be no use, either. I believe her, but that's different from making her statement into evidence.'

He persisted. 'If you *had* got positive proof? What then?'

'I was going to give it to you.'

'Well, Ellen, I believe it, I believe Madison has been jamming the works. I've resisted that idea for a long time. I hate to even think he could do it. Ernie Hale kept at me to face the facts, but I kept on turning away. There's something special about consultancy, even though I know the political side and the jockeying that goes on. I'm like a devout Catholic in that sense. Do you know what I mean?'

She nodded. 'I know. You don't want to ever see it proved that anything corrupt can really infest the top. Everything else is acceptable, just so long as the highest authority is basically clean.'

'Check.'

'What are you going to do?'

'That will take some thought, Ellen. But I won't waste time on it, I'll be quick. I don't want to think that somebody's going to die just because I don't make up my mind fast enough.'

They left the canteen, and as Ellen crossed to the nurses' home to put her case back in her room, Paul took a back route to casualty and walked right into Edith Roberts.

'I was coming to see you,' she said. She did not look well.

'Oh? What about?'

'Just something that's been on my conscience.' She was not in her white coat, but was wearing street clothes. 'I came in especially to tell you.'

'If it's about us, Edith, please don't say it. Just don't.'

'It's got nothing to do with what happened, Paul. I just wanted to warn you.'

'About what?'

'I think somebody means you harm.' She made an impatient gesture with her hand. 'I mean, I think Mr Madison is prepared to use more than argument against you.'

He felt quite stunned. It was a surprise to see her in the first place, and that in itself had pushed him rather off-balance. But to hear Edith Roberts, of all people, putting the bad word on the man she had defended so heatedly, on so many occasions, that was amazing. 'It must have caused you some soul-searching to come and tell me that,' he said, putting kindness in his voice where once he could have managed intimacy. 'By an odd coincidence, I've only just had to face the truth about Madison. I knocked him a lot Edith, but I never wanted to think he was really culpable.'

'I'm sure he is.'

'What has it done to you, discovering this?'

She looked at her toes, searching for a simple, rational way to describe something that was no less than an earthquake. 'It's cleared away a lot of illusion. That will be a good thing, in the long run. I can cope with reality if it's forced on me.'

Paul was grateful and was momentarily drawn to her. Everything that had attracted him in the beginning was there again, only the hasty recollection of the strictures, the uphill drive to a doubtful destination with her as soul-mate, steered him clear of making a bad move. Thinking swiftly of Mary Scott, he realised how far he was already from anything that had once existed between himself and Edith.

'Thank you for telling me, and thank you for everything else.'

She smiled. 'There's not much else, is there?'

'There's enough. What are you going to do?'

'I'm going to spend a lot of time thinking and reorganising. And forgetting, of course.'

He took her hand between his own and squeezed it. 'Don't forget everything. There's always something worth keeping.' The communicator in his coat pocket began to bleep urgently. 'I have to run. That's an emergency.'

'Remember what I said, about Mr Madison.'

'I will, Edith. And I'll remember what it cost you.'

22

A thirty yard section of the southbound carriageway was littered with wreckage. The Life-Support Unit arrived ten minutes after the police call went out, and within the next five minutes three more ambulances arrived, followed by a fire-fighting appliance.

Dan McGoldrick had parked the wagon as close as he could to the centre of the accident, and while he and Lester Hill started to unload a stretcher and blankets, Paul went with Ellen Haxton to the white and orange police Rover that was sitting on the reservation, beside an upturned Austin Healey. A sergeant was leaning through the window of the police car, barking into the radio. He turned as Paul came up and waved an eloquent hand to convey the extent of the confusion.

'What a flaming mess.' He stepped on to the road and pointed past the smashed sports car. 'As far as we can see, that lorry—' he pointed to an eight-wheeler sitting right in the middle of the centre lane, 'swerved while he was overtaking the black saloon.' Paul noted a squashed Daimler, huddled by the shoulder. 'He must have been avoiding something, but Christ knows what. He blew a tyre, braked, and five or six other vehicles had to avoid him. You can see what happened then.'

Some cars had broken up, others had been impacted. There was a lot of smoke, and the light breeze was whipping it through the twisted alleyways of mangled steel, aluminium and rubber. So far, no people could be seen. 'Have you got any tally of the injured?' Paul reached out and took the emergency bag which Lester had brought.

'The lorry driver went through the windscreen, and he's just a bundle of broken bones and torn skin. His head hit the road first. We've put a tarpaulin over him, he's lying on the far side of that saloon. We've had a quick run round, and so far it looks like three dead, including the lorry bloke, and seven or eight badly hurt.'

Paul waved to a group of ambulance attendants and drivers who were waiting on the fringe of the area. In emergencies where more than one ambulance was required to back-up the unit, he was required to take charge and co-ordinate the rescue. They all crossed to where he stood, and he fed them their orders quickly.

'Look for cases with no immediate breathing problems and get them into your wagons. If you spot any respiratory emergencies, sing out. Anybody at all that you think you can take back to Westfield General, anybody you're quite sure will not need support on the way, take them as fast as you can. Call Nurse Haxton here if you want painkilling injections or any special help with splinting. Right, get going.'

A fireman appeared, shaking his head. 'There's an old souped-up A40 lying down there. It's upside down and the hood's crushed. I can't see who's inside. We'll have to turn it over and burn off a section of the panel. On top of that job there's a woman trapped at the knees in her estate car, a man with half an engine lying on him and two people jammed in the Daimler.'

'How long will it take?' Paul was watching the firemen setting up their thermal lance beside the dark red A40.

'We'll be as quick as we can, but don't expect miracles. If we start rushing it, we'll only do more damage.'

Paul and Ellen crossed to the overturned Healey. The door opened easily, and Paul crawled in on his belly. A girl was folded over the wheel, which was pinning her against the roof. He came back out and estimated the distance between the unit and the car. 'Ellen, can you plug in the saw and lead it over here?' He opened his bag and took out a syringe and a couple of ampoules.

It was difficult to move within the tight space, and the fact that the patient was upside down did not help. There was a good deal of blood spreading from a wound on the girl's chest. but she was still breathing. Carefully, Paul felt about the body for fractures or other irregularities. The chest wound appeared to be the only serious injury. As he had suspected when he first sighted the free-flowing nature of the blood, the girl was suffering from the defibrination syndrome. The fibrin, which is an insoluble protein essential to the clotting of blood, had been lost to such an extent that no clotting was occurring at all. She was bare-legged, which saved time. Paul pushed back her coat and skirt and wiped an area of her thigh with an antiseptic swab from a pop-open pack in his pocket. Supporting himself on one elbow, he took up the syringe, tore it from its packet, and flipped the plastic sheath from the needle. He reached behind himself and picked up the ampoules. The labels said A.M.C.H.A., and the substance inside was called tranexamic acid. He took up the entire contents of one ampoule through the needle, then injected it into the patient's leg. The effect was dramatic, one of the most impressive in emergency work. The oozing stopped within two minutes, all traces of haemorrhage disappearing as the drug took effect. It had to be handled with care, and hope still existed for the creation of an injectable solution that would stop all serious bleeding, not just this special type. In the wrong patient, the substance could be lethal.

Ellen arrived, carrying the bright steel saw, its power cable snaking along the road behind her to the ambulance. Lying on his back, Paul positioned the edge of the instrument against the steering column and pressed the switch. The blade began to move, its carbon steel teeth eating through the casing of the column. He encountered strong resistance after a few seconds and regulated the drive control, causing the blade to saw more slowly. Within a minute he was halfway through, and at that point he switched off. Handing the saw back to Ellen, he twisted himself to a kneeling position, noticing as he did that there was a strong smell of warm blood from his coat, where he had lain on the edge of the puddle. Another shirt ruined, he thought. The column was quite mobile now, and he only needed to draw it gently towards himself in order to release the pressure on the girl's chest. Her body began to drop towards the hood and Paul quickly placed his hands under her, easing himself backwards to the door. Ellen knelt beside him and they drew the patient into the open. She was very pale, and her breathing pattern had altered since Paul had released her. 'Lester!' Paul shouted.

The stretcher was brought and Ellen accompanied it back to

the ambulance. While they moved, the nurse was checking the extent of the girl's chest damage. She would be ventilated and transfused, while Paul was attending to any other severe emergencies.

'Over here, doctor.' A white-haired ambulance attendant was leaning through the open doorway of a dented Morris. As Paul drew near, he could see a man lying back in the driving seat. 'Bit of a horror here, I'm afraid.'

The engine had come into the passenger compartment, and the heavy central block was lying where the driver's knees would have been. On the radiator grille, Paul noticed a deep indentation, which corresponded with one on the back of the Daimler further along the road. The degree of injury in an accident of that kind was always dispiriting. At the moment of impact, assuming the car was travelling at an approximate speed of fifty miles per hour, the inertia acting on the driver would make him weigh, in effect, several tons. It was only for a split second, but that was long enough for gross damage to intervene. Without making an examination, Paul could be pretty sure that the legs would be snapped, the soft abdominal tissues would be bruised and possibly crushed, the spine would be out of alignment and the brain would be struggling to overcome the effects of massive shock. That was assuming, of course, that the patient was still alive.

'The fire people will have to shift that block,' Paul murmured. 'Let's see if there's anything we can do in the meantime.' He examined the man's head. No injury there at all, and the pupils were responding to light. The chest was quite clear, too. 'I think, so far, he's been lucky. We'd better put some morphine into him, just in case he starts to come round. The pain down on his legs will be too much to take.' Paul had just inserted the needle in the man's arm when shouting broke out, over by the Life-Support Unit. He spun round, keeping his thumb on the plunger, and saw two policemen waving frantically at a vehicle—it looked like a large lorry—heading towards them at considerable speed. Paul withdrew the needle and ran across the road. There was another police car parked now beside the original one, and the irate sergeant was bawling at the driver, a white-faced young constable. 'What the bloody hell's happened? What are you doing here? Eh?'

'I left the barrier up,' the driver complained.

'Barrier? That wasn't any barrier, lad, That was a stop sign, and things like that get ignored or blown away if there isn't a police car there to back them up. There's a bloody stream of traffic coming down here now. What are you doing here?'

'My radio's folded up, sergeant.' The constable sounded petulant. 'I lost contact. I wanted to report. I didn't know what to do, did I? I was cut off.'

'Bloody kids!' The sergeant moved away and started to walk briskly towards the waving group behind the unit. He grabbed a metal STOP—ACCIDENT sign from the reservation and carted it to a point just beyond the perimeter of the action area. The lorry had braked, but another vehicle was coming round from its rear, and it was moving at speed. 'What's he doing?' The sergeant was screeching, running along the road, waving wildly. The breakdown of his diversion had allowed an unknown number of cars to pass the exit road. There would be chaos, trying to get them all back the way they had come.

The car which had shot out from behind the lorry was braking now too but the driver was panicking, causing the vehicle to swerve wildly. As it ground to a slanting halt halfway between lanes, the urgent whine of a siren came up and a white Vauxhall Victor Estate ambulance conversion appeared, slicing out from the rear of the car and mounting the reservation. For an instant, Paul could see the driver, struggling with the wheel, trying to straighten his course and get back on the hard road. It was an auxiliary unit, capable of carrying one stretcher patient and two seated passengers, and it must, he presumed, have responded late to the emergency call. With no diversion sign in view, the driver would have supposed that he was still at a distance from the accident. Until all the traffic started braking in front of him, of course. Now he was out of control, having tried to keep clear of the fast car he had been following. All activity around the area of the wreckage stopped for a breathless moment as the long white ambulance seemed to sail right across on to the north-bound side. The wheels hit solid ground at close to maximum speed, and in the instant they did Paul realised that the driver must have struck his head on the windshield frame when he mounted the reservation. He was lying over to one side, no longer in charge. The vehicle cut across the motorway at a wide angle, and cars, lorries, a motorcycle and a coach began to take steps to avoid it. With a noise like a snare drum amplified a million times, the nose of the ambulance chopped into the fortified radiator of the coach, both vehicles stopping dead on the instant. One heartbeat later the windshield of the ambulance bulged outwards, exploded into shimmering particles as the driver's body sailed through and smacked against the solid panel across the front of the coach. Ellen Haxton had screamed and the sound of it came back to the ears of everyone standing around, activating them, sending them into the instinctive actions of their individual training. The police sergeant was not shouting now, he was striding grimly back to his own car. Paul saw him pick up the microphone and begin talking urgently into it. Ellen Haxton, shocked at her first sight of an accident actually happening, recovered quickly and dashed to the unit for her bag. Inside, the girl with the chest injury was still receiving a steady flow of blood and oxygen. Lester stood beside her, keeping an eye on the equipment. He touched Ellen Haxton's shoulder as she made to leave the ambulance again.

'I've never seen anything like it,' he said. 'You'd think the angel of death had landed here.'

'It doesn't work that way,' Ellen said firmly and stepped down on to the road. Paul told her briefly to find out if anyone in the coach was injured. 'The ambulance driver's had it,' he added.

A call was sent out for more police support to clear the motorway, which was now blocked on both sides. Paul used the radio to ask for as many doctors as could be transported to the scene. He had noticed, as probably a few others had by now, that something in the coach was badly wrong. People had been standing in the aisle when the collision occurred, and three distinct groups of people were huddled about the interior, frightened and shocked looking, attending to people out of sight on the floor. The area was cluttered with individual tragedies, major and minor, and delay, the word that had haunted Paul's investigations of his failure for so much of the time, threatened to be the cause of a lot of heartbreak on this bloodstained highway.

While cars arrived, bringing doctors, police, a St John's ambulance team and a Catholic priest, Paul went round, trying quickly to locate the most severe injuries. The engine block was raised from the legs of the man who had been given morphine, and it was found that he had sustained a traumatic amputation. One leg had been chopped right off and lay on the floor. The other was crushed and would probably need to be removed later. He was placed in the unit and accompanied by Ellen Haxton, who could do no more than try to arrest his bleeding, he was rushed back to Westfield General. In the meantime, Lester Hill and Paul applied assistance where they could.

The coach had been taken over by three general practitioners, who had already supported Ellen's claim that it would need a full alert situation at casualty to cope with the numbers. It was estimated by a policeman that the coach had been accelerating when the radiators met. The opposing speeds of the vehicles had caused an immediate arrest of motion, so people in the coach had literally flown through the air, striking metal, wood, plastic and other passengers. One man had broken his neck, another's spine was suspected to be fractured, a woman had been killed when her forehead hit the metal rim on the back of the seat in front of her, two children had broken ribs, the driver was in extreme pain from a suspected fracture of some facial bones, an old man, who had been taking down a case from the luggage rack at the moment of impact, had a broken jaw and a suspected fracture of the collarbone. The list was growing larger all the time.

On the other side of the reservation, Paul and Lester were trying to stop the rivulets of blood that were pouring from a man who had been trapped with his wife in the black Daimler. In his jacket pockets, inside and outside, he had been carrying numerous bottles. His wife, who was conscious and suffering from no more than bruising and mild shock, explained that they were antiques, a collection which he was transporting in what, until then, they had though was the safest way. The stems, broken sides and severed lips of the curious vessels had been driven through his chest and abdominal walls. He was a very sick man at that moment, and Paul tersely explained to the woman, who admitted that the idea of using pockets was her own, that there is nothing in the world sharper than freshly broken glass. The man was laid on the roadway and as many shards as possible removed, while Paul simultaneously stopped the holes and applied one-handed pressure to two particularly bad wounds.

'The whole thing was his fault anyway,' the woman said,

standing shakily by the car, her expensive hair standing in stiff wisps all over her head.

'Whose fault?' Paul looked up and saw her pointing beyond the lorry in the middle of the carriageway. 'Do you mean the lorry driver?'

'No, not him. The one who cut across in front of him. That red car.'

The firemen had turned the A40 upright and were almost finished removing the roof panel.

'It's a hell of a thought,' Lester said. 'That one car caused all this havoc. All the death, all the injury. One sodding car.'

The Life-Support Unit returned a few minutes later. The man with the glass wounds was taken inside. Shortly afterwards, a woman whose legs had been trapped—and broken—was placed on the other stretcher. 'Lester,' Paul said, 'you go back with Dan this time. If there's anybody alive in that flattened car I'll need Nurse Haxton to help me.'

They crossed and stood by the side of the A40, waiting for the firemen to prise back the top. All around, ambulance men were carrying stretchers to and from the wreckage. On this side of the motorway, nine people had already been rescued. So far as Paul knew, this car contained the only case not yet inspected. A fireman stood up on the car's battered bonnet and locked his fingers under the lip of the roof. 'Heave!' he grunted, while two others pushed upwards as he pulled. The panel began to move, and as the firemen's faces turned darker and darker red, it finally gave and swung upright. The man on the bonnet looked down into the exposed cabin and his eyes widened noticeably. 'Bleedin' Christ!'

Paul stepped forward and so did Ellen. They glanced at the figure stretched back across the seat. He was obviously dead, the roof had flattened his face and the bones of his skull showed broken and irregular through the skin of his forehead. He was wearing a tee shirt with the name Andy in yellow capitals across its dirty green front. The cause of the fireman's surprise was not so clear from ground level. Ellen looked over the edge of the door, into the well in front of the dashboard. She flushed, stared hard for a moment, then stepped away. Mystified, Paul had a look. The man's knees were smashed, spread out on either side, their broken bones having torn through the cloth of his trousers.

The bizarre element, alongside injuries that were sadly commonplace, was that his penis was exposed, and it was tied between two strings which were anchored to the left and right doors. Paul looked up at the fireman. 'This weirdo,' he said, 'was the cause of all this. The accidents would never have happened . . .'

It was another hour before Paul felt he could leave the site. Most of the wreckage had been cleared, the police had organised namelists of the injured wherever possible, and traffic bypasses were in full operation. Accident consultants, men with tape measures, chalk and cameras, were moving over every inch of roadway between the points where the accidents started and where they had finished. The injured, the maimed and the dead had all been removed, the load spread over three different hospitals. In the back of their ambulance, Paul and Ellen checked the equipment, anchored the parts that had been freed in order to help the afternoon's patients, and sat down on the foldaway stools, waiting for Dan to take them back to casualty.

'That was very bad,' Ellen said. 'I mean, it shouldn't have happened, should it?'

'None of them should.' Paul examined a small chip on the wall close to where he sat, one of the tiny signs of usage, the battle scars that would, if time were granted, give the unit a lived-in feeling. 'But I know what you mean. My big worry right now isn't how freaks can cause damage on the roads, though.' He looked at her, seeing in her tired face that she knew what he was going to say. 'It's what a certain unbalanced character might get up to in the confusion that's building over at the hospital.'

Ellen nodded slowly. 'I'll be watching, doctor.'

'So will I, so will I.'

The scale of the chaos was higher than Paul had expected. Having changed quickly into a theatre shirt and a fresh white coat, he entered casualty to find the place buzzing with noise and the unmistakable air of discord. 'We've got too many, doctor. Far too many.' Sister Maclean had paused for a moment on her way to the treatment room. 'Men's surgical is jammed out, there's three operations lined up outside the main theatre and there's easily twenty people in here.'

Paul shrugged. 'It's our quota, sister. Nothing else we can do.

The circumstances are kind of exceptional, after all. Who do I look at first?'

'A young boy over there. He's from the coach that crashed. I think he's been drinking. He's seventeen, he says. Fifteen or sixteen at most is more like it.'

'What's the complaint?'

'Chest pains.'

Paul went to the appropriate trolley and looked at the boy. He did have the distant appearance and the characteristic smell of one who had been on the bottle.

'Where does it hurt?'

The boy looked up dreamily. 'It doesn't hurt at all, now. I just banged my ribs. The pain's going away.' He did not look particularly well. Paul decided to leave him on the trolley for a while. If nothing else, the rest would do him good.

In a corner, one of the junior surgeons was stitching a man's scalp. Further along, two nurses were incubating an elderly woman. In the broad open area by the waiting room, five trolleys were set up, each attended by a doctor. Overworked or not, Paul thought, they had certainly got things organised. He looked beyond, into the main treatment room, and caught sight of Madison. He was commanding a pair of doctors and three nurses, directing them around the place with the full flourish of his authority. It was hard to believe he was anything other than what he appeared to be—an efficient, rather pompous consultant general surgeon. Sister Maclean came up and touched Paul's elbow.

'Would you take a look at this girl, doctor?'

The young woman was shivering violently, huddled under a blanket on a chair by the office door. 'What's wrong, honey?'

'It's my legs,' she gasped, trying to control the vibration of her jaw. 'They won't work. They won't support me.'

He unwrapped the blanket and squatted in front of her. The legs were pretty, undamaged externally, and shivering like the rest of the girl. Tremor was usually associated with systemic disease, rarely with accidents. 'When did it start?'

'When I saw that man hit the windscreen of the coach.'

'Were you hurt at all?'

'No, I was sitting back in my seat. I just got jolted forward.

But I saw his face, just above the bottom of the window. I saw it coming forward and I saw it getting all spread—' The trembling increased and stopped her speaking.

Paul heard a bell ringing inside his memory. He had seen this happen to a young girl before, in America, after a particularly bad pile-up on a freeway. Recollection of the event brought up more information. A colleague, older and much more experienced had called it the Stuck Needle Syndrome. A powerful shock, visual usually and coupled to some other violence (in this case, the sudden arrest of movement and the noise of people crashing about the inside of the coach) could produce a shudder, a nervous reaction to fright and horror. If it was powerful enough, it stayed with the patient, instead of dropping away. Like the stuck gramophone needle, it would just go on, established as part of the nervous function. It was rare, but not too rare.

'Sister.' He waited until Sister Maclean disentangled herself from a patient who was scared of the needle and gut the doctor was weilding over his torn arm. When she finally came over, red faced and perspiring, Paul explained what was wrong.

'What's the treatment?'

'One session on the shock box.' He bit off his next sentence. In the confusion and general strain of the day, he had forgotten that Ernie was dead. Paul had been about to suggest that he be called over.

'Shall I ring the psychiatric unit?'

'That's right.' Paul turned to the quaking girl. 'Don't worry about a thing. We're going to replace your shudders with a small headache.'

He returned to the boy with the drunken look. He was paler now. 'How are things? Still no pain?'

'No. Nothing.' Paul stared at him, puzzled. Something was wrong, whether the lad felt ill or not.

Paul found an unattended sphygmo-manometer and wrapped the bag round the patient's bare arm. He pumped on the bulb and watched the column of mercury. The systolic pressure was 90, and the diastolic was 70. The boy's skin was quite clammy to the touch. It was more than alcohol, Paul knew, that was causing the low blood pressure. Pressure of arterial blood depended on four principal factors: there was the force of the heart beat, resistance to the flow of blood in the peripheral arteries, the elasticity of the arteries and the total amount of blood actually circulating.

Paul decided to start by checking the heart. He clipped the stethoscope over his ears and opened the boy's shirt. Placing the bell of the instrument over the appropriate spot, he listened; the heartbeat was oddly muffled. Confused for a moment, he tried again, with the same result. Then he slid the instrument over to the right of the patient's chest. The beat became louder. The young man's heart had shifted to the right hand side!

'Nurse!'

Ellen Haxton appeared.

'Get me a big, wide bore needle.'

She came back with the needle in a matter of seconds. 'Is it a pneumothorax, doctor?'

'I think it's a *haemo*pneumothorax.' Without troubling to warn the semi-stupefied patient, Paul slipped the needle between his ribs, at the side of the chest. Blood immediately began to spout from the bore of the needle. Ellen Haxton grabbed a stainless steel dish and held it underneath the small gusher.

'Nurse, I'll watch this. You go and organise a bed for this boy. I want suction on him, connected to an underwater seal bottle.'

The patient was beginning to look alarmed. 'Don't worry, kid. Ten minutes ago was the time to worry.' Blood had obviously been leaking from a tear in the lung, filling the chest cavity to such an extent that the heart had been slipped out of place. And the boy had felt nothing. Some people, Paul thought, were made of very tough materials.

After the patient was removed to a temporary emergency ward, Paul decided to get nearer Madison. He knew that Ellen Haxton was doing her best to watch him, but it was not always easy to attend the wounded and watch what was going on elsewhere at the same time. It was a pity, Paul reflected, that Madison had to be here at all, just at this time. But in an emergency of this size, everybody waded in, even the consultants.

It was amazing how obvious some things became when you knew what to look for. While he pretended to be engrossed in some x-ray films, Paul watched Madison moving around the big treatment room. Every case that had been brought in—and treated—by the Life-Support Unit bore a blue tag, attached to the patient's wrist by a ribbon. Every case that Madison was giving his eagle-eyed attention to, without exception, had the tell-tale blue tag. People were working between two trolleys in some cases, so the consultant was in plain view all the time. Nevertheless, Paul became jumpy, realising the narrow scope of the old man's surveillance.

Something at the door caught his attention. Ellen Haxton was there, doing some more snooping in an admirably offhand manner, but it was something else that had taken Paul's eye. He stepped past Ellen and looked along the passage. The shuddery girl, the one who could not stand up a few minutes ago, was walking casually towards the patients' canteen.

'Excuse me, miss.'

She turned, saw him, and came back.

'What happened to your tremors?'

'The psychiatrist came over—'

'He brought his equipment with him?' Paul couldn't believe it.

'No. He told me what he was planning to do to me. That did it. I stopped shaking.'

'Well, well.' He watched her turn and walk off, without so much as a shiver. If he ever got around to it, he would write that one up. Tell the patient something that sounds worse than the thing he or she witnessed, and tell the patient that it's going to happen to him or her, and you don't have to go through with it. Maybe not always, he thought, but in this case the effect was spectacular.

'Doctor!'

It was Ellen Haxton's voice, high and urgent. Paul spun round and saw her standing beside Madison, grasping his arm, holding it away from a blue-tagged patient. There was a syringe in the ready-for-injection position in his hand. Madison was glaring at her, his lips drawn back, his teeth grinding together.

'Get the syringe!'

Paul took five long strides and snatched the instrument from the consultant's fingers. The plunger was up, the needle was properly in position, but the barrel was completely empty. That was not strictly true, as Paul knew. There was air in the syringe, enough air, if it was injected into a patient, to cause an agonising, fatal embolism.

Madison shook himself free from the nurse and stepped back, his elbows half bent, eyes wild, mouth open and gasping. He could have been on the verge of great anger, nervous laughter, or tears. He rotated his head slowly, staring at the doctors and nurses who had frozen at what they were doing, at Sister Maclean who stood in the doorway looking astonished, at Ellen Haxton who had dared to lay restraining hands on him, and at Paul Avery, who held up the accusing syringe in front of him.

'You people . . . ' His voice choked off and he drew himself up, shaking his head once, then marched out of the room.

Minutes after he had gone, when everyone had been told to get back to the serious work on hand, Paul walked slowly through to sister's office and dropped into the chair by the desk. Ellen Haxton came in a moment later and stood looking down at him.

'He *is* mentally unstable, isn't he, doctor?'

He smiled at her understatement. 'As a hatter, Ellen.' He tossed the syringe on to the desk and sighed. 'What a freaky day this has been. What a goddamned freaky day.'

23

From where he stood in the bathroom, Henry could hear Amy's voice talking to him from the adjoining bedroom. He absorbed enough of what she said to enable him to make a reply, but he was not really listening.

'They told me they were doing everything possible. But I must remember that over half of these girls are never traced. They just vanish. Isn't it dreadful?'

'Yes, it's scandalous.' He had been looking at his face for five minutes, running his hand round the smoothness of his chin, tracing the lines down either cheek, staring at his eyes and noting how they were set to perfection above his fine nose. An admirable face, it was still as strong and filled with character as ever. Who would know, to look at him, that his calm features covered so much pain and humiliation?

'We must try to see things from her point of view, Henry. The girl is full of intelligence and knowledge that she's not equipped to use. She's experimenting with her life, her energy's running away with her. We have to make that allowance. Things like gratitude and loyalty get swamped by your emotions when you're that age.'

'You may well be right.' How could a life so perfectly conducted, so honourably dedicated to something that rose above the ordinary level of mundane human commerce, be so badly dealt with? Was it the working of a perverse fate, or was it an accident of circumstance? He turned his head slightly and saw the dignity in the angle, the ingrained wisdom of the line. Was it all the outcome of what he really believed, that he was one of the early victims of a barbarism that sought to overthrow his beloved tradition? Yes, that was it, he could never really doubt it.

'When she comes back—*if* she comes back, will you try to be kind to her, Henry? I'm not implying that you haven't been in the past. You've been generosity itself, but I think a little more warmth, a little less logic, would help. Girls of that age need so much love, and Katie is no exception, I'm sure.'

'I'm always prepared to try a good suggestion, you know that, Amy.' Where did he stand now? At what distance from the wolves and his own security? If he confronted the truth, he was in limbo. He had been exposed, caught in an act of self-preservation; he could chide himself for that, for it had not been necessary. The figures were already in, the future of the loathsome toy ambulance was already decided. If he had wished to continue his campaign, for the sake of consistency in the appearance of things, there would have been opportunities of a less public nature, would there not? So he had been caught. Nothing had yet come of it. But something would. In the meantime, he was deprived of his dignity and authority in many eyes, and rumour would combine with executive ardour to have him further humiliated. He could be proceeded against. Henry did not know how much Avery and his supporters had discovered, but, in truth, only a little of it would be sufficient to ruin him. Harshly distanced from his status but not yet acted against officially, he was in the worst of vacuums. The only consolation he could find was that now, in this hiatus, he could deprive the hunters of their quarry.

'I've promised myself, Henry, that I'll be more attentive in future. I'll really try to see all the little signs in the girl and act on them. I suppose it's a sort of prayer, I'm promising to be a better person if I can please have what I want. I suppose you think I'm being stupid. But I do miss her so.'

'I don't think you're stupid, Amy.' He opened the cabinet and took out the little metal cannister. The tablets had eased the pain in his shoulder and knee in damp weather, and they had helped him to sleep when his mind had been over-active sometimes. He unscrewed the cap and tipped one on to his palm. One for easing pain. He tipped another. Two for sleep. He turned the container up sharply. Ten, twelve for an honourable, unsmirched exit.

'You're a long time in there tonight. Are you all right?'

'I'll be with you in a minute.' He poured water into a glass and swallowed the tablets three at a time. Then he dabbed his mouth with a towel, loosened the sash of his robe, switched off the light and went through to the bedroom.

'It's quite a warm night,' he observed, slipping off the robe and placing it across the chair. His slippers were by the bed, as usual, and he eased himself under the covers gently, still mindful of his knee. Amy's warmth touched him and he moved closer to her.

'Shall I put out the light, Henry?'

'Leave it for a bit, will you? I like to look at the curtains. Odd thing, but a breeze moving curtains has always soothed me.'

She touched his face and leaned over to place a kiss on his forehead. 'I wonder how many thousands of times we've gone through our bedtime ritual, Henry?' An edge that was not a bitterness, but a little sadness, came into her voice, 'I sometimes wonder if very much has happened to me, over all the years. Bedtimes always seem to have felt pretty much the same. As if nothing new or very useful had ever preceded them.'

'It's no little thing to have enjoyed the world, Amy. Just to be and do, and abide by a code. Protect an ideal. That's achievement.'

She made a soft sound in her throat, the remnant of the chuckle he had once loved to hear. He used to quote poetry to her. That had made her chuckle, out of embarrassment, or pleasure. Time moved through a man, Henry's vision was beginning to soften already. Time passed right through like a stream, a man did not go with it, he was changed by it. At some point, some smoothly washed period of the past, he had hardened, becoming the sum total of the smaller hardnesses that had once been only passing things. And now? He had stepped away from the stream. He could sense the absence of time now, it was peaceful not to have it wearing on him. A little dignity, that's all I asked. Freedom to be what I fought to be.

He yawned. It did not seem to matter very much now. It was all softness and a kindly darkness. He could still see the curtains, still see them moving. Amy's lips touched his brow again and he felt her move away, preparing for the nightly rehearsal of what he had now decided to enter. Names, faces, music, colours, they came and went, making no impression, being merely there and something to look at. It became darker, and for one instant he was frightened, he knew he could not go back. Then it was pleasant again, and a few seconds later there was just silence, and no awareness at all.

At four in the morning Amy awoke, knowing something was wrong. She put out her hand and touched him. His face was cold. She began to shake him, and the coldness of his arm came through the material of his pyjama jacket. She switched on the light and swallowed once, gulped herself fully awake and saw his face, younger by years, the lips parted in a distant smile, the eyes closed. She rose and walked to the door, came back and looked at him again. She sat on the bed and began to cry, brimming with sorrow. If nothing else, the one thing she had wished to be granted was to be there when it happened. She had been by his side, but she had slept. It seemed wrong. He looked so peaceful. And now she was alone. Terribly alone.

The confusion of emotions gave way to her practical nature and Amy put on her dressing gown, left the bedroom softly and descended the stairs. She made herself a pot of tea, drank one cup of it, then telephoned Henry's private physician. There would be a lot to do, and the details would defer her sorrow and obscure her loneliness.

She listened to the ringing tone and thought of him lying up there. He would be missed, she thought. So many people's lives had been changed because of Henry Madison.

Sir Albert Macauley had convened the meeting hurriedly. There was himself, Dr Towers, two obscure members of the Board and the matron. They sat behind the long board table, muting their shock, as first Ellen Haxton, then Paul Avery, explained what had happened the previous day.

'I can hardly believe it,' Matron said. 'Mr Madison is a man of the highest standing. We all know that. The sort of behaviour you describe—oh, forgive me if I sound suspicious, but could it not be some mistake?'

'Mr Madison's guilt was clear enough, matron.' It was Ellen Haxton who spoke, displaying more assurance than usual. 'The way he walked out, the way he did nothing to defend himself. Besides, I can assure you that I saw him deliberately fill that syringe with air.'

Before any other committee member could say anything, Paul explained that there was more evidence: forgery, sabotage, it could all be produced. His aim, however, was not to start some prosecution. It would be hard to prove actual malpractice against Henry Madison. All that was really demonstrable was that the Life-Support Unit had been victimised.

'You're asking us, Dr Avery, to believe that Mr Madison may have been practising illegal acts, for some time, in order to discredit your scheme.' Sir Albert sounded as troubled as matron.

'Yes, I am.'

'But it's a terrible thing to face.'

'What's the alternative? Turn our backs on it?'

Dr Towers cleared his throat. 'What exactly do you want the Board to do, doctor? You're alleging that Madison is a criminal, so I presume you expect us to act on the possibility. What do you have in mind?'

'I think he should be dismissed. No more than that.'

'That, doctor, is a very great deal.'

'Not when you consider that he's allowed people to die, probably killed others, done God knows what else, all to protect his beloved status. Dismissal is light.'

'This is awful.' Matron placed both hands over her eyes. 'I've never come across its like. Never.'

After some hesitation, Ellen decided to tell them about the girl who had been coerced into saying nothing about the administration of a poisonous gas to a patient. 'I know when someone is telling the truth,' she added. 'I believe every word of it.'

Diplomatically, Paul added some details about the work sheets, admitting that he had broken the rules (he did not mention that it had been Ellen's doing) but pointing out that some breaches were often necessary in order to reveal larger ones.

'A sound surgical principle, doctor,' Sir Albert grumbled. 'It certainly seems, to me at least, that there is some substance to your complaint. But we will still have to challenge Mr Madison.'

'I realise that.'

'And he will no doubt deny everything.'

'That depends whether he's prepared to face prison as an alternative to simple dismissal.'

'Your proof is slender,' matron reminded Paul.

'Madison does not know that. If he were to be charged with just some of the things I've found out—'

'Yes, yes—' Towers waved the rest of the tactical analysis aside. 'We're in for trouble, whichever way we look at it. Mr Madison could very well retreat behind the cloud of doubt surrounding most of the evidence you possess. All that is certain, I think, is that we know the Life-Support ambulance has been got at.'

Paul spread his hands. 'Everything points at Madison. We were actually *waiting* for him to do something yesterday. And he did, or almost did'

They rambled on, the plain point emerging that no one of the official side was prepared to come out and say that Madison should be brought in to face the music. The resistance they showed was the same as Paul's had been when Ernie Hale suggested that Madison might be a live threat. The hesitancy was ingrained, and Madison had put it there, with his particular style of consultant power wielding. The little committee believed the story, they were already convinced that Madison was all that the evidence suggested him to be. But this called for more than a reprimand. Towers had already done that, and with little hesitation as that came well within the bounds of ordinary procedure. But to accuse a consultant of sabotage, that was something else.

The bulk of the problem was solved at nine-thirty when Towers' secretary handed him a slip of paper, bearing the bombshell information that Henry Madison had passed away in the night.

After some heavy mutual innuendo, to the effect that this news had the smell of everything but coincidence, the committee were content to let Paul make the appropriate observations and suggestions, requiring no more action from them than simple agreement.

'There is no gain, as far as I can see, in pursuing the matter any further. Beyond this room, there's nothing more than the odd suspicion, and some certain knowledge held by one little girl who isn't going to say anything. I'm prepared to forget all of it.

I'd be glad if steps could be taken to give the Life-Support Unit a proper chance. We can do a lot of harm and cause some grief if we begin digging into the details of what may have been done. So let's leave Henry Madison his dignity, now that he's beyond doing damage or being hurt.'

It was necessary, of course, for Dr Towers and Sir Albert to deplore the practice of covering-up, even though in this case, as they realised, it was the better course. Having aired the fact that they possessed consciences, it was unanimously agreed that Madison's name should have no stigma attached to it, and that the Avery Life-Support Unit should be allowed to continue in service, pending figures to be gathered over the ensuing month.

Outside again, feeling the promising warmth that was filtering through the dispersing mist, Paul had the curious sensation that he was going to start laughing, for no obvious reason. As they walked towards casualty, he mentioned the feeling to Ellen Haxton.

'Release of tension,' she said. 'There was more pressure on you than you realised. Now it's gone, and you don't need to resist.'

Sound reasoning, he thought, still aware of a strange lightness. 'Would you say I was like a somebody trotting up a steep road, who suddenly finds that it's tilting downwards, and he can't stop running?'

'Yes, I'd say that.'

It did not change the way he felt, but it was comforting to have a reason. 'I'm very grateful for all you've done, Ellen. I'd like to show my appreciation in some way.'

The pink flush touched her cheeks. 'Things have gone the right way, doctor. That's enough for me.'

'You're not pushy enough, you know.' He held the swing door and allowed her to pass through. 'You should hold out for material benefits, like most other women.'

She paused and smiled before opening the door to the changing room. 'I'm not like most other women. I'm receiving all the benefits I want, already.'

He watched the door close behind her. That was a very unusual young woman. She didn't draw any attention to herself, she never made waves; all the same, Paul did not think he would ever forget her.

24

Some of the comfort Amy had hoped to draw from the bleakness of the event had been denied her. They had taken Henry's body away, because his physician was not prepared to issue a death certificate. There would be a post-mortem, and she had been assured that whatever the findings, they would be kept confidential. It disturbed her to think that there was some irregularity surrounding his death, but the greater upset was caused by the cancellation of her plans to have his coffin placed in the study. That would have helped her so much, she thought.

It was not going to be easy. Where there was life there was hope, and while Katie breathed there was always the chance that she would come back. But would she? Amy had nowhere to turn for genuine comfort, the memories of life with Henry seemed to be more intense throughout the years and months that Katie had been part of their existence. She had thought about it, and she had decided that it would be an enormous improvement of matters if Katie would write, even if she remained away. There would be a link then. As it was, there was only the painful wound of abrupt loss.

The joy of reunion is always magnified if surprise plays a part; it is enlarged even more if it comes at a time when it is prayed for. Amy found Katie standing on the front doorstep at four o'clock that afternoon, twelve hours after making the discovery that had tightened the screw on her loneliness.

The girl looked ill. She was untidy, which was unusual, had

been crying and her eyes had lost their brightness and the self-confidence which had been replaced by a vacant, distracted stare.

Amy folded her arms around her niece and walked with her that way to the kitchen. She sat Katie on a chair and began swiftly to make coffee, saying nothing, crying a little. They both drank some and after the reality of her presence had almost fully impressed itself on her aunt, Katie said, 'He's dead.'

'Is that why you came back?'

'He was all I wanted.'

Amy frowned. 'Katie, who are you talking about?'

'Andy. I wouldn't go with him. I got frightened. So he said he would go alone. And he was killed.'

Amy began to tremble. 'You poor lamb.' She rose from her stool and went to the girl, placing her hands around the tear-stained face. 'Poor, poor lamb.'

By stages, steps as painful as any that Amy had ever known, she managed to absorb Katie's outer discomfort. She enticed some warmth back to the girl by telling her that her room was waiting, that there would be no question of accusation or penance. Then, when she knew that there was only the grief left, the bite which would be reduced in time to a little sting, then an itch, then a painless memory, Amy told Katie that her uncle was dead, too.

No amount of self-delusion could prevent Amy from seeing that the news brought the greatest comfort of all. Katie was stirred to fresh tears, but there was relief in them, a more open acceptance of her aunt, now that the harsh element was no longer present in the home. They sat up until midnight, talking, confessing their small hurts to each other, both knowing that there were private pains that they would have to keep to themselves. They went to bed tired, and Katie, without prompting, gave her promise that she would never run away again. Amy could have asked for no better nightcap.

Before she slept, before she laid her head down to spend her first night as a widow, Amy said a prayer. Usually, she prayed in her head, but now she spoke. She had no certainty of a God, but the hope was firmer tonight.

'Thank you for sending Katie back to me, and forgive the selfishness that lies in my need for her. Please make her happy again, and forgive her any wrong she has done, for she is only a child. Give my husband's soul rest, and make me never forget that he protected me always. If he has sinned, forgive him too. Whatever wrongs he may have committed in his life, I am sure he always believed he was doing what was right.'

She put out the light and crept under the covers, closing her eyes tightly, trying not miss his breathing beside her. She was sad, there was no denying it. But it could have been so much worse. She could have been without hope. That would have been unbearable. Henry had always said that hope was essential; without it, he insisted, life simply stopped.

'Mary? I thought I'd call and ask you to come round this evening. You might as well try out my home cooking before you're too deeply committed.' Paul grinned as she told him it was only his body that interested her. She would be round at nine, she promised.

It was just after seven. He was restless, still trying to cope with the jumpy exhilaration of his reprieve. He had already dusted and made the house tidy. What else could he do? The food was already in the oven. He did not think he could settle down to read any journals. Go for a drive? A walk? He lit a cigarette and wandered about the sitting room. A partly opened drawer caught his attention, and as he was about to close it, he saw the yellow packet inside. His hand hovered, then he took it out, tipping the contents on top of the bureau. Ernie Hale. A dozen pictures of the man, playing the fool, inflating the life of events. They had been taken when Paul, Ernie and some nurse whose name Paul had forgotten had spent a day out in the country. The gestures and poses meant very little now, they were shadows surrounding the liveliness of Ernie's face. Perhaps, Paul began to realise, I have more room now, more time to miss my friend.

He sat down, thumbing through the snapshots, recognising every expression, remembering the same facial postures applied to a crowd of different occasions. Ernie had been one of the goods guys, so who were the others? What crowd of okay characters did he belong to? There was just him. With a small shock Paul realised that Ernie had filled his entire scale of need in the friendship department. There were no others, and the standards of downright fulfillment that Ernie had set made it unlikely that any man would ever take his place.

He looked up, glancing around the empty room. He was some kind of loner. More than he had realised. He had always wanted to go his own way, but it wasn't necessary to be a hermit. Even the act of deciding to come to England, even that could be construed as a desire to isolate himself. He looked at Ernie's face again. That smile, that capacity for infectious pleasure. If Ernie Hale had not been around, just how much of a cave-dwelling exile would Paul Avery have become? It was startling to consider.

Earlier that day, he had written a short letter to Cynthia, Ernie's girl. He had expressed his sympathy for her and he had outlined the quality of his own bereavement. Now, thinking about that letter, Paul knew there was much more to it. Had there been no Ernie, this stay in England would have gone towards solidifying what had begun in the States. He would have cut himself off, an individualist who would share nothing. That was why Edith and Ernie were such opposites. The psychiatrist had been a lucky break, the lady surgeon was a symbol of the withdrawn trend he had set in motion. What made it all such a stunning realisation was that the only other man sharing this method Paul had known—the only comparable case of a professional who chose to keep his own company—was Henry Madison.

Something he had read came back now, and he went to the bookshelf and took down the volume, *Style and the Individual.* He turned the pages and found it, the passage that had impressed him before and shook him now.

> Ambition is a healthy climb, it is invigorating. But it is a journey that must never be taken alone. The climber must touch others, allow them to help, give them help in return, even though it may slow his progress. The solitary climber arrives tired, often embittered by the final effort. At the top, he becomes a tyrant, jealous of the peak he feels is his. He is fearful of ever taking the road down, for he made no friends on the ascent.

Ernie Hale stopped Paul from becoming a one-man conquest team. He poured smiling reason on the solitary impulse. God bless him, Paul thought. Looking ahead, using the few signs that existed, he could see at least a chance of prominence and success. He was only grateful that he would never, now, run the risk of achieving it on his own. There was the ghastly example set by Madison, and if that ever proved inadequate, there would always be Mary Scott to sustain his sense of proportion.

For all Madison had done, Paul could still pity the man his loneliness. He could not have had much to give him pleasure, and the little he possessed had cost him too great a price. Defending one type of loneliness had won him another kind. It was a grotesque picture. Paul wanted the top, he would never settle until he was there. He was grateful, to Madison as much as to Ernie, that he would not make the mistake of valuing isolation, mistaking it for distinction.

He put the book away, replaced the pictures in the envelope and checked the oven to see how dinner was going. The house felt more empty than he had noticed before. He thought of the parties he had thrown, the laughter that had filled the place. In spite of the way he had enjoyed all that, there had still been an undercurrent of impatience, a desire to have the place vacated again.

Not any more. It depressed him, the sounds that were all his own, the silence that could only be broken by something predictable. He looked at his watch and shuffled back to the sitting room, going to the curtains and peering out at the darkening street. It was very still out there too. Nothing was moving.

'Hurry up, Mary,' he whispered, 'I'm feeling lonely.'